MISSION 51

A NOVEL BY
FERNANDO CRÔTTE

This is a work of fiction. Names, characters, organizations, places, events, and incidents are either products of the author's imagination or are used fictitiously.

Published by Inkshares, Inc., Oakland, California
www.inkshares.com

Edited by Matt Harry, Sarah Nivala, and Avalon Radys
Cover design by Christian Akins
Interior design by Kevin G. Summers

ISBN 9781950301294
e-ISBN 9781950301300
LCCN 2021935638

First edition

Printed in the United States of America

For my mother and father—

Virginia Villanueva Buenrostro
and
Fernando Crôtte Zamora

—who bravely left their home and family in Mexico in 1954, and came to the United States as resident aliens to start a new life.

A NOTE FROM THE AUTHOR

I MET DR. Linda Deltare during a birding festival at West Virginia's New River Gorge in the spring of 2010. I was struck by the enthusiasm of this elegant, elderly lady as she observed a constellation of starlings sweeping through the sky. I remember her looking away from her binoculars, exclaiming, "Did you see how they responded in unison to the leader's chip call?"

She focused her gaze right at me, and since there was no one else nearby, and I was uncertain whether her question was rhetorical or not, I felt obliged to respond: "I'm afraid I didn't hear the chip call or see the flock's response. To be honest, I'm not that tuned-in to communication behavior in flight."

She started an animated ramble about flock behavior until she stopped herself short, apologizing. "I'm sorry. I get carried away by that sort of thing. I've been interested in communication theory since my college days, part of my master's work and doctoral thesis."

"Oh, please go on," I told her. "I may not know much about it, but I'm interested. I love learning new things about bird behavior." What I said was true. I was interested. I never lied to Dr. Deltare—or almost never.

So we had a friendly conversation about this and other avian topics as we worked our way back to our group of fellow birders. We then encountered each other on and off for the next few days, establishing a comfortable acquaintance. At the end of the festival, we exchanged the typical farewells: "I hope we run into each other again someday at another birding event," I said, and I meant it. She impressed me as a smart, pleasant, and interesting lady.

Curiously, we did run into each other repeatedly over the next few years, at almost every birding event I ever attended. I saw her at the MAYgration Festival in Cape May, New Jersey, then at the Pea Island National Wildlife Refuge in the North Carolina Outer Banks. I saw her at Hawk Mountain in Pennsylvania, at Merritt Island in Florida, at Magee Marsh in northwest Ohio, and again at the Rio Grande Valley in Texas. Our little acquaintance gradually grew into a warm friendship. We shared each other's cell phone numbers and email addresses. So after that, I was not as surprised to see her at other birding events, since clearly, we both shared the hobby and passion. But looking back, it was a little weird seeing her everywhere I went.

One day, she even showed up in my hometown of Winston-Salem, North Carolina, at one of our regular Audubon activities at Bethabara Park. I was taken aback at her presence, surprised at how far she must have come for such an unimportant event, or perhaps just to see me. After an enjoyable morning of birding, I asked her to join me for lunch and she readily accepted. It was then that she finally unloaded the burden she had been carrying, and for whatever reason, she decided to unload it on me.

"Ferd," she said with a coarse cough, while lighting up a new cigarette with the dying ash of the one she had just finished. "There's something I've been anxious to tell you—something

I've never told another living soul. But my days grow short. I have lung cancer, and it's going to kill me, and what I know *cannot* die with me. I simply have to pass it on to someone I can trust, and from the first time I met you, I felt you could be that person. I've been following you for a few years now, to get to know you better, and I'm convinced you are the one."

"Well, gee, thank you," I said, not knowing exactly how to respond to that.

"No. Don't thank me. This is nothing to be thankful for."

A wave of anguish washed over her wrinkled face, and then she fought off tears before she pressed on. She gazed into the distance, her eyes darting back and forth. I could tell a lot was going through her mind, so I sat patiently while she gathered her thoughts.

"I was abducted by the government a long time ago, against my will and under duress," she said. "Here, take notes." She handed me a pen and a pad of paper.

She proceeded to spin a fantastical tale about an alien from space, about government conspiracy, about technology and large corporations, about danger to herself, and a lifetime of running and hiding. She told me that she was the only one who could speak to this alien. She called him by name—Mat. She said the world was not ready to accept him, so what she was about to tell me should remain a secret. I nodded understandingly, wondering where she was going with all this craziness, and listened patiently to her compelling story. We sat there for hours while she told her tales, an epic story spanning decades. At times, she became visibly agitated, and she often looked over her shoulder in a comedy of suspicion. I was absorbed and fascinated by the energy of her storytelling, and frankly, by the story itself. She spun a good tale!

Lunch turned into dinner, and when she finally finished, she said, "I know this must be difficult to believe, but I have evidence. I hate bringing you into this. The government's been after me for most of my life, and I'm afraid they'll come after you someday, too. I'm sorry."

Now, I've heard this sort of thing before. I'm a doctor, for god's sake. I'd made my diagnosis hours previously: this was a classic case of paranoid schizophrenia, heavy on the paranoia with a solid persecution complex. She was clearly out of touch with reality, amplified by a fascinating delusional construct consistent with her obvious intelligence. The only part that didn't fit was her awareness that this would be difficult for me to believe, and that I would need evidence. I find that most paranoid schizophrenics aren't that aware of or sensitive to the viewpoint of others.

She pulled something out of her backpack. Then, after looking over both shoulders twice, she placed a glowing, pyramidal object in my hands, closing my fingers around it. "Guard this with your life!" she said with an intensity in her eyes. "And never say a word of it to anyone!"

I promised Linda I would do as she asked. She examined my face and looked deep into my eyes—to convince herself of my sincerity, I suppose. After that was settled, she seemed visibly relieved and strangely worried at the same time. "Promise me again. Don't show the Trangula to anyone. To anyone! Hear?" I assured her again that it would be our secret, and I meant it. I was only a friend, not her doctor, but I always honor confidences—or nearly always.

But now I feel I must unload this stuff myself. My friend Linda is dead, and someday I'll be dead, too, maybe sooner than I expect. Her story must be told.

There was proof. Beyond her notes, I had that elusive pyramidal object, until it disappeared from my locked safe—I don't know how. Now all I have to share are the words of a possible paranoid schizophrenic, but it would be crazy of me not to tell her story. I know too much.

So here's the first part, as it was told to me by one who was there.

Fernando Crôtte, MD
Winston-Salem, North Carolina
May 16, 2021

PART ONE

TORKIYA

ONE

TORKIYAN STORMS

THREE SEPARATE STORMS conspired in the distance—sky towers of dark, mushrooming clouds appearing as thin lines on the hazy horizon. Despite the distance, Zeemat sensed their approach by the escalating tingles on his alien skin. Like an insistent itch demanding to be scratched, something compelled him to move, to go outside, but he resisted the urge, choosing instead to remain indoors, against his own instinct and his father's command. A stronger desire overpowered his innate drive: he would stay indoors to watch the storms through his bedroom window, so he could paint an impression of what he saw through his artist's eyes.

Zeemat's large, compound eyes saw his world in all its vivid colors, from infrared to ultraviolet, from the glare of the midday sun to the near-blackness of night. Unlike most Torkiyans, including his father, who saw the world in the black and white of winning and losing, Zeemat relished the nuance of hue and value, the detail of temperature and tone. The subtlest similarities and differences fascinated him, and he marveled at how every stroke on the canvas was part of a larger whole. Painting brought him joy in the heartless world of militant Torkiya. It provided an escape from the pressure to compete and combat, things that had always felt opposed to his gentler nature. In his paintings, he could instill a certain beauty and peace in the world that he didn't find in the danger and drama of Torkiya's day-to-day. In his paintings, he could make life better. He was compelled to create these images of a better world, and the task consumed his thoughts. And now he focused on capturing the beauty in the violence of the impending storm. Something told him it would be historic.

Violent weather continuously assailed the planet Torkiya. On rare occasion, several storms collided to form a massive mega-storm, unleashing torrents of rain and shocks of multi-colored lightning on the agitated people below. This storm was one of those—a collusion of three separate storms uniting for an allied assault—and Zeemat was prepared to stand witness.

He moved his painting materials to the hemispherical win-dow of his third-floor bedroom, giving him an unobstructed 180-degree view of the mounting gloom outside. From his elevated position near the peak of his pyramidal family unit, he could see the three separate masses of dark, swirling clouds marching toward him from the distance, beyond the tall cylin-drical buildings of the capital's central district, and beyond the Space Academy, which he knew was farther away in the same direction. Though the storms were still outside the city limits, he predicted they would collide directly overhead—an accurate assessment provided by the evolution of his species in a planet of raging storms. Now his almond-shaped eyes found the tow-ering lightning rods visible from his window, part of a network of lightning towers spanning the expansive planetary capital city, dotting it in a uniform grid to capture every possible bolt. Zeemat darted his eyes right and left, up and down, follow-ing the distant, quick flashes of red, yellow, and blue lightning exploding from the strengthening storms, streaks of raw energy branching out and intertwining, striking closer and closer to the city, closer and closer to the lightning rods, and to the sidewalks. He hurriedly set up his easel and electronic canvas, then poured a dollop of the ten ionic paints into finger wells at close reach. He wouldn't miss this chance to capture the fiery spectacle. He rubbed at the itch on his arms but allowed the tips of his long fingers to tingle in anticipation.

The time between flashes of lightning and rolls of thunder was shortening. The last few diamagnetic cruisers still in the air hurried to land on their charging stations before locking into place, safe from the weather's impending violence. As the clouds and lightning grew nearer, he gazed up and down his symmetrical street, to the vanishing points in the distance, not surprised to see parades of citizens streaming out of their multicolored but otherwise identical pyramid-shaped homes. Drawn by the energy in the air, they rushed to the sidewalks connecting the entire city, a frenzy of ravenous bodies pushing and shoving with their slender arms to gain a suitable position.

Zeemat considered the sidewalks to be a work of art. He loved the swirling, copper metal pattern inlaid into the gray stone of the sidewalks. As the rain began to fall, sizzles of lightning lit up the sky, and the copper in the sidewalks glimmered the reflection of every flash. "Rainshine," Zeemat called it, and it had much to do with copper—that precious, conductive metal that was ironically rare in a planet of electric storms. Copper was used in the construction of the sidewalks, a flaunt of the capital's wealth. The swirling copper pattern in the sidewalks represented the storms themselves, which were an integral part of Torkiyan life. These metallic inlays connected every section of sidewalk all over the city, in turn connecting to the system of massive lightning towers—an elegance of form and function. When lightning struck, the powerful electric charge conducted down the towers and throughout the entire city through the copper wiring of the sidewalks for the benefit of every Torkiyan.

Life on Torkiya did not depend entirely on these frequent and violent storms. Most species simply tolerated them, but over the five billion years since the planet had come into being, from the first spark of life to the present day, evolution found clever ways for some living things to use the storms to their advantage. The most successful species on this planet shared two characteristics: a degree of intelligence and some capacity to use the electric power of the planet's frequent storms.

Evolution fashioned the citizens of Torkiya (which meant "the land of storms" in their language) with an acute intelligence, their overlarge brains crowding the smooth dome of their cranium, their heads resembling an upside-down teardrop. Their angled, almond-shaped eyes dominated the lower half of their face—eyes with millions of tiny sensors to capture a wide spectrum of light and movement, glimmering softly with reflected light, glowing with a rainbow of ever-changing colors to mirror their emotions. Their noses were small and fine, belying a precise sense of smell that provided chemical and geographic information about their environment. Their mouths were also small, as their efficient digestive and energy-producing systems required little food. Due to powerful musculature, the Torkiyans' thin necks were sufficient to support their large heads. Their torsos were also slim, housing the other major organs laid out efficiently by nature. Retractable external genitalia provided males and females with a similar appearance unless sexually stimulated, at which times a male plug made a dramatic appearance, and a female socket readied itself for reproduction. Their sexual activity, and their purposeful actions in general, were driven more by logic and reason than by instinct and desire.

As for their use of electricity, Torkiyans were endowed with conductive carbonic skin on their gray hands and feet, enabling them to absorb the massive energy of a lightning bolt. Evolution equipped them with a specialized nervous system capable of storing the energy, giving them a period of enhanced strength and aggression, or of using the energy against an enemy or predator. Through their intelligence, aggression, and superior use of electric power, the ruthless Torkiyans dominated their world.

They advanced their technology and reached out into space, colonizing the neighboring planet Senechia and conquering its sapient inhabitants, enslaving them to mine Senechian copper, their most treasured resource.

Whenever Zeemat thought about Senechian copper and slaves, he thought about his father, the most famous hero of the Senechian War.

"They fought bravely, but we were smarter and stronger," his father often boasted. "Now we have their copper, and they do our bidding. Everything is better."

But Zeemat didn't see it the same way. The original Senechian slaves, the ones who had fought and lost, were dying off. The younger Senechian generation, about Zeemat's own age, were genetically modified Senechians grown in Torkiyan labs. They didn't speak. Their faces revealed no emotion. They would follow orders until the day they died. Zeemat once tried to paint them, but he couldn't manage to depict them happy, or their world a better place.

A loud crack of nearly simultaneous lightning and thunder brought Zeemat back to the present. He looked down to see his barefoot neighbors fighting for their positions on the sidewalk, standing directly on the metallic patterns. He noticed that his father, Yonek, and mother, Iohma, were already there. They spotted him at his window and waved frantically for him to join them outside. His father flashed a menacing grimace, lips downturned, fists clenched, and piercing angry red eyes aimed directly at him—eyes that shot a conflict of emotions through Zeemat's soul. As a child, those lips had spoken kind and encouraging words. When he was a baby, those hands had held him close, keeping him warm and safe. And for most of his life, before painting had become his passion, those eyes were most often the placid pink of a good father's firm but gentle nature.

His mother touched the fingertips of both her hands together, cocked her head, and made a sad expression—the one she sometimes used to get her way—pleading for him to come outside. But Zeemat knew a current of anger hid in his mother as well, and it would be worse after the storm. She didn't approve of his painting any more than his father did. She encouraged more education, beyond the basic studies he had just completed, especially in science and math—fields in which Zeemat had shown hereditary aptitude but subjects he disdained. As he expected, his mother's expression slowly morphed from pleading to impatient to intolerant.

Several people took notice of the family's interaction and quickly averted their gaze, both from Zeemat's behavior and his parents' shame.

But Zeemat was determined. He would not join them; he would paint. And though his father's disapproval weighed heavy on his heart, Zeemat was content with his gentler calling. Zeemat understood his father wanted nothing more than for his son to energize into the an aggressive Torkiyan like him, and energizing under Torkiyan storms was essential for that to happen. But Zeemat wouldn't obey, and his father wore the angry, disapproving look he reserved for soldiers under his command who did not comply with his orders.

Zeemat didn't want to disappoint him, but he simply didn't fit into his father's world of science, technology, space travel, and warfare. All his life, his friends and schoolmates had beaten him during fighting play. While they all had gravitated to positions in Torkiya's militant society, Zeemat had not. Though he'd done well in basic science and math, he'd hated it. He only became more interested in art. He could see the beauty of life everywhere—in the endless variety of plant and animal life, in the excitement of the city day and night, in the storms, the changing light, in the people themselves. And his style, his artistic voice, was to somehow improve on what he saw—to intensify the colors and emotions, to highlight the contrasts, to balance the elements, and to pacify the strong undercurrent of anger that was the Torkiyan way. Now that he had finished his basic studies, he pursued his calling with diligence and dedication, and his beautiful paintings showed it. Art was something he could do well, while fighting was not.

Zeemat looked down to his parents and shook his head. He held up his hands, the brilliant ionic paints already dotting his fingertips, colorful emblems that ranked him as a painter, an artist, the opposite of a warrior. His father turned away and covered his eyes, unwilling to see his son this way.

A deafening crack of thunder signaled that the storms were upon them. As anticipated, they coalesced directly overhead, the crash of clouds exploding into bright bursts of lightning, often simultaneously. Lightning bolts connected with each other, embracing a wide swath of the darkened sky, their distinct colors blending to yield entirely new ones. The bolts wrapped around each other like intertwining snakes, whipping wildly through the air before buffeting the towers and sizzling down their lengths, their hot charge spreading instantly along the sidewalks and into the people themselves. They were drenched in a deluge of blinding rain now, and as the strong wind threatened to blow them off the sidewalk, they leaned into it, fighting to keep their ground so they could receive jolt after jolt of the energizing charge. The storm was at its peak. Zeemat was ready. He aimed his colored fingertips and attacked the canvas. He looked back and forth out the window and at the canvas, painting frantically with all the fingers of both hands, like two spiders madly spinning a colorful web. He sought to capture the spectacle and the emotion of the moment. He drew not only the lightning and the swirl of dark clouds but also the animated reactions of the people on the streets.

He loved the way the wind whipped their wet clothing in all directions, their upraised arms waving in the air, and the smiles on their faces, celebrating the power of the storm. His eyes were drawn especially to the expressions on their faces when a bolt electrified the sidewalk—the red glow of their eyes, which made their large heads look even larger, their looks of surprise, pain, and pleasure, followed by triumphant shouts and growls, with clenched fists pumping up toward the sky. This was Torkiya, and these were the Torkiyan people. A people unparalleled across their known universe. Zeemat tried to capture it all, so he could remember this proud moment forever.

This storm lasted longer than most others had. The frantic pace of his concentrated painting exhausted him, while outside, people received an energizing charge more powerful than any they had ever experienced. The Torkiyans would remember details about this storm—the exact place where they'd stood, the people around them, the spectacular colors, and the electrifying charge and aggression that afterward lasted twice as long as most other storms. The storm proved historic, as everyone had hoped it would be, and Zeemat was the only one in the city who'd missed being in it.

When the storm finally dissipated, a Torkiyan celebration erupted. Some people danced, moving their long limbs with fluid grace, as if they were swimming in the warm Torkiyan Sea, while others wrestled and fought with the powerful punches and kicks typical of their species. Zeemat started on another canvas, capturing images of people in their post-storm festivities, including his own parents. His lips turned up into a proud smile as he watched his father and mother face each other in their fighting poses. Part of him wished he could be a fighter like them.

He studied them as his mother attacked his father, delivering a series of powerful punches from all directions, while his father backed away, trying to deflect them. His father reached up to feel the bruise developing on the side of his large head before his eyes flashed red, and he countered with punches and kicks of his own, driving her back while she tried to fend off his powerful blows. He charged her and tackled her to the ground. They wrestled and tousled until his mother escaped his crushing grip. He circled around her, jabbing and distracting her with his left hand, while hiding his right fist so she would not see his punch coming.

Yonek swung a powerful right uppercut aimed at the underside of Iohma's fine, tapered jaw. But she knew to expect it. Iohma had seen him make this move many times before. She spun gracefully as the punch whizzed by the side of her head and, using the power of her spin, she landed a hard punch at Yonek's midsection, tumbling him backward, gasping. When he stood up straight, rubbing his side, they faced each other, breathing heavily, fists ready, eyes glowing, and smiling at each other in Torkiyan delight. Then, they suddenly stopped. They dropped their guards. As if in some sort of silent communication, they looked up to Zeemat's window at the same time.

They stared at him through his window as the swirl of Torkiyans around them continued their delirious dancing and frenzied fighting. The strength of his parents' emotion was strangely inspiring to Zeemat. He painted his father's scowl and stance, with his clenched fists and tight muscles, looking as if he were ready to explode. He captured his mother's bowing head as she looked at him through upraised eyes, leaning in, teeth bared and fists clenched in a posture of attack, any hint of shame now overtaken by a seething rage.

Zeemat hurried to finish his paintings, dreading the different sort of storm to come. He put the final flourishes on his painting and stood back to inspect his work. He'd taken a deep breath when he heard the entrance door open and his parents storm into the house. He heard the front door slam and heavy footsteps march up the stairs. As he shuffled around the room, putting his painting materials away, he heard his father's booming voice already yelling at him, even before he kicked open the locked door to enter Zeemat's room.

Yonek's eyes burned red, his teeth clenched, and his hard breathing forced out a growl. He charged toward Zeemat, who took a few steps back, bracing himself for his father's rage.

"*Grrk*! Don't back away from me like a weakling coward!" His father's Torkiyan speech boomed against the walls with harsh buzzing and angry *clicks*.

Zeemat stayed silent. Zeemat knew from experience that nothing he could say or do would avert his father's anger in moments like this.

Yonek advanced toward Zeemat, who stepped back farther until he found himself against the room's far wall.

Iohma caught up with her husband, and as she placed her hand on his shoulder, a snap of static electricity caught Yonek's attention, holding him back from doing something he might later regret. Yonek took a deep breath and reached up to touch his wife's hand, the red glow in his eyes dimming to orange. Iohma stepped in between Yonek and Zeemat, further diffusing the tension in the air. When she was sure there would be no physical fighting, Iohma stood next to her husband and held his hand. They faced Zeemat together.

"*Zzzt.* You didn't come out for the storm," Iohma said accusingly. Zeemat wished she had the shameful, pleading look on her face he had seen from his window earlier. Now she growled through clenched teeth, mirroring her husband's rage, her eyes aglow from the fresh electric charge. Zeemat sensed a threat rise as the left side of her upper lip curled. He knew the danger had not yet passed.

Zeemat slammed a stubborn foot to the ground, immediately recognizing the childishness of his little tantrum. Suddenly, memories flashed before him—riding on his father's shoulders as a toddler, fantasy-flying in a spaceship, then slamming his conquering feet on the pretend planet Senechia. These were memories from happier days, but that was then, and now he was no longer a child. He was a young Torkiyan ready to assume a respectable job in Torkiyan society. He didn't know how to do it, but it was time to stand his ground as best he could.

"*Zzzt.* I want to paint," he said, one hand tapping his chest and the other pointing to his paintings, his voice fizzling out in a weak crackle.

Yonek's eyes blazed red again, and he let out a harrowing growl. Iohma squeezed his hand more firmly, but Yonek ripped it free. He marched directly to the easel and grabbed Zeemat's fresh painting. He held it overhead and brought it down hard against his knee, breaking it in two.

"No!" Zeemat shouted as he rushed toward his father to try to save what remained of his shattered painting.

Yonek threw a powerful side kick, which landed squarely in the center of Zeemat's chest. Zeemat toppled backward and crunched to the ground, squirming and clawing at his chest and throat, gasping for air.

While Zeemat struggled to catch his breath, Yonek finished demolishing the painting, glaring at Zeemat and hissing as he did so.

"Our family does not paint! We don't watch life; we live it. We fight for it!"

Iohma nodded her agreement, piping in, "Your father did not become Supreme Commander of Mission 51 by chance. He earned it during the Senechian War. And I wasn't promoted to Chief Programmer because of my good nature. I crushed my competition—their bodies, minds, and spirits. None of that came easily."

"I'm not like you . . ." Zeemat blurted, his breath caught between short gasps. He glanced between his mother and his father. ". . . I'm not strong and smart."

"*Brrgh.*" Iohma shook her head from side to side, waving off the idea. She allowed her voice to settle into a more controlled buzzing *hum.* "You have my natural aptitude for numbers. You showed that in school. But you don't know what you can do because you haven't done the hard work."

"I have, though," Zeemat replied. "Did you see the painting before he destroyed it? Do you think I could do that without practice and hard work? Do you think that was easy?"

"*Grrk!* Enough!" Yonek boomed, his voice freezing Zeemat and Iohma in their tracks. His eyes pulsated a purplish red.

Iohma jumped back in between Yonek and Zeemat, putting a hand on her husband's chest to hold him back.

"Yes," she concurred. "He'll stop painting now, like we discussed."

She looked at her husband, forcing her eyes to mellow from a bright orange into a soft yellow, and it did the trick, calming Yonek and averting an escalating crisis.

Then she looked back to Zeemat, sneering at him, the cause of all this trouble. "Our positions in the Space Academy bring you opportunities other Torkiyans would covet," she hissed. "You don't deserve it, but we've decided to enroll you in the Academy, so you can finally grow up."

"No! I won't do it," Zeemat whined. "It's not fair."

Iohma released a high-pitched sound that pierced the air and their hearing organs, shutting Zeemat up. Father and son reached up with both hands to cover the tiny acoustic holes on the sides of their heads.

"Of course it's not fair!" she screamed. "It's not fair to the other students at the Academy, and to the cadets in the Space Program who earned their way in!"

Zeemat raised his own voice, though it was far from matching the shrilling tone of his mother's.

"If you're ashamed of me, I can leave Torkiya City. I can go somewhere else to live and paint and pretend I don't have a family."

"There's no place in this world I will let you paint!" Yonek growled in a low, even *rumble* somehow more threatening than his explosive outbursts. Zeemat rubbed his still-aching chest and prepared himself for whatever would come next. He could see the muscles of his father's body tensing. A faint, flickering red threatening to inflame his eyes.

Iohma hugged Yonek and held on tight, absorbing some of his anger, restraining him. She looked her husband in the eyes. "It's settled, then. We'll proceed with the plan."

Yonek took a few deep breaths. "*Zzzt.* There's no other way," he replied, his eyes defusing, finally starting to calm down.

Zeemat was confused by the subtle sadness that had crept into their tones.

"What?" Zeemat asked. "What plan?"

Yonek and Iohma turned to face him, the glow in their eyes now an identical golden yellow, reflecting a more somber mood.

"You will never paint again," Yonek said. "You'll become a brave Torkiyan at the Space Academy, even if it kills you. I'm assigning you to Mission 51."

TWO

DREAMS AND REALITIES

THAT NIGHT, ZEEMAT wriggled and squirmed in his sleeping cocoon before his worries surrendered to a restless sleep. He dreamed of the storm, and he saw himself painting it in a way he could only do in dreams. He painted with fast, impossible strokes, and the lightning bolts shooting from his fingers appeared on his canvas like real flashes. He drew the sound of thunder and the movement of the wind. In his dream, he was indoors, but his clothes rippled from wind, and he was drenched like the people outside had been that day.

The storm swelled, building to a crescendo, until a loud clap of thunder deafened him, and a bright bolt of yellow lightning blinded him as it burst through his bedroom window, paralyzing him. Then something seemed to yank him out through the window, shattering it, cutting him, and he was suddenly in the air, falling, powerless. He couldn't move. He couldn't breathe. And then, when he was about to crash to the ground and die, he woke up.

He sputtered awake in a panic of perspiration and waited a few moments to catch his breath, to slow his racing heart.

He looked around the room to reorient himself—yesterday's clothes lay crumpled in a heap on the floor, right where he'd left them. A half-eaten plate of food sat on his desk. His easel stood by the window, and he noticed the debris on the floor beneath it. A pang of grief struck him as he took in the shattered remains of his painting, only a memory now. The sleeping cocoon now felt too confining, preventing him from taking a deep breath. He crawled out, stood, stretched, and lumbered to the bedroom window, which was still intact, unlike in his dream. Outside, the skies were now sharp and clear, showing no trace of the previous day's storm, and the red sun sparkled over the crimson horizon. The view calmed and warmed him. His pounding heart eased to normal. He loved the beautiful ionic glow of light that always followed a powerful storm—almost unreal, like a dream. He had an urge to paint this sunrise, but he decided against it after the conversation he'd had with his parents the night before. He sighed, hoping he could somehow change their minds about the absurd notion of his attending the Space Academy and being part of the prestigious fifty-first mission to the distant planet Cerulea. It was ridiculous to think he could ever measure up to something like that.

He pressed on his stomach, trying to subdue the rumbles of hunger and dread. It was time for the morning meal, time to face his parents and his fears. He thought twice about what to wear and decided on the dirty pair of baggy pants and the loose, paint-stained shirt that lay on the floor. They were comfortable, unlike the tight-fitting military uniforms his parents always wore. They'd always disapproved of his clothing. He shook his head and sighed again before plodding downstairs to join his parents at the morning meal.

"Ah, here you are, my son," Yonek said, a little awkwardly, emitting unexpectedly pleasant tones, his eyes beaming a placid pink.

Iohma sat by his side, her hands folded serenely on the table. She smiled and nodded to Zeemat, motioning for him to sit and start eating. Zeemat sat down slowly on the other side of the table, eyeing his parents with suspicion.

They had been waiting for him with an unusually large meal laid out at the table, decked out with some of Zeemat's favorite foods—wild Cricksucker ova fried, seasoned, and salted just the way he liked them. Slices of roasted Gleek and a sweet Urkani dipping sauce made his stomach rumble. A variety of multicolored fruits were puréed and served in separate bowls for him to mix in his favorite combinations. A tall glass of chilled Hamaya juice was already poured and waiting for him next to his plate and eating utensils. It was as magnificent a meal as the ones they served on special occasions.

"We prepared this feast to remind you of our love," Iohma said, pointing with open hands to the beautiful display of food on the table.

"We'll always love you, no matter what happens after today," Yonek added.

Zeemat sat down and started to eat, his eyes trained on his parents. After what had happened the night before, Zeemat was confused by their sudden change in demeanor. The storm's charge certainly had not yet worn off, and this wasn't like them—lately, they had been critical of his every word and action. Something odd was happening, and he couldn't quite put his finger on it. He almost preferred their anger—at least he was used to that. Their pleasantries unnerved him.

"What's going on?" Zeemat mumbled with his mouth full. "Last night you were angry and ashamed, and now . . . this."

"Nothing to worry about," Yonek said in a seemingly cheerful voice, his face unnaturally taut. "We made a decision last night and now we're at peace."

Zeemat stopped chewing mid-bite. The guarded looks on his parents' faces concerned him more than the anger he'd expected. They looked down at their plates as if hiding something from him. They didn't talk about their plans for the day like they usually did. Zeemat remained motionless but on high alert. He held his face still except for his eyes, which darted from his father to his mother, back and forth.

"Please don't tell me you were serious about that Space Academy and Mission 51 nonsense," Zeemat said.

"It's not a rash decision, Zeemat. Your father and I have been talking about it for a long time," Iohma replied, proceeding into what sounded like a practiced speech. "Don't think of it as a punishment but rather as a chance for you to find your place in the family history of warriors and conquerors. You're lucky we can give you this one final gift. No one else on the planet could have an opportunity like this."

"As the Supreme Commander of Mission 51," Yonek said, "I have the right and power to select the crew. I've already chosen three of the four, and today I will announce that you are the fourth and final member of the crew."

"You're going to Cerulea on Mission 51. Isn't that exciting?" Iohma spoke in a high, chirping voice, her pacifying tone grating to Zeemat's ears. "You'll be remembered as a warrior and a conqueror, a hero."

Zeemat couldn't believe it. His mother spoke as if this should be a consolation to him, but how could they seriously think he'd be right for the job? A crew member of a once-in-a-lifetime Cerulean mission. Crews were chosen based on knowledge, skills, talents, aggression, and accomplishments, and Zeemat had none of those things. Becoming a crew member was a highly competitive process, and Zeemat had never even set foot inside the Space Academy.

"*Zzzt!* This is ridiculous!" Zeemat exclaimed, slamming down his eating utensils. "Look at me." He pointed at his weak body clad in baggy, paint-stained clothes. "You know I'm not the right person for this. You know I'll fail."

"You'll determine your own fate," Yonek said, a little less cheerful now.

"It's time for you to leave us." Iohma's face bore a firm look matching her husband's. "The three crew members already selected are fully capable of seeing the mission through. You'll train to be the fourth, and you'll learn to be useful to your crewmates. You're going to Cerulea whether you like it or not. You'll fight for survival or die trying. You'll be a beacon of Torkiyan Knowledge, Wisdom, and Truth and make us proud. You'll seek copper for your people. You'll learn what it takes to be a Torkiyan, and you *will* bring honor to our family."

Zeemat shuddered, momentarily immobilized at the thought. He shook his head slowly.

"I can't do it! I won't do it!" His mind raced through his dwindling choices. It was obvious he couldn't stay in his house any longer, maybe not even in the same city. "I'll leave," he said, his voice crackling. "And I'll live somewhere else if that's what you want me to do." He rose from the table and began to turn away.

"Yes," Yonek agreed. "Somewhere else—the Space Academy."

Yonek stood from the table, marched over to the desk in the adjoining room, waved his right hand over the desktop holograph, and brought up the ready image of two of his officers.

"It's time," Yonek said to them. "Zeemat is ready."

"No, I'm not ready!" Zeemat yelled, pushing the table away and spilling his juice in the commotion. He dashed toward the stairs.

"I'm packing. I'm leaving!"

Yonek propelled himself toward Zeemat, stopping him with an outstretched hand.

"Your bags are already packed," he said, nodding to the two small bags waiting by the entrance door.

"No!" Zeemat repeated. His parents had put their plan into action. He knew he needed to move fast before Yonek's officers arrived to take him away.

Zeemat bolted to the front door, threw it open. Through the window, he spotted a speeding diamagnetic military cruiser, decorated with the Space Academy emblem and the traditional colors of space blue and star yellow, halting in front of the house, the coils still spinning with the vehicle a short distance off the ground. Two young officers leapt out and straightened their uniforms. Zeemat's heart raced and his head swam as he looked frantically in all directions, assessing his best route of escape. He turned to his right and broke into a desperate run to freedom.

The officers looked at the running Zeemat, calm amusement playing across their faces, and then over to their commanding officer Yonek, who stood at the entrance door. He nodded for them to take chase. They nodded in return and took off after Zeemat like bloodhounds let loose on their doomed prey.

Zeemat ran in full sprint, panic rising like bile toward his throat. He glanced over his shoulder, shocked to see the officers running faster, taking long, powerful strides with their trained, muscular legs. Zeemat tried to lose the officers by turning at the last moment around neighboring habitations, but they kept him in their sight as they closed the gap between them.

When they caught up to him, Zeemat turned around and took a wild swing toward one of the officers, who dodged the assault with ease. With a swift countermovement, the officer twisted Zeemat's arm into a defenseless position. The second officer grabbed his other arm and twisted it in a similar fashion, rendering Zeemat powerless in the grasp of these two strong soldiers. They held him in a vise grip, lifted him off the ground, and marched him back to their waiting vehicle in front of his house.

Zeemat tried to free himself, twisting his body and kicking his feet in the air, squirming like a fish in the grasp of a Flying Water Tyrant. But despite his resistance, the officers had no trouble carrying him back to the waiting vehicle, its doors opening automatically as they approached. Zeemat propped his feet against the doorframe of the vehicle in a last-ditch effort to resist his capture, but the officers forced him into the car with a practiced efficiency. They secured his arms and legs, restraining him like a prisoner.

"Here are his belongings," Yonek said to the officers, handing over the two small bags he had packed for his son. "It's more than he'll need."

He averted his gaze from Zeemat, who was hiding the whirlwind of emotions coursing through him, already mourning the loss of things as they used to be.

Zeemat shot his father an angry look as the vehicle's doors whooshed shut. Yonek's expression was firm for the benefit of his officers, but it morphed into grief as he watched his precious son being driven away against his will. *It's for his own good*, he thought, trying to reassure himself that what they had done was right.

Iohma joined her husband outside, and together they waited for the cruiser to disappear in the distance.

"*Zzzt.* It's for the best," she said, echoing her husband's thoughts. In her heart, she believed the words were true. "He'll find his way. The Space Academy will be a fine home. He'll find his talents and learn how to live like a Torkiyan. You'll see."

"Yes, I will see," Yonek repeated.

Iohma examined her husband's curious expression, not quite sure what to make of it.

"I *must* see," Yonek insisted.

THREE

LEAVING HOME

ZEEMAT STOPPED STRUGGLING in the back seat of the Space Academy vehicle. There was no use resisting the officers or his circumstances. He leaned his head against the window and gazed out at the rows of pyramidal dwellings identical to his own family unit. Their uniformity and symmetry had always seemed so boring to him, but suddenly they were like precious objects from a world he didn't want to lose. He didn't know many of the people inside those dwellings, but he felt as if they were all potential friends he might have met someday, but now he never would.

The cruiser swept past several tall lightning towers as it picked up speed. Zeemat inspected their intricate design and the beauty of the connected sidewalks. The swirling pattern of the copper inlays shimmered as they sped past them. He'd never noticed that effect before. He tried to capture mental images of everything he saw, in case he never came back.

The cruiser made its way out of his neighborhood and onto a thick metallic ramp that rose over the city. The diamagnetic force worked better over the heavy, electrified metal, and the cruiser picked up altitude and speed. They glided over other neighborhoods of pyramidal, spherical, and square-shaped habitations painted in a spectrum of colors. He thought of all the normal people inside them, eating their normal morning meals, looking forward to a normal day. He envied them, feeling sorry for himself.

In the distance, he spotted the school he'd attended as a child, and a painful pang of a memory tugged at the bottom of his heart. He had been a disappointment to his parents even then. He remembered the time his teachers had summoned his parents for a conference because he wasn't "living up to his potential." His father had echoed that phrase countless times since that miserable day.

Zeemat observed the public buildings and open spaces of the city as the diamagnetic cruiser glided silently overhead toward the city center, like a Mourning Spark hunting its prey without making a sound. Somehow, Torkiya City looked more beautiful now that he was restrained. Suddenly, he valued the freedom he'd always taken for granted.

The cruiser moved past the museum—The pride of Torkiya, a showcase of Torkiyan technology and conquests. Several people were walking up the steps of the enormous pyramidal building. His eyes followed the contour of the building to an opening at the topmost point, where a brilliant blue light shot skyward, projecting a column of light visible even in daylight. "The Illumination of Knowledge," Zeemat whispered to himself. It was a work of art unto itself.

The museum was in the business and government part of the city. Cruisers at different altitudes zipped by in all directions, and countless citizens on the ground went about their business, entering and exiting the buildings like a swarm of Power Ants, scurrying along the decorated sidewalks in a single file.

His eyes were drawn to the city's river, reflecting the burnt-orange color of the morning sun. As the cruiser zipped by, he gazed upriver toward one of his favorite landmarks, Torkiya City Park, remembering the countless times he had painted there, at all hours of the day and night, in all seasons of the year. He loved how the silvery grasses shimmered in the breeze, and he recalled the red, yellow, pink, and purple hues of the plants and trees. The air smelled different there—the pure, clean air of nature and of perfect freedom. He took a deep breath and pressed his face against the window to catch the last few glimpses of his precious park and city as he left it all behind.

The cruiser broke out into the vast, open country of the Production Lands, an enormous area divided into an orderly grid of even squares, with each square moving to its own rhythm, its supplies and output in perfect tune with the needs of the Torkiyan people. In each square, slave workers produced every different type of food, material, and product the Torkiyans used in their everyday lives. Zeemat peered through the window, trying to spot some of the working slaves, the genetically modified Senechians. He'd never seen any of the original captives, the ones his father had brought back from the Senechian War, the ones who still had memories and a free will.

Now these were second- and third-generation Senechians, fully modified by the Torkiyan Genetic Engineers with traits they would pass on to their offspring. These mindless slaves lived and died in the service of Torkiya. Zeemat caught a brief glimpse of a few of them, working in a Krkazi field, with an armed Torkiyan Supervisor nearby, his Charge Spear reflecting a flash of sunlight as they flew past. Zeemat knew that the supervisors shot energy bolts from these spears to "encourage" lazy workers.

Zeemat felt the energy drain out of him. He felt sorry for these young slaves. He wondered if they felt out of place, or if anything remained of their language and culture, any stories of their home planet. He wondered if they had hopes and dreams. Zeemat shook his head and scrunched his face, disgusted by how his Torkiyan people had treated the Senechians. The whole idea of production slave workers who had been robbed of all memory made him feel sick and angered him. He knew better; it wasn't the way to treat another living being, especially from a sapient species. As the sight of the slaves faded in the distance, Zeemat recalled the fruitless conversations he'd had with his parents on the topic, and how his father had always shot him down for having "weak, anti-Torkiyan" ideas.

The vehicle continued to pick up speed, passing the Production Lands in a blur. Beyond the Production grid, the vehicle turned onto a different ramp leading to the Space Academy. As soon as they reached the ramp, the officers took their hands off the cruiser's controls and placed them on their laps. Only official vehicles could proceed beyond this point, and the vehicle was now under the direct control of The Torkiyan Air and Space Command. As they entered the zone, Zeemat gazed at the sprawling Space Academy complex in the distance ahead, looming larger by the moment. His heart began to pound again, and a wave of nausea caught him by surprise. He brought a hand up to his mouth to discourage a vomit.

The Space Academy was famous for a spirit of intense competition, both physical and intellectual. It was the place where space travelers of all sorts earned their positions. It was the place where those special, select few Torkiyans would earn their spots on the missions to Cerulea. Those people were the best Torkiya had to offer. They became immediate heroes when they were selected, and they became historical figures after their departure. None of those heroes of the previous fifty missions to Cerulea had ever been heard from again. They were presumed dead, and they were honored for their sacrifices. As their vehicle drew closer to the Academy, Zeemat felt his own death looming near. Absentmindedly, he pulled at his restraints, which somehow seemed tighter, and he tugged at the top of his shirt, suddenly feeling claustrophobic in the confines of the cruiser. He felt anxious, alone, and most of all, gripped by a powerful fear of injury and death.

The cruiser now glided past the first of the large buildings of the Space Academy. All his life, he had seen images of the Academy on holo, but they'd failed to capture the sheer size of it. He was dumbfounded by the enormity of the complex—buildings of all shapes and sizes arranged in the shape of a star, with rays of buildings emanating from an enormous central construction. He knew each ray was devoted to the various aspects of the Academy's operation—Science and Technology, Rocketry, Testing and Experimentation, Weaponry, Manufacturing and Construction, Education, and Administration. His parents often had spoken of their work at the Academy, but he'd never had much interest in hearing about it. Now, flying directly over it and knowing this would be his new home, he wished he had paid more attention.

They joined other cruisers in an orderly air-traffic pattern, some heading to and from areas within the complex, some departing for places unknown. Unlike city vehicles, these were cargo and military cruisers of different sizes and shapes, certainly specialized for different purposes. The largest ones were decked out in visible weaponry. The entire place seemed foreign, with square and rectangular buildings instead of the more elegant cylinders, spheres, and pyramids of the city. Along each ray of the star-shaped complex, the buildings seemed to be laid out in a haphazard arrangement of size, orientation, and spacing, so unlike the symmetry of Torkiya City. Irregularly shaped open spaces dotted the complex, perhaps used for testing equipment or for training personnel, Zeemat imagined.

He wondered where exactly he was headed. He wondered where he'd find the cadet's classrooms, or the labs where the scientists developed new technologies, or where the engineers fashioned parts for the ships, the training centers, eating halls, and dormitories. The massive building at the very center of the complex looked familiar, and he remembered having seen numerous launches from that place on holo. The tall building was where engineers constructed the rockets and the ships. It was right next to the launchpads. He imagined his own launch from that place in the not-so-distant future. It would be his last contact with his home planet, and his body shuddered at the horrifying thought of launch into the dead of space.

They jerked inside their vehicle as it was directed down a split in the metallic ramp, leading them directly into a large opening on the side of one of the larger buildings in the Administration Ray. The vehicle entered a spacious room that housed several other ones like it. Finally, they slowed and came to a stop. The coils of the vehicle's superconductor spun down, and they dropped slowly to the floor, ending with a metallic *clunk* as the vehicle snapped into its charging base. The cabin lights dimmed, and the side doors opened upward with a whoosh.

The officers released Zeemat's restraints and escorted him up a ramp to an office on another floor. Zeemat followed without protest as door after door slammed shut behind him. He looked around sheepishly, feeling hopeless. There was no place for him to run or hide.

FOUR

ORIENTATION

AS ZEEMAT WAS escorted through the facility, still unclear of his destination, he felt yet another wave of nausea imagining how the Space Academy cadets would receive him, especially the three crew members already selected for Mission 51. They had all earned their positions, surpassing everyone else to win the grand prize—crew members of Mission 51. How could he face them, knowing he was simply handed the position, without having made any effort? He felt small and insignificant, like a Fumebug to be squashed beneath their feet.

The soldiers led him to a stark waiting room and, after a few moments, pointed him to the office of the Director of the Space Academy, Major Goki Tran. Zeemat recognized him immediately from his many holo appearances during launches. He would be hard to miss, with the ridiculous number of pins and medals attached to a uniform that was too tight on his rotund body. He carried himself with an air of superiority. Zeemat remembered conversations between his parents about Tran. They'd referred to him as the kind of man who loved the spotlight and always said what people wanted to hear, all the while manipulating for his own selfish agenda. Zeemat approached the powerful man with caution.

"*Grrk*. So this is Zeemat," Tran said, emitting irritated, chattering grunts as the soldiers led Zeemat into the office. Tran's hands rested on his wide hips as he slowly inspected Zeemat up and down, his face scrunched in a grimace of disgust, as if he'd just smelled something rotten.

Zeemat felt embarrassed and exposed under the Director's gaze. He was certain he was the only person in the entire complex not wearing a uniform. For the first time, he felt ashamed of his baggy, paint-stained clothing.

"So *this* is who Yonek has wisely picked as the fourth crew member of Mission 51," Tran mocked. A crooked smirk cut across his face, sarcasm and condescension dripping off his every word.

An awkward silence followed as Tran walked slowly around Zeemat, still inspecting him. After the long moment, Tran spoke.

"Ridiculous. How can you possibly explain your father's choice?"

Zeemat knew immediately that he didn't like this man. He decided not to give him any satisfaction, if it was at all in his power to do so. But his reply surprised him, as he spoke in a steady, respectful tone.

"Director Tran, my father and mother are your fellow officers here at the Space Academy. They hold high positions, so they must know what they're doing. They asked me to cancel my plans and to enroll in the Academy, so I did. I trust their wisdom, and I'll work hard for their honor."

Zeemat stood straight and tall, imitating his best military stance.

"*Crrrghk!*" The derogatory guttural *clicks* of Tran's voice made it clear he disapproved of Zeemat's assignment. "We'll see how well you measure up to 'wisdom' and 'honor.' *Glrrghk!*" Zeemat tried to keep his composure, but Tran's outburst of obscenities made him tense up and shake inside.

Tran gestured dismissively with a wave of his hand and pressed a button on his desk. With that, a young female officer entered the room. Zeemat noticed she was young, about his own age. She had intelligent eyes, and she moved with a strength and grace that immediately impressed him as she approached. He could tell by the decorations on her uniform and her proud demeanor that she was important. She grabbed Zeemat firmly by the arm and pulled him out of Tran's office. This time, Zeemat was happy to comply.

"*Zzzt.* I'm sure that was not pleasant," she said once they were out of Tran's earshot. "Be thankful it was brief."

Zeemat liked the musical quality of her voice, the rise and fall of her *beeps* and tones. She led him through a maze of hallways and enclosed bridges that took them to another building in the complex.

"You'll find your way around," she said. "The place has a logical organization."

She led him to a window that overlooked much of the complex and stopped to point out several buildings and landmarks to start his orientation.

"I recognize the tallest building in the middle," Zeemat said, pointing to the spaceship construction facility.

"The complex is star shaped," she said. "That's the center of the star, where they bring together all the parts of the ship for assembly. It's right next to the pad where they launch ships. Out from the center in all directions are lines of buildings where they work to design, test, and manufacture the different parts of the ship. They dedicate each ray of buildings to one aspect of the process."

Zeemat already knew some of this, and he was only half listening, the rest of his attention paid to admiring this attractive young cadet giving him his orientation. He followed her long, pointing finger back up to her graceful hand, up the lean, muscular arm, and he kept following all the way to her beautiful face. The motion of her delicate lips intrigued him as she continued explaining the layout of the Space Academy complex.

"Pay attention," she commanded, gently elbowing him in the chest with her other arm. Zeemat complied at once but not before noticing a small smile and a faint blush on her face.

"As everyone knows, every resource is being used right now for the construction and deployment of Mission 51. What you don't know is that the ship will be a first-in-class vehicle able to achieve the speed required to enter the Fifth Dimension. This historic feat will allow the ship to cut small corners through the geometrical construction of space-time. The predicted overall speed is astounding—two-tenths the speed of light!"

Zeemat didn't understand half of what she'd said. He stole a glimpse back at her face and noticed the awe with which she spoke those words. He also noticed the name tag on her chest. Her name was Ehya.

She continued. "That ray of buildings is where our scientists and metal workers fashion the new ionic metal into the proper shapes for the ship. It's not an easy task—the ionic metal was difficult to tame. The alloy is unstable, and its natural tendency is always to revert to its previous shape, but we discovered how to mold it into new shapes that will hold their form. It will allow the ship to tolerate the extreme distortion and rapid reformation she will experience in 4D and worse in 5D. A bonus is that the ionic nature of the alloy responds to touch. This makes it possible for the ship to monitor the physical state of her crew and for the crew to interface with the ship. This skin-to-skin, ship-to-crew interaction is a tremendous advance in interface technology. Your mother had a lot to do with that."

Ehya's enthusiasm was infectious. Zeemat began to focus increasingly on what she was saying, nodding his head. Ehya pointed to the next ray of buildings.

"My mother?" he asked, but Ehya ignored him and pressed on with the orientation.

"That's where the ship's engines, reactors, and fuel tanks are in their final stages of construction. The very last building, the one set off at a distance, is where the antimatter fuel for the main engine is in continuous production. It has taken about one hundred years to produce enough antimatter for this mission."

Ehya looked over to Zeemat, satisfied to see he was now at full attention, hanging on to her every word.

"In that ray of buildings, they developed the navigation instruments and the ultrasensitive Gravitational Wave Sensors that will be critical for achieving and maintaining ourselves in 5D."

"What?" Zeemat asked. "What did you say?"

"Gravitational Wave Sensors? 5D?" Ehya asked.

"No. You said 'maintaining ourselves in 5D.' Are you part of the crew?" Zeemat's eyes widened as his mouth fell agape.

Ehya paused, turning slowly to face Zeemat. "Perhaps we should introduce ourselves," she said.

"That would be nice," Zeemat replied. "I'll start. *Zzzt.* Hello, my name is Zeemat." He offered his hands to shake.

"I know who you are," she said as she took both of his hands in a cross-armed handshake. "My name is Ehya."

"Yes, just like it says on your name tag."

They both looked down to the name tag on her chest.

"Then I guess we don't need introductions," she said. They laughed, and the tension of the day finally seemed to ease a bit.

"So how did you win the grand prize of having to show me around?" Zeemat asked.

"Your mother informed me you'd be coming and entrusted me with your care. She said you were very special."

That caught Zeemat off guard. "My mother? How do you know my mother?"

They were still standing at the window, and Ehya pointed to the last ray of buildings radiating from the center of the complex.

"That's where your mother works. As you know, she's the Space Academy Director of Programming. We work together on our ship's Synthetic Soul. We program her every response and action. She taught me what I need to know about the ship's computers and about navigating us safely to Cerulea."

"You said 'us' again."

Ehya stood straight and tall. "Well, yes, I am one of the crew. I'll be the Technology and Navigation Officer of Mission 51."

Zeemat realized he was standing next to one of the planet's heroes. Ehya had defeated all her competitors to attain this prestigious assignment. She would become part of Torkiyan history. And she knew his mother.

"Honestly, I'm more than impressed," he said, seeing her now in a much different light. "Tell me more about the ship's Synthetic Soul." Zeemat was curious not only about the ship's program but also about his mother's involvement in it.

"Her name is Janusia," Ehya said.

"The Synthetic Soul or the ship?"

"Yes, the Synthetic Soul, the ship, both. They're the same thing."

Zeemat nodded and smiled. "Ah, they named the ship Janusia after the ancient god of doorways, travels, beginnings, and endings. Perfect!"

Ehya finally flashed a warm smile of her own. "I'm glad you appreciate the significance!"

"She's my favorite of the ancient gods," he said.

"You'll learn all about her, and she about you. You'll study a lot of things in these next three years. You'll learn about the science of space travel, about survival, about our mission to explore, colonize, and conquer Cerulea, about our quest for copper."

Zeemat noticed that Ehya's smile had disappeared as her brow furrowed, and a serious expression overtook her face.

"I know nothing about these things, you know. I'm starting from zero."

"Yes, we all know," she said, the furrows on her brow growing deeper. "But we follow orders, and they ordered us to accept you and mold you into a useful member of the crew."

"Do the others feel the same way?"

"Meah and Dirk do. They're the other two crew members assigned to Mission 51, so they're the only ones who really matter. But many other cadets in the Space Academy don't. They're angry because you stole their chance."

Zeemat hung his head in shame, while Ehya glowered at him. Perhaps sensing his sincerity, Ehya's face gradually softened.

"Here's what we've decided: Meah, Dirk, and I can handle all aspects of the mission. We want you to learn as much as you can in these three short years about the science, the ship, and all our jobs. We want you to know enough to try to step in if any of us become incapacitated. Can you accept a position like that?"

Zeemat jerked his head up with a quivering smile and a glimmer of hope, but before he could speak, Ehya stopped him with a hand gesture.

"But we must know that you will try, that you'll give *everything* to this effort. Our lives are at stake."

Zeemat paused, resetting his hopes. She was right. He was unprepared to be a crew member, and their lives were at stake. Accepting him could not have been an easy task for the three others. He nodded.

I'll do what it takes to learn everything I can. I promise.

Ehya stared at him with colorless, unreadable eyes. She didn't want to discourage him, but she knew that Zeemat had no idea what lay ahead of him.

"And no painting," Ehya said, shaking her head as she waved her index finger, accentuating the point.

Zeemat froze. She knew about his painting, and that it would be difficult for him to give it up. Suddenly he had to make a choice, to give up the thing he loved most. It felt as if the meaning of his life had boiled down to this one, single moment. Ehya waited for his response.

"I paint to make things better," he finally said.

"You can't have any distractions. There's too much to learn."

Zeemat paused again, taking another moment and a deep breath before responding.

"It won't be a problem," he said, already thinking about how he might draw in secret, and maybe paint later. *Maybe when we get to Cerulea*, he thought.

"Good," Ehya said. "I'm glad that's behind us. Now let me show you where you'll be spending most of the next three years."

Zeemat followed Ehya down another maze of hallways and bridges to a different part of the Space Academy complex.

As they walked along, she pointed out the locations of the multimedia classrooms, the real-life simulators, the zero-G and Estimated-Cerulea-Gravity laboratories, dining hall, and dormitories. She ended the tour at his assigned living quarters. It surprised Zeemat to find the small suite of rooms quite accommodating, even with no windows.

"No windows, no distractions," Ehya said. "This may not be like your beautiful home in the city, but it's your home for now. They assigned each of the crew members of Mission 51 quarters like this, and it's an honor. For the military, this is luxury."

Zeemat took a quick look through the rooms, stopping at his desk in the study room, provisioned with the latest holographic computer. Shelves stacked with mountains of reference materials lined two sides of the room.

"Here's a map of the complex and your schedule for the next year," Ehya said, waving her hand and bringing it up on Zeemat's computer. The hologram displayed an accurate 3D rendering and a summary of the work he had to do.

Zeemat's jaw dropped, and his eyes shimmered in a shock of silver as he scrolled down an endless list of courses, assignments, simulations, workouts, meetings, and training sessions. He took a deep breath and let out a long sigh. "It seems impossible," he said.

"Everything is possible," Ehya responded. She spoke as if it were a universal truth. "You just have a lot to learn. So make yourself at home, clear your mind of everything else, and prepare to attack the hardest years of your life. It's as simple as that."

FIVE

THE SPACE ACADEMY: DAY ONE

AFTER A RESTLESS first night's sleep in a rough military cocoon, a loud voice shouting his name from inside his room startled Zeemat awake. He bolted up in bed and jerked his head around, looking for the intruder.

"Who's in here?" he demanded.

"Venik," a voice said, seeming to come from all directions. "Your automatic assistant. It's early, but it's your first day, and you have a busy schedule. You must hurry if you wish to arrive on time to your first appointment."

Zeemat bolted out of bed. He didn't want to be late for anything, especially on his first day.

"Why didn't you wake me earlier?"

"I tried, but you did not respond to lower volume, so I progressively increased it until you responded. I was becoming concerned you might be dead."

"Oh, so you're not all that bright," Zeemat said. "You can't tell if I'm alive or dead."

"Not until they place your chip, and that's at your first appointment."

"Where do I go?" Zeemat inquired.

"I displayed the location on your desktop holograph," Venik said in a tinny, mechanical monotone.

Zeemat donned his baggy, paint-stained clothes, the only ones he had, and examined the map on the holo before heading out. He ran to the location and made it just in time, gasping for breath.

The attendant looked up from his workstation, eyeing him up and down before mumbling a derogatory "*Grmpht.*" After confirming Zeemat's identity using the planetary database, he looked up his information on the Academy's private database to set up his radio-frequency chips. His eyes glistened silver when he realized Zeemat was a crew member of Mission 51. He glanced at the computer, then at Zeemat in his messy clothes, then back at the computer to reconfirm. He shook his head, shrugged his shoulders, and keyed in the required data to the chip system.

"Sit right here," he said to Zeemat. "This will be quick."

The attendant removed two tiny chips from the computer and placed them inside a handheld device with a trigger. He brought it up to Zeemat's hand.

Zeemat yanked his hand away. "Wait! No one told me anything about inserting a chip."

The attendant mumbled a few more remarks to himself, and his eyes dulled into an irritated purple.

"How will our systems know where you are, or how you're doing, if you don't have a chip? How will you access computers, and open doors, and turn things on?" he asked.

"Oh . . . yes . . . now I remember," Zeemat lied. He offered his left hand.

He felt a brief jolt of pain when the attendant deployed the chip into the palm of his hand. He suppressed a groan, relief washing over him when it was over.

"Now the other hand," the attendant said, impatient *clicks* in his voice. "Fliers get both hands for the flight controls."

Zeemat presented his right hand. *Flier*, he thought, smiling while the device fired. He suppressed another groan.

"That's it. You're done."

"Now where do I go?" Zeemat asked.

"Perhaps to get some decent clothes?" The attendant smirked sarcastically as he sized up Zeemat and his clothes. "You can't walk around like that—how embarrassing for you." After a few moments and a heavy sigh, he said, "Here, let me show you how your chip works."

The assistant walked Zeemat to a nearby computer and asked him to wave his hand in front of it. The computer turned on and welcomed him

"Now ask for your schedule," the assistant said.

"Let me see today's schedule," Zeemat said.

His schedule displayed instantly. Sure enough, next up was a fitting appointment at the commissary for his Academy clothes. Then he had a workout before the morning meal.

"How do I get to the commissary?" Zeemat asked.

A map instantly displayed.

"That's it," the assistant said. "Any idiot can work it, so you should do just fine. Just wave your hand in front of anything that needs to open or turn on. The chip relays your location and vital signs to the Academy computers from moment to moment."

Zeemat balked at the electronic intrusion on his privacy, but he knew he had no choice about it.

"Thank you," he said to the attendant, rubbing his aching hands as he hurried out the door to his next appointment. The attendant hissed and went back to his work.

At the Academy commissary, other attendants discarded his old clothes, leaving Zeemat to stand naked in front of a full-length mirror. His body looked thin and scrawny compared to everyone else he had seen on base, male or female. A different attendant measured him in every direction and issued him clothes to wear for study, for ship simulations, and for workouts.

Zeemat looked at himself in the space-blue jumpsuit they'd issued him, and he thought it looked silly.

"Do I get a uniform?" he asked.

"Not until you complete your first year . . . *if* you complete your first year," the attendant said. Zeemat didn't hear a bit of humor or sarcasm in her voice. She spoke the words as if they were a well-known fact.

"Thank you." Zeemat hurried off to his next appointment.

He found his way to the gym for the morning workout, locating his locker in the locker room so he could change into his workout clothes. As he entered the gym, he was relieved to find he was a bit early.

But he heard sounds coming from the far side of the gym. Three people had arrived even earlier and were already warming up and stretching out. He saw that one of them was Ehya and figured the other two were the other members of the crew. He felt a lump in his throat as he approached them.

"I see you found your way," Ehya said.

"New chips, new clothes." Zeemat displayed the healing areas on the palms of his hands and his new clothes for the others to see.

Ehya turned to the others to start introductions, but one of them spoke up first. He had a boyish look and a playful grin on his face. "Nice legs," he said, bringing a hand up to his mouth as if to suppress a laugh.

Zeemat looked down to his scrawny legs.

"I think they'd look better on a chair than on a pilot," the crew member said before laughing and bolting off to start a warm-up run around the gym's track.

"Don't mind Dirk," Ehya said. "That's the way he is. He was joking."

"Half joking," the other one said before she introduced herself. "You must be Zeemat. My name is Meah. They've assigned me to be the captain of Mission 51."

Meah didn't smile or offer her hands to shake.

Zeemat nodded. "I'm honored," he said. "And I'm looking forward to spending time with you all."

"Yeah, like the rest of our lives," she said sarcastically. "Now, let's get to work." She took off in a run after Dirk.

Ehya looked at Zeemat with a half smile and shrugged her shoulders, as if to say there were things they could not control. "Let's go. Exercise will help you feel better," she said. She led him on a run around the track.

"What's the distance around this track? And how many laps will we do?" Zeemat inquired.

When he heard Ehya's response, he realized their "warm-up" run was farther than he had ever run in his entire life at any one time. He kept up with Ehya for one lap before his legs and lungs started to ache, and he fell behind.

"Do the best you can," Ehya said before running ahead to catch up with Meah and Dirk.

The others finished much sooner than Zeemat did, and they had time to catch their breath for a minute before starting their weight training routines.

Zeemat didn't have that luxury. He was panting heavily when he finished his warm-up run but had to start on the weights right away. The others were lifting and pulling twice the weight he could manage, as they churned through twice the number of repetitions and sets.

They finished with a cooldown routine and more stretching. When Zeemat finished and joined them, he collapsed flat on his back in utter exhaustion. It was still early in the morning, but Zeemat felt as if he had put in a long day's work.

After quick showers, they joined up again at the morning meal. The four sat together at a table in a large, bustling mess hall. Squadrons of Space Academy cadets sat at other tables, eating, laughing, shoving one another, and gobbling down their food. By comparison, his table with Ehya, Dirk, and Meah was quieter and more reserved. They focused on eating their meal and studying. Meah had a portable holo device from which she looked over the details of the day's simulation.

Zeemat looked around and noticed a group of cadets in uniforms pointing in his direction. Then they talked among themselves and laughed.

"Someone's noticed you're here," Dirk said, jabbing an elbow to Zeemat's side. "You're popular!"

"Yeah, I bet they love me," Zeemat said.

"They'd love to see you dead," Dirk said, laughing at his own comment. Then he looked at Zeemat and noticed the worried look on his face. "Forget them," he said. "Eat your meal and drink your fluids. You'll need the energy. We have a lot of work to do. And you can't worry about who loves you and who doesn't."

Zeemat tried to shrug it off, but the table of cadets kept pointing and laughing until they rose as a group and marched directly toward him. The leader of the small gang stood right over Zeemat, leaned down, and spoke into his ear.

"You won't survive your first year, you little shit. Why don't you just quit right now and give your seat to someone who deserves it?"

Zeemat looked up in alarm. The cadet who spoke was large and brutish with a mean face and clenched fists.

"Oh, and that would be you, you big shit?" Dirk said to the brute. He stood up and walked right up to the brute, their faces nearly touching. "Like it or not, he was assigned to Mission 51, and he has our support." Dirk pointed to himself, Ehya, and Meah. "So back off. It's a Space Academy decision."

The brute's eyes flashed red, and he cursed, but he backed off, and the gang skulked away. They knew the Academy prized the crew members of Mission 51 above everyone else. No harm to them would be tolerated. In fact, the opposite was expected. The entire system was there for their support as they prepared for the fifty-first mission to Cerulea.

Dirk sat back down to finish his meal, humming a song to himself as if nothing had happened.

"Thanks for that," Zeemat said.

Dirk nodded, then looked him in the eye. "Don't let him be right about the first year," he said. "Survive!"

After breakfast, the crew gathered in the group's private classroom. Meah gave a detailed presentation about the day's upcoming simulation, dealing with a landing scenario after coming out of cryopreservation sometime in the distant future.

"For this simulation, we'll come out of cryo, and they'll give us a set of challenges to sort out before attempting a landing on Cerulea's surface," Meah said. "Countless things can go wrong, so the challenge will be to figure them out, fix them, and proceed with the landing as best we can. Fail or succeed, we'll learn something,"

Meah turned to Zeemat and snorted, making no effort to hide her impatience and her superiority. "There's very little you can contribute at this point. You know nothing about spaceship engineering, electronics, military computer systems, navigation, propulsion systems, or . . . anything. So you can just sit there quietly, watch, and learn after you come out of cryo. After the sim is over, go research every single question you have. You have a Trangula at your disposal, which you can access through the computer in your room. Use it!"

Zeemat nodded. He felt relieved to be watching, though he was worried about cryopreservation. Surely they didn't expect him to do that on his first day, he thought.

Meah interrupted his thoughts with some final words. Looking Zeemat in the eyes, she said, "Of course, we'll all skip the midday meal today because of the cryopreservation element to this simulation. No one wants to see Dirk's lunch."

The others laughed, but Zeemat's jaw dropped open.

Later that day, they regrouped in the simulation room. His crewmates had already arrived when he entered a small circular room. He stopped at the entrance to look around the cramped, enclosed space.

"It's an exact replica of what the inside of Janusia will look like when she's built," Ehya said, beaming proudly.

Zeemat's eyes darted around the room, and he almost lost his balance, overwhelmed by a wave of dizziness. The small room seemed to tighten somehow, closing in on him from all sides. The low ceiling barely allowed him to stand up straight. The lights inside the cabin were dim, and Zeemat noticed a vibrating *hum* that bothered him. There was only enough room to take a few steps in any direction. Four workstations against the wall were spaced evenly around the circular room, lights shimmering on their countless and incomprehensible controls and displays. Buttons and levers dotted the wall on either side of the workstations. But his eyes settled on the four tanks clustered in the center of the room—the cryopreservation units, interconnected by a series of hoses. Part of the tubing system penetrated the floor to a tank underneath. At that very moment, the tanks were filling with a clear, viscous fluid that emanated a nauseating vapor hovering over the tanks. He noticed a mechanical arm from the ceiling holding lids that would cover the tanks once the occupants were inside. Zeemat shivered in panic as the room became bitter cold.

"Better get used to it," Meah said, noticing Zeemat's anxious facial expression. "These tanks will be our home for about two hundred fifty years."

She allowed herself a half smile as she watched the color drain from Zeemat's face.

Dirk approached Zeemat and draped a friendly arm around his shoulders.

"Don't you worry about a thing, my friend. It won't seem like two hundred fifty years. We'll be in cryo sleep for most of it."

That didn't reassure Zeemat. He inched his way to the center of the room to peek inside the coffin-like tanks. As he watched the tubes pouring cryopreservation fluid into the tanks, a few drops splashed onto Zeemat's arm. The frigid fluid felt more like a burn than a freeze. He recoiled and rubbed the stinging spot on his arm.

"The tanks will be filled in a few moments," Meah announced, disrobing. "Time to take off our clothes and start the simulation."

Dirk and Ehya began removing their clothes, but Zeemat stood motionless, his heart pounding. He knew he should follow their lead, but he felt paralyzed. His glimmering eyes were a sizzling shock of silver, his shaking body failing to respond to his thoughts.

Ehya was now completely naked, and she noticed Zeemat's distress. She approached him to help him out of his clothes.

Zeemat was only vaguely aware he should be feeling other things as a beautiful, naked female undressed him, but he could only feel a tightening sensation in his throat.

"Is this for real?" he gasped.

"Yes," Ehya murmured. "Watch how Dirk and Meah do it, then I'll help you this time. I'll go last into my tank."

As if in a dream, Zeemat found himself naked with his three accomplished crewmates who had done this, perhaps many times before, during their years at the Space Academy. But this was Zeemat's first, and he was utterly unprepared.

The tanks were full now, and Dirk was the first one to jump in.

"Don't think about it," he said to Zeemat. "Just jump in, submerge your head, and take a deep breath. It'll knock you out in no time."

He proceeded to do just that, blowing bubbles and waving from undercryo as he lost consciousness.

Zeemat's legs wobbled, and he almost fainted just watching Dirk submerge. He held on to Ehya's arm.

Meah was already half submerged but took a moment to direct a few final words to Zeemat: "When we come out of cryo, just sit at your workstation over there and observe as we try to figure out whatever problem they throw at us."

She went under, inhaled, closed her eyes, and went still. The automatic mechanism slid heavy lids over Dirk and Meah's tanks, sealing them in.

Zeemat felt his mind slipping into a dreamy fog, the reality of his day falling away. Ehya's voice seemed distant.

"Your turn," Ehya said.

"Is it going to hurt?" Zeemat's voice quivered.

"Yes, but don't worry about that. It's just pain and just for a short time. The pain won't kill you."

Zeemat tried to take a step toward his tank, but his feet felt impossibly heavy, as if they were glued to the floor. Ehya had to pull him along. She waited by his side until he mustered the courage to swing his legs into the tank. He screamed in pain when his toes touched the fluid.

"Hurry," Ehya said. "You don't want your feet and legs to freeze before the rest of you. It must happen all at once. Go under. Take a deep breath. Now!"

She pushed his head and shoulders down into the cryo fluid, and Zeemat gave in to it. His eyes glimmered wildly, and his body shook uncontrollably. He resisted taking a breath, but the frigid cold forced it. He felt the burning-freezing fluid enter his lungs and barely had time to register the horror of it before everything went black.

When he awoke, the others were already working at their stations, bathed in a red, warming light. They were still naked and dripping cryo fluid from their bodies, but they were busy checking all the ship's systems, as they were trained to do. Zeemat sat up from his now-empty tank, shivering. He lumbered out of the tank and hobbled to his workstation. He waved a trembling hand, and it turned on.

"Mirror Ehya's workstation," he ordered the automatic assistant while wrapping his arms around himself for warmth.

"At your command, Zeemat," the assistant replied. The screen lit up with a copy of Ehya's screen so Zeemat could follow along.

"You know my name?" he asked.

"Yes, and much more," a sweet, calming, disembodied voice said. "There will be time for formal introductions later. For now, dry off and put on a dry set of clothes."

A red spotlight lit up by his side, highlighting the clothes he had removed earlier, and then widened to engulf him in a warm zone. Zeemat followed her suggestion and put on his clothes, enjoying the warmth as if it were the world's greatest joy.

"Now let me see Dirk and Meah's screens," he said. The automatic assistant displayed the two new screens along with Ehya's, evenly splitting them on Zeemat's holographic screen.

Meah interrupted the working silence. "We are critically low on fuel!"

"What does that mean?" Zeemat asked, but everyone ignored him.

"We have not established orbit around Cerulea," Ehya announced.

"There's no fuel for orbits anyway," Dirk announced. "There's barely enough for a landing attempt."

Meah requested navigation parameters to set up the landing, and Ehya keyed them in.

Zeemat was caught up in the moment's anxiety. "What are you going to do?" he asked, shaking Ehya's shoulder to get her attention.

Ehya turned away from her screen to respond. In that instant, updated navigation parameters appeared on her screen, but she drew her attention to Zeemat.

Ehya began to explain the details of what was happening, but Captain Meah stopped her short. "Stick to the script!" Meah commanded.

His crewmates deftly maneuvered the ship through a partial orbit and a rough descent, but the simulation ended in a crash. There were no survivors.

Meah screamed a clicking chatter of obscenities, pounding the top of her desk. She ordered everyone to stay in the simulation room until they analyzed every action to determine what had gone wrong. When she learned that Zeemat's interruption had caused Ehya to miss a critical change in navigation parameters, she bolted to Zeemat and slammed him against the nearest wall.

"I will not let you kill us!" she hissed, grabbing his throat with one hand and pointing a long finger in his face with the other.

Dirk and Ehya appeared on either side of Meah. They didn't raise a hand to stop their captain, though both attempted to diffuse her anger.

"It's his first day, Captain," Dirk said, laughing as Zeemat choked under Meah's hand. "He'll learn, and there's nothing like death to teach a good lesson."

"He was ordered to be here, and we were ordered to accept him," Ehya reminded Meah. "And he's the son of the mission's Supreme Commander. You have to give him a chance."

Meah considered their words for a moment then relaxed her hold on Zeemat's throat. She took a step back while he wheezed, struggling to catch his breath.

"You're lucky you are your father's son," she said. "And you're lucky that the best engineer on the planet and the most ferocious fighter pilot in the known universe seem to be on your side. I'll heed their advice . . . for now."

Meah and Dirk left the simulation room, but Ehya asked Zeemat to stay behind. "Let's give them some space," she said. "And anyway, I want to formally introduce you to Janusia."

They returned to their adjacent workstations and sat down.

"Should I wave my screen on?" Zeemat asked.

"No need. She's with us at all times. She's everywhere in the simulation room just as she'll be everywhere on the ship. She will *be* the ship."

"My name is Janusia," the now-familiar voice intoned. "Welcome to the crew, Zeemat."

"Thank you," Zeemat replied, looking all around the room, trying to imagine Janusia's presence. "Though I don't feel I belong here, especially after what just happened. I'm sure you saw it."

"It's all part of the learning process," Janusia said. "And you should know that I value your presence."

Ehya beamed proudly. "I coded those words. They're part of the 'feelings' module your mother invented and I embellished upon."

Zeemat smiled at Ehya before responding to Janusia. "Thank you, Janusia. What are your duties? How much do you know?"

"There is not enough time for me to list my duties, and I interface directly with the ship's Trangula, so I know everything. I'm here to assist with anything you and the others may need."

Zeemat could tell Ehya was happy to see that Janusia had a calming effect on him. She smiled and said, "Let's pair you up."

Ehya stood up. She leaned in close over Zeemat sitting at his workstation, so she could reach his hands. Their heads touched, their arms paralleling each other's as she held his hands.

Zeemat felt a thrill tingle through his body.

"Put your hands here," she said, helping him to place them on hand-shaped indentations on the desk surface in front of his screen. "Now hold them there while Janusia reads you."

Zeemat felt a rush of warm electricity in his hands. The room vibrated, and a complex series of *chimes* and musical notes surrounded him as different colored lights circled the room. After a few moments, everything returned to normal.

"That's it. You're paired. You're part of Janusia. She'll become the ship's Synthetic Soul, and she'll know more about you than you can imagine. She'll be able to anticipate your needs and predict your actions. You're going to love her."

Zeemat rubbed the tingles out of his hands. *She's just a machine*, he thought.

"Now let me show you *this*!"

Ehya's excitement brought Zeemat to full attention. She walked over to the wall next to Meah's workstation, waving her hand in a circular motion over part of the wall that had a triangular marking. A portion of the wall then slid open, revealing a pyramidal object pulsating a deep red color.

"I didn't notice a door there," Zeemat said.

"That's because the ionic metal heals itself every time the door closes," Ehya explained. "The entire ship will be constructed of the same material. You'll never see a seam or edges on doorways in Janusia."

Zeemat had heard about the new ionic metal but seeing it in action impressed him. More than that, his eyes were drawn to the pulsating object inside the small compartment that had opened in the wall—the ship's Trangula.

Ehya and Zeemat stood in front of the Trangula in reverent awe. There were only a handful of these objects in the world because they were so difficult to create and required enormous amounts of energy to maintain. It contained all Torkiyan knowledge—everything they had ever learned as a species over eons of time.

"It will be priceless as we travel, and even more important as we establish a colony on Cerulea," Ehya said, her whisper reverential as her eyes fixed on the mesmerizing object.

Like all Trangulae, it had been built in the shape of a small pyramid. Trangulae came to life when plugged into a large power source, or when held in the hands of an energized Torkiyan. They emitted a dim holographic representation of anything requested. Even if the charged individual was at a nearby distance, a Trangula glowed in a slow pulse. As a charged Torkiyan came steadily closer to a Trangula, the glow turned from yellow, to orange, to pink, to a deep red, and the pulsations cycled more rapidly. The presence of more individuals energized it faster. The information within Janusia's Trangula would serve as the heart and soul of the ship and of the mission itself. It would be difficult for them to survive without it. Ehya, Dirk, and Meah were already adept at managing the information in the Trangula, and Zeemat would learn.

Zeemat and Ehya stood close to each other as they watched the pulsating Trangula and imagined the vast amount of Knowledge, Wisdom, and Truth it contained. Their arms and shoulders touched. Ehya took hold of Zeemat's hand, and they lingered there, gazing at the mesmerizing Trangula.

When Zeemat returned to his room, he found a warm, delicious meal waiting for him on the desk next to his computer screen. "How did this get here?" he asked out loud, not expecting a response.

Venik responded, "I knew you missed the midday meal for the scheduled simulation, and I sensed you were returning to the room, so I arranged for this meal. I placed it next to the screen so you can work while you eat."

"Thank you," Zeemat said. "I think I just changed my mind—I'm going to like having you around."

Zeemat waved his screen awake to check out his planned assignments. He had so many questions, especially about navigation and what was needed for a safe landing. He hated the fact that he'd caused a simulated crash and instigated his captain's wrath on his first day. Looking at his list of assignments, he realized he had a lot of basic material to learn before he could even begin on the advanced topics his crewmates had already mastered. He sighed and began to chip away at the lengthy list of the day's homework.

Later that afternoon, a reminder alarm interrupted his studies. It was time for an afternoon workout in zero gravity. Zeemat arose from his desk with a groan, his body aching from the morning's workout and the cryopreservation shock. *At least this should be much easier in zero-G*, he thought.

He joined the others who, as before, were already there waiting for him. They entered a large tank and were sealed in. The inside of the tank had a series of exercise and activity stations. Zeemat heard loud clanking noises from the outside and felt the entire tank shake violently, until it eased into a gentle vibration. Then without warning, his body lifted into the air.

The others pushed off a wall and flew to the other end of the long tank to the first exercise area. Zeemat struggled to get back to a place from where he could push off. It wasn't as easy as the others made it look. He bounced off the walls and used a lot of energy to catch up to the group, who were already moving on to the second station.

Zeemat continued to struggle, fighting his way through the exercises. Again he finished long after the others did.

When he returned to his room, he fell into bed, exhausted. He slept through the dinner alarm. He woke up later that evening ravenously hungry and with aches and pains all over his body.

"You missed dinner," Venik said. "But I can arrange for a snack to be brought here if you wish."

"Yes, please," Zeemat begged.

He moved his exhausted body back to his computer to resume his studies. He ate his snack and rubbed his aching muscles. He stayed up well into the night studying and managed a few hours' sleep before the morning alarm went off. He rubbed his eyes and lumbered out of bed to look at his schedule, groaning as another heavy day started all over again.

SIX

THE FINAL YEAR

TWO YEARS LATER, Zeemat was again the last one to be awakened from cryo. As the least-experienced member of the crew, he was always the last one for everything. Ehya, Dirk, and Meah sat busy at their workstations, dripping wet from their cryo beds as always, reviewing the procedures for the final approach to Cerulea. Zeemat made his way to his own station, turning the screen on with a practiced wave of his hand, and reviewed the status of the ship's supplies.

"Well done, Zeemat," Janusia said in a calm, pleasant voice. "I made a list of additional tasks for you today. Please ask me if you require assistance." She finished her communiqué with a flourish of lights and *chimes* around his station, which blended into the red warming light.

Zeemat smiled, encouraged by Janusia's constant support. If he didn't know better, he'd swear she was a real person, and that he was her favorite among the crew.

"Let me know if there's anything I can do for *you*," he said, to which she responded with another series of *chimes* and lights, just for him.

He saw Ehya working on her station to his left. Her holographic screen had a close-up 3D representation of Cerulea's star and planetary system. Zeemat looked over her shoulder to watch as she expertly adjusted the coordinates. His eyes drew directly to the third planet from the star—Cerulea.

"Setting course and velocity," Ehya announced to the others, who remained focused on their own tasks.

Zeemat took a long, admiring look at his accomplished and beautiful crewmate, trying to imagine their future together, as they were now assigned to be a mating pair once they established a colony on Cerulea.

"Course and velocity confirmed," Janusia replied in a calm, pleasant voice. "Updating Cerulea density and gravitational data."

"Cabin temperature, pressure, and oxygen concentration within acceptable limits," Captain Meah reported. She doubled as the ship's Environmental Systems Engineer, in charge of Environmental Systems both on board Janusia and once they landed on Cerulea. She would be responsible for establishing physical housing and shelter on Cerulea, making the necessary adaptations to whatever they might find on the surface of the alien planet. They already had a sense of what to expect, but measurements of Cerulea's physical properties could not be precise from Torkiya, fifty light-years away. Captain Meah was busy making adjustments to the plans, given the data for this simulation. She took a moment from her calculations to glance toward Zeemat.

"*Zzzt*. Are you going to make it?" she asked half jokingly.

Zeemat was still coughing up the last bit of cryo fluid from his lungs. After hundreds of these simulations, he still feared and hated every aspect of the cryopreservation system. The painful shock of the cold fluid on his naked skin, the drowning sensation as he breathed the fluid in and lost consciousness, and the knowledge that during the actual flight he would be unaware of anything for ages, trusting his life to a system of chambers, tubes, cryo fluid, and a computer—all of it was horrifying.

"I made it this time," Zeemat replied. "But I can't guarantee the next time."

"One drowning at a time," Dirk said, and they all shared a few *clicks* and *gurgles* of Torkiyan laughter.

Ehya patted him on the back to help him cough up the last of the bitter fluid. She rubbed the back of his large, smooth head.

"Save the coupling for after the landing," Dirk teased.

Dirk's station was to the right of Zeemat's. Overseeing Power, Propulsion, and Weaponry, he was responsible for the powerful main engine at the stern, and the three smaller positional engines at the stem, starboard, and moonboard positions along the edge of the ship. He would also manage the antimatter and fusion fuels and reactors. Dirk would carefully inspect the computers essential for entering the 4D and 5D realities after generating the phenomenal speeds connected with those alternate states—speeds that would shorten their fifty light-year trip to two hundred fifty years, half the duration of previous missions. In fact, they would probably overtake Mission 50, launched one hundred years earlier, which was hopefully still making its way to Cerulea.

The computers on Janusia were a crucial interface between the engines and the Gravitational Wave Sensors located strategically along the outside edges of the ship. They were key to achieving Harmonic Resonance, for smooth navigation through an ocean of G-waves at sub-photic speeds. Without such coordination, the ship would not tolerate the inevitable distortion in 4D and 5D. It would vibrate, shatter, and disintegrate. Despite Dirk's playful nature, they had chosen him because of his natural fearlessness and his brilliant mathematical mind. They could trust him to handle not only routine operations but also potential disasters.

Zeemat was impressed by how Dirk, despite his remarkable achievements, could still be such a playful smart-ass. After two years of working together and getting to know each other, they'd gained the other's trust and confidence. They knew the importance of training hard and that they must be able to rely on each other during the dangerous mission. Even so, Dirk still found the time and energy to offer jokes and amicable jeers, ever the purveyor of comic relief in stressful situations. Dirk had become a good friend.

"It'll be interesting seeing you all deformed and stretched out in 4D," Zeemat teased Dirk. "It'll be an improvement."

Dirk leaned over and reached out to punch Zeemat on the shoulder. "Yeah, I look forward to that. It'll be easier to reach your scrawny ass to punch you when I'm stretched out."

Zeemat rubbed his shoulder and they laughed. Janusia joined in the fun, letting out a cheerful burst of sounds and lights over both of their stations.

Zeemat turned his attention to his own screen. They had assigned him the position of least responsibility, but he was immensely proud of it. He couldn't believe what he had accomplished since the day his parents had forced him out of the house two years ago, and he smiled at the thought. With a lot of arduous work, much had changed. He had found a fragile peace with his parents, forgiving them in his mind for what they had done to him, even though it still felt like an abandonment. They had begun to speak to each other, and when he was in the right mood, he could even see a glimmer of wisdom in their decision to enroll him in the Academy, to "grow up," as his mother had once said, and to "live up to his potential," as his father never ceased to repeat.

Captain Meah had also softened to him a bit, perhaps because he hadn't killed the crew again during a simulation like he did on that first day. Zeemat let out a few gurgling *beeps* of private laughter at the memory of it. In truth, Meah had noted his efforts and had approved his promotion. Now he had a real uniform, decorated with the emblem of the Chief Officer of Materials and Supplies on Mission 51. Zeemat knew this was a made-up position, and that any of the others could do his job in addition to their own. After two years of intense catch-up study, he knew a little about a lot of things but had mastered nothing. His presence and role on the mission were probably unnecessary, but he was determined now to help in any way he could. He "inspected" the ship's simulated inventory of Materials and Supplies, ensuring that the water recycler was operational, before he went through the list of additional duties Janusia had given him to increase his elementary knowledge of the ship and its functions. He still had a lot to learn.

Janusia was "learning," too. She was in a state of constant evolution, thanks to her ability to add her own observations to her databases, to predict and prioritize, and especially because of the ongoing adjustments to her programming. During the previous two years, Zeemat had seen her develop into a rich, complex personality who acted like another member of the crew—perhaps the most important member of the crew. She held everything together. Zeemat was grateful for her guidance and amazed at her intuitive awareness of his needs.

"Your mother is here," Janusia informed Zeemat.

Zeemat looked around the simulation cabin. "Where?" he asked.

"Not here in this room," she explained. "She's in the Programming Office here at the Academy. I just felt her update my code."

"You notice when they change it?" Zeemat asked, curious about how a machine could experience a purely technical set of commands.

"Oh, yes. The changes are subtle, but somehow they make me feel more . . . complete."

"'Feel'?" Zeemat asked.

"Ha!" Janusia laughed, emitting a wave of colorful lights around the cabin and a short series of cheerful *chimes* and tones. "I know—machines aren't supposed to feel. But your mother gave me emotions. She named me a Synthetic Soul, far beyond a mere automatic assistant. I can be happy, sad, angry, and ashamed, to varying degrees, just like you. She's says this helps me to better understand my crew and to better anticipate your needs."

"Well, I didn't always feel this way, but I have to admit you do a great job and I'm glad you're here," he said.

"Go see your mother," Janusia said.

Zeemat nodded. He waved his screen off and headed to the section of the Space Academy that housed the Programming Office, making his way to his mother's suite on the top floor. The sign on her door read "Chief Programmer." Zeemat smiled proudly as he gently knocked and let himself in.

"Hello, Mother," he announced after quietly opening the door and peeking inside.

Iohma startled. She quickly finished the line of code she was working on, waving her screen off, and turned to give Zeemat her full attention.

"Zeemat! It's so good to see you. How are you doing?" Zeemat noticed a faint blush redden her cheeks before evaporating into the room.

"Good. Better. Better all the time," he replied. "We're starting the third year of our training, and the ship's construction is well underway."

Iohma beamed a proud smile. Her son appeared well and had so far measured up to her hopeful expectations.

"I was just at the construction facility with your father. Janusia's going to be a beauty!" she said.

"She's incredible—like a person, thanks to your programming."

"We're going to take good care of you," she said. "My job was to raise and protect you, and I did the best I could. Now Janusia will help me with that."

"She's just a machine. She'll never replace you," he said, hoping his forced smile was enough to hide his growing anxiety as the launch date loomed near.

"She'll be a fine crewmate, a friend when you need one, and she'll provide a good home during your journey."

"She'll never be home. Never," Zeemat said. "You know I don't want to leave, right?"

Iohma forced a smile of her own. "This third year will fly by, and you'll be prepared," she said, matching Zeemat's anxiety with her own worries.

"And then *we* will. We will fly by," he said, his voice breaking into uneven, nervous *clicks*, his tenuous smile now completely disappearing from his face.

SEVEN

ZEEMAT AND YONEK

DURING ZEEMAT'S THIRD and final year at the Academy, construction workers and technicians finished the assembly of the ship Janusia. It was an arduous process because of the tricky ionic metal and the tight specifications demanded by the theoretical science of 5D. Supreme Commander Yonek drove the project to completion, doing his best to heed the cautions of the engineers who reminded him that the ship was only as strong as its weakest part.

But one look from the powerful Supreme Commander was enough to make the engineers and parts manufacturers cower, to avoid Yonek's famous physical aggression. "Motivate with power" was one of his famous quotes. With Yonek's size, strength, reputation for ruthlessness, and position of power, he always got his way. The construction of Janusia rushed along.

Now the completed ship, shaped like a biconcave disc to allow maximum deformability, gleamed on pedestals in the construction facility adjacent to the launchpad. Lights aimed on it from strategic angles created shimmering reflections off the ionic metal, as if she were breathing, as if she were alive.

Fully fueled, provisioned, and ready to go, she looked to be moving even though she was standing still. The launch of Mission 51 was imminent.

Yonek caressed the surface of the ship, satisfied that she was safe. He couldn't wait to reveal her to its crew, but especially to Zeemat. He called for his son to join him for a private tour. He wanted to see his reaction.

When Zeemat caught his first glimpse of the completed ship, he stopped dead in his tracks, as if paralyzed. He felt a rush of emotions, not the least of which was a sense of awe at Janusia's sheer beauty. She was a work of science and art, both of which he well appreciated. But she would also be his prison for an incomprehensible amount of time, and perhaps his tomb. He had yet to see the cryopreservation chambers inside, but he knew they'd be there. He gagged at the thought of submerging himself in the frigid fluid, for real this time, for two hundred fifty years. As much as he tried to fight it, fear and anxiety overwhelmed every other thought and emotion.

His father approached him from behind and draped an arm around his shoulders, a warm gesture that reminded him of their relationship years ago when Zeemat had been a child. The tenderness took Zeemat by some surprise.

"Well, what do you think?" Yonek inquired.

"She's beautiful, Father." Zeemat's voice wavered ever so slightly.

Yonek knew his son. He could sense the fear and trepidation. Zeemat felt his father's arm hold him tighter.

"There's nothing to fear, Son. Whether you live or die, this ends in honor. You are already a respected hero in the world's eyes."

Zeemat's eyes pixelated into a shade of green, as a depressed blue blended in with his anxious orange.

"I was never meant for this," he said softly.

"They prepared you, and you've done well enough," Yonek said, removing his arm off Zeemat's shoulder and walking toward the ship.

"I barely survived the training program," Zeemat said, following behind. "And I'm not accomplished like my crewmates. I'm surprised and grateful every day that they accept me."

"*Grzzt.* Of course they do," Yonek scoffed. "They follow orders."

Zeemat sighed. "I hope it's more than that. I didn't earn my place like they did—we all know that. I'm here because you assigned me. But they don't hold it against me. They want me to know as much as I can about their jobs, in case something were to happen to any one of them, so I could take over. Maybe they say that to be nice, but it has motivated me."

"Motivate yourself," Yonek said, his natural impatience and intolerance showing, "with strength!"

He grabbed Zeemat by the front of his uniform and drew him near, so close that their faces nearly touched. He smiled, trying his best to sound amicable.

"You got a coveted spot on the mission. Now, do something good with it. There's a whole new world to explore and conquer."

Yonek touched his forehead to Zeemat's, and their eyes glistened pink, a surprisingly tender moment, before Yonek finally released him. Yonek turned away so Zeemat couldn't see the conflict of emotions brewing inside him.

Zeemat straightened his rumpled uniform and composed himself as well. He knew he was not a warrior or a conqueror. In fact, he hoped to find peace on Cerulea. *And maybe a place to paint*, he dared to think. He held on to a slim hope that he might be free to paint again at some point in the distant future, once they established themselves on Cerulea. Three years at the

Academy had not extinguished his desire—his need—to paint the world as he saw it, as he wanted it to be.

"I plan to make a difference, Father, to make things better," Zeemat said, knowing it was something his father would want to hear.

"*Zzzt*. And I'm making sure you do just that," Yonek replied. "To explore, to fight, and to conquer, like a Torkiyan."

EIGHT

FULL CERULEA

THE DAY CAME when Zeemat, Meah, Dirk, and Ehya began the cleansing ritual for the long voyage, eating only the special pre-cryo diet for several days. They rested and prepared their minds in the traditional Torkiyan manner before a launch. The team approached the desired peaceful state as best they could, limiting sadness, anger, or regret over the past, fear or anxiety about the future, and focusing on the present moment, on the immediate task at hand.

The crew were not allowed to bring additional physical items on board the ship. Personal images, holograms, and personal files had been uploaded to Janusia's Trangula for viewing by the crew at any time. Zeemat was grateful to have images and holos of his family, friends, and of his paintings.

They donned their comfortable space suits. The cabin would be pressurized the entire way. There was no need to use the heavier pressure suits and helmets in their personal lockers on board unless something forced them to leave the ship for some unexpected reason. Janusia the ship was built using the latest self-healing ionic metal construction, so there should be no reason for external repairs in space, no reason to use the suits or the upper hatch until they reached their destination.

His crewmates impressed and humbled Zeemat. Dirk, for all his craziness, looked like a handsome adventurer, reminding Zeemat of the historical images of so many adventurers before him. Captain Meah had become a picture of ruthless Torkiyan confidence, prepared to manage all Janusia's systems and any situation that may arise. And Ehya, with one eyebrow cocked and leaning forward as if in attack mode, looked like the fierce navigator and fighter pilot she truly was. Zeemat stood next to her and took a deep breath to catch a whiff of her intoxicating aroma, a powerful force of attraction. Her scent made him tingle.

The crew had completed all their preflight preparations. Now it was time to receive their formal orders and to be escorted to a large reception room at the base of the launch complex.

In the center of the room stood a statue of none other than Zeemat's father, the Supreme Commander of Mission 51, made famous by his exploits during the Senechian War. The base of the statue was a half dome made of pure, precious copper, symbolizing the planet Senechia, which held a good supply of it. The statue of Yonek stood tall, holding his battle helmet in one hand and his rifle in the other. His form stood over a dead Senechian, with one of his heavy boots stomped on his victim's throat. A large group of Space Academy representatives and members of the Torkiyan media surrounded the statue, anticipating the arrival of the crew of Mission 51.

"*Zzzt.* Smile, Torkiyan," Dirk prompted the anxious Zeemat. "Do you want to look good in the history books, or do you want them to see that ugly face?"

Zeemat saw his crewmates waving at the holo cameras and followed suit. The event was broadcasted over the entire planet, and Zeemat wanted to at least *appear* strong and prepared, even if he felt closer to the exact opposite. Everyone would pore over images of the launch spectacle, and his conflicting feelings would only sully those historic images. He didn't want to show the planet that he was not as intelligent as Dirk, as brave as Ehya, or as capable as Meah. All they needed to see was that he was willing to do what he'd been commanded to do. So he smiled and waved at the cameras.

The last moments on their home planet were for the official orders from the Supreme Commander of Mission 51, supreme commander Yonek. The crew's response to the traditional mission orders would amount to the mission promises, personal oaths of the greatest importance, never to be broken. Zeemat had been pushed into this, but he was now prepared to accept it all. He considered how far he'd come as his father took the podium, straightened his uniform, and cleared his throat. The moment was finally here.

Yonek saluted the crew, and they saluted back.

"*Zzzt.* Crew of Mission 51," Yonek announced in a loud, commanding voice. "I salute you! Your mission is to represent Torkiya and to secure the planet Cerulea. Do you accept your mission?"

The crew responded to the ritual mission directive in unison: "With pride, strength, and honor!"

"You will enlighten the planet Cerulea with Torkiyan Knowledge, Wisdom, and Truth. Do you accept your mission?"

"With pride, strength, and honor!"

Yonek continued. "You will establish a colony and defeat all sapient species you find on Cerulea. You will use them to gather copper and anything of value for the future benefit of Torkiya. You will connect our worlds. Do you accept your mission?"

"With pride, strength, and honor!"

"Then go bravely and . . . FULL CERULEA!" Yonek announced that final traditional command at the top of his voice, with arms outstretched.

The crew saluted and repeated, "Full Cerulea!" The saying was a declaration of brave acceptance of their dangerous mission—a promise to do or die for their planet and their people.

When the Ceremony of Orders and Promises was complete, the crew waved a final goodbye to the cameras. They were led into a small elevator that took them to Janusia, sitting at the tip of a large rocket. The crew entered their ship, assumed their positions, and performed the immediate prelaunch tasks they'd been trained to do.

They completed their checklists, strapped in to their seats, and notified Mission Control when everything was all set. The soon-to-be space travelers sat patiently until the launch team was ready as well. Zeemat shut his eyes tight in anticipation—and to fight the dizziness and disorientation he felt, even though they were still on the ground. He was glad they had eaten a light preflight meal because he felt it in his throat. He concentrated on his heavy breathing, trying to slow his racing heart, to calm himself down. He'd already drenched his uniform in sweat, and he feared he might soil himself at any moment.

Finally, the slow countdown began, and the rocket engines ignited. The launchpad was engulfed in flame and smoke, and the large rocket lifted off the ground. The clocks and timers on board Janusia and in Mission Control started to spin.

The much-anticipated blastoff proceeded smoothly, though inside the cabin, the crew experienced the wild vibration and bone-crushing G-force of the launch as Mission 51 departed in a deafening, land-shattering roar.

To Zeemat, the moment was colored by high anxiety—or utter panic—and it felt unreal, like a dream, a nightmare from which he would not wake up. They had just left their home planet forever, and his future was far from certain. This might well be the end of their lives, he reasoned, and everyone but him seemed to be okay with that. His home was disappearing fast behind him, and Janusia would never be a home to him—he had never felt so disconnected in his entire life.

Shortly after, as they continued to ascend into space, the boosters separated, and Janusia rocketed at a rapid 3D speed. Zeemat imagined the cheers of joy ringing out all over Torkiya, as the heroes—even though he'd never feel like one—were on their way.

After the violent noise and flames of blastoff subsided he pictured his father back at Mission Control. He imagined him remaining at the observation window until the ship was but a tiny bright dot in the sky and finally disappearing altogether, along with his only son.

He may never know what happens to me, Zeemat thought.

NINE

CERULEA 1521

WHEN ZEEMAT AND the others departed the planet Torkiya, it was the year 1521 on the planet Cerulea. A fleet of Spanish supply ships lay harbored in Veracruz on the Mexican gulf coast. Groups of soldiers and supply carts were strung along the dirt road leading from the coast to the heart of Aztec territory in central Mexico. At the end of the line, Hernán Cortés sat on his horse, observing the destruction of Tenochtitlán, the Aztec capital, from his vantage point at the top of a hill.

Thick streams of smoke emanated from the burning huts down below. His troops had easily overtaken the indigenous people, who'd fought with sticks, stones, and obsidian knives to defend their homeland—no match for armored men on horseback yielding metal swords and spears. The Spanish had cut through the Aztecs like a sharp knife through warm butter. Now they would find their gold.

By Cortés's side, Father Bartolomé sat on his own horse, overlooking the massacre. He hoped some natives would survive to justify his own presence there. His task was to change them—to bring religion, education, and culture to these Aztec heathens, whether they liked it or not.

TEN

THE FIFTH DIMENSION

EVERYTHING BECAME STILL when the final rocket booster separated. The vibration from the powerful rocket that had shot them into space had dissipated. Now it seemed as if they weren't moving at all, even as they careened through space, traveling away from Torkiya and toward Cerulea at a rapid but still conventional 3D speed.

The crew unfastened their safety harnesses and stored them away, hoping they would need them again one day in the far future, for their hopeful landing on Cerulea. But for now, they could move without restriction in Janusia's small cabin.

Dirk ran through a routine checklist to ensure all systems remained functional, especially the engines and computers. He performed a careful preliminary setup and testing of the fragile Gravitational Wave Sensors. He also confirmed that the shock-wave weapon system was intact. Ehya reviewed the navigational programming. Meah ensured all life support systems had survived the rough moments of the launch.

"*Zzzt*. Status!" Captain Meah said, breaking the silence as the others continued their work.

"Computer systems and propulsion fully functional," Dirk replied.

"Navigation parameters set," Ehya added.

"Good. And life systems intact," Meah said.

Zeemat double-checked everything on his own screen. "Materials and Supplies one hundred percent," he said with a short, gurgling laugh. "Because we just started the mission."

"Stick to the script," Captain Meah commanded, scolding Zeemat for making light of the moment. "Janusia, report," she added.

"All operational algorithms one hundred percent," Janusia intoned, emitting a brief pulse of a warm, red glow to the cabin and a pleasant, audible *chime* to diffuse the tension.

Meah sent a communication back to Mission Control: "All systems responding one hundred percent. We will now proceed into 4D."

Dirk began the process of the gradual acceleration required to enter the dangerous 4D and the unknown 5D realities. "Janusia, start the antimatter engine and bring us up to one-quarter Terminal Velocity."

"Starting the antimatter engine," Janusia confirmed, emitting a pulse of green light.

They all felt a sudden jolt as the powerful main engine kicked in. Everyone watched their screens as the engine increased thrust, and Janusia rapidly gained speed.

After some time, and several meals later, Janusia announced, "Stable at twenty-five-percent Terminal Velocity."

"Crew, reports," Meah ordered.

Janusia was the first to respond. "Tolerating faint vibration without adverse effect."

"Direction is on course," Ehya announced.

"Computer systems and propulsion remain fully functional," Dirk said. "Weapon system intact."

"Remaining supplies and materials within planned parameters and water recyclers at one-hundred-percent efficiency," Zeemat added.

"And life systems intact," Meah concluded, glancing at the multisystem data on her monitor screen. She examined all the data carefully for signs of any trouble. It concerned her that Janusia should exhibit any vibration at all at this speed.

"We are now approaching 4D," she said, voicing what everyone already knew. She paused a moment and waited for any comments from her crew. "If there are no concerns, we'll press on."

After another few moments of silence, Janusia piped in: "No objections registered."

Meah examined her screen once more before commanding, "Slow burn the main engine to fifty-percent Terminal Velocity."

Dirk set the parameters, and the engine obeyed. This time there was no jolt as their speed slowly increased.

Shortly after, Ehya was first to notice the ship bending.

"Captain," she began. "Distortion detected at the ship's stem."

Meah calmly checked her screen to confirm. "Noted."

At first, the ship's distortion was barely noticeable, but as they gained speed and entered the Fourth Dimension, the ship began to distort visibly and wildly. The entire ship bent in one direction, then another. It elongated, then shrunk. It twisted and regained its shape, ultimately developing an unsteady vibration.

Inside the ship, the crew also suffered the distortion effects of 4D as they knew to expect. Their physical bodies stretched to their limits, contracted, bent, and twisted. To make matters worse, traversing through the gravitational waves of deep space at that speed increased the violent vibration. They had to adjust to a sense of double vision as their physical bodies shook wildly.

A still-calm Meah requested an update: "Janusia, report!"

"Stable at 4D velocity, 0.1 Light Speed," Janusia replied. "We are experiencing the expected distortion and vibration. All systems and algorithms remain functional at one hundred percent. G-sensor deployment advised."

The crew confirmed Janusia's brief report. Everything seemed to be in order, though Meah remained concerned about the early onset of the vibration. She looked around again for any sign of trouble but found none.

Meah turned to Dirk. "G-sensor status?" she inquired.

"G-Wave Sensors online," Dirk responded.

"Engage G-sensors," she commanded.

"Engaging G-sensors," Dirk confirmed. He entered the computer commands to turn the Gravitational Wave Sensor system on.

The fusion-driven positional engines began to spit and spurt in small, short blasts, seemingly at random. Janusia emitted a harsh, audible sound, a grating description of their rough course through the gravitational waves of deep space. The sounds of the engines and Janusia's audible representation confirmed that the G-sensors were at work. The ship now made subtle corrections in direction and velocity to better align with the gravitational waves through which they were traveling. They were approaching what Torkiyans called Harmonic Convergence.

The ship's vibration began to subside. At the same time, Janusia's grating sounds gradually turned into a more pleasing *hum*. The distortion continued, but at least the vibration was much more tolerable, making it easier for the crew to get back to their jobs.

Ehya turned her screen into comparison clock mode and beamed. "*Zzzt*. Time differences between Janusia and Torkiya noted," she announced. The clocks back home were spinning faster than their own clocks on board the ship.

Zeemat and Dirk burst out into cheers, and Meah allowed it. They all felt the same way—it was a tremendous thrill to know they were flying through the geometric construction of space-time in a 4D reality.

Before making the next move, accelerating into 5D, Meah took a moment to send a message back home. "Stable in 4D and about to enter 5D. From the crew of Janusia, we send our love and gratitude, and we will keep you in memory."

Zeemat understood the subtext of this message, and suddenly he felt overwhelmed by a powerful wave of sadness and loneliness, killing the joy he'd felt just a few moments before. He knew this would be the last message from Janusia that his father or anyone else on Torkiya would ever hear. By the time they awakened from cryo in two hundred fifty years, all the people he had ever known back home would be long dead, and for Zeemat this was an almost unbearable thought.

Why were they doing all this if not for the people back home whom they knew and loved? He put his elbows on his workstation and held his head in his hands. If that wasn't bad enough, there was no assurance he'd be coming out of cryo—in two hundred fifty years, he might be just as dead himself. So many things could go wrong. But he hoped they wouldn't. He hoped that someday they would send a similar message about surviving 5D when they reached Cerulea's star system, but that would go to an entirely different set of technicians at Mission Control, and their radio message would take fifty years to get there. He felt a rising anxiety, almost a panic, but he felt grateful for the presence of his seemingly unaffected crewmates—without knowing it, they helped calm him.

"Are you all ready to make history?" Meah asked, finally speaking at ease. There was no further need for formality. They had no one to answer to except for themselves.

At the thought of "making history," the crew again erupted into cheers and applause. Janusia chimed in with a colorful display of lights flashing around the ship's interior. Each of them confirmed their systems remained fully functional. They were now ready to take the perilous step into the unknown Fifth Dimension.

"Then, let's proceed!" Meah commanded. "Janusia, fill the cryo beds."

As if he hadn't already had enough, Zeemat sweated through another wave of anxiety as he waited for the cryo-system tubing to begin spurting the cold fluid.

Janusia filled the beds with the cryo fluid stored in a special tank under the floor. There was just enough fluid to fill the four beds.

To tolerate the increased distortion and vibration they would experience in 5D, each of them would have to be immersed in fluid. The cryo fluid also served the purpose of preserving their bodies for the long travel ahead.

Meah, leading by example, was the first to remove her clothes and lower her body into the freezing fluid.

"See you in the far future!" she announced to the crew, confident and precise, as if this were just another simulation. She nodded to Dirk as she sank herself into the fluid, inhaled, and closed her eyes, drifting into cryo sleep. Dirk and Janusia made sure her cryo-bed lid was safely secured.

Ehya stepped out of her clothes. "I'll be dreaming about our mission," she said to Zeemat, and she gave him a long hug.

Between his anxiety and his feelings for Ehya, Zeemat felt as if his heart were pounding out of his chest. He was grateful for Ehya, his very first friend at the Academy, and his intended mate on Cerulea. She'd given him a powerful sense of hope for the future. He helped his beautiful crewmate ease into her tank. They looked into each other's eyes as she lost consciousness. He stood by as Janusia sealed the lid to her bed, making sure it was secure. After that, he took a deep breath. Soon it would be his turn. Zeemat was afraid to go under and afraid of what he'd find when he awoke, but he was a little encouraged by Meah's and Ehya's fearlessness.

Dirk was already halfway into his tank, shivering.

"Before you go under . . ." Zeemat began, hoping for one last confirmation. "Are the computers, engines, and G-sensors in order? Are we truly all set? Can Janusia handle 5D?"

"Everything's perfect," Dirk said, brimming with his usual good humor and confidence. "Just do what they trained you to do. Get into your tank. Janusia will seal you in."

With that, Dirk submerged himself and inhaled. As he rapidly lost consciousness, he grabbed at his throat and made a face as if he were drowning, then smiled and faded into cryo sleep.

Zeemat shook his head, amazed at his friend's persistent sense of humor, even under these intense circumstances. He returned to his console to make one final check of supplies and materials as they'd trained him to do before entering his cryo bed. He was alone now, and he surely felt it. His friends were in their "cryo coffins," his own pet name for them, and they would be there for a long, long time. Even before feeling the cryo fluid against his skin, he felt chills.

Janusia interrupted: "Whenever you are ready, Zeemat, I will seal you in safely. Then I will accelerate us into 5D and proceed to Cerulea."

Her calm, cheerful voice belied the historic significance of the achievement—the first long-range voyage in 5D.

Zeemat looked around. He assumed everything was in order. He had to trust that the others and Janusia had everything in hand because he certainly didn't understand all the details of running a spaceship. He took another deep breath, acutely aware of how nice it was simply to breathe. Finally, he resigned himself.

"Okay then, Janusia. I guess I'm ready."

Zeemat stripped out of his clothes, folded them neatly, and placed them on his chair. He then slid into the tank, shocked as usual by the frigid fluid. Before going under, he gave the ship one last look around and said his last words to Janusia: "Take good care of us, Janusia. We'll talk again when we approach Cerulea."

"Yes, Zeemat," Janusia replied with a tender informality. "We'll talk again when I bring you out of cryopreservation in Cerulea's star system. I'll keep you safe." She sent a warm red glow over the entire ship for Zeemat to see as he lowered himself into the fluid.

When Zeemat was asleep, Janusia slid the automatic lid over his bed and confirmed three times that the seal was secure. He was the most important part of her mission, after all. Iohma's programming told her so.

Now that her valuable passengers were secured safely in cryo, Janusia powered the main engine. She brought up her speed to the planned Terminal Velocity of 0.2 Light Speed.

They entered the Fifth Dimension.

Despite the perfect performance of the G-sensors, computers, and fine adjustments in direction and velocity by the positional engines, the distortion and vibration effects on Janusia were wild. Yet the ship remained whole because of the inherent elasticity and self-healing properties of its ionic metal construction. Parts of the ship bent, stretched, and twisted, but then regained their original shape. Micro-cracks self-healed. Everything was holding up fine—everything except for a few defective bolts holding the cryo beds in place.

ELEVEN

FORTY LIGHT-YEARS IN

JANUSIA KEPT CONTINUOUS watch over her systems and witnessed the relative passage of time on the clocks. She monitored the health and effectiveness of the G-sensors and computers, which sent moment-to-moment instructions to her positional engines for fine adjustments to speed and direction. She monitored the degree of vibration to be sure it remained within her tolerance. She monitored navigation to be sure they were headed in an overall direction toward Cerulea's star system.

She also monitored the cryo-bed seals and the fluid levels within them, especially the one that housed Zeemat. *Above all, take Zeemat safely to Cerulea.* That was her prime directive. It was a hard-wired command installed by Iohma herself, Zeemat's loving mother, the Chief Programmer of the ship's Synthetic Soul.

To conserve energy, Janusia turned off all the lights and lowered the temperature to just above freezing. She did not need light or warmth to do her job. She also monitored the status of the crew's stored food and water supply, which they would need for the final, short part of the journey, when she brought them out of cryo.

She monitored the ship this way for forty light-years, about 80 percent of the distance to their destination. She heard the perfect sputtering of the positional engines and the steady *hum* of tolerable vibration for a very long time.

Then suddenly, without warning or explanation, one of the G-sensors failed. Janusia could no longer detect all the surrounding gravitational waves. Without the information from even one sensor, the entire Gravitational Wave Detection System shut down. The moment-to-moment instructions to the positional engines came to an immediate stop.

A shock of vibration blasted the ship. Janusia sensed a violent pounding on her hull from the surrounding G-waves at 0.2 Light Speed. She knew the vibration would worsen if she didn't do something fast. They were in critical danger of breaking apart.

In an instant, Janusia took control of her positional engines and tried to redirect herself so that her main engine faced in the direction they were traveling. She intended to fire the engine and slow herself down. She would then see if there was a way to repair the malfunctioning G-sensor and resume her high-speed journey.

But before she could maneuver herself into position, she encountered an area of thick gravitational waves. Janusia struck them head-on at 5D speed, suffering a massive jolt to her hull, followed by even wilder vibration, throwing her way off Harmonic Alignment. The entire ship began to distort uncontrollably and intolerably.

The weakest link is always the first to go. On their ship, the weakest links were a few of the bolts that held the cryo beds in place. They didn't measure up to the tight specifications, unable to withstand that final jolt and sudden increase in vibration. The faulty bolts shattered, skyrocketing in multiple directions all over and through the ship.

One deadly bolt cut the cryo-fluid line that connected the beds to the empty tank below. Immediately, cryo fluid leaked out of the beds. The levels inside the cryo beds fell, and the typically calm Janusia went into panic mode.

Another bolt flew through Dirk's computers, damaging the system that allowed fine control of propulsion. Another bolt went through Meah's environmental-control computers. Another bolt destroyed internal sensors Janusia used to keep track of activities inside the cabin. With each injury, Janusia felt herself lose a measure of awareness, capability, and consciousness. She lost full control of herself.

A large bolt blasted through the barrier toward the main engine, breaking through the interior wall and lodging inside the workings of the engine itself. The main engine was lost. Fortunately, the adjacent antimatter reactor remained intact—a sudden release of antimatter would have annihilated the ship.

But the worst of it resulted from a bolt that shot upward from the base of Ehya's cryo bed, piercing a hole in the underside of her bed, shooting through her torso, continuing through the top lid of the bed, and through the ceiling, all the way to the outside of the ship. The deadly bolt continued in a straight line, at a high rate of speed, into never-ending space. The hull instantly repaired itself, something Ehya's damaged body could not do.

Now the fluid in Ehya's cryo bed was leaking out rapidly through the hole in the bottom as it drew even more fluid from the three other interconnected beds.

Janusia's complex consciousness began to fade. She was shaking and vibrating at 0.2 Light Speed, about to break apart. If she didn't act quickly, all would be lost. She fought desperately to keep herself alive. She would have to survive first if she was to accomplish her primary mission directive—to 'take Zeemat safely to Cerulea.'

Janusia snapped into emergency mode. She shut down her modern systems and worked off her basic programming, hoping to restore herself later. Before going basic, she gave herself a priority of commands.

The first thing she did, while still shaking and vibrating at 0.2 Light Speed, was to shunt all remaining cryo fluid to Zeemat's bed. There was just enough remaining fluid to fill one bed. It would not be feasible to wake everyone up because there was not enough food and water to last them to Cerulea, especially since they would have to slow down for the remainder of the long trip.

So she drained Dirk, Ehya, and Meah's beds dry, leaving the lids tightly sealed. She filled Zeemat's bed to the brim. She shut off the valves that connected his bed to the ruptured fluid line and to the other beds. Zeemat was safe. Priority number one was complete.

The next thing she did while in basic mode was to confirm that the main engine had died, then to test the positional engines. She quickly discovered that the small positional engines were still functional and controllable, so she used them to position herself in the optimum configuration to slow herself down. It took a long while, but she gradually slowed out of 5D and settled safely in 4D. Considering the state of her injuries, the remaining vibration became tolerable when she slowed to 0.05 Light Speed.

The third task she gave herself was to test navigation. She discovered that the system was no longer functional. She retrieved the files of navigational stars, estimating her position and that of Cerulea, and redirected herself to a place somewhere within Cerulea's star system.

Now that she had stabilized the catastrophe, Janusia tried to restore herself to her full, complex form, until she quickly realized she could not. The damage to the various computers and internal sensors was permanent. She would be forever impaired. Yet she decided she was still most valuable as an impaired version of her full self rather than the automaton she was in basic mode.

Janusia felt incomplete. She had lost her main engine. She felt that a critical part of her being had been removed. She was unable to send commands to multiple parts of herself, and she even discovered that she could not send a message to Torkiya. Though she was able to compose a message, for some reason she could not send it. She couldn't always speak, and what she said didn't always match what she was thinking. As she couldn't turn on every light, she couldn't see everything. She couldn't regulate her temperature. She continued to monitor her systems as best she could, but there were definite gaps in her awareness. The reality of her handicaps frustrated her immensely, but it would have to do.

She was aware that Dirk, Ehya, and Meah were dead or dying inside their cryo beds, which made her feel like a failure. But Zeemat was safe. In case something else happened, Janusia set parameters for Zeemat's automatic arousal from cryo. She again turned down all systems to energy-saving mode, including many of her own processes, but she kept herself at full alert, such as it was, running inspection routines at regular intervals.

With a sense of responsibility, loss, and dread, Janusia settled in for an even longer voyage.

TWELVE

CERULEA 1776

AT THE TIME of Janusia's catastrophe in space, it was the year 1776 on the planet Cerulea.

On the east coast of the North American continent, European invaders were fighting among themselves after displacing or eliminating entire tribes of indigenous people.

On the west coast, a ship was anchored safely in the San Francisco Bay. The Spanish had a solid stronghold in Mexico and were spreading their influence north. Juan Bautista de Anza led the expedition, bringing colonists, soldiers, livestock, and a Catholic priest to their northernmost outpost.

Padre Francisco Palóu was given the task of establishing the sixth mission along the coast of Alta California. Now it was time for the local Ohlone Indians to be educated, civilized, and converted to the Catholic faith, whether *they* liked it or not.

Padre Palóu organized the construction of Misión Dolores, the Mission of our Lady of Sorrows, while de Anza directed the unloading and distribution of the ship's supplies. The soldiers made sure they had enough labor to carry out their plans.

"*Vamos!* Ya! *Apúrate!*" a soldier yelled in the ear of an Ohlone native man. He prodded him with the blunt end of his spear to encourage him to move faster.

The defeated Native American man carried a heavy load of supplies, his tenth load of the day, and deposited it at the site of the mission. Padre Palóu gave him a drink of water. The native man shot the priest a look of pure hatred.

In other parts of the city, the colonists whipped the Native Americans for failing to finish their tasks quickly enough. They were helping build a school to be used for their education and a jail to be used for their punishment. Older women were told to make food for the soldiers. Younger women fed the soldiers' other appetites.

The Spanish leader, de Anza, toiled and suffered through every aspect of the difficult expedition. He had seen many of his fellow Spaniards die while trying to colonize the New World. He made every effort to ensure the survival of the brave colonists in his charge.

At the end of a brutal day of arduous work, an exhausted Ohlone man sat by a campfire. His losses were mounting—his family, his friends, his people, and his entire way of life were dying, and there was nothing he could do to stop it. He lay back, defeated, as he watched a tower of sparks rise from the campfire, fading and disappearing into the star-filled sky.

THIRTEEN

DEAD

ONE-HUNDRED AND SEVENTY-SEVEN years later, Zeemat stood naked, wet, cold, and confused, gazing out the ship's windows at the same star-filled sky, trying to orient himself and determine his position in space. With the back of his hands, he wiped a foggy film of cryo fluid from his eyes and confirmed by the stars that he'd made his way to Cerulea's planetary system, but they were not as close to Cerulea as he thought they should be. By the small appearance of the system's star, he could tell they had a great distance yet to go.

Janusia had awakened him from cryo, but she wouldn't or couldn't speak to him. He shivered and fumbled around in the darkness to discover his computer no longer worked.

As the fog began to clear from his mind, he realized the others had not come out of cryo. He assumed Janusia was in some sort of sleep mode, and he tried to figure a way to make her wake up, but she still hadn't responded. His computer didn't work, so he tried Dirk's, then Ehya's—none of them worked. Then he sat at Meah's station. "*Zzzt*. Janusia, respond!" he said, his voice laden with rising concern.

"Welcome," Janusia replied in a flat tone of voice.

"*Zzzt.* Janusia! What's going on? Get the others out of cryo. Turn everything on."

Janusia did not respond.

"Janusia, turn on the lights!"

A single light turned on over Zeemat's head.

Zeemat was able to wave Meah's computer on. Her default screen detailed a summary of all the ship's life systems, and Zeemat gasped at discovering the condition of the ship. Fuel was low, food and water for a crew of four were not enough to last for the estimated time of arrival to Cerulea at the current speed, the main engine was dead, and so were three of the cryo beds.

Zeemat snapped his body around to face the cryo beds and rushed to Ehya's. In a growing panic, he tried to pry the lid off her bed, but it wouldn't budge. He noticed there was a partially healed hole in the lid. "Janusia! Help me!" he commanded.

"How may I be of assistance?" Janusia responded.

"You can see what I'm doing!" Zeemat screamed, still struggling with the tight seal of the cryo bed. "Help me remove this lid!"

"Which lid?" Janusia asked.

Zeemat was desperate now, his confusion twisting into dread. Why wasn't Janusia helping? Why couldn't she see what he was doing and anticipate his needs? She was programmed for so much more than this. He tried being more specific.

"Janusia, release all the cryo-bed lids."

At once, all the cryo-bed lids released. There was no hiss and no steam as he'd expected. He pushed Ehya's lid aside, looked in, and then took two staggering steps back, eyes in a panic of silver, and he covered his mouth in a shock of horror.

Ehya was dead. A horrible odor emitted from her open cryo bed. Her once-beautiful body was dry, shriveled, and shrunken, and there was a hole in what remained of her chest. This had happened a very long time ago.

Zeemat became acutely dizzy. The room spun around him, and he fell to his hands and knees. He vomited the little cryo fluid that remained in his stomach.

When he partly recovered his senses, he crawled his way to Meah's bed and slid the lid aside, fully anticipating what he would find. Her chest did not have a hole in it, but time had shriveled her body just like Ehya's. Her dried-up face was frozen in a permanent look of terror. Her palms faced upward, and her hands had hardened in a clawlike position. Her fingernails were missing. It looked as if she had been trying to claw her way out of the tank.

Zeemat sobbed uncontrollably now, and it took all his strength and resolve to move the lid of Dirk's bed. He had trouble seeing through his dizziness and the dim light. His mind reeled from what he was witnessing. The rank odor from Dirk's bed nauseated him, but he had to confirm the status of his good friend.

Dirk's body and posture looked just like Meah's. He, too, had tried to escape his cryo bed before he died.

Zeemat again collapsed to his knees and held his head in his hands. Through sobs and screams, he asked, "What happened, Janusia? How did this happen?"

But Janusia would not or could not respond.

FOURTEEN

DISABLED

ZEEMAT CAME TO realize that Janusia was profoundly disabled. When he sat in what was once Meah's chair, Janusia turned on lights for his convenience and turned them off when he stepped away. The heater would turn on for short periods of time if he was freezing. At times when he felt particularly despondent, a brief flurry of random lights and sounds from Janusia would surprise him and cheer him up a little. Janusia was not dead, but she was severely injured. Her communication was almost nonexistent, and despite consulting the Trangula, which was thankfully intact, Zeemat was unable to repair her.

When he sat in Meah's chair, he could give Janusia a simple command, and she would sometimes execute it, sometimes not. When Zeemat sat in any other part of the ship, Janusia would never respond to any of his commands. Zeemat realized that Janusia's awareness of the ship was spotty and limited.

"I remember thinking you were just a machine," Zeemat said in a hoarse voice. "Now I wish you were here. I miss you."

He rose from Meah's chair, took a few steps into the cold, dark, silent cabin, and then returned to the chair.

"There's nothing I can do," he said, staring out the window into the deeper darkness, numb, paralyzed, and hopeless. His eyes would have turned to a mournful magenta, but he was too tired for that.

A long time had passed since Janusia had awakened him from cryo, when he first realized he was utterly alone. Looking out the window, he identified two planets close by. He'd seen them before, through the powerful space telescopes back home. The one with the beautiful rings was the sixth planet from the star. The largest one, the one mainly composed of gas, was the fifth. He found himself to be somewhere between those two planets. And far in the distance, he was able to spot the tiny light of Cerulea itself, just peeking out from the right side of the system's star as it orbited around.

For most of this time, he couldn't appreciate much progress by looking at the distant stars. Meah's monitor told him he was traveling at a miserably slow 3D speed. He had attempted to repair the main engine but found out something had happened to its inner workings. It was dead and there was no reviving it. So there was no purpose to the large amount of antimatter fuel that remained in the reactor. He decided not to use the small amount of nuclear fuel left for the tiny fusion-driven positional engines, saving it for an approach to Cerulea, establishment of orbit, descent, and landing, if he could figure out how to do any of those things. He had seen his crewmates execute perfect landings on multiple simulations, but he had never done one himself. It seemed less and less likely he could make all that happen on a damaged ship without its heroic crew. But he tried to hold on to a fading hope. Zeemat continued at this frustrating speed and waited . . . and observed . . . and studied. The ship's Trangula was his only hope of survival.

"For today's lesson, we're going to learn how to intercept a moving planet and establish an orbit around it," he said out loud to himself.

He'd recently picked up the habit of speaking to himself. There was no one, not even Janusia, to join him in conversation, or to lead him through a lesson, so he had to do it himself. Sometimes he encouraged himself, like his parents had done when he was young—or scolded himself, like his parents had done when he grew older. He even argued with himself, having full conversations—anything to keep from going insane in the solitary confinement inside the shell of Janusia.

"I've always known it—this is my crypt, my tomb," he once lamented. Janusia would have normally replied with a positive statement, or a cheerful display of lights and sounds. But now . . . nothing. He felt as if the silence and loneliness were swallowing him up, like the drowning sensation when he submerged himself in cryo fluid. So he spent as much time as he could studying data on the Trangula and distracting himself in any way he could.

Sometimes he passed the time by taking inventory of the ship's supplies. That was his assigned role, after all. He rationed out his own food and kept the water and oxygen recyclers working. He tried his hand at other repairs around the ship. His first thought had been to restore Janusia from the Trangula's backup, but the problem had occurred with the damaged computers on board the ship. A fresh program wouldn't make a difference. But if he couldn't repair the ship, he could at least learn other things to help him survive. The Trangula held a world of information. He watched and listened to holographs of all kinds of Torkiyan knowledge, especially about flying the ship, computer languages, rocket science, and communication technologies. He hoped other information would be useful on

Cerulea, but that seemed less important, as he truly doubted that he could make a successful landfall.

He continued to devour information as the tiny light of Cerulea gradually grew larger, circled around to the left side of the star, and then disappeared behind it. Unlike during his years of unmotivated study before being forced into the Space Academy, he'd grown to motivate himself. Those were his father's words, he recalled with a sad smile—*Motivate yourself!* He finally saw the wisdom in those words and wished his father could see what he was doing. He sighed at the memory as he scrolled through more information on the Trangula, trying to figure out how to manually work Janusia's positional engines. If he was to survive, he would have to somehow intercept Cerulea next time it came back around as it orbited the star.

He looked out the windows at the vast, empty space and dreamed of floating out there, breathing his last breaths in wide-open space instead of being trapped in the crypt of Janusia. He longed for the freedom of the outdoors back on Torkiya. He wondered if he would ever experience anything like that on Cerulea.

He wondered if the predictions were true, that Cerulea was warm enough for life, that it had liquid water, that it almost certainly harbored life. Who cared about the quest for copper at this point? He'd never cared much about that, anyway. He wondered if he would be able to breathe in Cerulea's atmosphere. But he realized his imaginations were foolish. His chances of intercepting Cerulea and establishing an orbit around it were unlikely, and the chances of a successful landing were almost nil. Yet somehow a spark of hope persisted as the time and distance to Cerulea grew shorter.

He had been alone on Janusia for a long time, nearly a full revolution of Cerulea around its star, but he didn't feel as if he'd made much progress—it felt as if Janusia was plodding her way through the thick mud of space.

"I can only tell I'm moving when I see the nearby planets," he said, his weakening voice now just a coarse whisper. The fourth planet from the star came into view. He leaned against the window and plastered his face to it, his thin legs shaking, hardly able to hold his frail weight. He was fascinated by this reddish planet. He knew it was still too cold to harbor life, so there was no sense trying to land there, especially since that would not be the case for the next planet, his destination—Cerulea.

He could see that the system's star appeared larger now. His people believed Cerulea orbited in the same warm zone that Torkiya did around its own star. As time passed, as he approached the position where he calculated Cerulea would be, he became more anxious about that known fact.

"After what we've suffered to get here, Cerulea better be warm. It better have water. It better have life, or my own life has been for nothing."As Zeemat spoke to himself, he struggled to suppress his growing anxiety, to hold on to any hope at all. A thought came to mind—*I wish I could paint*—but he had no painting materials, and he could not fathom how he could possibly make this situation better by painting.

Despite his thinning body and his waning strength, he had no choice but to persist. Janusia was crawling along whether he wanted her to or not, toward a destiny that was out of his control. He felt like a captive of his own ship, probably heading to his death, but he had to forge on. No choice.

One day, his legs were so weak that they gave out, and he fell to the floor, hitting his head against a corner of Ehya's old cryo bed, cutting his forehead and drawing blood. He cried softly, letting the blood drip down his face, losing his last bits of hope.

He voiced his fears again: "Janusia, you're my prison, time is my enemy, and the end is near."

But after some time, he got himself to his feet, turned on the Trangula to keep studying, kept eating his dwindling supply of rationed food, and he pressed on.

And then one glorious day, an edge of the blue planet peeked out again from behind its star.

Zeemat felt a spark of energy ignite deep inside his body. The tiny spark grew stronger in the following days as Cerulea circled farther and came more clearly into view. He could make out some details now. With his naked eyes, he could clearly see the blue sheen for which it was named.

He made another inventory of his nearly empty supply of food and water. If he rationed strictly, it just might last, he thought. The spark of energy flashed into a flame of hope.

FIFTEEN

FINAL APPROACH

AS IT CIRCLED in its orbit from behind the sun, Cerulea was in full view. Zeemat began to smile frequently, as if a switch had been turned on. Cerulea appeared much larger now, and he could see more and more detail. After the planet rotated many times, he had memorized the shapes of the land masses and the bodies of water. He stared at the beautiful blue orb as it slowly spun on its axis, imagining what else he might observe as he drew nearer. His joy mixed with a building anxiety, doubting he could make a landing in such a damaged ship, but he had to try. He felt damaged himself—thin, emaciated, weak. He had learned all he could from the Trangula, and he no longer had the time nor the energy to study more. He eyed the gauges and worried about his scanty supply of fuel. He cursed at the cold, dead main engine and the useless supply of antimatter fuel.

"Zzzt. It's just you and me now," he said to the small positional engines that were not designed to propel Janusia, or to effectively slow her down during descent."

As he drew closer and closer to Cerulea, Zeemat felt the critical moments were approaching. But he felt sluggish, finding it difficult to move. He was so weak he could hardly lift his arms. He shivered in Janusia's cold cabin, keeping the heaters off most of the time to preserve as much fuel as possible.

"I'll need these three small engines and every bit of fuel," he said, his dull, tired eyes fixed on Cerulea.

When he finally came close enough, he used a minimum amount of fuel to thrust Janusia into a path to intercept Cerulea in its orbit around the star. He sat at Meah's old station and reviewed the calculations he'd made by hand, without the help of functioning navigational computers. He found it easier to adjust the calculations now, as Cerulea became visibly larger with each passing day. Repeatedly, he reconfigured his calculations, eager to get it right.

Janusia was vaguely aware of Zeemat's written calculations, with fewer than half of her cameras partially functional. At times she caught glimpses of his work. She was slightly more aware of her position in space, and of nearby objects. She was keenly aware of Cerulea and still held on to her main mission objectives, which included establishing an orbit, analyzing Cerulea's physical properties, providing the data to make the necessary adjustments, and landing. Now that she'd seen Zeemat's calculations, Janusia became agitated and alarmed, for his calculations were wrong.

As Janusia drew nearer to Cerulea, she could more accurately measure planetary and atmospheric conditions. Zeemat would be very pleased to know that the atmosphere was compatible with his physiology. But Cerulea itself was considerably more massive than predicted by scientists on Torkiya, fifty light-years away. Cerulea's gravitational pull would be much stronger, which Zeemat hadn't taken into account.

Janusia tried desperately to message Zeemat with an irregular series of lights and sounds, a meaningless code.

"*Zzzt.* Now what?" Zeemat said. "Janusia, you're insane." Zeemat manually turned off the lights and sounds.

Now he was almost there. His time alone in Janusia had been painfully long, progress so difficult to judge. But now Cerulea seemed to be fast approaching, even when traveling at a slow, conventional speed. Against all odds, he was finally arriving at his planned destination.

"Cerulea, Zeemat has arrived," he announced with a weak whisper of a voice. He was too tired to generate the enthusiasm this moment deserved.

On final orbital approach, he ever-so-gently tweaked the positional engines, using as little of the precious remaining fuel as possible to achieve his first stable orbit around this alien world. *I did it!* he thought. He sat back in awe and wonder as views of the planet came and went through the window of the spinning ship. He stopped to consider his whirl of emotions, which to his surprise were mostly morose.

"Historic," he said, sarcastic and miserable in his loneliness. "The others would have loved this."

Despite the obvious beauty of the planet below him, feelings of sadness and loss overwhelmed him.

"What's the point if there's no one to share this with?" He cringed at the sudden memory of loosening the ties to release his friends' dried-up bodies into the darkness of space.

The memory of seeing them disappear silently into oblivion haunted him like a recurring nightmare. He remembered saying some ceremonial words that had seemed important at the time, but he now felt he hadn't honored them enough. Zeemat considered that at his own death, no one would be there to utter ceremonial words for him—not that he deserved any.

"Damn cryo beds!" he cursed. He couldn't understand why the fluid had leaked out of the three other beds while his had remained intact. In any event, his friends had died ages ago. "But they should be here now," he cried.

He wiped a single cold tear inching down the side of his face. He felt utterly alone, and any previous idea of making a new home in a strange planet seemed absurd without the company of others. If it were possible, even being this close to his target destination, he would place himself back in the dreaded cryo and send himself back home.

He broke himself from his depressive thoughts because now, finally, here he was, floating just a few miles over the legendary planet so very far away from his own. The time had come. Zeemat tried sending a final report to Mission Control, knowing the radio message would have to cover a fifty light-year distance, and uncertain if the communications system still worked at all.

"Goodbye, Torkiya," he said with a final, weak salute to his old home planet before turning his attention to the job at hand.

He allowed Janusia to make several orbits around the planet, taking careful note of the lay of the land and the blue water. He was specifically looking for a place to land, imagining landing at a much faster speed than he would prefer. He thought about the small positional engines. "I can't slow down enough for a true landing. I'll try to land in the water.

"Large body of land, small body of water. Small body of land, large body of water," he said.

He memorized the pattern with each passing orbit. He targeted a landing in the middle of the largest body of water. Now it was just a matter of doing it. "I'll execute a perfect landing," he said, trying to encourage himself but disbelieving his own words at the same time.

Despite his doubts, his training and self-education kicked in. He had learned the series of maneuvers he needed to perform, and he cycled through the preparatory routines to deorbit, descend, and land.

"I can do it," he encouraged himself.

He took his space suit out of the locker and managed to wriggle into it, finding it easier than the last time he'd used it because he had lost so much weight. He put his helmet on and secured it. Then he got back into his chair and strapped himself in. The effort was exhausting.

Slowly and weakly, he worked the damaged controls. Truly, there was no choice. He was almost out of food. The ship was dark and cold, nearly out of fuel. He and the ship were dying.

"If I'm going to die, I want to die down there," he said, looking down at Cerulea, the beautiful blue alien planet.

He calculated the exact point at which to start the process. He oriented the ship to take maximum advantage of his small positional engines and started a long burn to descelerate. When he could feel the ship descending, he stopped the burn. He now oriented the engines so they could slow down the growing acceleration of descent. But shortly after, he realized he had made a crucial miscalculation.

"*Zzzt.* Janusia, what is happening? We're dropping too fast!"

Though he didn't know it, other Torkiyans who had come before him had made the same mistake many times before. Cerulea's mass and the gravitational pull that went along with it were much greater than Torkiyans had estimated from afar, so he was accelerating to the ground much faster than he'd expected. Zeemat slammed the control lever down to burn the small engines at full throttle, trying his best to slow his rate of descent.

About halfway down, he felt the effect of the planet's atmosphere.

Zzzt. I'm glad there's an atmosphere this high up, he thought. *But we're heating up!* He could see Janusia's forward hull glowing red hot.

Zeemat tried a series of long *S*-shaped curves to shed more speed, flying by feel for the first time in his life. He was reenergized now, with the high stress of an extremely dangerous descent and landing. He had no time for fear. He was at full attention, trying his best to survive. Then, as he looked out the windows to check his position, a sudden bright light blinded him. The heating ship burst into flames.

The inside of the ship grew hotter and hotter as his descent speed continued to increase. Between the flames, he could see the rapidly approaching land. He realized with a panic that he wouldn't reach the water at all. He was falling to the ground at an alarming rate.

Zeemat attempted to flatten out the steep trajectory of his descent. Janusia tried to respond, but it was in vain. He was going to crash. Zeemat could now see the shapes and contour of the terrain as he flew by at an incredible speed. *This is it*, he thought. *I'm dead.*

In the final moments of Janusia's flight, he spotted a mountain range in the distance ahead. He hoped he could clear the highest peak, or at least fly between the highest ridges, to the flatter land that lay farther ahead.

Just before impact, Zeemat instinctively crossed his arms in front of his face and turned away, preparing for impact.

As they collided, the mountaintop and Janusia exploded into a million pieces.

SIXTEEN

HIT ME AGAIN

SHORTLY AFTER ZEEMAT'S fateful crash, someone in Texas reported seeing a flash of light streak across the sky. Several people in New Mexico and Arizona saw a similar flash or heard a whooshing *rumble*.

The bleary-eyed people in the Las Vegas casinos were mostly oblivious. At a blackjack table, a drunk man thought he might have felt a brief jolt as a tiny wave rippled through the remains of his vodka martini.

"What was that?" he asked, though no one cared to respond. He shrugged his shoulders, pointing a shaky finger to his cards, then hiccupped and slurred an order to the dealer: "Hit me again."

PART TWO

CERULEA

SEVENTEEN

THE CRASH

ON A SWELTERING summer day in 1954, Janusia careened toward the Las Vegas Mountain Range in southern Nevada, crashing into the southeastern side of a mountain peak. In a fraction of an instant, the ship broke into countless small pieces, the antimatter fuel tank rupturing. As the antimatter spewed from the ruptured vessel, it reacted instantly with the mountaintop, annihilating the rock in a burst of gamma light and a cloud of dust. It left an unnatural, smooth, empty groove in its wake, allowing Janusia's main cabin to continue speeding forward.

What remained of the ship plunged through the annihilated mountaintop, hitting the ground on the other side. Blazing pieces of the ship ripped through the rough desert terrain in a northwesterly direction, leaving a charred gouge in its wake, like a blackened groove of a barbecue grill. The gouge extended for forty miles from the mountaintop as the debris gradually lost speed and altitude.

Bits and pieces of deformed metal came to rest and dotted the area along both sides of the dark gouge. Each of these objects glowed red hot, spewing rivulets of black smoke spiraling up to the sky.

The largest of these objects was the main cabin of the ship. It was designed to hold together as long as possible, to protect the passengers inside. The cabin crashed through the mountain, then tumbled along with the other smaller bits and pieces of the broken ship. Within the cabin, Zeemat had lost consciousness during the first moments of the violent impact. The protective cabin could not withstand the repeated collisions—it broke apart as it scraped along the hard, uneven desert floor. The shattered cabin and the few remaining pieces of the ship finally crashed to a thunderous stop, creating a gaping terminal crater about ten feet deep. The force of the final impact threw Zeemat's body a short distance from the worst of the burning wreckage. The debris gave off a tremendous heat, and a thick cloud of black smoke towered over the impact crater.

Zeemat was on his back as he regained an intermittent and foggy consciousness. He opened his eyes to a smoky, billowing darkness, with flickering moments of light blue high above. He tried to move, but lancing pain in his left arm and leg stopped him. He lay still for a moment and took a few deep breaths, trying hard to regain his full consciousness so he could figure out what to do. He noticed his breathing was becoming more labored. It was then he heard the hissing of his space suit losing pressure. It was torn in several places. As he started feeling extremely hot, a sharp, stinging burn erupted all over his body.

His mind faded again, but just before he lost consciousness, he saw again the faint flickering of a color blue above. Instinctively, he crawled toward it, up the inside of the crater, slowly, like an injured insect, using his good right arm and leg. His crawl became progressively more desperate as he realized he was in the burning wreckage of his crash site. His space suit now laid flat against his skin, completely depressurized. He believed he was breathing his final few breaths.

In desperation, he managed to crawl to the top of the crater and flopped down in pain and exhaustion when he reached the outside. With his last bit of strength, he gritted his teeth and rolled his injured body a few times to clear the edge, coming to rest on his back. Now he could see the unimpeded bright blue sky above him, and in that moment, he allowed himself a small satisfaction. With what he thought were his dying moments, he felt grateful to have reached his goal—he had landed on the planet Cerulea.

There was no more air to breathe inside his space suit, so with his right hand, he fumbled with the latch to release the visor of his helmet. The visor snapped open and fell away. He suddenly felt the heat of the Cerulean atmosphere on his alien skin, pleased and horrified at the same time—he hadn't known what to expect. He held his final breath as long as he could, finally exhaling in a slow *hiss* as his consciousness faded to black. He passed out as he gasped in his first lungful of sweet Cerulean air.

EIGHTEEN

GROOM LAKE

IN THE BLISTERING hot Mohave Desert about seventy-five miles northwest of Las Vegas, the Air Force personnel stationed at the Groom Lake airfield heard Janusia's *rumble* and crash. They felt a strong jolt under their feet, like a small earthquake. A few minutes later, one of them noticed a rising tower of black smoke in the distance. A trained crew of first responders quickly gathered emergency materials and sped in Jeeps to a presumed crash site.

At first, they approached the crash site with the trained efficiency of a military rescue. Their eyes drew immediately to the body at the edge of the large hole, the source of the black smoke. They fought through the intense heat, dragged the body onto a stretcher, and pulled him away to a safer place.

It was then that Zeemat opened his eyes and saw his first human beings, and they saw him.

"What the hell!" one of them cried out.

Zeemat looked alarmed and afraid as he heard the jumble of strange sounds coming from the man's mouth.

Zeemat tried to speak, but the burns and the smoke had injured his voice box. Not a sound came out.

Despite the many questions they might have had, the crew went right to work on Zeemat. They cut him out of his still-smoldering space suit. As they moved his left arm and leg, Zeemat winced and tried to fight them off, the pain giving him a brief shot of awareness and energy. He had been taught his entire life to consider alien life forms as his enemy, and he couldn't understand what they were doing to him. But he had no strength left to fight them off. They pinned his arm down as they continued to remove the burning space suit and covered him up with a blanket.

"Should we try to start an IV?"

Zeemat heard more of the strange sounds coming from another of these Cerulean creatures. Though he was still trying to fight them off, pushing weakly with his right arm, he gathered a vague notion that they were trying to help him. As he lost his grip on consciousness again, he realized he had no choice. He stopped fighting and made a foggy decision to resign himself to their care.

The rescue crew delivered excellent first aid as they sped Zeemat back to the base at Groom Lake. They immediately sent word to their superiors, and it blazed through the Air Force chain of command all the way to General Nathan F. Twining, one of President Dwight D. Eisenhower's Joint Chiefs of Staff.

Zeemat's consciousness came and went, and he became vaguely aware of several cycles of light and dark, day and night. He saw and felt people working over his body. He was also aware of mind-numbing pain, in part inflicted upon him by the Cerulean creatures in their efforts to help him but mainly because of the extensive injuries to his body from the crash. He cooperated with them as best he could. They continued to speak their unintelligible language and tried to communicate with him through gestures, but his weakness and his injuries interfered with any meaningful exchange. He couldn't speak because they had inserted a thick tube in his mouth that extended down his windpipe. It was attached by a long, flexible tube to a machine by his bed. When the machine hissed, his lungs inflated. He understood that it was helping him breathe, but it didn't let him talk. He wanted desperately to communicate with these people. He was convinced now of their friendly nature.

Many day–night cycles transpired before Zeemat finally got a measure of relief from his intense, continuous pain. He had tubes stuck into his right arm. The tubes were attached to bags containing a clear fluid. Sometimes they injected a small amount of another clear fluid into one of the tubes. After that, his pain would let up and he would sleep. He had bandages over much of his body. His injured left arm was bent slightly at the elbow and immobilized in a crusty, heavy, white material. His left leg had several rods through it, which were attached to a metallic contraption hoisted into the air by a series of thin ropes. The ropes fed through pulleys attached to a heavy weight on the other end.

Gradually, he noticed differences among the Ceruleans. He assumed some were male and some were female. He noticed that some were superior, and others followed commands. The helpful ones were dressed in white. He also noticed two other individuals standing off to the side. They did not assist in his care, nor did they share the friendly, smiling faces of the ones dressed in white. One was dressed in a dark green uniform with decorations pinned to the chest, arms, and shoulders. Zeemat assumed they were military decorations. Next to him stood another Cerulean creature dressed in black. As Zeemat became increasingly aware of their threatening posture and facial expressions, an alarm went off inside him—something told him they were waiting for their time to strike.

NINETEEN

AREA 51

AFTER ZEEMAT'S ARRIVAL, activity escalated at the crash site. A large area was blocked off to the curious public, who had noticed strange events happening around the Groom Lake airfield. Some had stumbled onto the dark gouge in the earth made by Janusia's final run and collected bits and pieces of the fallen aircraft. Despite roadblocks, people continued to trudge through the intense heat and the rough desert terrain to see what they could see, until armed guards surrounded the area, day and night.

President Eisenhower deployed the National Guard to the crash site. The entire area was now strictly off limits to all civilians. The US Army Corps of Engineers quickly developed an extensive compound and erected a fence around a wide perimeter, encompassing the old Groom Lake Air Force airfield and the new MASH unit—a Mobile Army Surgical Hospital. Almost a year later, in April 1955, the US Air Force claimed the general area to be a test site for military aircraft. The CIA became involved, shrouding the entire project in utmost secrecy, and planes started flying in and out of the area for reasons unknown.

At some point, an unceremonious sign appeared on the front gate of the compound, amid a tangle of sagebrush and creosote bushes, some distance away from the entrance off Highway 375 near Tempiute Village, Nevada. The sign read simply "Area 51—Government Property—Keep Out."

TWENTY

ZEEMAT AND MORGAN

BY THE LATE summer of 1954, Zeemat had counted sixty cycles of day and night. During that time, he could feel himself growing stronger and mentally sharper. He heard a Cerulean speak in their mysterious language: "He sure heals quickly!"

Eventually, they removed the air tube from his throat and mouth. He cleared his throat and tried to speak, but his voice erupted in harsh *crackles*. His voice box had yet to heal.

He could sip liquids through a straw, and, little by little, they gave him food to eat. He enjoyed some foods, while others made him gag. His favorite was a brightly colored fluid he associated with their sounds, "orange juice." The color reminded him of Torkiyan sunsets. When he could eat and drink enough, his attendants removed from his right arm the small tubes that carryied liquid.

The heavy white cast was cut off his left arm. One of the helpers clad in white then started moving his limb in all directions. It caused pain, but Zeemat cooperated with the helpers in white as best he could. He tried to lift a small weight, but a jolt of pain stopped him.

He also noticed that he struggled in the stronger Cerulean gravity. Every movement—even breathing—was a struggle and seemed to require more energy. The atmosphere itself weighed heavy on his body. He grimaced, horrified by his overall condition—the pain, his frailty, and his profound weakness. He felt helpless, vulnerable, and completely out of his element, like a newborn baby.

Sometime later, the attendants released his left leg from its metallic cage and removed the pins from his leg. The helpers went to work on the leg just as they had on the arm.

Ninety days had now gone by, and Zeemat could sense his progress. With a grimace, he moved his injured arm and leg through a full range of motion. His muscles trembled and spazzed as he lifted medium-sized weights, while the helpers in white cheered him on. He got on his feet and trudged in small steps, even though it required the support of a metal contraption on wheels.

Eventually, the helpers in white grew fewer in number. One day, their leader entered with a small device that flashed a bright light and made a clicking sound. He aimed it first at Zeemat, then at all the helpers and all around the room, each time with a *click* and a flash. The leader stood right next to Zeemat for one of these flashing *clicks*. He gave Zeemat a tight hug and a beaming smile. *Flash. Click.* Zeemat never saw him again.

After that, all the helpers in white disappeared, and Zeemat felt alone and vaguely afraid of what might be coming next. The only ones left in the room were the threatening people dressed in dark green uniforms and the one in black. Two of the soldiers in green approached and grabbed him, one by each arm. Without a smile or an attempt at a greeting, they yanked him to his feet and headed to the door. Another walked behind, carrying a long object that Zeemat assumed was a weapon. They pushed and shoved him out of the now-empty healing room.

The soldiers dragged Zeemat outdoors and rushed him to another building. His sensitive eyes were unaccustomed to the bright light after so many days indoors, so his optic sensors dimmed for most of the way. More soldiers with weapons opened the door of the other building as they arrived and shut it after they entered.

They hurried him along a short hallway. At the end of it was a metal door, which opened into a small room. Zeemat's sensors dimmed again as a shock of bright daylight poured in through a barred window at the far end. The soldiers pushed him inside and left him alone in the room, slamming the metal door shut behind them. He heard a *click*.

When his eyes adjusted to the light, the small room came into focus. Moving faster than he thought he could, he rushed to the window, pressed his face against the bars, opened his optic sensors wide, and took in his first real look at the planet Cerulea. Immediately, his terror at having been handled so violently slipped away as he beheld the view: a cloudless, bright blue sky and the Cerulean landscape.

He broke into a huge grin, even though he was seeing but a small part of the airfield, the barren land beyond it, and low mountains in the distance. He felt ecstatic, like the whole world had just been handed to him on a copper platter. He felt the solid Cerulean ground beneath his feet. He stuck his arms out through the bars and felt the heavy heat of the desert sun on his skin. As he took a satisfying deep breath of the dry Cerulean air, he heard the *rumble* of a strange vehicle and then spotted it moving nearby, on the ground, on wheels, carrying several soldiers.

"I'm alive . . . on Cerulea!" he exclaimed, making chiming sounds of joy as he took in his new discoveries.

He finally left the window when the sun sank low in the sky. He no longer saw activity outside, so he sat through a quiet evening with nothing to do before enduring a restless night. The cot was uncomfortable and the thin blanket they'd provided was insufficient for the cool night air.

The following morning, as the rising sun brought the first hints of daylight, Zeemat looked out his window. Nothing was moving yet. He heard no sounds at all in the silent Mohave Desert. For the first time in over one hundred days, Zeemat found himself alone again. He was in a stark room with a small table, one chair, and a cot. He wondered if all Ceruleans lived this way. He grabbed the strong metal bars of the room's only window and tried to give them a shake. The bars were solid. He walked ten paces to the other side of the room and tried opening the metal door. It didn't open.

His new awareness that he was being held captive was suddenly interrupted by a familiar loud sound coming from outside his window. From his perspective, he couldn't see the approach of a large flying vehicle somewhere to his left, but he could hear the earth-shaking *rumble*. Then a plane became visible as it landed and continued down a smooth runway, the sound gradually fading as he lost sight of it to his right. *Ceruleans can fly!* he thought, with a vague notion of connecting their worlds in a sort of coexistence that would have enraged his father. In his excitement, he tried shaking the bars again. He wanted to be outside, to see the flying vehicle up close.

Sometime after the sound of the airplane died down, Zeemat heard the clicking sound on the door again. He turned to see it open, and the man dressed in black whom he had seen before entered his cell. He didn't have the ominous look Zeemat noticed when this same man had stood in the shadows of the healing room. Now CIA Special Agent William Morgan approached, carrying a tray of food and drink. Zeemat wrinkled his brow in suspicion.

Special Agent William Morgan was dressed in a black suit, crisp white shirt, and a narrow black tie. He was the chief CIA operative assigned to the task of communicating with the alien from Area 51. The pleasant lavender fragrance of the Yardley oil mussed into his thin black hair stood in stark contrast to the hard, gaunt features of his unsmiling face. A black, fine mustache complemented round, tortoiseshell glasses. He clenched his teeth between sentences, bulging the muscles at the sides of his jaws as he spoke.

Morgan placed the tray on the small table, then stood at a distance while he and Zeemat sized each other up. Morgan stood straight to make himself as tall as possible then tapped his own chest with a closed fist. With a deep voice, he said, "Morgan."

Zeemat remained suspicious. He understood Morgan's effort to introduce himself, but he sensed something unfriendly in this man's posture and tone—perhaps something dangerous. So he simply stood there, making no expression of understanding and saying nothing.

Morgan tried again, tapping his chest and saying his name, but he received the same lack of response from Zeemat. The man narrowed his eyes and glared at him.

"Listen here, whoever you are—there'll be no more coddling like in the MASH unit. This room is your home now, and you're going to answer our questions, one way or another." Morgan tried speaking to Zeemat in slow, even tones. "Who are you? Where did you come from? Are there others like you? Why are you here?" Zeemat recognized a word or two that he'd heard other Ceruleans speak, but none of it made sense.

Morgan didn't expect Zeemat to understand his words just yet, but he had hopes they might be able to communicate in some way. He reached inside his suit jacket and produced a pencil and a small pad of paper from the inside pocket. He used the pencil to draw a circle with the outline of North and South America in it. He added a smaller circle just outside of it. He drew numerous points all around. Zeemat understood he was trying to depict the planet Cerulea, its moon, and its stars, but he didn't give Morgan the satisfaction of knowing that indeed he had understood.

Morgan sighed again, this time emitting a frustrated grunt. "My name is Morgan—Mor-*gan*," he said again, tapping his chest and overpronouncing his words and syllables. "And who the hell are *you*?" This time he approached Zeemat and poked his chest with an index finger.

Zeemat furrowed his brow even deeper.

"Aha! I got a little response out of you! Maybe that's what it will take, a little encouragement." He poked Zeemat in the chest a few more times.

This time, Zeemat emitted a low, hissing growl. But then he thought better of it. He made an effort to control himself and settled back down to his unresponsive stance. He decided not to give Morgan anything at all.

Morgan kept trying for a while, but he gave up eventually and left Zeemat in his cell.

Morgan returned the next day, with another breakfast tray. Zeemat noticed a glass of orange juice and his face betrayed a greedy smile, which Morgan noticed immediately.

"I've been watching you. I know you want this orange juice. Well, here you go. Enjoy it, because it will be your last one unless you start talking or drawing." Morgan left the room for Zeemat to eat his breakfast and enjoy the juice.

The following morning, Morgan tried again, bringing Zeemat's breakfast with orange juice, but he held back the juice in his hand.

"Morgan," he said, tapping his own chest. "And you?" He pointed at Zeemat.

Zeemat stood motionless, like a statue.

"Draw something," Morgan said, pointing at the paper and pencil.

Zeemat just looked at him, trying to keep a flat expression.

"Then no orange juice," Morgan said, pulling the glass away dramatically. He walked out of the room.

The next day, Morgan withdrew the entire breakfast. Zeemat was placed on rations of bread and water, but Morgan teased him with hearty meal trays and orange juice every day.

After weeks of this, Zeemat could see himself losing weight and strength again. He knew his nutrition was lacking in what he needed to continue his healing and recovery. But he was certain he didn't want to give anything to this Cerulean. *Mor-gan is the enemy*, he thought. *He is not like the helpers in white.*

One day, Morgan found Zeemat looking out his window, so he had the window boarded shut. Now Zeemat only had the light of a bare bulb in his small, lonely cell.

When Morgan came back the following morning, he finally got a response from Zeemat.

"Are you going to draw something for me today?" he said, pointing at the pencil and paper. He teased Zeemat with a tall glass of orange juice and by tapping on the boarded-up window.

To Morgan's surprise, Zeemat scrunched his face into an angry grimace, clenched his teeth, folded his arms, planted his feet defiantly on the ground, and shook his head no.

"Well, well, well," Morgan said. "We're finally getting somewhere. So, again, for the umpteenth time, I'm Morgan, and who the hell are you?" He poked his finger forcibly into Zeemat's chest.

Zeemat shoved him back with all the strength he could muster, and he took bold, threatening steps toward Morgan. He leaned in close to the man's face, their noses mere inches apart, and again shook his head. *No!* he screamed in his mind.

Morgan backed away, a little shaken. It was clear he was making no progress. He left Zeemat locked in his cell and rushed to his office to place a phone call.

"There's a call for you, Director Dulles," a secretary announced after she knocked on his door. She sauntered in with high heels, a stylish, tight-fitting pencil skirt, and a crisp white blouse with the top three buttons open. She wore heavy makeup, a too-bright tone of red lipstick, and her short hair was in tight, unmoving curls, held captive by a generous dose of hair spray.

"Can you take a message?" he replied. Allen Dulles was the director of the CIA. He wore an expensive three-piece suit with a white shirt and tie. He had short-cropped, graying hair, a well-trimmed mustache, wire-rimmed glasses, and clenched a pipe between his teeth even though the tobacco had long since burned away. His large cherrywood desk held three telephones and several piles of paper in neat stacks.

"It's Special Agent Morgan in Nevada," the secretary said.

Dulles looked up from the document he held in his hand. "Put him through."

When the phone rang, he picked it up on the first ring. "Hello, Morgan. Dulles here. Hope you have something positive to report."

"No, sir. The alien still refuses to cooperate." Morgan knew they were speaking on an ultra-secure line. He described what he had done so far and Zeemat's behavior.

"Then we'll step it up a notch. I'm sending your old friend Dooley your way. You know he's the best field interrogator we've got."

"Good," Morgan concurred. "I think it'll respond to some old-fashioned motivation."

TWENTY-ONE

MORGAN AND DOOLEY

DOOLEY ARRIVED BY the following day in an unusually rapid deployment. It was close to Thanksgiving, 1954. He presented himself to Morgan for further orders.

"The reason you're here, Dooley, is to help us find out why that thing is here." Morgan nodded toward the door of Zeemat's cell.

"That's what I do, and I'm grateful for the opportunity," Dooley replied, mindlessly caressing his fisted right hand with his left.

Junior Special Agent Kenny Dooley was a short, squat man, heavily muscled, with a few missing teeth and a face full of scars. He enjoyed his job at the CIA. They paid him to do what he loved best—hitting people. He'd discovered the joy of it during high school football. After graduation, he honed his skills at a boxing gym in Boston. When the United States entered World War II, he enlisted in the Army, where he discovered that drinking and fighting were accepted behaviors, and he earned a reputation as a mean drunk. His superiors recognized this talent and used it to their advantage when questioning prisoners. After the war and an honorable discharge, the CIA recruited him as a brute enforcer and interrogator. And now they assigned him to a secretive place in southern Nevada where his skills were required for a certain prisoner.

Special Agent Morgan slid open the tiny window of the heavy metal door, offering Dooley a peek into Zeemat's cell.

"Well, I'll be damned," Dooley said. "I didn't really believe it until just now."

"And this isn't the only one," Morgan added. "This one came earlier this year. The other one in Area 50 in Roswell came in 1947. We're afraid they're gearing up for an invasion."

"The one in Roswell . . . just like this one?" Dooley asked, pointing at Zeemat, who studied them with his head tilted.

"Identical, except that the one in Roswell's dead. Didn't survive a crash landing. We learned things from an autopsy, though, and we recovered parts of its ship. But we don't know their plans or intentions. That's what we aim to find out from this one."

"Are these the only sightings?"

"Not even close. Best estimate is fifty-one, all over the world, over hundreds, if not thousands, of years."

Dooley nodded. "Is this the first live one?"

"Maybe. There's evidence of spikes in technology in the areas of previous encounters. Some of those aliens might have lived here for some time. But we didn't find bodies until the dead one in Roswell, and now this one."

"What about the ships?"

"The one in Area 50 was mostly destroyed. The bits remaining suggest there were at least two occupants, but only one body was recovered."

"And the other one?"

"No doubt destroyed with the rest of the ship. We heard some superstitious stories from migrant workers around Roswell, like the Chupacabra nonsense, but there's no evidence of any other survivors."

"So now that we have this live one . . ." Dooley began. "How are we going to get anything out of it?"

"He's going to draw, or paint, or learn to speak English. This is a higher life form, isn't it? He flew a spaceship to get here, for god's sake."

"And if he doesn't cooperate?"

"He hasn't. And that's why *you're* here," Morgan said, squinting as he glared back at Zeemat through the tiny window of the cell's steel door.

TWENTY-TWO

FAILURE TO COMMUNICATE

DOOLEY'S POWERFUL RIGHT jab made contact with the left side of Zeemat's face. "Maybe that will loosen your tongue, you little shit!"

Zeemat grunted like he had after many of Dooley's punches. His arms and legs were tied to a chair with his arms strung behind his back. A line of blood dripped from a cut on his lip. His left eye had nearly swollen shut. His face was bruised and bloated from Dooley's "interrogation." A small table stood nearby, with a blank sketch pad and unused pens, pencils, brushes, and paint.

"What was that?" Dooley asked, cupping his ear and leaning in. "Another little grunt? Is that all you've got to say? Maybe you need a little more encouragement."

Dooley let off a flurry of punches, a combination of lefts and rights, capped off by a punishing right uppercut which pounded Zeemat's head upward and backward, nearly toppling him out of the chair.

Zeemat felt dizzy. The pain was excruciating, but like the cryo-fluid pain, he knew it would pass. He remembered Ehya's words—*It's just pain, and for a short while. The pain won't kill you.* After many days of this treatment, he knew this session would soon be over. He knew he would heal, like he always did. And then he expected the next day would bring more of the same.

Zeemat didn't understand their words, but he knew his captors wanted some sort of information. They continued to make gestures with a pencil and paper, suggesting he write or draw something. But whatever it was they wanted, Zeemat wasn't about to comply with the demands of these evil people. He hoped he could stay alive long enough to finish healing from the crash, but his recovery was set back every day by a new round of beatings from this horrid Cerulean creature. He willfully dimmed his optic sensors to try to stop the dizziness.

BAM! A sucker punch hit the right side of Zeemat's face as Dooley unleashed a roundhouse left. "Don't fall asleep on me now, asshole," Dooley mocked.

Zeemat nearly lost consciousness with that one. A wave of nausea overwhelmed him, and he threw up the remains of his previous meal, mixed with fresh blood from his facial cuts.

Dooley pinched Zeemat's cheeks between his thick thumb and fingers and pulled until their faces were close together. He waited until Zeemat seemed to regain his bearings, and his eyes brightened a little.

"Listen, asshole, maybe when you give us something we can use, we can stop these beatings. But honestly, I don't give a shit. If I have to keep beating on you, that's all right with me."

Zeemat looked briefly at Dooley, then his eyes dimmed again as he continued to fight for consciousness.

Dooley gave Zeemat's face one final brutal punch before pushing him backward. Zeemat's head toppled to one side. Dooley took a deep, satisfied breath, exhaled, and walked away, removing his bloodied leather gloves.

"I guess that's all he can take. Untie him," Dooley said to a soldier as he snickered.

The soldier complied and removed the shackles that bound Zeemat to the chair. He stepped back and kept his rifle at the ready.

Dooley approached Zeemat, grabbed him by his bloodied shirt, and lifted him up to his feet. Zeemat wobbled but was able to stand.

"Okay, asshole, try to hit me," Dooley taunted. "C'mon, right here. Show me what you got." He pointed at his own jaw and came up close so Zeemat could try to punch him.

Zeemat knew he couldn't. He was too weak. Even when he was perfectly healthy back in Torkiya, he was too weak. He wasn't a fighter, and he knew it.

Dooley pushed him back into his chair and walked away from the semiconscious Zeemat with a smug smile.

"Crazy how that little shit can take a punch," Dooley said to the soldier. "He should be dead after what I've given him." He shook his head and looked toward Zeemat. The soldier took that as his cue to return him to his cell.

"Even crazier's that he'll be back here tomorrow, and all his cuts and bruises will be mostly healed," the soldier remarked.

"Yep. That's a beautiful thing. I can start the 'interrogation' all over again, every day!" Dooley chuckled.

The soldier placed the loose shackles back on Zeemat's wrists and ankles, yanked him out of his chair, and shoved him toward the door.

Zeemat shuffled out of the interrogation room, down the hall, and back to his cell. He heard the familiar *click* as the door to his cell locked behind him. He plopped onto his cot and lay there motionless for a while, preserving his energy for healing.

He knew that not all Cerulean creatures were cruel like this. The ones that had saved him and cured him had been good. He couldn't understand why things had changed.

He stopped fighting for consciousness and allowed himself to fall asleep. His last thoughts of the day were that he would never give them what they wanted. *I'll either die or escape*, he thought. *Mor-gan and Dooley will fail at their mission.* He winced in pain as those thoughts brought a weak smile to his battered face.

Several months later, in the spring of 1955, a new plan of action was approved by CIA Director Dulles, President Eisenhower, and the Joint Chiefs of Staff.

TWENTY-THREE

ABDUCTION

ON A BEAUTIFUL, breezy spring day in May 1955, Linda Deltare stood on the sidewalk and examined her reflection on a storefront window as it overlapped her view of the mannequin in a stylish business dress in the display on the other side. It appeared as if she was wearing the dress herself. She turned her head from side to side and put her hands on her hips, pretending to move in it. She liked how the dress complimented the curves of her hips and bust while maintaining a professional appearance.

She flashed her best interview smile, showing off her high cheekbones, full lips, and perfect teeth. *Or if this job doesn't pan out, maybe I can be a model in a window!* She chuckled at the thought. She was happy. She was visiting Chicago for the first time for her first job interview, and the pleasure of window-shopping on Michigan Avenue, Chicago's Magnificent Mile, was a surprise. She needed something to wear for the interview, so she walked into the store, tried the dress on, and bought it in a size six. "A graduation present for myself," she said to the helpful clerk.

"It fits like a glove," the clerk responded. "And the color goes nicely with your green eyes and auburn hair. It looks beautiful on you, Miss Deltare."

You mean "Doctor" Deltare, she thought to herself, smiling. She still couldn't believe the years of research and study, years of classwork, fieldwork, papers, presentations, dissertations, and being on someone else's schedule were finally over. It had been all the harder being the first and only woman in her PhD program. Now she was done with the condescension, the jealousies, the unwanted advances, and having to work twice as hard as the males in her program for half the credit. Now, at twenty eight years old, she found it hard to believe that her life was finally her own.

She walked out of the dress shop, bag in hand, beaming in carefree delight as she leisurely strolled down Michigan Avenue, observing the throngs of people hurrying up and down the busy street. The commotion seemed so alive, so real, such a far cry from the lonely libraries and the stodgy world of higher education in Boston.

As she turned around to head back to her room at The Drake, she didn't see them coming. She didn't notice the black Ford Fairlane Crown Victoria that slowly cruised past her and stopped at the curb a short distance ahead. Two tall, muscular men in black suits and sunglasses stepped out of the car, approaching her steadily. One reached out and snatched the bag from her hand. The other one came up close and grabbed her firmly by the arm. "Please come with us, Dr. Deltare. Don't make a scene. Your help is needed."

"Hey!" Deltare said, shocked by the sudden assault. She tried to free herself from the man's grip, but he was too strong. "Let go!" she demanded, but the other man had grabbed her other arm.

In an instant, they lifted her off her feet as if she were weightless and rushed her back to the waiting Crown Vic. She twisted and kicked while a third man opened the back door. They whisked her into the back seat in such a nonchalant manner that no one even noticed the abduction.

"Help!" she screamed, but the door had already shut, and no one heard her over the noise of midday traffic.

The car sped away, heading north on Michigan Avenue. Deltare struggled for a short while, but it was clear she was at the mercy of these men.

"What's going on? Who are you? Where are we going?" she asked, as her alarm turned to panic. The men looked straight ahead without saying a word.

She noticed the Great Lakes streets as the car sped along. She passed a few more streets until the car took a sharp right turn onto Delaware. A few seconds later, the Crown Vic made a screeching stop in front of a nondescript building. The driver jumped out of the car, looked up and down the street, then came around to the other side of the car to open the back door. The others came out with Deltare still in their grasp. They rushed her to the front door of 195 Delaware, which opened as they approached and quickly shut after they entered the building.

"What is this place? What do you want?" Deltare's fright grew in the silence of unanswered questions. The two men still would not release their tight grip. Outside, she heard the Crown Vic pull away.

Now another man appeared, dressed like the others in a black suit, white shirt, and a narrow black tie. He seemed to be in charge. Without introduction, he said, "Dr. Deltare, please excuse us for this sudden intrusion."

"You have no right!" she declared.

"Sorry, Doctor, but that's the way it is. Just calm down and everything will be all right."

"'Calm down'? Release me at once!"

The man put his finger to his lips. "Shush, Dr. Deltare. You're not going anywhere."

A chill crept up her spine. She'd learned that Chicago was famous for gangsters, and she believed they were now holding her captive. She had a good idea of what they probably wanted. She had no money in her purse, no valuables, but she was a pretty, young woman traveling by herself—an easy target.

"If you promise not to run, these men will let go of your arms," said the man in charge. He waited patiently for her reply. "And if you promise not to yell, we won't have to gag you." He produced a handkerchief from out of his jacket pocket.

Deltare was desperate now. She looked around the room. There were no windows. She was unlikely to make it past the two brutes to the single door of the room. They had her.

"Are you going to hurt me?" she asked. Part of her didn't want to hear the answer.

"That depends on how well you cooperate," the man in charge said in a seemingly nonthreatening way, which didn't fool Deltare for an instant. "Let's try it. Men, release her arms."

The two blank-faced men, still wearing their dark sunglasses, released her arms and stepped away. Deltare took the opportunity to make a dash for the door, but the men instantly grabbed her again.

The man in charge pointed to a plush desk chair. "Tie her up, then."

"No, wait," Deltare implored, but it was too late. The two brutes proceeded to tie her down to the chair.

The man in charge waited patiently for Deltare to be tied up. He pulled out the handkerchief again. "Now are you going to stay quiet? Or do I have to use this, too?"

Deltare kept quiet, glaring at him.

"Dr. Deltare, we're going to ask you a series of questions, and this may take awhile, so you might as well make yourself comfortable." He pointed with a circular hand gesture to the ropes tying her down, while calmly lighting up a cigarette.

Yeah, 'comfortable,' she thought, scoffing to herself.

The man in charge spoke to the two brutes: "Hey, I'm hungry. Why don't you boys pick up a pizza at Uno's or something?" Then, looking at Deltare, he asked, "You hungry?"

Flabbergasted, Deltare's mind dizzied with questions. *Hungry? Really? Is that some kind of joke?*

But she thought it best not to say anything. After a few moments, the man shrugged his shoulders and said to the brutes, "You better get two pizzas. She's gonna be hungry."

And it did take awhile. Two days later, Deltare, though no longer tied up and no longer afraid for her life, was still held captive and at a loss as to what exactly these men wanted from her. She had met with several people questioning her about everything in her life. One man had asked for details about each of her family members, close and extended. Another one had asked about her finances and congratulated her afterward for being truthful. Still another, obviously a scientist, delved extensively into her graduate work, particularly about her linguistics studies and communications work with dolphins.

"Is it true you were able to collaborate with dolphins to accomplish a common task?" the scientist asked.

"Yes, as you surely know. I see you have my published paper in your hands."

"Yes, but is it true?" the skeptical scientist looked at the paper with a raised eyebrow and squinted eyes. "I don't always believe the veracity of published papers, especially from a rank beginner like you. So why don't you give me some details and examples?"

After long hours of questions and answers, the scientist seemed satisfied. He sat back, removed a cigarette from a silver case, and offered one to Deltare. She readily accepted. He lit it for her with an engraved cigarette lighter, and she took greedy puffs of the much-needed smoke. Then he closed his notebook and stood to leave, extending his hand to shake Deltare's. "Thank you, Dr. Deltare. You seem to be legit."

Over the next several days, Deltare underwent more interviews, becoming disoriented as her captors kept her in a windowless and clock-less room for what she estimated was about a week. But the inquisition seemed to be over at last—no more psychological tests, no more questions about her ethics, or her politics, or her loyalty to her country.

After that, the place became decidedly quiet, and that was almost more disconcerting than the weeklong parade of strangers asking personal questions. She had a feeling something terrible was about to happen.

The man in charge entered the room again, a serious look on his face.

"No more pizza!" begged Dr. Deltare, surprising herself by joking at a time like this.

"What? No. I'm not here for that. Let's get you ready to go," the man said. He moved quickly, as if on a mission.

"Go where?" Deltare asked.

"You're going on a special trip. They're waiting for you," he said, and that's all he would divulge.

Suddenly, one of the two brutes appeared, holding her luggage from The Drake in one hand, and the bag with the dress in the other. He led her out of the building and into a cool, clear night.

It was her first time outside in about a week. "What time is it?" she asked, trying to reorient herself.

"Oh-three-hundred, ma'am," answered the now-polite brute.

"And where are we going in such a hurry at oh-three-hundred?"

"To Meigs Field, ma'am."

"The airfield on the lake? Where are they taking me?"

"I don't know, ma'am. That's classified." The tone in the young brute's voice suggested he was following orders and telling the truth.

The black Ford Fairlane Crown Victoria was back at the curb. She crawled inside, this time into the front passenger seat and of her own accord. There was no use in fighting whatever was happening.

A few minutes later, the car cruised along Lake Shore Drive and quickly arrived at Meigs Field, having met no traffic in the middle of the night. The gates at the tiny airport were open, with soldiers standing guard nearby. They drove right up to the airstrip itself, where the blades of a military helicopter were spinning and ready to go. A different man in black, one Deltare had never seen before, was there to take over. Special Agent William Morgan shook Deltare's hand and yelled a hello over the helicopter noise.

A few hours later, they arrived in Washington, D.C. and landed on the White House lawn.

Morgan led Deltare into the White House and asked her to wait in a large office while he waited just outside. The office was surprisingly pleasant. She sat in a comfortable chair by a wood-burning fireplace, rubbing her hands and warming herself up after the chilly, nighttime flight. She eyed the pot of coffee on the table in the center of the room and took a long whiff of its delicious aroma.

A moment later, the office door opened, and three men entered. One carried a pile of notes and papers, one juggled a pile of rolled-up maps and prints, and one she recognized as Dwight D. Eisenhower, President of the United States.

"Hello, Dr. Deltare. I'm Dwight Eisenhower." He pointed in the direction of the two other men. "This is General Nathan Twining, Air Force, and General Matthew Ridgway, Army. Thank you for coming. Would you like some coffee?"

Deltare wondered if this was all a dream. Maybe she was asleep. Perhaps the stress of having been abducted and then kept in disorienting confinement for a week had taken its toll. But just in case this was real, she replied, "Yes, please, Mr. President."

"How do you take it?"

"Black, please. No sugar or cream."

"Atta girl, Deltare. That's how we take it in the field. No place for frills. How was the flight over?"

"Well, I have to say . . ."

"Good. Now down to business." The president was a military man, not one for superficialities or for wasting time. He gestured to an empty chair at the table, for Deltare to join the other men who had already sat down.

As Deltare rose from her comfortable chair by the fireplace and moved to a chair at the table, the president began talking. In his presence, she felt bewildered and small. How was it possible that she could be in this room, sitting around a table with these important men? She felt another rush of disorientation. But dream or not, she decided she better keep quiet and let the president and these military men say what they had to say.

"I'm sorry if this all seems kind of strange, Dr. Deltare, but it had to be done. I understand you passed all the screening tests. Good. Now, are you ready to do an important job for the United States of America, and for all of humanity? It will be the most important job of your life."

At his words, Deltare became more sure that she'd entered a dream. She could only look at the dream president, cocking her head with curiosity, without saying a word.

"You're supposedly perfect for the job, right up your alley."

"I'm sorry, sir. I don't know what this is all about. Can you be more specific about what it is you think I can do for our country and for humanity?" Deltare decided to play along with the dream.

General Twining began to respond, but President Eisenhower waved him down. He was clearly in charge of this meeting. Eisenhower continued: "Dr. Deltare, let's just say we have discovered a new species, and we need your help in gathering information. It's important for the national defense. You have the knowledge and skills to help us learn what we need to know."

"'National defense'? Mr. President, how can I possibly help? My work was with dolphin communication. They're smart, friendly creatures that pose no threat. It sounds like your new species is probably not like that. What's the danger? A chemical substance? Perhaps you need a chemist." Deltare began to pry for details as the dream began to feel like a nightmare.

President Eisenhower frowned, irritated that Deltare would be asking any questions at all. Her job was simply to comply, to follow orders, like everyone else. He approached and loomed over her, standing uncomfortably close.

"No, not a chemist, Dr. Deltare. You were identified, so I want *you*. Understand?" He didn't wait long for her to respond before adding, "Can I count on you or not? Yes or no? Now!"

She stammered, "Yes, sir. I . . ."

"Good. And can you keep a secret?"

"Um . . . yes, sir, but . . ."

"Yes, I know you can. That's what it says on your psychological profile. So let me tell you that of all secrets, this one is at the very top of the top-secret pile. We've gone to great lengths to do what we've done already, and I expect you to follow suit. So you'll be under the strictest surveillance, as will your family and friends. For the duration of this project, I expect you to have no contact with them. They'll be given an appropriate explanation for your disappearance. Let me be clear—if you approach any family member or friend, or anyone at all, you'll be placing them in utmost danger. We must keep this contained. Clear?"

"Mr. President, I . . ."

"Good. Your whereabouts will be kept secret. No one should be able to track you down, not even the FBI."

"Sir?" Deltare leaned back, her eyes growing wide. A secret from the FBI seemed counterintuitive, not to mention disloyal.

"Yes. This operation is strictly under my supervision, along with the Joint Chiefs and the CIA. Capisce?"

"Yes, sir." Deltare squinted her eyes, concerned that something was not quite right.

"Good. So we're agreed."

"Um . . ." Deltare wondered if she had really agreed to anything. This thing was out of control; it was starting to feel like a runaway train.

Eisenhower now deferred to one of the others. "General Twining will go over some of the particulars. From this point on, there is no turning back, Deltare."

She felt confused, but this was the president of the United States, so she agreed, immediately wondering if she would live to regret that decision.

General Twining proceeded. "Brace yourself, Dr. Deltare," he said.

Twining distributed identical files around the table, and Deltare opened hers like the rest of them did. Inside, she found a series of black-and-white photos.

"These were taken about one year ago in southern Nevada," Twining said. "Please examine them carefully, Dr. Deltare."

"What am I looking at?" she asked. The photos had been taken in the desert. There were dark areas that looked like something had been burned. In one of the pictures, she noticed a heap that looked like the burnt remains of a man.

"In this dark, depressed area you can see the burnt remains of the invader's spacecraft," Twining pointed out.

Deltare scrunched her face in a smirk. Suddenly this all seemed rather silly. She looked around the table at all the serious faces and again wondered if this was all a crazy dream.

"Yes, and this is the alien pilot," Twining said, pointing to the burnt heap Deltare had previously noted.

"'Alien pilot,'" Deltare repeated, unable to contain the mocking tone in her voice.

"I imagine this might sound rather unbelievable, Dr. Deltare, but this isn't a joke. Do you think we'd all be here right now if we were kidding? The alien somehow survived a high-speed crash. It was severely injured, but we were able to rescue it. Well, General Ridgway here and his team get the credit for saving its life, and the CIA for the start of its interrogation." He paused and looked Deltare directly in the eyes. "And I guess that's where you come in."

"Me? Interrogation? This must be a joke!" Deltare was now more than a little irritated, and it no longer felt like a dream. "I don't do that sort of thing!"

"Well, you do now, cupcake!" General Ridgway looked angry, which was his natural state of being. Abruptly, he stood up. His army MASH team had miraculously saved the alien's life, but the subsequent CIA interrogation was not going well.

They had exhausted their means of extracting information. They were at a loss, and the president had grown impatient. Ridgway had finally agreed with the others to bring in a civilian expert, but it was clear he wasn't happy about it. In fact, he resented anything having to do with the word "civilian." In his opinion, civilians were lazy, undisciplined morons, several ranks below a Private First Class.

"Your job is to learn the alien's language, earn its trust, extract the information we need, and that's all," Ridgway growled.

Deltare looked over to President Eisenhower, then to General Twining. They were both nodding their heads, agreeing with Ridgway. She'd get no support from them.

And so it was settled. The meeting was over, and Linda Deltare, PhD, had landed her first job.

After the meeting at the White House, Generals Twining and Ridgway said their goodbyes and took their leave from the Commander-in-Chief. President Eisenhower then turned to Deltare, visibly surprised and irritated that she would still be in the room.

"You have your orders!" he barked.

As if on cue, Morgan came back into the room to retrieve Deltare. "This way," he said with a side nod of the head. They exited the White House and headed back to the waiting helicopter on the back lawn.

In the fresh air, the tension dissipated, and Deltare now became aware of her utter fatigue. She hadn't slept for god knows how many hours. Certainly she had been up all night. Now she was apparently embarking on another noisy and shaky helicopter ride, heading to who knows where, hopefully to a place where she could get some sleep. Maybe then she could clear her head and figure things out.

As the helicopter lifted off the White House lawn, Deltare noted the first light of the rising sun in the east, framing the Capitol Building in a beautiful pink silhouette. It was the dawn of a brand-new day, but she had never felt more in the dark.

Despite the helicopter noise and vibration, Deltare fell asleep, but only for a few minutes. In no time at all, the helicopter landed at the Bolling base.

"Dr. Deltare . . . Deltare!" She felt someone shaking her by the shoulders, and she forced herself awake. "Our plane is waiting. You can sleep a few hours on this next flight," Morgan said.

"Where are we going now?" Deltare asked as they hopped off the helicopter. They walked toward a C-47, waiting for them on the adjacent runway.

"I'll tell you what you need to know when you need to know it," Morgan said. "For starters, if you don't know it already, I'm your handler."

"My 'handler'? I have a handler now?" Deltare stopped dead in her tracks and crossed her arms. "I'm not going anywhere until you answer a few simple questions." She glared at Morgan.

"Women!" he said, rolling his eyes.

"So let me ask again. *Where are we going?*"

Morgan scrunched his face and exhaled loudly. He reached into his inside jacket pocket to retrieve an envelope then handed it over to Deltare.

"It's addressed to me . . . from the CIA!" she exclaimed, her eyes widening. She carefully opened the envelope and retrieved the letter.

"You're now CIA Junior Special Agent Linda Deltare, and you're under my direct supervision and command," Morgan said.

Deltare skimmed through the formal acceptance and welcome letter, then read it more slowly to take in every detail.

"I guess I have a job I didn't apply for. It says, 'Salary and benefit information is forthcoming.'"

"Who cares about that?" Morgan replied. "What you were selected for is priceless. Let's go."

Morgan resumed his walk to the waiting C-47, and Deltare followed, hollering over the runway noise.

"Now I have a thousand more questions," she yelled. "Let's start with one I already asked. Where are we going?"

Morgan turned around and put a hushing finger to his lips. He walked up close to Deltare and spoke into her ear. "We're going to Roswell, New Mexico—about a seven-hour flight. You can get some rest on the plane. I'll fill you in once we get there."

"What's in Roswell?" Deltare pressed. Morgan shook his head and ignored her.

She followed him up the gangway steps and into a luxuriously appointed cabin of the custom C-47. It reminded Deltare of a lawyer's office, decked out with high-end furnishings and beautiful wood trim all around. It had a lounge area with a leather sofa and comfortable chairs, and a work area with an adjustable-height table and task chairs, all fixed solidly to the floor. At one corner stood a small but impressive self-service bar.

Morgan headed straight to the bar and fixed himself a scotch on the rocks. "Help yourself," he said to Deltare.

She joined him at the small bar and looked around, then decided on a bottle of Coke. She used the metal opener attached to the side of the bar to pry off the cap. She was so tired; the sugar and caffeine surely would not interfere with her much-needed sleep.

"Let me show you where you can rest." Morgan led her to one of two doors at the back of the plane. The door opened to a small sleeping room with a smaller-than-twin-sized bed. There was an airplane mini-sink in the corner. Her suitcase was standing at the side of the bed, and her dress was hanging from a hook on the wall.

"My graduation present," she sighed.

She washed up at the tiny airplane sink and snuggled herself into bed. She closed her eyes and started going over the insane set of events that had transpired over the previous week—her abduction, the meeting with the president, now a mysterious job with the CIA, and Morgan—when the revving of the plane's engines distracted her. She opened her eyes to look out of her little porthole window as the plane rolled into position, picked up speed on the runway, and lifted off. Over the next few minutes, she watched the cars, the buildings, the streets, then the whole city get smaller and smaller as the plane gained elevation and left it all behind. Somewhere along the line, she fell into a deep sleep and rested well for the first time in days.

Deltare heard a knock on her cabin door and woke with a start, disoriented. She rubbed her eyes and got her bearings.

"Rise and shine," Morgan called out from the other side of the door.

Deltare felt as though she had only just gotten to sleep, but she marveled at how rested she felt. She got up, washed her face in the tiny airplane sink, brushed her teeth with the tiny airplane toothbrush, and then joined Morgan in the main cabin. He was seated at the worktable, and she took one of the empty seats next to him.

Morgan greeted her in a businesslike manner: "Good morning, Dr. Deltare. We'll be landing within the hour. I wanted to take this time to go over your day's agenda."

Good! she thought. *Finally!* She was happy to regain some semblance of control over her life.

"We'll land at Walker, and we'll walk to a facility on base."

"'Walker'?" asked Deltare.

"Walker AFB," explained Morgan, with an irritated frown.

"'AFB'?" asked Deltare, this time more sheepishly.

"Air Force Base!" said Morgan, this time more audibly perturbed.

"Sorry, Special Agent Morgan," Deltare said sincerely. "This is all new to me."

Morgan ignored the comment, taking an exasperated breath, and proceeded with his briefing. "After we land, we'll walk to a facility on base, and you'll get the nickel tour."

"Ooh! A nickel. Big spender!" Deltare joked.

Morgan glared at her, and her smile evaporated. "This is serious, Deltare! It's not every day someone gets a chance to see an alien and its ship."

Deltare's mouth dropped open. She heard the words, but they didn't make sense, and she felt the same dreamy feeling she'd felt when she sat with the president and the military men.

Morgan produced his pack of Lucky's and offered her one, which she took without hesitation.

"The alien in Roswell's dead, but you need to know what we found. Then you'll be ready for the next part, because the one in Nevada's alive."

Deltare pulled a long drag from her cigarette and squinted her eyes as the bright southwest sun lit up the windows. She was deep in thought when the pilot's metallic voice on the loudspeakers startled her.

"Fasten your seat belts, everyone. We're beginning our descent to Roswell, New Mexico."

TWENTY-FOUR

CONTACT

TWO DAYS LATER, after her thorough indoctrination in Roswell, Linda Deltare was flying on a plane again, gazing out the window with a serious look on her face. Flashes of sunlight reflected off the wing of the polished C-47 as it rumbled through the cloudless sky above the Mohave Desert. The unmarked airplane had left Walker Air Force Base in Roswell, New Mexico, four hours earlier and was now approaching its destination—Nellis Air Force Base in Las Vegas, Nevada. The plane rolled and yawed as the experienced pilot fought a gusty crosswind before making a perfect landing.

The plane was directed to its usual spot on the tarmac next to a hangar used by the CIA. After they came to a stop, a tarmac worker placed heavy chocks against the wheels while the massive twin propellers decelerated to a jerky stop. At the same time, two others rolled a gangway staircase into place and pounded on the airplane's door once the staircase was secure. The plane's heavy door squealed on its massive hinges as someone pushed it open from the inside.

Special Agent William Morgan squinted at the relentless desert sunlight assaulting his eyes. He reached into the inside pocket of his black suit coat to retrieve a pair of mirrored sunglasses. After making a quick inspection of his surroundings, he marched down the gangway stairs.

Following close behind, Deltare exited the plane and stood at the top of the stairs. She was now wearing her recently issued uniform—a knee-length black cotton skirt, a white linen blouse, and an unflattering black suit jacket, but she had not yet mastered the blank expression typical of all the CIA agents she'd met. Instead, she wore a curious, questioning look as she observed her surroundings, her keen mind registering every detail.

Her luxurious auburn hair tousled in the wind. She'd parted it on the side, draping it in loose waves down to her shoulders. She shook her head and blew a stray wisp out of the side of her mouth. She brought her right hand to her forehead both to tame her hair and to shield her eyes from the blazing midday sun. It was the first time she had ever set foot in the American Southwest desert, and she felt unprepared without sunglasses. She used her left hand to steady herself with the railing as she guided her short heels down the gangway steps and into unknown territory.

They made their way to the hangar, where Morgan's black 1955 Fairlane Crown Victoria was parked. The CIA had provided the new vehicle for his use during his assignment—the matter of the alien in Area 51. He unlocked the vehicle and took the driver's seat. Deltare walked around to the passenger's side. When she saw that no one would be opening the door for her, she helped herself into her seat.

They made their way out of the Air Force Base to Interstate 15 North, then up US Route 93 toward Coyote Springs. When they approached State Route 168, Morgan slowed the car and rolled down his window, letting in a blast of hot air. He pointed to the Las Vegas Range to the left as he relayed to Deltare the story of Zeemat's arrival. She looked toward the mountains and then studied Morgan's face, feeling another dreamy rush of disbelief.

Morgan picked up his speed again as they headed toward Crystal Springs, where they then turned west on State Route 375. As they approached the old Tempiute Village, they turned off the road onto a nondescript dirt road flanked by a sign that read "Area 51—Government Property—Keep Out." After a few turns, they encountered the first of two barbed-wire chain-link fences, with heavily armed guards protecting the entries. Morgan showed his papers, and they let his car through. The Crown Vic then proceeded down the dirt road, kicking up desert dust along the way.

At some point, the road acquired a thin, single-lane asphalt paving, gradually expanding to a wide two-lane road, ending at a formal guardhouse with a heavy red boom bar blocking entry or exit. Another armed guard met them. Though he recognized Morgan from his previous visits, he didn't smile or nod. He didn't recognize Deltare sitting in the passenger's seat, and his right index finger instinctively crept to the trigger of his short-barreled automatic rifle. He carefully inspected the papers Morgan presented, reading them over a few times. He took them into the guardhouse to place a confirmatory phone call. When he returned, his face was no less serious, but he returned the papers and said, "Agent Morgan, Dr. Deltare, welcome to Area 51." He raised the gate's boom bar and waved them through.

It was midafternoon, and the temperature was well over one hundred degrees. They saw several large airplanes parked in the distance and two long asphalt runways crisscrossing at an angle. There were several buildings and airplane hangars on the compound, most of them made of bare sheet metal, except for one building composed of a heavier cinder block construction. There were small windows all around that sturdier building, and Deltare noticed the windows were barred.

Morgan pulled up to the side of the cinder block building and parked the car. "And here we are!" he announced, in an atypically cheery voice.

They got out of the air-conditioned car and into the oven of the desert heat. Deltare felt a scorching sensation from the pavement through her shoes. She turned full circle to look around the compound, wondering why the government would place a small airfield in the middle of a hot, dry, dusty desert. She was impressed by the cloudless blue sky and the perfect quiet. *Almost peaceful,* she thought, before deciding that the feeling was more of a lonely isolation in a desolate environment than an actual feeling of true peace.

Morgan allowed her a few moments to take in her surroundings, then said, "Let's go inside and get started."

Deltare followed Morgan into the building, noting the number "51" over the doorway.

The building looked bleak on the outside but was surprisingly well-appointed on the inside. She was relieved to find it had central air-conditioning. The cool tile floors were fashioned in Southwest colors and style. Smoothly plastered walls were painted in a pleasing light turquoise, though there were no framed pictures or decorations on the walls, and the stark windows were bare of window dressings. Her first thought was that it needed a woman's touch.

One side of the building was an open space with two metal military-issue desks. One was tidy and neat, with a nameplate that read "S. A. William Morgan." The other was decked with a mess of disorderly papers and the nameplate "J.S.A. Kenneth Dooley." A rough-looking brute of a man sat behind that desk, chomping on the butt of a wet cigar. As they walked in, he stood to attention.

Morgan made the introductions. "Junior Special Agent Kenny Dooley, this is Junior Special Agent Dr. Linda Deltare. She'll be your replacement, by order of the president of the United States."

"So *this* must be our 'expert' civilian interrogator," he said, throwing a sideways glance at Deltare. The dour look on Dooley's face turned into one of undisguised contempt.

Deltare offered Dooley a handshake. "Not an interrogator," Deltare clarified. "I consider myself a language analyst, and maybe an interpreter in this case, but not an interrogator. Anyway, pleased to meet you," she said, still holding out her hand. Dooley was slow to return the gesture, but Deltare kept it outstretched until he reluctantly shook her hand. She suppressed a cry of pain as Dooley squeezed hard, making obvious his displeasure with this new arrangement.

"And what is your role here, Mr. Dooley?" Deltare asked, rubbing her hand.

"My orders are to extract information from the alien." Dooley pointed to a steel door at the end of the hall on the other side of the building.

"You mean they *were* your orders, in the past tense, right, Mr. Dooley?" Morgan corrected. "You have new orders, correct? To guard the premises?" He presented Dooley with a letter, embossed with the presidential seal, but Dooley waved it away.

"I know what the letter says," he admitted with a growl. "But if we didn't get anything out of the alien in the past six months, I'm sure she won't either."

Deltare had not expected this kind of welcome. She squinted her eyes, starting to piece together her role in all this.

"What have you accomplished so far?" she inquired.

"Not much," Dooley admitted. "It hasn't given up a thing."

"May I see the records of your interrogations?"

"They're classified," Dooley barked.

Morgan frowned at his agent and shook his head, reaching into his pocket again to retrieve the letter. "Read it and get used to it, Mr. Dooley. By order of the president of the United States, absolutely everything here is at Dr. Deltare's disposal. She's now in charge of this interrogation and has full access. You'll provide her with everything she needs, or you'll be in contempt of presidential orders. We don't want that."

Deltare frowned at the continuing use of the word "interrogation," but she was glad to have Morgan's support.

"Please, Mr. Dooley . . . we're on the same team. Let me see the records." Deltare spoke in a gentle but firm tone, knowing her assignment was directed by none other than the president of the United States.

Dooley opened a desk drawer to retrieve a single binder, with telegraphic notes detailing the past six months.

Deltare was taken aback. "That's it? This can't be everything. Where's the rest?"

"That's everything," Dooley replied. He sneered with a weird, self-satisfied smirk on his face.

Deltare looked over to Morgan. "How can this be everything? There's next to nothing here. How can this account for six months' work?"

Deltare took a few moments to skim through the binder. Each of the daily notes were almost identical, repeating a handful of brief sentences and phrases: "Efforts to communicate with the subject failed" or "The subject was uncooperative" or "Nothing to report."

"Mr. Dooley, what techniques have you used to communicate with the alien? What protocols did you follow? Where are they written?"

"We have free rein over our techniques, the same ones we use in the military to extract information from our enemies during war."

Deltare narrowed her eyes even tighter, getting a clearer picture of this man's role. "Can you be more specific?" she asked.

"No."

Morgan saw Dooley starting to lose his composure. He knew his agent well enough to know that Dooley would not tolerate being the one interrogated, especially by a woman. So he intervened.

"Do I have to remind you again, Mr. Dooley, about your orders?"

Dooley took a deep breath before he continued. "The military has its ways, Doctor, and so does the CIA. That's all I'll say about that."

"Contempt, then?" Deltare pressed.

Dooley glared at Deltare, his fists clenching, his face turning red.

"How about we all cool our jets and have a look at the subject?" Morgan said, breaking the tension a bit.

Now Deltare was the one to take a deep breath. The stress of the ugly confrontation with Dooley had only heightened the anxiety she felt in this unique moment. She was about to see for herself if what she'd been told was true—if an alien from space really existed. She began to hyperventilate.

As they walked down the hall, Morgan pointed out the various offices and rooms along the way. One of them was to be her office. Deltare barely registered the tour, feeling a little dizzy and off-balance. Her eyes fixed on the heavy door at the far end of the hallway, drawing closer with each step.

When they reached the strong metal door, Dooley carefully opened the door's tiny sliding window at eye level and peeked inside.

"It's at the far end of the room, on the right, sitting on its bed," Dooley said. "Let me go in first to be sure the shackles are in place."

"'Shackles'?" Deltare wondered if this alien might be friendly, or perhaps not.

Dooley smirked. "Don't fool yourself, Dr. Deltare. This is the enemy. You can't trust it. You better always remember that and keep your guard up."

Dooley's continued use of the word "it" irritated Deltare even more. "Has he hurt people?" she asked.

Dooley considered the question for a moment. "No, because we've been careful. We're in control."

As Dooley unlocked the door, he grabbed a long metal stick leaning on the wall next to the door.

"And what is that?" Deltare asked.

"A cattle prod."

"Why would you need *that*?" Deltare asked, with a rising level of concern for her own safety.

"That's how we get it to move to where we want it to. It listens to the cattle prod."

Deltare felt dizzy and disoriented as she tried to reconcile her expectations of what Dooley was saying and doing. This was not at all what she had hoped for. She had imagined meeting an officer from another world, a wise being of superior intelligence, perhaps even gracious and polite. She had seen something in his eyes and facial expression in the photos she was shown in Roswell during her indoctrination. Perhaps she had it all wrong. Perhaps she was fooling herself. Perhaps this being was indeed dangerous and full of evil intent.

They eased into the room.

Zeemat turned his head toward them and then straightened up as he noticed the presence of someone new. Deltare noted a serious, cautious, perhaps fearful look on his face. His body language showed a tense preparation, ready to respond to whatever came his way, perhaps to strike.

Deltare stood wide-eyed and mouth agape. It was all true. She was standing face-to-face with a being from another world. Her heart felt like it would pound out of her chest. She made an effort to steady her breathing.

Dooley addressed Zeemat: "Sit over here, in the desk chair." He gave the command with an excessively loud and slow speech, overpronouncing each word, while pointing to the desk chair with the cattle prod.

Zeemat looked at the desk chair but didn't move.

Dooley repeated his command, louder and slower, now tapping the desk chair with the cattle prod.

Zeemat still didn't move.

Dooley then took several decisive steps toward Zeemat and swung forcefully with the cattle prod, striking him on the shoulder and the side of his head. Zeemat attempted to ward off the blow, but though he could only partially deflect it, he still did not move.

Deltare was shocked. "Wait! Is that necessary?"

Dooley didn't bother to respond. He turned the cattle prod switch to "On" and snapped off a few sizzling charges. He then approached Zeemat, aiming the tip of the electric prod.

"Wait!" Deltare repeated. "Stop!"

Dooley didn't obey. He jabbed the prod into Zeemat's side and snapped off a few charges, this time making contact with the alien, who grimaced at the shock but took it remarkably well, like he'd become used to it.

"I SAID STOP!" Deltare screamed, charging toward Dooley and shoving him out of the way.

Caught off guard and off-balance, Dooley was surprised by the boldness of a mere woman. He stumbled to the side, regained his balance, then turned quickly to face Deltare, his red face in a rage, like when he'd had too much to drink.

"You can't tell me nuthin'!" he shouted back.

Surprised by her own gusto, Deltare took a breath to steady herself. She had never physically pushed a grown man. The violence of it felt almost nauseating. Her whole body started to shake, but she knew she had to say something, as she feared that Dooley was about to attack her.

"G-Get out!" she shouted, pointing to the door. Her head still dizzy and her heart still pounding, she was unsure if she really had any authority, or if she was doing the right thing. This was all new to her. She clenched her hands into fists to suppress the shaking.

Dooley glared at Deltare, but it was obvious he was out-ranked. For a few tense moments, he simmered, fists clenched for a different reason, staring hard at Deltare. Then he walked toward the door, brushing uncomfortably close and intention-ally bumping her with his shoulder. Deltare reacted by instinct, giving Dooley another forceful shove, this time pushing him hard to the wall. Dooley whipped around, ready to fight, but Morgan stepped in front of him in time to ward off Dooley's first punch.

"Now, now, that's no way to treat a lady," Morgan said with a half smile on his face and a wink only Dooley could see.

"That ain't no lady!" Dooley countered, pointing an accu-satory finger at Deltare's face.

"Well, she's giving the orders right now, so just do as you're told. Leave the room. Leave the building. Go cool off."

"I want the keys to the shackles," Deltare said.

Dooley threw the keys to the floor as he walked away, and they heard him storm off, kicking things and slamming doors on his way out.

Deltare took a few moments to let the intensity of the confrontation die down as she thought about what she should do next. She picked up the shackle keys off the floor and stared at them in her shaking hands before looking over to Zeemat, who was carefully examining her at the same time. Now she saw caution and worry in his facial expression and body language—not danger.

She had to decide. This was a crucial moment, and she knew it. Morgan had to see that she was the right person for the job, and she had to demonstrate to the alien that she was friendly. Perhaps more than anything, she had to prove to herself that she had the courage to do this.

"Please leave us now," Deltare said to Morgan, her voice cracking a bit. "I want time with him alone. Shut the door behind you. You can look through the window."

"Dr. Deltare," Morgan said, his tone steeped in concern. "Is that a good idea?"

"Please," Deltare repeated. "Do it now. I think I'll be okay."

Morgan shrugged his shoulders and walked out the door, closing it behind him. A moment later, Deltare heard the door window slide open and knew Morgan was looking, but she fixed her attention now on Zeemat, who still had not taken his eyes off her.

They looked into each other's eyes, each trying to discern the other's intentions, neither knowing what was to happen next. Deltare walked over to the desk, pulled out the chair, and dragged it over to a spot as close as she could get to Zeemat without coming into his reach.

They sat there for a few moments, looking each other over from head to toe. When she saw the bruises and cuts on his face, she finally understood.

Deltare did the talking, knowing full well he would not understand a thing, but hoping her feelings or intentions would come through to him.

"I'm sorry they've treated you this way," she said in all sincerity. "I have a strong feeling you didn't deserve any of it. Well, I want you to know that things have changed. It's *my* job now," she said, pointing to herself, "to figure out a way for us to communicate."

Deltare was still pointing to herself when she realized that was an appropriate place to start. She tapped herself on the chest several times and said, "Linda."

Zeemat regarded her, making no response, with a vague look of suspicion.

"Linda," Deltare repeated. "Linda Deltare. Doc-tor Lin-dah Del-TAH-ray." But still, she received no reaction from Zeemat. Instinctively, she understood he would likely feel suspicious, threatened, as if this might be a trick of his interrogators. She looked Zeemat in the eyes and nodded understandingly. "Linda," she said one last time, softly.

Deltare then pointed her attention to the shackles around Zeemat's wrists and ankles. She rubbed her own wrists in empathy, then her ankles. The look on the Zeemat's face betrayed a subtle change—surprise, confusion.

Deltare rose from her chair and stood for a few seconds, holding the keys in front of her so Zeemat could see. She took a deep breath and took a step closer to him, now within his reach if he so chose. But Zeemat didn't reach. He leaned away by a fraction of an inch, enough for Deltare to feel she was doing the right thing.

She took another step closer, now an arm's length away from Zeemat. She could see the texture of his fine skin. She saw more clearly the bruises and cuts at various stages of healing on either side of his face and head. She now made a turning motion with the keys in her hand and looked down to the shackles. "May I remove them?" she asked in a gentle, soothing voice.

Zeemat's expression remained guarded, but he slowly lifted his wrists to allow Deltare to unlock the shackles. He knew what she was suggesting.

"Please don't hurt me," Deltare implored as she unlocked the first of the shackles. "I'm just trying to do the right thing."

Zeemat's right wrist was now free. He put his right arm down and offered the shackled left wrist. Deltare then unlocked those. She put the keys and the now-empty shackles on the floor beside her, giving Zeemat a little time to rub his gouged and irritated wrists. Deltare felt sad and ashamed for what they had done to this creature. She pulled the desk chair closer and observed Zeemat with genuine empathy and concern. Slowly she offered her hands, palm up, suggesting Zeemat put his hand in hers. His face, which had been taut and severe, now softened. He took a few moments before slowly placing his injured hands in hers. She gave them a soft squeeze, then gently rubbed the sore wrists with her thumbs. "I am so sorry," she repeated.

On the other side of the door, a wide-eyed Morgan stared in disbelief at these historic moments.

Deltare then pushed the chair back, got on her knees, and unshackled the alien's ankles. She motioned with her hands for the alien to stay seated, and he did. She then picked up all the shackles and ceremoniously walked them over to the door. Morgan opened the door, and Deltare handed him the shackles. "Throw these damn things away. We'll not be using them again."

"Yes, ma'am," Morgan replied, surprised and impressed by the sudden change of events.

"And please bring us something to eat and drink," Deltare added.

The door closed and clicked, and she returned to the chair by Zeemat's side. She smiled at him now. "Well, how do you like that?" she asked him, rubbing her own wrists and ankles.

Zeemat gave her a hint of a smile, which gave Deltare a thrill.

"Oh my gosh," she said to no one in particular.

A million things now raced through her mind. "How in the world am I going to talk to you?" she asked Zeemat. "Especially since we can't even get past introductions?" She tried again: "My name is Linda . . . Linda."

She tapped her chest, but Zeemat remained blank-faced. Deltare then took a small risk and slowly pointed to the alien's chest, tapping it gently a few times and then opening her palms in a questioning gesture. Still no response.

Morgan came to the door and peeked inside. "I found a few snacks in the pantry and sodas in the icebox."

"Thank you," Deltare said, taking the items from Morgan and placing them on the desk, the glass soda bottles clinking in her excited hands.

"Oh well, so much for conversation for now," Deltare said to Zeemat. "Let's have something to eat." She dragged the small desk over to where Zeemat was sitting on the side of the bed, then pulled up the chair so they were sitting across from each other.

Deltare was thrilled at the progress so far. She still had a million questions, but those could wait for another day. For now, it was time to celebrate the removal of shackles, the seeming gentleness of this alien. Deltare dug into the snacks and opened the sodas, taking several sips and gesturing for Zeemat to join in. And at long last, the starving and thirsty Zeemat reached over, took a few snacks and coughed his way through his first carbonated drink. Deltare laughed, first at seeing Zeemat's expression of surprise, and then at how he seemed to relish the fizzy drink.

After the snacks and drinks, Deltare returned the desk to its proper position. She approached Zeemat, who was still sitting on the side of the bed. She gestured for him to rise, and he surprised her by standing up straight, right in front of her, about six inches taller than her own five-foot-two frame. At that moment, just like when she'd examined the photos during her preparation in Roswell, she saw more similarities between them than differences.

"I have to leave now," Deltare said, pointing to herself and then to the door. "But I'll be back tomorrow, and every day after that."

Deltare now felt fully engaged in her forced assignment. Now she understood—nothing could be more important in her life than this. "We must figure out a way to talk to each other," she said.

She reached out to shake the alien's hand, to show him a human gesture of friendship, and he surprised her by reaching out his right hand, shaking hers, and not letting go. Then he offered his left hand, and she responded with her own left hand. They engaged in the two-handed, cross-armed handshake that was the traditional sign of friendship and respect in Torkiya. Zeemat smiled, and Deltare laughed nervously.

Finally, they released each other's hands, almost reluctantly.

"Goodbye," Deltare said. "See you tomorrow." She turned to leave.

As she neared the door, she saw Morgan close the observation window. The steel plate slid shut. Just then, a striking sound came from behind her. In a deep voice, she heard an unmistakable word: "Lin-dah." She spun around, wide-eyed.

"Lin-dah . . . Del-TAH-ray," the alien said. Then he tapped his chest and said, "Zeemat."

TWENTY-FIVE

FRIEND OR FOE

DELTARE DISCOVERED THAT Zeemat was good at imitating sounds and learning languages. Much of his Torkiyan brain was dedicated to that. His double-larynx respiratory system allowed him to produce and mimic virtually any sound. His first words sounded like a perfect imitation of Deltare's, though he gradually fell into his own voice and rhythm of speech as he pieced together phrases and sentences in passable English.

"You're a fast learner," Deltare said after their first week of working together on his language skills.

"Linda teacher good," Zeemat replied. They were well past the simple naming of objects and building a basic vocabulary. Zeemat had mastered the look and sounds of the alphabet and had begun to learn the basic rules of grammar. He was reading and writing at primary school level, devouring every book Deltare brought him.

But Zeemat would only speak to Deltare, and only when the door's observation window was shut. "Only you," he told Deltare, and she was glad about that. It helped cement her importance to the project and her continued involvement with Zeemat.

In turn, Deltare asked Zeemat to repeat each of the English words and phrases in his own Torkiyan tongue, and she jotted endless notes in her own phonetic code, trying to make sense of Zeemat's complex language, but she had yet to get a handle on how to reproduce it. She recorded every session, hoping someday to have the technology to put it all together and make sense of the *buzzes, beeps, honks, trills, chimes,* and all his other curious sounds. She had Morgan listen to the tapes, while she pretended she was making progress in deciphering and translating the alien sounds.

Over the following weeks, Zeemat blazed through grade school and high school English. Deltare expanded his curriculum to include other subjects. She brought in books, and Zeemat couldn't get enough—learning about humans, their activities, Earth's animal world, and the geography of the planet. He took naturally to mathematics and easily mastered the counterparts to the Torkiyan numeric symbols he was used to. Deltare learned to translate his Torkiyan symbols into the Hindu-Arabic numeral system most people used on Earth.

Zeemat wrote notebooks of English words and phrases, divided into topics like food and drink, numbers and letters, days and dates, objects and things, people and animals, greetings and farewells, and feelings and thoughts. He had learned how to write and speak sentences with a subject, a predicate, and a direct object, and he'd also begun to use creative clauses.

Zeemat was thrilled to be free, finally, to draw again, and he made countless drawings for Deltare. He drew the view from out his window at various times of the day and night, and of the people, vehicles, and planes he saw.

"Amazing detail! I'm impressed!" Deltare saved each drawing he made for her.

Zeemat's considerable progress thrilled her. With Morgan's support, she supplied Zeemat with books, magazines, and maps, which seemed to springboard his interest.

"Zeemat wants to go here," he said to Deltare, pointing to a picture of a boat in a storm at sea in a *National Geographic* article. In one of his notebooks, he started a list of places to see. The more he learned about planet Earth and its inhabitants, the more he wanted to see it for himself. "Earth is beautiful!" he told Deltare.

"Maybe someday," she said. Deltare pictured herself as the ideal person to show Zeemat the world, but for now, she was content simply communicating with him and showing him what humans were all about. She could do this for a long time, forever maybe. But she was aware that this was unlikely—that the government had other plans for Zeemat.

After a productive session with Zeemat, Deltare was called into a meeting with Special Agent Morgan.

"We can see you're making progress with the alien," Morgan said. "But when will you be able to teach us his language? When will he tell us what we want to know?"

"Soon," Deltare said.

"That's not fast enough. We want answers now."

"Who is 'we'?" she asked.

"Who do you think? Me, Director Dulles, the president of the United States, his Joint Chiefs of Staff—we all want to know! Why do you think we went to so much trouble to keep him alive, and to bring *you* into the picture?"

"'Trouble'? You think Zeemat is trouble? He's closer to a miracle, wouldn't you say?"

Morgan drew close to Deltare, towering over her. "Well, if you want to keep working with him, your miracle better start answering the big questions. He can start by telling us why he's here. And if there are others like him here on Earth right now. What are their intentions? We want to know if he's friend or foe. Until he can prove otherwise, he's a foe."

"What? He's been nothing but gracious and kind," Deltare quickly pointed out.

"We want answers, Deltare . . . *today*. That's an order!"

With a series of words, gestures, and pictures, Deltare got answers to some of Morgan's questions. It proved difficult, but Zeemat communicated that he was on a mission of exploration, to start a new life on this distant planet, to be a representative of the Torkiyan people.

For his part, what Zeemat had said was true. He didn't need to tell Deltare about the Torkiyan master plan to subjugate and conquer the people of Earth. "Zeemat does not like to fight. Zeemat is alone on Earth. Earth is his new home."

Deltare took meticulous notes. She continued to gather an ever clearer picture of this unique individual, and she liked him more each day.

"Won't you tell that to Morgan? Won't you speak to him?" Deltare asked.

He shook his head. "Only you."

"Why just me?" Deltare asked.

"I want you . . . to stay . . . with me," Zeemat said in perfect English.

Morgan wasn't convinced by Deltare's report. "That's what he *says*—that he's friendly—but can he *prove* it?"

"How's he going to prove anything?" Deltare asked, incredulous. "And why should he have to?" She furrowed her brow in a scowl, and crossing her arms tight against her body, she squared up to face Morgan.

"You're acting like a mother hen. Get over it," Morgan said. "He can show his good intentions by providing information. If he can help the military, it'll go a long way toward proving he's here in peace."

Morgan opened his desk drawer and pulled out a folder, holding it firmly in both hands and shaking it in front of Deltare's face. "These technical documents are top secret. President Eisenhower and Director Dulles cleared you and only you. Disclosing any of this information would be high treason, punishable by life in prison . . . or worse."

Deltare took a step back and pulled her hands away abruptly, as if the top secret documents might somehow burn her. She hadn't expected to participate in anything 'technical,' and Morgan's threats were crystal-clear. She was a bit confused. Nothing could be more secret than Zeemat himself. How were they going to trust her with the knowledge of his existence? She'd been recruited to figure out a way to communicate with him, or so she'd understood—not to draw out sensitive, technical information.

"Tell me you understand and that you agree to keep this completely, absolutely confidential," Morgan said.

"Do I have a choice?" Deltare asked, looking at the folder labeled "Top Secret" in fear, as if it were a deadly viper about to strike. Yet she recalled how she'd been abducted several months earlier, when she was "recruited" for this position by the CIA, and she realized her "choice" didn't seem to matter.

"No, not really. Remember what the president said to you after your recruitment? This is for the good of the American people and for all mankind." He pushed the folder toward her.

Deltare twisted her face in resignation. She would comply because this was a once-in-a-lifetime opportunity, but she didn't have to like every part of it.

She took the folder from Morgan. The words "U-2 Project" were printed neatly on the folder tab.

"What's this?" she inquired.

"You better start teaching him about airplanes and flying."

"I don't know anything about that. And anyway, I'm sure he knows way more about those things than we do."

"Precisely the point."

She opened the folder and skimmed through documents about the Air Force's new, top secret spy plane.

Later that day, to Zeemat's delight, Deltare directed much of his learning to airplanes and flying. He developed an advanced aviation vocabulary in English, and Deltare learned right along with him.

Zeemat was fascinated by the clever technology of these primitive flying machines and impressed by the brave men who flew them. As his reading skills improved, he devoured every book on the subject that Deltare brought to him. She requisitioned a bookshelf for him, and he began to accumulate his favorite reads.

They often took small breaks to look out the window, between the strong steel bars that were set five inches apart, like in a prison cell. They enjoyed watching and listening to the planes taking off, landing, or circling overhead. They had only a limited view of the airfield, but it was far better than nothing. Zeemat loved what he could see of the comings and goings on the base.

On a hot summer's day in July of 1955, about a year after his arrival, Zeemat sensed a definite increase in activity around the base. Support vehicles and Jeeps with serious-faced soldiers sped in all directions. An interesting airplane had arrived, and no other planes were flying. This new plane was the sole focus of everyone's attention.

Pressing his head against the window bars, Zeemat got a glimpse of part of the plane. Its beauty enthralled him. From what he could see, the dark gray airplane had an elegantly long and slim physique. A small cockpit sat atop the base of a long, slender nose. He could see almost all of one long, thin wing. Narrow engines paralleled the fuselage at the tail. Zeemat knew this was a plane unlike the others he had seen on the base. With its slim body, it would have a low payload capacity, so it was not for carrying things—it was built for a special purpose. It would also have a narrow profile when seen from below. He could tell the design was intended to be difficult to see in the sky. And the rather long wings were likely designed for lift. This was a plane that could reach the planet's upper atmosphere, which he envisioned as "lower space."

Zeemat's assessment was soon confirmed. He turned his head toward the door when he heard Deltare's familiar gentle knocks and watched as she entered. She brought with her a man he had never seen before.

"Good morning, Zeemat!" Deltare said with a cheerful lilt to her voice. "This is Mr. Kelly Johnson. He designed the new plane that just arrived. I'm sure you saw it out your window. It's called the U-2." She turned to Johnson. "Mr. Johnson, this is Zeemat."

Zeemat walked up to a wide-eyed Kelly Johnson, who took a step back as Zeemat approached.

"Don't worry, Mr. Johnson," Deltare reassured. "He won't bite."

Zeemat offered his right hand like Deltare had taught him, and after a few tense moments, Johnson cautiously shook it. He slowly began to relax.

"I didn't know what to expect," Johnson explained. "General Twining ordered me to show up here today with the U-2. A few minutes ago, I was told I would meet a special consultant, and that he was an alien from space. I laughed until I noticed everyone was serious. I didn't really believe it until just now. I'm sorry if I appear a bit shaken."

"I totally understand, Mr. Johnson," Deltare said as Zeemat smiled and nodded, his lips tightly closed.

Zeemat kept quiet and Deltare sighed. She wished he would speak to the others like he spoke to her, but she imagined why he didn't. The others had abused him, and she'd been kind. It was a simple matter of trust. She had done the same with negative people in her own life, effectively shutting the abusive ones out, so she understood Zeemat's decision to speak only to her.

Deltare continued: "I'm certain you have many questions for Zeemat, but we are not at liberty to discuss anything other than the U-2 and the technical problems you are having. Like you, I was just informed this morning of your arrival. I do know a little about your issues with the plane. Perhaps Zeemat can help."

"And how might that be?" Johnson asked, squinting his eyes and raising the corner of one side of his mouth.

"Well, as you might imagine, Zeemat has more experience with aerospace navigation than anyone else on planet Earth. It makes sense we would want to ask for his thoughts."

"Can he talk?"

"He and I understand each other fairly well now. We have built a relationship." Deltare and Zeemat shared a brief smile. Johnson looked far from convinced. "This is ridiculous. He knows nothing about this project. We've been working on it for years."

"Well, we have all been ordered to pursue this consultation, so why don't we just give it a shot?"

Deltare wasn't thrilled with this arrangement either. She much preferred working with Zeemat on language and basic communication. She didn't think he was ready to be a military consultant, but orders were orders. "So let's start at the beginning. What is the purpose of this airplane?" Deltare asked as a starting point, though she already had a good idea.

"You don't even know what this plane is all about?" The pitch of Johnson's voice rose in irritation.

"It's a spy plane. We know the basics. We have full clearance, but please understand we only recently became aware of the U-2's existence."

Johnson took an exasperated deep breath. He sized up the alien and Deltare one more time before continuing. "Okay then, I think this is stupid but here goes. The U-2 is the nation's best spy plane, designed to take pictures over enemy territory. It's capable of reaching very high altitudes. It's designed to avoid or minimize detection, to not get shot down. We solved a lot of the technical issues with this latest version of the plane, but it's still not as undetectable as we'd like it to be, and our pilots are having trouble tolerating the thin air at very high altitudes for long enough to accomplish their missions, even while using oxygen masks."

Deltare interrupted and summarized. What Johnson said would already be difficult enough to address with Zeemat. She didn't want this consultation to become any more difficult than it had to be. "I believe I understand, Mr. Johnson. You want better undetectability for the airplane, and more high-altitude tolerance for your pilots."

"Exactly." Johnson nodded.

"Can you provide us with technical drawings?" Deltare asked.

"I have them with me. I was told to be prepared."

Johnson retrieved a sizable pile of documents and drawings from his large briefcase.

"Oh my gosh," Deltare exclaimed. "It'll take awhile to review all this. Give us the rest of today to look at these, and we'll have a time frame for you later this afternoon."

"I'll return at sixteen hundred for your thoughts," a still-irritated Johnson said. "After that, I'm leaving with the plane. That's *my* time frame." He took one last squinting, skeptical look at Zeemat, then turned on his heel and left the room.

Alone again, Deltare shot a worried look at Zeemat, who appeared calm.

When they were alone again, he said, "Don't worry, Linda. I have ideas. Let's look at the papers." His English was improving by the day.

Over the next few hours, Zeemat examined the detailed information Johnson had provided. He learned much more human technical vocabulary and jargon in aerospace science and chemistry than what he had already acquired, and he was grateful for the three years of training at the Torkiyan Space Academy and the year of solitary study with Janusia's Trangula. He now had a better feel for Earth's atmospheric distances, according to human measurement, and the effects on humans at varying altitudes. He could mentally compare similar effects on Torkiyan pilots on his own home planet, taking into account the differences in atmospheric composition and gravitational forces. Torkiyan technology was advanced in this regard. Zeemat found it enjoyable to go through the process of problem-solving the things he'd taken for granted on Torkiyan ships. He realized that what he knew, basic as it was compared to what his crewmates had known, was still far more advanced than any human knowledge.

With time running out at 1500 hours, Zeemat began to write, with pen on paper, in English, complete with mathematical symbols and detailed drawings. Deltare was impressed.

Precisely at 1600, Mr. Kelly Johnson returned for his report.

Deltare stood at the ready, holding the several-page report in her hands. "As requested, Mr. Johnson." She held out the report for Johnson to take.

Johnson read the report, a smirk tugging at his lips. The first part had to do with the U-2's undetectability. Zeemat reported that there were only two ways to avoid radar and light detection at typical human aviation speeds. The first had to do with the shape of the airplane itself. They could do more than simply provide a narrow profile to avoid the enemies down below. The main idea was to design the ground-facing surface of the plane with angles, both macroscopically and microscopically, to bounce radar and light waves in different directions, minimizing reflection back to the source.

The second way was equally important. Materials that absorb radar and light waves should be the only ones used on the ground-facing exterior surfaces of the U-2.

Zeemat provided several detailed drawings he'd made to help describe what he had written.

The ingenuity and simplicity of the alien's report caught Johnson by surprise. He hadn't expected to receive anything useful. But the design images Zeemat had drawn particularly impressed him. His next spy plane was in development, and he now planned to incorporate some of these design elements into the next version. And materials could be tested for radio wave absorption as Zeemat advised.

The next part of Zeemat's report dealt with the issue of pilot tolerance of high-altitude flying. Zeemat started by stating the obvious: With increasing distance from the Earth's surface, the atmosphere gradually blends into deep space. He suggested thinking about the U-2's flight ceiling as being low space rather than high atmosphere. He mentioned that human space exploration would require space suits that could maintain a micro-atmosphere like the one on the Earth's surface. He suggested that a full-body suit would do much better at maintaining normal physiology at high altitude than what a partially pressurized aircraft and a simple oxygen face mask could provide.

Alternatively, he suggested fully pressurizing the aircraft to ground pressures, like all Torkiyan vessels did. At the very least, he suggested the pilots breathe pure oxygen for several hours prior to high-altitude flights to eliminate body nitrogen and avoid nitrogen bubbles in the bloodstream and the resultant air embolisms. He also suggested having at least two of these systems in place at any given time, for the added safety of the pilots. Zeemat provided an additional series of drawings with detailed construction of a functional space suit, trying to keep in mind the materials the humans might have at their disposal.

Johnson looked up in astonishment. Zeemat's recommendations were practical and immediately deployable. He appreciated Zeemat's simple and commonsense approach.

Before he left, Johnson shook Zeemat's and Deltare's hands vigorously, thanking them profusely for this useful consultation. He opened his briefcase, filing some of Zeemat's report in a folder marked "U-2," and some of it in a folder marked "A-1." He filed the space suit drawings in yet another folder marked "Ideas for NASA," a project he was helping the government to develop.

As Johnson was taken to his plane by Jeep, Special Agent Morgan called to report to CIA Director Dulles, who had advised and organized this consultation. "I thought this was too soon," Morgan said. "I didn't think the alien was ready, but things turned out amazingly well. This was an excellent idea. Good job, Mr. Dulles!"

"You too, Morgan," Director Dulles replied.

At the same time in Zeemat's room, Deltare gushed. "Great job with the airplane, Zeemat!"

"U-2," he said, looking out the window, admiring the beautiful spy plane as it lifted gracefully off the runway.

TWENTY-SIX

THE DAWNING

AFTER KELLY JOHNSON left with the U-2, Deltare figured she should expand Zeemat's education in another direction.

"Wait right here," she said, as if Zeemat could go anywhere else. "There's something I want to show you."

Deltare ran to her office two doors down the hall and retrieved the spinning Earth globe off her desk. She wanted Zeemat to have a better feel for where he was within the world's geography. She wanted to show him that the world was divided into countries, and that the US government considered some of them friends and others enemies.

As she walked the short distance down the hall to her office, she overheard Morgan whispering on the phone in the next office down the hall. She tiptoed closer, looking in all directions to be sure she wouldn't be spotted eavesdropping, and gently put her ear against the closed door.

". . . It doesn't really matter, does it, whether he's friendly or not, as long as we get valuable information?" she heard Morgan say to someone on the other end, probably his boss, Director Dulles.

After a pause, Morgan spoke again. "Yeah, the Air Force is on board, and I'm sure Deltare can get more information out of him."

There was another pause.

". . . I'll keep putting up with her for now because the alien's valuable. If we want the upper hand over the Russians, this asset might well provide that."

It dawned on Deltare that the government had plans for Zeemat that differed from her own. They considered Zeemat an "asset," and his information was for the armed forces, to defeat the Russians, not for "the American people and for all mankind" like they'd led her to believe. Her jaw dropped in surprise, then she clenched her teeth in anger.

They want a goddamn weapon!

TWENTY-SEVEN

DELTARE DEALS

AFTER THE SUCCESSFUL consultation regarding the U-2 project, Morgan prepared Deltare for more to come.

"I have several other consultations lined up," he told her.

But Deltare saw the big picture more clearly now, after having overheard Morgan's conversation with Dulles. She knew Zeemat was valuable and that she was needed "for now," so this arrangement was only temporary, and it was time to press her advantage.

"The consultations should wait," Deltare said. "We're making great progress with language and communication. Zeemat will be even more valuable when he can communicate better with us."

"This isn't a discussion, Deltare. These are orders from on high. We want usable information."

Deltare narrowed her brow and put her hands on her hips.

"If we're to put our language work to the side so we can help you with technical consultations, then I think you need to give us something in return," Deltare said. "That will show

Zeemat your good intentions and foster his cooperation," she added.

Morgan narrowed his own eyes, and he took a moment to respond. He seldom negotiated with his underlings, especially with women. But Deltare had the president's support, and she had demonstrated her worth as an asset.

"What do you have in mind?" he asked.

She'd gotten her opening, what she was hoping for.

"I want better living arrangements for Zeemat—expand his quarters, give him a more comfortable bed and a desk and two comfortable chairs for us to sit and work in." She suppressed a devious smile—these were easy asks, and she expected a yes to her simple requests.

"We can do that," Morgan replied. "We'll get to that as soon as possible. Now, let's talk about the next consultation we've set up . . ."

"Wait, Mr. Morgan," Deltare interrupted. "There's more." Morgan frowned.

"As for myself, I want control over furnishing my office." She waited for Morgan to nod his head yes, then she pressed for more. "And I want control over my wardrobe. I know it's the company uniform but dressing in black in the hot desert is absurd."

Morgan rolled his eyes, but these were doable demands, and he wanted to encourage Deltare and her work with Zeemat.

Deltare sensed her opportunity. "I want a Louis Vuitton briefcase."

"You're pushing it, Deltare."

Deltare didn't get a no, so she reached for one more thing—the biggest one. "And I don't want to stay overnight here on base. I want a suite in the best hotel in Las Vegas. Someone can drive me in and out every day. I can do my best work if I'm rested and well fed."

Morgan released an audible sigh. He paused a minute, before responding. "I'll give you these things and you give me more information. Clear?"

"Clear!" Deltare replied, releasing a smug smile, keenly aware of the government's intentions and of her value to the program.

TWENTY-EIGHT

CREATURE COMFORTS

A FEW DAYS later, as the sun was setting and night was falling, a military guard drove Deltare to her suite at the Dunes Hotel and Casino, one of the most luxurious rooms on the property. The guard took his post in the hallway just outside her room.

She opened the door to her new suite, reached in to turn on the light, and covered her gaping mouth with her hands. The elegant room was adorned with a lush carpet, fine furniture, and artful objects. After the initial shock at the unexpected elegance, she entered the room on shaking feet. The polished mahogany of the combined TV and stereo console in the living room felt smooth and rich to her caressing touch. A picture window had a glorious view of downtown Las Vegas, already alive in a dazzle of lights. A small kitchenette sat off to the side. As she walked down the short hallway to the bedroom and bathroom, she noticed there was no telephone anywhere, and that there was also no mechanism to open the windows. She was glad the air-conditioning units made the rooms comfortable. In the bedroom, she decided the king-sized bed was too large. Instead, she would ask for a queen-sized, and a large desk and bookshelves to balance out the space. *Gold mine!* she thought, allowing herself another smug smile.

Along the entire width of one bedroom wall, a set of mirrored sliding doors opened to a wide closet. The dresses, slacks, and blouses she purchased earlier in the day at the hotel's swanky shops, courtesy of the US government, were already hanging, with room for plenty more. New shoes to match her outfits sat in their boxes lining the closet floor.

The bathroom was all marble and crystal, with sconces that emanated a warm light from what appeared to be open Aladdin lamps. A fine Turkish rug warmed the cool marble tiles in front of the sink and vanity. She glanced at herself in the bathroom mirror before becoming instantly distracted by the inviting, step-in tub she saw reflected behind her. She turned around, sat at the edge of the tub, and turned the hot water on.

Standing to look again in the mirror, she took off her clothes and let them drop to the floor in a messy heap at her feet. A thought came to her mind: *I wish Zeemat could see all this.*

After a long bath, Deltare snuggled herself into a soft white terry cloth robe she'd found in a small bathroom closet and wrapped her dripping hair in one of the hotel's thick Turkish bath towels. She stepped into a pair of soft slippers with the Dunes logo on them and shuffled over to her new TV/stereo console.

The console's cabinet door opened smoothly, and as she had requested, a collection of LP records had been delivered—recordings of all her favorite Rodgers and Hammerstein

Broadway show tunes. Flipping through the covers, she settled on *The King and I*, her excited eyes darting through the song list, searching for a specific track. A warm smile took over her face when she found it, and she ran her finger tenderly over the title of the song, letting it linger there. Using a long fingernail, she cut the cellophane along the edge of the new record's cover to preserve the protective cellophane, then gingerly removed the record, taking care not to scratch or smudge the glistening surface. She placed it on the turntable, turned the record player on, then gently positioned the player's arm so that the needle landed in a groove in the small space just before her desired track. After cranking up the volume, she stepped back, hugged herself tight, and sang along to "Getting to Know You." She closed her eyes and swayed to the music, gradually opening her arms and lifting her head, performing the song to an imaginary audience as if she were the star of the show.

TWENTY-NINE

THE AGE OF AQUARIUS

OVER THE NEXT few years, Zeemat met with a steady flow of scientists and engineers. He helped each of them with their own technical challenges.

IBM's Thomas Watson Jr. and Arthur Samuel came in the fall of 1955. Zeemat instructed them in the Torkiyan basics of electronic language and logic as best he could. He was proud of his mother's work as Janusia's Chief Programmer and had paid some attention to it. He detailed what he remembered of the electronic language in a complex Torkiyan formula, which he and Deltare later painstakingly translated into English letters and numbers. IBM engineers refined it into a scientific computer language they called FORTRAN, the "translated formula," and used it to develop a machine that could not only play checkers but also learn from its experience. It was the first artificial intelligence ever developed on planet Earth.

In return, Zeemat received rewards from Morgan, as requested by Deltare. "They help to keep him motivated," she argued.

Zeemat's first rewards consisted of magazines and newspapers. Deltare presented Zeemat with a set of back copies of *National Geographic* magazines starting with the month of his arrival in 1954. Newspapers started with *The New York Times*, but his daily reading eventually included *The Wall Street Journal*, *The Washington Post*, the *Chicago Tribune*, and the *LA Times*.

Morgan saw no harm in giving Zeemat information about Earth and humanity, figuring that he would never leave his cell and go on to use what he'd learned about the humans against them. So he continued to allow Deltare's "incentive program" of "rewards and motivations."

Deltare was ultramotivated to continue working with Zeemat, not only because of the unique scientific opportunity, but also because, despite herself, she felt a similar rush of excitement working with Zeemat every day as she'd had with her first crush in school.

"This is my life's work," she told Morgan. "I know that now."

She liked everything about Zeemat. He spoke to her kindly and politely, he seemed to brighten up whenever she entered the room, he drew pictures of himself with her, and he'd become her only friend.

In time, Morgan allowed Deltare to stay at her room in the Dunes without a guard at her front door. They installed a phone connecting only to the base and developed a system where she would call to check in and check out on her way back and forth from Area 51. Deltare was visibly eager to come to work, and she gained her employer's trust.

Zeemat met with Harry Vickers and James Rand of the Sperry Rand company to put the computer language he'd helped create into products for the military. Zeemat's work with IBM and Sperry Rand resulted in countless military contracts and products.

Soon after, Deltare walked into Zeemat's room with a box wrapped in gift paper and tied with a colorful bow. "This is for you," she said, as excited as a kid at Christmas. "Hurry! Open it!" She clapped her hands.

Zeemat was puzzled by the strange package and by Deltare's emotion. "What is it?" he asked, cocking his head as he cautiously examined all sides of the colorfully wrapped package.

"Open it!"

Zeemat removed the bow and unwrapped a sealed cardboard box. He opened it, reached in, and pulled out a Zenith tabletop radio. He looked at Deltare, puzzled. "Thank you," he said. "But what is it?"

Deltare chuckled. "Well, how would you know, really? It's a radio!" She clapped her hands again, clearly more excited than he was.

Zeemat held the long electric cord in one hand, figuring it would plug into an outlet like his lamp did.

"Here, let me plug it in for you." Deltare took the heavy radio from him and placed it on the floor next to the bookcase. She inserted the plug into the nearby electrical socket. "Now look . . . and *listen!*"

Zeemat observed as Deltare worked the dials. He could see a thin vertical bar move left and right on a numerical display. At first, all he heard were *hisses* and random noises, but finally, she honed in on a particular spot on the radio's display, and a clear human voice sprang out of the radio's speaker. She turned another knob to raise the volume.

"Here it is . . . 1460. KENO. It's my favorite radio station around here. It plays all the top songs. Listen!"

Zeemat focused his attention on the radio announcer.

". . . and moving quickly up the Top 40, here are the sweet voices of The McGuire Sisters with their new song, 'Sincerely'!"

Zeemat was fascinated. He loved the music. He looked over to Deltare, who had her eyes closed as she swayed to the music, a dreamy smile on her face. He smiled, too, glad that she was happy.

In late 1957, Morgan brought several other people to meet with Deltare and Zeemat. A group of engineers had recently left the Shockley Semiconductor Laboratory and were recruited by Mr. Sherman Fairchild, a visionary entrepreneur, to continue working on semiconductor technologies. With some difficulty, Zeemat recalled enough from his studies at the Academy and from his solitary year with the Trangula to help this group develop the design to manufacture functional silicon chips with microscopic integrated circuits. This success resulted in another barrage of military contracts and eventually led to the formation of dozens of companies, including Intel and AMD. Executives from each of these companies constantly pressed Deltare for more access to Zeemat's knowledge.

Deltare began to meet with these company executives in secret at the Dunes, knowing full well that this could land her in a heap of trouble with the government. But the risk felt worthwhile—she could provide herself with an insurance policy in case things didn't work out with her current employer. She believed their need for utmost secrecy placed her at unusual risk. So, she devised a way of meeting with these executives while playing the slot machines at the hotel's casino. They sat at adjacent machines and made a minimum of eye contact, passing information back and forth in packs of cigarettes. Deltare sold special access to Zeemat's knowledge, and in return they funded a secret bank account for her in the Caymans.

In 1958, Zeemat received his next reward. Morgan and Dooley lugged it one on each end, and delivered it to Zeemat in his cell. The dour look on Dooley's face was an unwelcome reminder that this abusive man was still under Morgan's employ.

But Deltare was overjoyed. She held her hands with interlocked fingers, as if in prayer, and jumped up and down. She didn't allow Dooley's presence to dampen her excitement.

"Zeemat, these are two gifts in one!" she said.

She directed the men to position the console against the only remaining free wall. Dooley shoved the heavy piece of furniture into position, its legs grating loudly along the cement floor. Then he hurried out of the room, not waiting around for any more unwelcome orders from Deltare. Morgan followed behind him, leaving Zeemat and Deltare to themselves.

Deltare closed the door behind the men and turned her attention back to Zeemat. He slid his hands along the smooth, shiny top of the cherrywood cabinet. She reached behind it, plugged in the power cord, and attached a long antenna wire to the antenna screws on the back of the TV. The wire extended along the baseboards and out his window. Deltare told him the other end of the wire was attached to a tall TV antenna he couldn't see.

Zeemat stood off to the side with a knowing smile on his face. He instantly recognized the television console. He'd seen newspaper ads for TVs, and he'd read articles about popular programs. Now he could watch them himself.

"Zeemat," Deltare began. "There's a TV on one side, but look!" The long console was an elegant piece of furniture, and the top of the left side of the console was a lid on a hinge. "Ta-da!" she said, opening the lid to reveal a record player.

Zeemat also knew about record players but never imagined he would ever hear one play.

Deltare left the room for a minute, promptly returning with a pile of unopened long-playing records.

"I picked these out for you," she said. On top of the pile was the latest Frank Sinatra album. Deltare tore the cellophane along the edge with her fingernail and expertly extracted the record. She showed Zeemat how the record player worked.

She placed the needle in the space just before the track of the title song, "Come Fly with Me," and turned up the volume.

The sound blaring from the cabinet's stereo speakers overwhelmed him. It felt like a dream—memories of Torkiyan music and dancing flooded his brain, while he watched Deltare twirling around the room with arms outstretched as if she were flying, like an airplane.

"'Come, fly with me,'" she sang, pulling Zeemat by the hand to join her.

Zeemat jumped right in. Deltare sang along with Sinatra while she "flew" around the room, Zeemat following right behind.

Morgan watched them from the door's window, aware of their growing bond, with a look somewhere between disgust and disbelief.

THIRTY

DELTARE AND DOOLEY

MORGAN STILL HAD Dooley in charge of security, a job he despised. To make matters worse, Dooley obsessed over the memory of Deltare displacing him when she arrived in 1955. *A woman!* he thought, fuming.

In the winter of 1959, Dooley paused during his routine patrol of the grounds around Zeemat's cell block. Most everyone had finished their work for the day and were either in the barracks or had left the complex. Area 51 was quiet. He watched as the December sun dipped below the horizon, and he felt the sudden drop in temperature, raising the collar of his woolen coat as he shivered.

Reaching deep into his coat's side pocket, he retrieved the flat bottle of gin he always carried with him. He swallowed several gulps, enjoying the rush of warmth seeping from his throat into his stomach and spreading through his body. He didn't mind what it did to his head either. It helped pass the cold, quiet, lonely nights. He screwed the lid back on the bottle and returned it to his coat pocket when he noticed the light turn off in Deltare's office window.

Deltare had worked late into that evening, after a productive day with Zeemat. She finished writing her notes, filed them, and tidied up her desk, placing several more of Zeemat's technical drawings into her personal briefcase. She put on her heavy cardigan sweater, turned off the lights, and headed out to her car, looking forward to a warm bath at the Dunes.

She reached her car in the small parking lot to the side of the building, opened the door, and threw her briefcase onto the passenger seat. She was about to jump in when a deep voice startled her from behind.

"Looksh like you're done for the day," Dooley said, suppressing a belch.

Deltare whipped around, smelling the liquor oozing off him. He slurred his words with a gleam to his bloodshot eyes. And she noticed a certain look to them—disdain, and maybe something else?

"You startled me!" she said, bringing a hand up to her chest.

Dooley's eyes followed Deltare's hand to her chest and lingered there for too many moments.

"Enjoying the view?" Deltare said, twisting her mouth in irritation. She wrapped her sweater tighter around herself.

"Yeah, I am," Dooley said, wobbling slightly on his feet. "You might be an irritating bitch, but did I ever mention you have a nice rack?"

"You're drunk, Dooley. Go sleep it off."

"You think thish is drunk?" Dooley laughed. "I'm jus' gettin' started. How 'bout you join me?" He opened his arms and took a bold step toward her.

"Stop!" she shouted, shooting out an outstretched hand.

But he kept coming.

"C'mon, honey. Be a doll for once in your fuckin' life," he said. A sneer tore across his face, and he shoved aside her outstretched arm, puckering his lips and leaning in.

Deltare tried pushing him away with both arms, but Dooley's brute strength overpowered her.

"You know you want it," he said. "I'll give you something that goddamned alien never will." He pushed her against the car, pressed his body against hers, and fondled her breasts over her sweater.

Deltare turned her head from side to side to avoid making contact with Dooley's lips. His breath reeked of alcohol and tobacco. She struggled with all her might to take his hands off her, but he was too strong.

"Come on, shweetheart," he said.

Instinctually, Deltare kicked her knee forcibly into Dooley's groin, watching his eyes widen as he groaned. His grip on her breasts loosened, but he didn't back off.

She kneed him again, and a third time. With each kick, Dooley deflated. He released his grip and staggered back, nearly losing his balance. He bent over, hands on his knees, and shot Deltare a menacing look.

"You bitch!" he said.

Deltare's heart pounded, and bile crept up her throat. She lunged for the open car door, tumbling inside before she slammed it shut and locked the door. She fumbled for her keys with her shaking hands, her eyes flailing wildly back to Dooley. But it was hard to see in the dim evening light, and through the tears that now flooded her eyes. After several anguished attempts, she shoved the key into the ignition, finally managing to start the car. She raced out of the complex, sobbing all the way back to Las Vegas.

The following morning, Deltare marched into Morgan's office without knocking. She walked right up to the edge of his desk, her stomach twisted in knots and her face fuming.

"Dooley assaulted me last night!" she choked out, trying to control the shake in her voice. With some difficulty, she detailed the events of the previous night to her boss, all the while he maintained his usual expressionless face.

When Deltare had finished, Morgan didn't take long to respond.

"Well, it's over now, and you look like you're all right. Let bygones be bygones," he said with a wave of his hand.

Deltare's jaw dropped. She stood there for a moment, as if paralyzed.

"He gets moody sometimes, but nothing happened. I'll talk to him," Morgan added.

Deltare felt a wave of confusion, astonished by her superior's ambivalence. She lingered, frozen, for a few moments before finding her voice again. She leaned over Morgan's desk. "What are you going to *do* about it?" she growled through gritted teeth.

"I just told you—I'll talk to him." Morgan said, frowning, his voice a little louder.

Deltare slammed her fists on his desk. "That's not enough, and you know it!"

Morgan's squinted his eyes and stood up. He pointed a finger in Deltare's face. "Get over it, Deltare. So Dooley was drinking. Big deal, it was cold outside. So he was a little charged up. That happens. You can't blame a guy for trying, especially if he's drunk. And anyway, no harm, no foul. Get over it!"

"You're defending him? After what he did?" Deltare's initial shock at Morgan's dismissive response had quickly turned into something else. Her face reddened as she shook her fisted hands in the air, letting out a raging growl.

"I want him in jail!" she yelled.

Morgan maintained his irritated frown but didn't say another word. He stared Deltare down.

By the glaring look on Morgan's face, she knew she would get no satisfaction. She began to shake uncontrollably. She gritted her teeth and screamed in frustration as she threw a pile of papers and a dirty ashtray off Morgan's desk then spun on her heels and stormed out of the room, slamming the office door behind her.

Deltare was too upset to make her morning session with Zeemat, but she thought she had composed herself enough by the afternoon.

One look at her face, though, and Zeemat knew something was wrong.

"Your eyes are swollen and red," he said. "What happened, Linda?"

"I'm all right," Deltare replied in an overly cheery voice. She suddenly looked away from Zeemat, but not before he noticed her biting her lower lip and the hurt expression on her face.

"What?" he asked, his voice soft with concern. "What is it?" He approached her and placed a gentle hand on her shoulder. And that was all Deltare could take. She broke down into sobs and tears.

Zeemat turned her around so they were facing each other, and he guided her into his arms, holding her close and letting her sob, unsure of what to say. They stood holding each other for a long time, until the tears had dried and her sobbing had stopped. Still, Zeemat waited patiently for her to speak.

"Thank you," Deltare whispered.

"For what?" Zeemat asked.

"For holding me and not asking questions until I was ready."

"I wanted to, but I didn't know what to say," Zeemat confided.

"Of course you didn't," Deltare said. "But you did that just right." She smiled warmly, stroking Zeemat's cheek as she thanked him again.

"So now are you ready?" he inquired. "To tell me?"

Her smile faded instantly, and Zeemat's eyes shimmered an anxious orange. He knew something was not right, and she felt that it would be wrong not to tell him. She took a deep breath and summarized for Zeemat what had happened.

As she spoke, she noticed Zeemat's breathing quicken. His face hardened, and his eyes pulsated a purplish red. She noticed his fists clenching. Deltare had never seen him like that before.

"I can see this upsets you. Maybe I shouldn't have said anything," she said. Zeemat's silence and darkening mood worried her.

"What are you thinking?" she asked.

"Dooley," he whispered.

Deltare pulled Zeemat into another hug. "Please don't worry about it. Anyway, there's nothing you can do."

"I want to make it better," he said.

THIRTY-ONE

ENERGY

WHILE THE HUSTLE and bustle of life on the planet spun around him, Zeemat spent much of his seemingly endless time alone with little to do. Most of the time, he either took his spot at the window or paced back and forth inside his limited space, which he had been doing when he tripped on the stereo's electric cord, pulling the plug out of the socket on the wall. He reached down to plug it back in as he had seen Deltare do the day the stereo had arrived. As he plugged it in, a tiny spark flew from the socket to the metal parts of the plug in his hand. He pulled the plug back out and tried it again and again. Sometimes he saw a spark, sometimes not. His heart raced as he thought of the possibilities.

He looked around the room for something metallic and remembered the extra antenna wires that had come with his TV. He had saved the precious thin little copper wires. Now he stripped the rubber coating off them and held one in each hand. He sat down next to the electric socket on the wall and inserted them.

He heard a buzzing sound then felt a faint rush of weak electricity course from his fingers to his hands before a vague tingle spread partway up his arms. His grip felt a little stronger. He felt a sudden urge to use his charged fist.

At the same time, he noticed the single lamp in his room dim. He removed the wires from the socket and the lamp brightened back to normal. Every time he inserted the wires into the socket, the same thing happened: he felt a weak charge as the lamp dimmed.

He shook his head, disappointed.

Not enough, he thought.

THIRTY-TWO

THE MOON DEAL

JOHN FITZGERALD KENNEDY became the thirty-fifth president of the United States on January 20, 1961, and as part of his indoctrination, he received countless briefings and updates. He learned of his duties, agendas, and protocols, some of which were known to the public, and some of which were not. The issue of the alien in Area 51 was one of those utterly confidential reports, and it fascinated JFK to no end—he needed to see the alien for himself.

On April 27, 1961, President Kennedy arrived at Area 51 in a new Boeing 707, designated Air Force One because of its special occupant. All other air traffic was cleared off the base, apart from the fighter jets that protected the country's most valuable asset. After landing, a squad of Secret Service personnel greeted him on the tarmac. They had prepared for his arrival over the previous few days.

The jet's door opened after the gangway stairs were secured to the plane. Within seconds, an energetic Jack Kennedy bounded from the plane and galloped down the stairs, shielding the bright sun from his eyes as he flashed his handsome, toothy grin. He wasn't campaigning. He was simply excited to be in Area 51 to see if what they said was true.

A military Jeep waited for him at the bottom of the gangway stairs. He boarded the Jeep while the Secret Service boarded their own vehicles, and they caravanned to the building marked "51." Some of the Secret Service escorted the president inside, while the rest assumed their perimeter posts outside.

Inside the building that housed Zeemat's cell, two people the president already knew greeted him: Air Force General Thomas D. White of his Joint Chiefs of Staff and CIA Director Allen Dulles, who was trying to make good after the intelligence disaster at Cuba's Bay of Pigs a few days prior.

Dulles was glad to see President Kennedy's high spirits. It had been Dulles's idea to coordinate the president's visit to Area 51 just after the Bay of Pigs fiasco—Dulles hoped to redeem himself and keep his job. What better way than a face-to-face meeting with an alien, he thought, especially one who was providing priceless intelligence that kept their country in the forefront of aerospace technology.

"Good morning, Mr. President," Dulles said, reaching out his hand.

Kennedy promptly shook Dulles's hand in the practiced manner of a born politician, but the smile momentarily faded from his face. "Good morning, Mr. Dulles," he answered flatly before turning away from him to face General White.

"Welcome, Mr. President," the heavyset general boomed. "It's an historic occasion. You're the first president to lay eyes on our prisoner. I think you'll be amazed."

"I'm sure I will be!" Kennedy's Boston accent filtered through in his excitement. "So come on, gentlemen, where is he?"

"Gentlemen *and lady*," the general corrected, stepping aside to reveal the petite person standing behind him. "You'll see the alien in just a moment, Mr. President, but first allow me to introduce Dr. Linda Deltare, the CIA operative who serves as the alien's translator."

President Kennedy's magnetic gaze bore into Deltare, a broad smile beaming across his face. He took a step toward her, extending his hand. "Ah, good morning, Dr. Deltare. I was briefed about you and your work. You are the only one who can communicate with the alien, is that right?"

"Good morning, Mr. President. This is a high honor." Deltare bowed, her heart racing and her face flushed with excitement.

"So what has he told you?" the president asked. "I want to know!"

"His language is very difficult to understand," Deltare said in truth, though she failed to mention that Zeemat understood and could speak fluent English. "It's a series of beeps, musical notes, clicks, chatter, and other similar sounds. Part of it reminds me of birds and dolphins, species with which I've become familiar during my doctoral studies. I've been working with him for six years, and I'm only now piecing his language together. It's complex. We communicate a lot by gestures. He seems to understand me a lot better than I understand him."

"But somehow you extracted technical information from him?" Kennedy spoke fast, glancing hurriedly over Deltare's shoulder to the steel door at the end of the hallway.

"Yes, he's been very cooperative in providing technical information. You may not know the details, but he's helped with space suit design, high-altitude flying, computer design, computer language programming, germanium and silicon integrated circuit design, and so much more."

A look of astonishment bloomed across Kennedy's face. "And you know about all these things yourself?"

"I'm learning as I go, Mr. President. I'm honored to be the intermediary between Zeemat and the technical experts who've been sent to us."

"Did I hear you right? His name is Matt?"

"Zeemat, Mr. President," Deltare corrected. "But maybe we should call him 'Mat' for short. I like it!"

"May I see him now?" The president rocked on his feet like a racehorse at the gate.

"Of course, Mr. President. You're the boss!" Deltare swept her arm in the direction of the hall and led the president to Zeemat's cell. A guard unlocked the door and the small group walked in.

Zeemat sat quietly on the side of his bed and turned his head to examine the curious group of humans who had entered his room. Immediately, he recognized President Kennedy from the pictures Deltare had shown him just before this sudden meeting. As Deltare had instructed, Zeemat stood up, faced the president, and offered his right hand.

"Is it safe to shake it?" the president asked, his eyes trained on Zeemat.

"Yes, Mr. President," Deltare replied.

He looked past her to the others, looking for their confirmation. They all nodded, though Kennedy noticed his attentive Secret Service guards resting their hands on their holstered guns.

Kennedy faced Zeemat and took a cautious step toward him. Zeemat mirrored this with a slow step of his own. Behind them, the guards tensed, firming their grips on their firearms. As Kennedy took another small step, so did Zeemat. Slowly, they closed the gap until at last, their hands met. Kennedy bravely grasped Zeemat's hand and pumped it vigorously. They both smiled and nodded their heads.

"It's nice to meet you," the president said, slowly and loudly, as if that would help Zeemat understand him better.

Zeemat bowed, emitting a long series of alien noises to impress the president with his complex language, as Deltare had instructed him.

Deltare leaned in, "concentrating" on Zeemat's words, ready to provide a "translation" for the president. "He said, 'Thank you very much, Mr. President. It is an honor and pleasure to meet you as well.'"

"He said all that? Are you embellishing?"

"Yes, sir, he said all that," Deltare lied. "And no, I'm not embellishing."

Zeemat let out another series of alien phrases.

"He wants you to know he comes in peace," Deltare translated. "He wants you to know that he is here to help so that one day our people and his people can connect."

Stunned, Kennedy looked from Zeemat to Deltare, then to Morgan and to the general, as if to confirm what he'd heard.

"Tell him I say thank you," he said softly.

"You can tell him yourself, Mr. President. He'll understand you," Deltare said.

Kennedy, still shaking Zeemat's hand as if in a trance, cleared his throat and looked into his large, alien eyes. "Thank you," he said. "Thank you for all you are doing. Thank you for your cooperation."

Zeemat bowed politely.

"Is there anything we can do to help?" the president asked, his tone sincere and reverent. He looked around Zeemat's room. "Are you comfortable here?"

Zeemat also looked around the room before emitting several more impressive alien noises.

"He said he is grateful for his comfortable arrangements, and for his radio and TV. He is glad to be learning about our world, our country, and its people. He said he considers this planet to be his new home and hopes he will be accepted."

"How wonderful!" Kennedy exclaimed.

Zeemat smiled. He was enjoying Deltare's "translations." He made a few more noises to see what Deltare might make of them.

"He also requests that he be allowed some degree of freedom to explore his new world. He would like that very much."

Zeemat met Deltare's gaze, transmitting his gratitude with a warm smile. No one knew him like she did.

"Well, I don't know about that," Kennedy said, now more somber. "Countless security concerns, I'm sure."

Deltare looked to Zeemat, wanting him to make more noises that she could translate for the president. Zeemat nodded and made another long series of alien sounds.

Deltare pressed on with her plan. "He wants to make you a deal, Mr. President. He said he will continue to provide useful information and will help us reach an amazing goal if you promise to grant his freedom at that time."

"Well, that is very interesting. And what goal might that be?"

Deltare and Zeemat had planned their strategy just before the surprise visit from the president. The goal had to be impressive and doable. Deltare herself had been shocked when Zeemat suggested it. She had her doubts it could be done so quickly, but she had to trust that Zeemat knew what he was talking about.

Zeemat made more noises, stood up military straight, pointed out the window to the sky, and smiled.

"He can get us to the moon," Deltare translated.

Kennedy rocked back on his heels and stood there speechless, both his mouth and eyes wide-open like saucers.

Zeemat emitted more sounds, as if on cue.

"In less than ten years, by his estimation," Deltare said.

"Before the end of this decade?" The president's eyes darted around the room as he struggled to contend with the gravity of their proposal.

Zeemat smiled.

Suddenly, President Kennedy looked to General White and Director Dulles and broke out into a rapid chatter, his voice jolting with unbridled energy. "Is this true? Can he do that? Can *we* do that? The moon?"

General White had his strong doubts, but he took a leap of faith. "From what we've gotten from him so far, I believe it's possibly achievable . . . maybe."

Kennedy could hardly contain himself. He paced around the room, mumbling to himself, and whipped his right hand in the air as if furiously writing on an imaginary chalkboard. This was an incredible opportunity to out-distance the Russians in the race to space. This could be the highlight of his entire presidency. This could cement a lasting legacy.

"Deal!" the president proclaimed.

Deltare piped in. "Landing on the moon in exchange for his freedom?"

"Yes, if he can get us to the moon, we can talk about the terms of his freedom," the president confirmed.

Deltare turned to Zeemat. "Zeemat, do you understand what President Kennedy just said? You'll be free if you can get us to the moon before the end of the decade."

Zeemat emitted a loud, excited chatter. He reached over and shook both of President Kennedy's hands in the familiar Torkiyan cross-armed, double-handed style.

After that, Kennedy and Zeemat spent an hour in a more informal conversation, with Deltare serving as translator. Zeemat thoroughly enjoyed listening to Deltare repeat some things he had told her in the past couple of years, while making other things up on the fly. She made him look fantastic.

A Secret Service guard interrupted the conversation, reminding the president of the time.

"I'm sorry, Mat," the president said. "But I have to go now. It has been a unique and incredible pleasure to meet you!"

Zeemat smiled and nodded as the president said his final goodbyes, then made his exit.

When they had left, he and Deltare held each other's hands in a tight grip, jumping up and down with pursed lips, trying to hold back screams of joy, before finally falling into a warm embrace. She held on tight, knowing they had struck a great deal with President Kennedy, while also enjoying Zeemat's close embrace.

A few minutes later, they watched through the barred window, hand in hand, as Air Force One rumbled down the runway. They listened to the sound of the engines fading away in the distance.

Zeemat eyed the faraway mountains and imagined walking along the ridges. Deltare dared to imagine a life of freedom outside of Area 51 and Las Vegas—hopefully a life with Zeemat. She nuzzled up closer to him. He put his arm around her, and she rubbed his back. The future seemed bright.

THIRTY-THREE

JFK'S CHALLENGE

ON MAY 25, 1961, President John F. Kennedy addressed the US Congress regarding what he felt were "urgent national needs." His speech gradually built up to the real reason for his address.

"First, I believe that this nation should commit itself to achieving the goal, before this decade is out, of landing a man on the moon and returning him safely to the earth. No single space project in this period will be more impressive to mankind, or more important for the long-range exploration of space . . ."

THIRTY-FOUR

PRESIDENTIAL PROTECTION

FOLLOWING JFK'S CHALLENGE, Zeemat and Deltare's work became increasingly focused on landing a man on the moon. It pleased Deltare to know that the technologies to be developed would be of universal interest, not just for military advantage.

However, CIA Special Agent Morgan, his new boss, Director John McCone (who took over as agency director after Allen Dulles was fired), and the president's military chiefs of staff were opposed to the new arrangement. They sought different information from Zeemat, particularly on how to improve guidance systems for their missiles and how to create more powerful bombs. They specifically wanted more information about Torkiyan use of antimatter for fuels and weapons, considering what they already knew about the smooth groove of annihilation at Zeemat's mountain crash site. They were also eager to learn anything pertaining to the newly discovered laser technology, imagining all Torkiyans carried ray guns.

Deltare asked Zeemat about some of this but protected him from the CIA and military members as best she could. When

Zeemat provided dozens of drawn pictures and mathematical formulas detailing answers to many of the military concerns, Deltare chose to keep them to herself. She amassed many of Zeemat's drawings and schematics in her Louis Vuitton briefcase. *Perhaps they'll be useful at some other time*, she thought. She sold some of them directly to her business contacts during their surreptitious meetings at the Dunes. But for now, according to presidential directive, Zeemat's primary purpose was to help achieve a successful moon landing, and she kept Zeemat's schedule focused in that direction.

Activity increased significantly in Area 51. Company executives, scientists, and engineers came to consult with Zeemat and Deltare. She handled the meetings and "translations" with them at the base, and several of these powerful people became part of her growing list of secret clients she saw at the Dunes. One of them funded a generous gambling line for her at the casino that she really considered to be a savings account in case she needed quick access to a sum of money someday.

They kept up the ploy of Deltare being the only one who could communicate with Zeemat. They both knew this would keep them together, and Zeemat surmised this would also keep Deltare safe. He remained suspicious of the military men.

As far as the government was concerned, Zeemat's presence was considered top secret and a matter of national security. Visitors were threatened with the penalty for high treason—death or life imprisonment—if anyone were to divulge his presence. At the same time, they knew Zeemat's value came from interaction with science and technology experts, so the risk of his exposure was restricted to these highly vetted individuals.

Rocket scientists from Boeing were among the first of such visitors to Area 51, and after a flurry of meetings, Boeing opened a manufacturing facility in New Orleans to build the first stage of the future Saturn V rocket. IBM engineers also continued to visit, and they led the way in computerizing the burgeoning Mercury space program.

Lyman Spitzer, a famous astrophysicist, came to meet with Zeemat and Deltare. Professor Spitzer was frustrated by the poor data obtained from balloon telescopes and described them to Zeemat in detail. He'd been talking about the potential of an orbiting space telescope for twenty years. Zeemat was thrilled to meet this brilliant man of vision. Together, they developed the ideas that turned into the first space telescope, the Orbiting Astronomical Observatory, and later into the Hubble Space Telescope. Zeemat hoped to use it someday to get a glimpse of his home planet.

In a rapid flurry of activity in 1962, Zeemat and Deltare met with representatives from AT&T, Bell Telephone, and NASA. Their work resulted in the launch of the first communications satellite, Telstar. Zeemat hoped to use it to communicate directly with Torkiya someday.

Zeemat didn't appear to need any more motivation for his continued cooperation. Knowing he would someday be free was motivation enough. Nevertheless, Deltare presented Zeemat with an upgrade to his appliances. She replaced his stereo/TV console with a top-of-the-line Sony stereo receiver, matching speakers, and a separate TV set in color.

Zeemat was thrilled. "This is so much better than the console!" he yelled at Deltare over the deafeningly loud high-fidelity music. The sound quality from this stereo was far superior to his previous set. Zeemat bobbed his head, grabbing Deltare by the hand, and they started to dance.

"It's got a great beat, and you can really dance to it!" he said.

Deltare laughed. "Where'd you hear that?" she asked. "And where'd you learn those moves?"

"American Bandstand," he replied.

After that, Zeemat used every spare moment to listen to his favorite radio show: Wolfman Jack and the Top 40. Or he spun a record from his growing collection. But most of all, in his spare time, he watched TV. The color set was beyond what he had ever dreamed, giving him a clearer picture of the world around him. His favorite shows were Westerns, especially *Gunsmoke* and *Rawhide*; and cartoons like *The Jetsons*, which reminded him of home and made him laugh; and Wile E. Coyote and the Road Runner, which reminded him of what he could see out his window. He filled his prolonged captivity with moments of joy.

During this time, Morgan was pressured by his boss, CIA Director McCone, for more military information from Zeemat. In turn, he increased the pressure on Deltare.

"Just got off the phone with General LeMay, and it wasn't pretty," Morgan told Deltare, his angry tone clear. "Everyone's tired of waiting. You better give us something the military can use, or it's going to get ugly pretty damn quick!"

"We've talked about this a million times, Mr. Morgan—we're focusing on the moon project, by President Kennedy's order." But Deltare was starting to worry, as she heard the threat in Morgan's tone. They wanted both the moon *and* the weapons—maybe the weapons more.

"We'll keep him only as long as he provides useful information . . . and the same goes for you." Morgan pointed at her with his hand cocked in the shape of a gun.

The gesture wasn't lost on Deltare. The threat was real.

THIRTY-FIVE

SHATTERED DREAMS

AT 12:30 P.M. on November 22, 1963, a loud siren shrieked an alarm, putting Area 51 on high alert. News of President John F. Kennedy's assassination while riding in a presidential motorcade in Dallas spread through the base like fire from a lit match to gasoline. Armed soldiers interrupted Zeemat's session with Deltare and isolated him in his quarters while the base deployed emergency procedures.

Zeemat turned on his TV set and watched Kennedy's final moments replayed over and over on every channel. His eyes hazed over in a veil of violet as he experienced yet another loss and tragedy. Kennedy's death brought back painful memories—the shock of finding his dead crewmates, the nauseating odor of their decaying bodies, the horrible feeling of utter loneliness. He felt paralyzed by the heavy weight of his sadness, and his stomach turned at the horror of it all.

He had known President Kennedy, and he liked him. He was among the few humans who had ever treated Zeemat with respect. And Kennedy had promised him his freedom. He was providing valuable information to the humans with that freedom in mind. Now he wondered if that freedom would ever happen—whether the next president would honor the arrangement. An anxious orange dotted his violet eyes as his breathing hastened, and his heart began to pound.

Eventually, he found the energy to turn off the TV, but not his thoughts. He spent the long night soaked in sadness and battling his anxious fears.

The following day, Morgan allowed Deltare to see Zeemat again. She sulked into his room, distraught with drooping shoulders. "Oh, Zeemat . . . President Kennedy . . ." She couldn't finish her sentence before breaking down in tears.

Zeemat held her tight, and she melted into his arms.

When she composed herself, she said, "President Kennedy's dead, and everything's changed."

"You'll have a new president," Zeemat said, hoping for the best.

"I mean the moon deal. Your freedom. Everything's changed!"

Zeemat sat up straight and cocked his head as if to better hear her. He kept his gaze steady on Deltare as she gathered her thoughts to continue.

"They've already ordered me to stop all work regarding the moon project. A new schedule of consultations is being drawn up by Morgan and the military men."

"They don't care about the moon, or about my freedom," Zeemat said, his previous fears materializing once again.

"They care about weapons, war, and beating the Russians."

"And I hate all of that." Images of his warlike Torkiyans flashed through his mind before he saw yet another image of Kennedy's assassination replayed on the TV. He lost his balance, overcome by a wave of dizziness, his mind reeling against reality. No matter how hard he tried, or how far the distance, fighting and violence somehow returned, and a better world eluded him.

"I'm sorry, Mat. Your freedom is off the table," Deltare said, her voice shaking with another series of sobs and tears.

Zeemat didn't quite understand the phrase "off the table," but he knew exactly what Deltare meant. The promise of freedom had died right along with President Kennedy.

THIRTY-SIX

EVERYTHING CHANGES

TWO WEEKS LATER, in mid-December of 1963, Zeemat stood at the window of his cell with his hands on the bars, gazing at the desert mountains in the distance—the mountains he had crashed into—the last time he'd been free. Now he might never walk along the ridge of those mountains like he had hoped. He may never see what was on the other side.

He pulled at the bars with all his might, knowing they would not give, like the thousands of times he had pulled at them before. A feeling of desperate loneliness returned, the same desperation he'd felt during his year alone on Janusia. His gut seemed to twist into knots, and he found it hard to breathe. He felt so lonely, he thought he might explode. He pounded the cinder block walls and screamed.

Since Kennedy had died, he'd had trouble sleeping. Day and night, he paced the floor, back and forth in the small space, trying to soothe the anxious feeling in his heart. He shook the rigid bars every time he reached that part of the room, each time shattering any hope he might have had. He felt like a complete failure—a disappointment to his parents, who'd preferred to ship him away rather than accept him as he was. He'd been resented by nearly everyone at the Academy, hesitantly accepted by his crewmates only because of his parents, and he'd been unable to figure out how to fix Janusia. And now he was imprisoned so he could provide information to evil human beings. It was all too much, and he fell into a dark depression, unable to see a way out.

He felt angry, too. President Kennedy had made promises, and those promises were broken by his captors. So, he made a decision—if he wasn't going to be free, he wasn't going to cooperate with their demands, even if they beat him to death. Yet his only friend, Deltare, kept pressuring him for the information he didn't want to give, and the only person he wanted to please was her. He felt torn.

"You have to give them something," Deltare implored. She had stalled Morgan with several of Zeemat's old drawings that she took from her briefcase, but she didn't want to give away any more of that valuable information.

"What's the use?" Zeemat whispered, gazing off into space.

Deltare bit her lip, worried about Zeemat's withering will to survive and not sure how else to motivate him. It hurt her to see cuts and bruises on his face, knowing the beatings had resumed. She pulled him away from the window, and they sat on the side of his bed, their bodies touching.

"Because if you don't give *me* something I can give to *them*, they might end up killing you." There was desperation in her voice.

Zeemat noticed Deltare staring at the cuts and bruises. "I survived Dooley before, and I'll do it again," he said.

"Mat, please. Do it for *me*," Deltare said. "I don't want to see you hurt like this."

Zeemat softened, seeing the painful expression on Deltare's face. He caressed her cheek and let his hand linger there, gazing into her worried eyes. After a few moments, he took a deep breath and relented.

"If they can make us a new deal, maybe I can help them with what they want."

Deltare straightened up, and a hint of a smile returned to her face.

"Oh, that's good. I'll inform them right away," she said. She gathered her things and scurried out of his room.

Zeemat assumed Deltare's leaders would be glad to hear it, and that Deltare would feel better, though he had yet to decide how cooperative he wanted to be.

That night, Dooley and his men still came to Zeemat's room. Zeemat hoped his treatment might change, but they yanked him out of his chair and began to shackle his arms and legs as usual. Zeemat was losing patience. He pulled his arms and legs away, resisting the shackling, but they managed to restrain him. He tried to hold his ground, but they forced him out of his room with the cattle prod and the butt of their rifles.

Once they secured Zeemat to the interrogation chair, he found that nothing had changed. Dooley donned his thick leather gloves and started talking.

"I know you understand me, asshole!" he fumed.

Zeemat had never spoken a single word to Dooley, but Dooley didn't seem to care. He always asked a question, waited for a moment of Zeemat's silence, then punched him hard.

"Tell me about your ship. Write something down. Draw something—anything." Dooley waited a moment, but Zeemat remained quiet.

Bam! Dooley landed another heavy blow to the left side of Zeemat's face.

"Describe the weapons on board your ship. Draw it. I know you can draw!" he said, pointing at the paper and pencil that were always on hand. Dooley drew an example, surprising Zeemat with how remarkably close it was to Janusia's shape. Though it confused Zeemat, he didn't show it. He kept silent. But this time he looked Dooley straight in the eyes and shook his head no. Dooley smacked him again.

Zeemat noticed that the nature of the questions had changed. Dooley now only asked about weapons and his ship. He found the series of questions confusing because Deltare had told him that his ship completely disintegrated when he crashed, yet Dooley seemed to have specifics he could not have known without examining a Torkiyan ship. He clenched his teeth and squeezed his lips shut, now even more committed to not cooperating. His head snapped right and left, absorbing Dooley's repeated blows. He saw no evidence of a new deal, and now he had questions of his own—for Deltare.

THIRTY-SEVEN

AWARENESS

THE FOLLOWING DAY, Zeemat woke early and looked out his window in anticipation as the last of the fading stars surrendered to the dawn. He couldn't wait for Deltare's morning visit, yet he dreaded it at the same time. He wondered exactly what she knew, what she told her superiors, and if they had agreed on a new deal, why the beatings continued. Why had they taken everything out of his room, and—most importantly—what had she kept from him?

Deltare walked in at her usual time and immediately noticed that the room was emptier than the day before.

"Those jerks! They took your TV and stereo!" she said. "This is the new deal?"

Zeemat studied her, a scowl darkening his face.

"I told Morgan you would cooperate if they came up with a new deal," Deltare said. "I reminded him of President Kennedy's agreement with you . . . with us. But it didn't seem to matter. Morgan said, 'I know what he can do. I know you can communicate with him. So, no deal.' Instead, I see they have a new plan, to take away things you've already earned."

"They know about my ship," Zeemat said with darkened eyes, carefully studying her reaction. "How do they know about my ship? You told me it was completely destroyed."

Deltare paused for a moment, noticing a change in Zeemat's usual tone. There was a certain rumble in it, like a lion's growl, and it frightened her. He was upset. She answered her friend, noticing the higher pitch in her own voice and her trembling hands.

"L-Let me clear up a few things," she stammered. "There's something you should know that maybe I should've told you before . . ."

"*You*, Linda? *You* lied to me?" His body tensed, his English infused with Torkiyan *buzzes* and *clicks* that Deltare recognized as tones of anger, pain, and disappointment. His eyes flamed red before slowly diffusing to a deep purple. She sensed the same disappointment she had noticed in the first picture of him she'd ever seen, before they met—the picture of him she was shown in Roswell.

"I'm sorry, Mat. I didn't exactly lie, but I wasn't completely truthful either. I meant to tell you someday, but I thought the information would only be hurtful to you, and I was under strict orders not to tell you."

"Tell me now, Linda! Where's my ship?" His eyes flashed crimson again as he slammed a fist on the top of his desk.

"I didn't lie about that. Your ship *was* destroyed. That's what I was told, and I believe them."

"Then I don't understand. How do they know details about my ship?"

"Not yours. There was another ship. It arrived seven years before yours did, in Roswell, New Mexico. I saw it myself when they were preparing me to meet you. The ship was incomplete, half of it had been destroyed, but they reconstructed it from the debris they found at the crash site, and they mirrored the other half."

Zeemat started pacing wildly around the room. "*Now?* Now you're telling me this? I thought you were my friend!"

Deltare looked down to the ground, ashamed for keeping such important information from him. She looked up sheepishly to meet Zeemat's glare.

"There's more," she said.

Zeemat cocked his head in the way he did when he was trying to understand things.

"What more?" he asked. He drew close to Deltare, the *clicks* and *buzzes* louder, and she cowered back. But he didn't touch her. "Tell me. Now!"

Deltare could see that Zeemat was trying to keep his eyes from flaming red. He was trying hard to control himself.

"There was a body," she replied. "A dead body. I saw him, too. He was like you . . . Torkiyan."

Zeemat halted mid-step. After a moment, he walked to the window and put his hands on the bars. But this time, he yanked on the bars with all his might while letting out a loud, piercing wail. Deltare put her hands to her ears, and when the scream stopped, she gripped her hands hard to try to keep them from shaking. Her eyes clouded over with a torrent of tears.

At last, Zeemat regained some of his composure and turned around to face Deltare.

"A body?" he asked. "*One* body?"

"Yes," Deltare replied.

"And what about the others?" Zeemat inquired.

"Others?" she gasped, raising a hand to her mouth.

"Tell me everything," Zeemat demanded.

THIRTY-EIGHT

DISCLOSURE

DELTARE STARTED FROM the beginning. Zeemat learned all about her linguistics studies and her doctoral thesis on interspecies communication.

"That's why they recruited me in the first place," she said. "They thought I'd be able to learn your language."

She described her "recruitment," when she was abducted by two men in dark suits while window-shopping on Michigan Avenue in Chicago, then interrogated and analyzed over the course of an entire week before being whisked away in the dead of night to a waiting helicopter at Meigs Field.

"That's when I first met Morgan. He later told me he was my 'handler.' I remember that the helicopter ride was cold and noisy—no way I could sleep—and a few hours later, before the sun came up, we were in the White House with President Eisenhower and two of his top military men. The president offered me an opportunity, but it was more like a direct order I couldn't refuse, and that was that. Before I knew it, I had a job with the CIA, and I was on a plane, headed to Roswell,

New Mexico, to learn more about my assignment—about *you*, really."

Zeemat sat in rapt attention while Deltare described what she'd seen in Roswell, just before she was first brought to Area 51.

". . . and in the center of the room there was a large, cylindrical glass tank filled with a clear fluid, and a body was floating in it. As I approached, I saw his back in close detail. The left side of his body and head were deformed, crushed. The right side was intact. I noticed a slender build, thin arms and legs, long fingers, like yours. To me, the body looked graceful even from the back, even in death. Then I walked around the tank to get a close look at the front.

"When I first saw his face, I remember feeling kind of dizzy, like this couldn't be real. My whole body was shaking, and I gasped. His right eye seemed to be looking right at me. But then his head didn't track me as I continued moving around the tank. I noticed the autopsy sutures on his chest and abdomen. Then my scientific training began to take over. When I stood directly in front of him, I saw that his head was bigger on his body than a human's head would be. The head was rounder at the top, and somewhat pointier at the chin, with a fine jawline. Maybe because the head was bigger, the eye seemed to be lower set. And that eye! A black, almond-shaped structure without an iris or pupil.

"I have to admit, it was frightening. Because of the injuries—the left side of his face being crushed—I couldn't get the full impression, but I thought the eye seemed bigger on the face than a human's eye would be. And that was the moment! That's when I was suddenly struck by the fact that I was noticing differences—the head and eyes a little bigger, the chin a little pointier—but a different idea sprung into my mind. I was amazed that this alien person was not so different, but so much *the same* as a human! He had a head, an upright body, arms and legs, fingers and toes. He had eyes, a nose, and a mouth. I tried to picture him when he was alive, how he must have moved and seen and talked and thought. I wondered about his personality.

"At that point, I remember Morgan interrupting my thoughts. He said something like, 'These creatures have been invading us for thousands of years, gathering information. And now we know their plans are escalating after an attempted invasion here in Roswell in 1947, and now another in Nevada in 1954. We believe that a major invasion could be imminent. It's essential that we find out who and what they are, so we can eliminate the threat.'"

Zeemat stayed silent as he fought waves of conflicting emotions. His eyes toned down to a dull rust color. He was angry at Morgan and his people for assuming the worst in him and for treating him so badly, even though he had to admit that they were right to be concerned about the other Torkiyans. And he was also angry at Deltare for having lied to him, though she was now being very generous with a detailed description of what she had seen. At the same time, he knew she was as close to a friend as he had on this planet, and that if anyone could help him, it would be her. But more than anything, at that moment, he felt heartbroken to learn of yet another fellow Torkiyan's death, and likely the deaths of his fellow crewmates as well.

He assumed the Torkiyan in the tank in Roswell had been a member of Mission 50 to Cerulea, and the thought carried more hope than he could bear. During some of the time on his own ship, they had traveled at 5D speed. They certainly could have almost caught up with Mission 50 and arrived only seven Earth years apart. He knew one crew member of Mission 50 was dead—but what had happened to the other three? He interrupted his own thoughts to prevent himself from missing any vital information as Deltare continued to speak.

"They found remnants of their ship, and Morgan showed me an album of pictures detailing the ship's reconstruction. There were pictures of a few men at work, in white full-body overalls. They placed all the ship's debris in what they believed was the proper order and position, then shaped sheet metal to replace the missing parts of the ship. Other pictures in the album showed the men looking over prints and using tools to rebuild the ship. The final page showed the spaceship on heavy metal supports. They could access a door on top.

"Then Morgan took me to see the ship itself. I approached it slowly, not knowing what to expect. I could easily tell apart the sections that had been added by our people, and the smoother part of the original ship. We climbed a ladder and entered a small cabin from the door on top. The interior of the original half of the ship had two seats, and the desk space and wall were riddled with instrumentation. Morgan said that scientists couldn't figure anything out. They didn't know how the ship was powered. They imagined the instruments were designed for navigation and reconnaissance because they couldn't find weaponry, so they assumed this was a specialized model of ship designed for gathering information. They also assumed that other ships would likely carry weapons."

Zeemat couldn't contain himself any longer.

"They made a lot of assumptions." A short, harsh buzzing sound escaped his lips, but he clamped them shut until Deltare finished everything she had to say.

She nodded. "That's exactly what I told them! Morgan said the assumptions were based on observations and opinions from the best military minds."

She looked up at Zeemat, to gauge whether he was ready for what she was about to say. He seemed tense and guarded.

She felt her own face and shoulders harden, but she proceeded, knowing this would be hard for him to hear.

"Then he showed me another album. This one was all about the person in the tank. The first pictures showed his crushed body in a bloody suit. They said he was dead when they found him. The next pictures showed a team of technicians cutting the suit off his body. Then there were a few pages of X-rays, showing broken bones on one half of his body, including his skull. There were pictures of him lying on a steel autopsy table. Then I saw pages of pictures showing him being cut wide-open with long incisions, dissected carefully, and all of his organs placed into glass specimen jars."

She watched as Zeemat's expression morphed from one of anger to horror, then to sorrow, his eyes wavering from rusty orange to a deep blue.

"They concluded that life on your planet has evolved in a way that parallels our own. They said the laws of physics and nature show themselves in patterns that repeat at every level, so we shouldn't be surprised to find such similarities between our species. Your DNA structure is not identical to ours, but it's similar. Your blood is similar. You have paired organs. Your brain looks different, but it's connected to a nervous system that is in some ways much like ours."

"They cut him open and tore him apart?" Zeemat asked, his voice shaking. He left his seat and began to pace the floor. He pounded a wall with fisted hands, the lunged at the window and pulled at the bars again, trying to shake them free, though they remained rock-solid as always.

Deltare allowed Zeemat some time to process the information she had just unloaded on him, and when he stopped pulling at the bars, she dared to continue.

"There's more, Zeemat. This is where I learned about you."

Zeemat kept his hands on the bars but stopped staring out the window and looked back to Deltare, waiting on her next words.

"After Morgan showed me those picture albums, he reached into a desk drawer and retrieved a circular tape cassette. He attached it to a reel-to-reel tape recorder, fed the tape through the mechanism to the empty receiving cassette on the other side, clicked it on, and the cassettes began to spin.

"At first, I heard crackles and hisses as the first part of the tape fed through, followed by a few seconds of silence. And then there was *you*! I heard a series of fascinating sounds. I heard buzzing, beeps, honks, bubbly sounds, gurgles, sweet notes, echoing flute-like sounds, and rough chattering noises. They'd taped you as they were helping you through the injuries of the crash, after you came off the breathing machine, and while you were still on pain medication. The tape went on and on for minutes, and I sat there in silence, mesmerized by your voice. When it was over, I asked Morgan, 'What the heck was all that?' And he said, 'You're the one who's going to tell us!' Mat, I was forced into this job, but I knew at that moment I wanted to do this. I wanted to see you, to understand you."

Zeemat's expression softened just a little, his eyes transitioning to a bright pink, and Deltare's tension eased a bit, too.

"Finally, Morgan had me look at one last picture album. I held my breath, knowing this one would feature you. I saw pictures of your crash site, some of which I had already seen during the briefing with President Eisenhower at the White House. Morgan pointed out your burned ship and your burned body. Then he showed me pictures I hadn't seen before. One page of the album had pictures showing you being placed on a stretcher and being cut out of your space suit. I saw pictures of blood everywhere. Other pages showed details of your bodily burns and injuries. I saw X-rays that showed your broken bones. I saw pictures of you in surgery, with a tube in your throat that hooked up to a ventilator, and another tube up your nose. You had IV lines in both arms and chest tubes on both sides."

Zeemat drew away from the window and took a seat by Deltare's side. He rubbed his chest, where one of those tubes had been. He had only spotty memories of what Deltare was describing, but he grimaced as he remembered the pain.

"I saw pictures of you in a hospital bed, with bandages all over your body. You had one arm in a cast and one leg in a contraption of pulleys and weights. Then there were pictures of you without the bandages, showing fresh surgical scars on your chest and abdomen, other pictures showing the scars nearly gone, and others showing complete healing—no scars at all!"

"I do remember some of that," Zeemat said. "I remember the men and women working over me. I remember the man who was taking pictures."

"Dr. DeBakey—he's a great man," Deltare said. "I'm almost finished. The final pages of the album showed you when you had nearly recovered. I saw a picture of your back, in a hospital gown, hunched over, walking away from the camera, holding yourself up by an IV pole. And toward the end of the album, there were a few pictures of the team of doctors and nurses, posing around your bed, all warm and fuzzy with satisfied smiles.

"Then . . . I saw the last picture in the album, a close-up of your face. I remember feeling almost paralyzed—shocked by your large, intelligent eyes looking right into the camera. You had a black, swollen left eye, and small cuts on both sides of your face and ears. I was struck by the look on your face. I couldn't put my finger on what I was seeing . . . Anger? Sadness? Fear? Pain? No. I looked long and hard at that picture, at your eyes and the complex expression on your face. At last, I came to the conclusion that you had a look of disappointment. And I remember feeling ashamed, just as I feel now."

They sat in silence, separated by worlds of emotion between them.

In time, Zeemat broke the silence. "You shouldn't have kept that from me, Linda." His eyes wavered between red and pink.

Deltare's vision blurred. "I was under orders," she whimpered. "I was going to tell you someday, I promise. I just wish I'd said something sooner." Her voice trembled, and she wiped a tear with the back of her hand.

"I want to be angry at you." Zeemat glared at her, letting her stew in her guilt and shame for a few beats. "But you're truly my only friend," he added.

He let out a sigh, his eyes slowly fading to purple. It looked to Deltare as if his entire body had deflated in disappointment. He stood up to look out the window again and allowed his thoughts to linger somewhere far away. Gradually, he stood up straighter. His fists tightened on the bars, and he gritted his teeth.

"Now I have to get out of here. I have to go to this Roswell place."

"There's nothing for you there. I've told you everything," Deltare said, a little alarmed by the sudden change in his tone.

Zeemat turned around to face her, his eyes now a level green. A strange energy seemed to have empowered him. "The Torkiyan person in the tank, he was probably part of our Mission 50. He was one of four on board the ship. Where are the others?"

"*Four* people?" Deltare gasped. It took a moment for that to sink in. Meanwhile, Zeemat smiled at the fact that she'd called them 'people.'

"They're gone, Mat," she said. "They evaporated along with half the ship. There was no sign of anything or anyone else. And anyway, how would you get out of here? This place is secure."

Zeemat tilted his head and looked at Deltare with a cocky half smile on his face that she had never seen before.

"It's not very secure," he said. "I'm getting out."

"Don't do anything foolish." Deltare's concern for what might lie behind his cocky smile grew.

Zeemat paced the floor, making imaginary diagrams in the air with his hands.

"Let's think this through," she said. "If you try escape and fail, they'll hurt you even more. And if you succeed, I'm afraid of what they'll do to *me*."

Zeemat shot Deltare a puzzled look and marched right up to her, bringing his face up close to hers. "What do you mean?" he asked.

"I was told my fate is tied to yours. I've been warned that all information about you must be contained. I know too much. I'm afraid . . ."

"Then whatever we do, we do together," Zeemat said decidedly. He drew back to the window, gripped the bars, and glared at the sight of the military base, at his captivity, then toward the faraway mountains. But a definite determination had now taken over his face.

After a few minutes, he said, "I need more information about your world. What is the *Encyclopedia Britannica*? I read something about it in a magazine article."

"I'll try to get you one," Deltare said. "Just promise not to do anything without me."

"If you promise never to lie to me again," he said.

She nodded, and they fell into a cautious embrace.

THIRTY-NINE

CHARGE

ZEEMAT STOOD AGAIN at the window, gripping the bars and gritting his teeth, determined now to escape. It was late December 1963, and for the first time in a long time, maybe in his entire life, he looked forward to having his full Torkiyan strength. He knew he could easily overtake his human captors if he was fully charged. After Deltare had divulged her secrets, Zeemat decided to do the same. He told her about Torkiyans' ability to strengthen with an electric charge.

"Let's go over our plans again," he said.

"*Shhh.*" Deltare brought a finger to her lips. She looked back to the door of Zeemat's cell to check that the window was closed. "Keep your voice down. I'm all set. I have a bag packed in the trunk of my car. I have money on hand to last us for months and lots more in my accounts overseas. I have our escape routes planned. But I still don't know how you're getting out."

"Don't worry, Linda. You'll see. Just be ready when the sun goes down."

Deltare took a deep breath. "I'm ready."

The sun sat low on the horizon when Deltare left the building as she usually did each evening. She made her way out to her car, which she had parked as close to Zeemat's window as possible.

As soon as Deltare had left the room, Zeemat took the electric cord from his lamp and stripped all the rubber from its entire length. He bent the cord until he could break it into four separate wires.

It seemed to take forever for the sun to set, but the time finally came. He looked out his window to try to glimpse Deltare's car, even though he knew it was on the other side of the building out of his view. He had to trust she would be there.

He unplugged everything from the electric sockets, then carefully placed a wire into each one of the socket's openings. All he had to do now was hold them all together in his hands, absorb as much energy as he needed, and then rip the bars from the windows. The bars were set into the cinder block walls, but it would be easy to break them loose with his full strength.

He wet his hands with water from a drinking glass, rubbed them together, and grabbed hold of the wires. The rush of energy was immediate. The tingling spread up his arms to his shoulders. He felt it in his spine and then spread to other parts of his body. He wanted to scream—not in pain but in joy. He felt a wildness, a need to move, to run, to fight. He could feel that he'd nearly reached a sufficient charge.

Suddenly, the electricity cut off, and even the lights on the outside of the building snapped off, throwing Zeemat into unexpected darkness.

He fumbled with the wires and the sockets, trying to regain the electric current, but after a few moments of confusion, he realized there was no more electricity to draw. He bolted to the window and placed his hands on the two center bars. With all his might, he shook them violently. He groaned and strained. He put both feet against the wall and pulled on the bars with all his might. The bars loosened. A little space appeared where the bars joined the cement. Small cracks formed here and there, and a tiny cloud of cement dust billowed around the window, but the bars held.

He groaned louder, his muscles aching from the tremendous strain. He continued to push and pull with all his might, and the bars were now a little looser. But without a full charge, his energy quickly faded. He felt his muscles weakening.

With a desperate groan and the last of his strength, he gave the bars a final gut-wrenching tug, then collapsed to the floor, spent and in complete despair.

The bars remained in place.

FORTY

GREAT BALLS OF FIRE

WEEKS LATER, IN early February 1964, Zeemat remained focused and undaunted despite the great disappointment of his failed escape. He'd learned from Deltare and the *Encyclopedia Britannica* about human electrical systems, including circuit breakers, and he'd begun working out a plan to draw more energy from the sockets. "It'll work next time," he reassured Deltare.

She forced a sad smile. "Sure it will," she said. But she was becoming more worried by the day. Zeemat still refused to provide his captors the information they demanded, and the nighttime beatings were getting more violent. She could see the evidence of it each morning on Zeemat's face, and she was amazed that he remained so motivated, but she doubted Zeemat could truly gain the strength he needed from the weak electricity in the two electric sockets in his room.

Deltare was about to say something to him when Zeemat shot up straight in his chair. He rubbed his arms as if something was crawling on them. He bolted to his feet and ran to the window.

"There!" he said. "Look, Linda, in the distance!" He pointed toward the southwest.

Deltare joined him and peered out the window, squinting her eyes, looking in the direction Zeemat was pointing, but she saw nothing.

"What?" she asked. "What am I looking at?"

"The storm," he said. "The storm!"

Now Deltare noticed a tiny speck of dark clouds far on the horizon. "We don't get many storms around here," she mumbled.

"It's coming this way. It will be here today. I can feel it. It's our chance!"

"You said you can use a storm. But how? What if it doesn't strike here?"

"It will. I just know it, and we must be ready. The antenna!"

Zeemat and Deltare set a hasty plan in motion. She searched several of the hangars on the base for a pair of wire clippers and a roll of heavy gauge wire. When she found them, she made sure no one was looking, then brought them over to the TV antenna situated close to Zeemat's cell. It was a tall antenna, set in concrete and reaching far above the roofline. She identified the ground wire and clipped it. She used the wire she'd brought from the hangar to attach it to the end of the clipped ground wire coming from the antenna. She spooled the rest of the wire around the side of the building to the open window of Zeemat's cell. She looked both ways one final time and threw the spool with the remaining wire through the bars into Zeemat's cell. Then she strolled back to her car, hiding her trembling hands as a serviceman in a Jeep drove by, offering her a friendly salute.

Zeemat unwound the remaining wire and looped it around the two steel bars in the center of the window, the same ones he had partially dislodged during the failed escape attempt. As he was finishing with the wires, Deltare walked back into the room.

"Do you still have the packed bags in the car?" he asked.

"No. They're in my room at the Dunes."

Zeemat looked out the window. "The storm will be here in a few hours. We can't risk you going to Las Vegas and making it back here in time."

"How can you be so sure about the storm?"

"I don't know how. I just know," he said, feeling the escalating tingling of his skin.

They watched through the window as the storm inched its way toward them. It seemed to be picking up speed. The skies clouded over and darkened. A gusty wind kicked up. They could now see the distant thunder and lightning coming ever closer, and the first few raindrops began to fall.

"It will be over us in less than an hour," Zeemat said. You should pack up anything you need from your office and wait for me in the car.

Deltare nodded and gave Zeemat a tight hug before heading out of the room. Before leaving, she looked around the room, wondering if this would be the last time she'd ever see it and hoping that would be a good thing and not a disaster.

Now the rain began to pour. Deep, rolling thunder shook the ground, and several lightning bolts struck nearby. Zeemat put his hands on the center bars and waited, eyes fixed on the storm outside.

The worst of the storm passed overhead and faded. Still, Zeemat kept a strong grip on the bars and clenched his teeth. His face was wet from the rain that blew in through the open window. He shook his head to clear the raindrops from his eyes, and that's when it hit—a bright bolt of lightning zapped through the air, striking the towering TV antenna. A blaze of electricity shot through it, down the ground wire no longer connected to the ground, and spread directly to Zeemat's waiting hands.

Zeemat roared as the shock of powerful energy engulfed him and charged his system, his deep, guttural shouts blending effortlessly with the crack of thunder. His eyes glowed. His body vibrated, and he held on to the bars until the shock had completely dissipated.

With the wild power of a full charge, Zeemat shook the bars with all his might. The cement that held the bars cracked. Chunks of it landed at his feet and along the outside of the window. The bars loosened. He pulled them free and looked at them in his hands, shook them in the air, and after another roaring growl, he threw them aside. In a flash, he pulled himself through the window, plopping down to the ground outside. He was free!

Zeemat looked up and let the rain beat down on his face, opening his mouth and drinking it in. He spread his arms wide and let out the gurgling sounds of Torkiyan laughter.

"What the bloody hell?" a gruff voice said.

Zeemat jerked his head around to find the source. A guard stood there. He could not see the man's face under the large hood of his heavy raincoat, but the sound of that voice was unmistakable. "Dooley!" Zeemat cried out in English, so Dooley could hear it.

"Well, I'll be damned! I knew you were holding back, you little shit! But too little, too late. Don't know how the hell you got out, but it don't matter. You're dead. I'll say you were trying to escape, and you attacked me." Dooley fumbled with his raincoat, trying to get to the handgun on his belt.

Zeemat spoke again, distracting Dooley. "I'm not *trying* to escape, I *have* escaped. But you're right about me attacking you."

Zeemat bolted toward him, closing the gap between them in two large strides just as Dooley managed to unholster his gun. Zeemat felt a wave of energy sweep over his body. Just as Dooley raised his shooting hand, Zeemat slammed him on the chest with a closed fist. On contact, a paralyzing jolt of electricity shot out of Zeemat's fist and stunned Dooley as the shock spread through his body. The force of Zeemat's impact broke several of Dooley's ribs and knocked the wind out of him.

Dooley tumbled backward, and Zeemat kept coming. He pounded Dooley's shooting arm, shattering the bones, and Dooley dropped the gun. Zeemat threw a powerful punch to the side of Dooley's head, sending it crashing against the side of the building. There he collapsed in an unconscious heap, blood pouring from his ears and nose. The carnage happened in a matter of seconds.

Zeemat stood over Dooley's body, his eyes glowing red and his fists still clenched in Torkiyan rage.

A final bolt of lightning lit up the scene as Deltare rounded the corner and stopped dead in her tracks.

"Mat! Stop! What have you done?"

FORTY-ONE

BREAKOUT

THE PANIC IN Deltare's voice interrupted Zeemat's rage just long enough for him to gain control over himself. He glanced down at the motionless Dooley and knew he was no longer a threat. His shoulders relaxed and his fists unclenched.

"Come on, Mat, follow me!" Deltare said in a shriek of a whisper. "Hurry!"

Zeemat and Deltare raced back to her car. She opened the trunk and Zeemat scrambled in as they had planned.

"Stay quiet and don't move!" Deltare ordered, now whispering more softly. "We have to get past the guard at the gate. Keep still until I open this trunk again. And the ride will be bumpy. Okay?"

Zeemat nodded. He reached up, grabbed hold of the trunk lid, and closed himself in. A memory of Janusia's cryo coffins shot through his mind.

Deltare shuddered at the loud *clunk* as Zeemat slammed the trunk shut. A quick scan told her no one had seen or heard any of the commotion. She glanced down at the battered Dooley and almost felt sorry for him, but there was no time to linger on that. She hurried back into the driver's seat, pulled out of the parking space, drove around to the front of the building, and tried to ease out of the parking lot, doing her best to fight the rush of adrenaline coursing through her body. She concentrated on slowing her breathing as she drove to the guarded gate and slowed the car to a smooth stop.

"Good evening, Dr. Deltare," the guard greeted her. He was friendly enough but professional. Deltare could see the impression of a rifle under his raincoat. The guard's trained eyes automatically darted around the inside and the outside of her car, but it was a cursory inspection, as he knew Deltare well and he didn't want to be out in the rain.

"I'm surprised to see you leaving right now, in the middle of a storm," the guard said. Deltare looked at him carefully, trying to read his level of curiosity about the timing of her departure.

"I'm pretty sure the storm has passed," Deltare explained. "And it's been a long day," she said, trying a fake yawn and immediately regretting it.

The guard flashed a brief frown at Deltare's lame yawn. "I can see you're tired," he said.

Deltare heard a hint of condescension in his tone. She studied his face and swallowed hard, trying to ease the large lump in the back of her throat.

The guard now seemed to be inspecting her for longer than usual, and he leaned in to give the inside of her car a closer look. Then he took a step back and looked at the car from front to back.

"The trunk seems to be riding a little low," he observed.

Deltare's heart felt like it would pound out of her chest. The steering wheel suddenly felt slippery with her sweaty palms.

"I . . . I'm lugging a bunch of books back to my place in Vegas," she stammered. "And maybe I need to check my shocks."

The guard squinted his eyes, his expressionless face giving nothing away as he stood there for a few seemingly endless moments. Deltare twitched a smile at him, but she wanted to scream.

Finally, the guard spoke.

"Drive safely, ma'am," he said with an unsmiling glare. "And check those shocks."

"Thank you. I will," Deltare replied. "Good night."

She took her foot off the brake, stepped on the gas, and drove through the open gate. The guard kept his eyes on the car until it disappeared around a curve.

Deltare's heart raced wildly. She couldn't stop looking in the rearview mirror, expecting car lights to chase her at any minute. They'd made their way out of the complex now, but they were far from safe. She picked up her speed, squealing her tires as she made the familiar turns on the long driveway leading out of the complex.

Endless minutes later, she found herself at the entrance to the Area 51 complex on Highway 375 and followed her usual route to Las Vegas. She wanted to get back to her room at the Dunes as soon as possible, to retrieve the packed bags.

In the car's trunk, Zeemat rattled around, hitting the sides of the dark trunk with every wild turn.

"*Owich*," he said, practicing his English while rubbing his head as it hit the inside of the trunk on a nasty bump in the road. But he laughed at the thrill of every curve in the road and the sudden turn of events. Though he was locked in a trunk, he was free.

A short time later, Deltare made the turn south to US Route 93 at Crystal Springs. It was a better-paved road, so she could pick up her speed even more.

As she approached Route 168 at Coyote Springs, she slowed the car to take a brief look at the low mountains of the Las Vegas Range to the west, backlit by the fading orange of the setting sun now peeking through the receding storm clouds. She tried to locate the specific spot where Zeemat had crashed but couldn't discern it in the distance and in the fading light.

She thought about Zeemat crashing around in the car's trunk, and she realized it was his first time ever in a car. Everything she knew—every single thing—would be new for him. Her face scrunched in worry.

"Well, there's nothing we can do about that now," she said out loud, flooring the gas pedal, speeding to Las Vegas.

When she turned onto the Las Vegas strip, she slowed the car to make the turn into the Dunes. She found a parking spot away from other cars, pulled in, and turned the engine off. She thought about leaving Zeemat in the trunk a little longer while she went inside to retrieve her bags, but she worried about him confined in a small, dark space, so she decided this was as good a time as any to bring him out into the world.

She scanned the parking lot to make sure no one was looking, then knocked three times on the trunk, as they had discussed, to let him out. She noticed a small bruise on top of his head as he crawled out of the trunk, but Zeemat beamed a radiant smile as he took in his first sights outside of Area 51. His eyes sparkled in a rainbow of colors, mirroring the dazzle of city lights they could see from their spot in the parking lot.

To Zeemat, the city's lights seemed like a galaxy of stars. Then, his vision drew to the crowds of people walking around on the street, while his ears tuned in to the traffic noise and the hum of the city's life. He turned his head from right to left and back again, trying to take it all in. This is what he'd wanted—to explore his new world—and he was transfixed by what he was seeing.

"Get in the car, Mat," Deltare commanded, opening the passenger door for him. Zeemat observed every detail of how she turned the door handle and swung the door open. "Sit!" She said.

When Zeemat was inside, Deltare closed his door and returned to the driver's seat. She reached over to the back seat for her raincoat, which had an attached hood.

"Here," she said. "Drape this over your shoulders."

She helped him into the jacket and to cover his head with the loose hood. Then she retrieved a pair of sunglasses from the glove compartment and placed them over his eyes.

"Now stay in the car and stay low. Try not to let anyone see you. Don't talk to anyone if they come close. Let's at least try to make it out of Las Vegas."

"Is this where you live?" Zeemat asked, still looking around.

"Yes. And I need to get our bags from my room. You need to stay here, quietly."

Zeemat was full of questions and observations, and it made her nervous. She knew they had to move quickly if they were going to escape successfully. Eventually, probably soon, they would find Zeemat missing from his cell, and Dooley would be . . . found. A massive chase would begin right away, with all the resources of the military and the CIA.

"Mat, you have to act like this is all normal." Her grave tone matched the stern look in her eyes. "I know it must be hard, but don't act so surprised. You'll stand out. We need to go unnoticed."

"I know, Linda, but . . . I never imagined. Are all human cities like this?"

The naive question broke Deltare's heart and eased the tension for a moment. She smiled warmly and held his hand.

"No. This is Las Vegas. It's a strange town, all flash and glimmer. You'll know what I mean when you compare it to other places."

She enjoyed holding his hand for just a few seconds before worry overwhelmed her again.

"I'll be right back. If anyone comes near, you duck down and don't let them see your face." Zeemat pictured a waddling duck in his mind but nodded as Deltare dashed into the building.

She made her way to her room briskly, avoiding eye contact. She felt relieved that Morgan no longer kept a guard in the hallway in front of her room. They trusted her to check in and out by phone. She placed the check-in call on the red hotline phone that connected only to the guardhouse at Area 51. That would hopefully give her a head start before anyone wondered where she might be. But she knew they could notice Zeemat's escape at any time, so there was none of it to waste. She marched straight to the closet, picked up the two prepacked bags she had ready for just this occasion, and headed back out to her car.

On her way out, she stopped at the casino's cage and laid her bags down in front of the window. The humorless person on the other side waited for Deltare to speak first.

Deltare produced her driver's license and slid it across the counter through the small opening below the bars. "I'd like to withdraw my entire line," she said.

The cage clerk examined the driver's license, then Deltare, and repeated the inspection a few more times before he was satisfied. He checked the ledger and raised his eyebrows. "I'll have to get the boss for this kind of money," the clerk said, leaving with her license.

Deltare waited for a few short minutes that felt like an eternity. Her heart pounded like a jackhammer. Her head felt dizzy and her legs shaky. She had to lean against the counter to be sure she wouldn't fall. She looked around nervously, expecting to see men in black at any minute, and tapped nervously on her wristwatch. She didn't think she could wait a moment longer, so she picked up her bags and looked toward the exit door.

She was about to bolt out of the casino when the boss appeared on the other side of the cage. He held Deltare's license in his burly hands and examined her as the clerk had.

Deltare dropped her bags again. "I'm going on a short trip, and I need my money right away," she explained. "I'll be back," she lied.

The boss recognized Deltare and knew she was a frequent visitor at the casino, and he nodded his approval to the clerk. In short order, Deltare walked out with her savings, a fortune of hundreds of thousands of dollars.

Hurrying back to the car, she waved off a doorman who offered to help her with her bags. "No, thank you," she said. "I can manage." The doorman made a face and reluctantly opened the door for her, peeved at missing the chance for a tip.

She picked up her pace to a slow jog, stepping in front of a couple who were approaching their own car, parked close to hers. She blocked their view of Zeemat, who had his face pressed to the window, still marveling at the sights he could see from his guarded position.

When the coast was clear, Deltare threw the bags into the back seat and pealed out of the Dunes parking lot for the last time.

Zeemat's eyes continued to dart everywhere as they sped through the main streets of the city, seemingly oblivious to Deltare's angst. He couldn't believe the spectacle of people and bright lights. As they turned off the city's main drag, he turned his whole body right and left, taking it all in, gurgling musical notes of delight.

A few blocks later, Deltare pulled into the Plaza Hotel and Casino and drove to the rear of the building, where Zeemat encountered a different spectacle—the Las Vegas train station. But his enthusiasm rapidly waned as they left the bright lights behind and entered a different part of the city. He pinched his nose. This new place had a burnt, chemical odor and a more ominous feel.

FORTY-TWO

DIVERGENCE

THE LIGHTS FROM the Las Vegas strip of casinos were a short walk away, but Zeemat encountered an entirely different mood at the train station. Most of the people he saw were sitting or standing in one place, not walking, and they weren't talking to one another. They looked tired.

"Before we get out of the car, let me show you what I have in your bag," Deltare said, interrupting Zeemat's observations. She reached behind her to retrieve his bag from the back seat. It was a plain military duffel bag that could be carried by its long handles or slung over the shoulders like a backpack.

"Here are two sets of clothes to get you started." She pulled out shirts, pants, a belt, socks, and shoes. "Here is an extra-large sweatshirt with a hood. And here is your coat," she said, retrieving an army coat from the bag.

Zeemat's eyes sparkled at seeing his new clothes, especially the army coat like the ones he'd seen soldiers wearing at the base. He brought it up to his face and inhaled the scent of the new garment, while Deltare continued to rifle through the bag.

"And here's the important part," she said. "The wig and sunglasses I told you about."

Zeemat examined the tangled brown hair attached to an elastic cap.

"I'm pretty sure this will fit. I made sure it was extra, extra large." She helped Zeemat don the wig, pulling and tugging it into place, and straightened the hair. She oriented the tiny rearview mirror so Zeemat could inspect his new look in an Afro wig.

While Zeemat angled his head from side to side, inspecting his reflection, Deltare withdrew several sets of sunglasses from the bag. "Let's see which one covers your eyes best," she said. They tried them all and settled on two—a wraparound style that covered his eyes completely, and an aviator style that worked as long as the mess of hair from his Afro wig covered the sides of his head.

Deltare didn't look away as Zeemat wrestled on his new clothes in the front seat of the car. She knew their time together was quickly coming to an end, and she fought back surges of fear and sadness. She would deal with their separation later, she thought. Their safety was now of paramount and immediate importance.

When Zeemat finished changing, they got out of the car and looked around the station. Zeemat observed every detail—the lines of massive trains and the tangle of railroad tracks, the commotion of sounds as vehicles came and went, the pungent aroma of oil and petroleum, people talking in small groups, some others sitting or sleeping on benches. He witnessed a crowd of people exiting a train that had just arrived. He noticed they were much happier and more energetic than the ones waiting for their train to leave.

His observations were interrupted by a thunderous blast. He shuddered at the shocking volume of the train's whistle, covering his ears. The wheels of an enormous train engine began to turn, and the connectors between each railroad car squealed and clanked as the engine stretched the slack between them. In a few moments, the entire train crawled forward and picked up speed. He saw an occasional weary face in a window as the train departed.

"Where are they going?" he asked Deltare.

"That one's going to Los Angeles," she replied, pointing to a sign along the boarding dock detailing the destination and departure time. "Other trains will take people in other directions."

"Where's mine?" he asked.

Deltare led Zeemat to a large board showing arrivals, departures, tracks, and times. "Every train station, bus station, and airport will have a board like this," she said.

Zeemat examined the board, his eyes darting around it. "There it is," he said. "Flagstaff."

They made their way to the ticketing line. Zeemat noted how Deltare and the other humans stood in line, how they acted, and how she made the transaction for two tickets.

"That wasn't so hard, right?" Deltare asked, biting her lip, looking for any sign of anxiety or confusion in Zeemat's face, and finding none. But she felt only slightly relieved. She still could not fathom how he would survive in the real world. But the plan was in motion. There was not much more she could do. She handed Zeemat the tickets.

Zeemat held a ticket in each hand, puzzled. "Why two tickets if we're splitting up?" he asked.

"I bought the seat next to yours, too," she explained. "So no one will sit next to you."

"I wish you were coming with me," he said, holding one of the tickets out for Deltare to reach if she decided to change her mind.

She put her hands on her hips. "We talked about this. They'll be looking for a couple traveling together. We have a better chance to get away if we split up now. And I have to get rid of the car."

Zeemat tried to smile but couldn't manage it. He'd had too many sad goodbyes in his life.

"Your train leaves tomorrow morning at eight a.m. It'll start boarding a half hour earlier. You wait here and don't wander. Don't miss the train!" Deltare paused after sensing Zeemat's sadness. "I wish I could stay to see you off, but I have to leave *now*. They'll be looking for my car. If they find it and me, at least you might still get away," she said.

"You're leading them away from me," Zeemat realized. "So I can escape."

"That's what friends do," Deltare said. "We run away from the CIA and the military to help our friends escape."

Zeemat looked puzzled, and Deltare managed a nervous laugh.

"That was a joke," she said. "No one does that. No one tricks the CIA or the government. No one tries to escape from them."

"That's a joke?" Zeemat inquired.

Deltare sighed.

"Oh, because in one way it's crazy and another way it's true?"

Deltare broke out in a true, honest smile. "Yes, exactly!" she said. But the laughter was short-lived. She looked down at her wristwatch again.

"This is when we go our separate ways . . ." she said. "For now."

She had pictured this moment as more dramatic, but the anxiety of knowing they would soon be found missing, and then pursued, overwhelmed everything else. They had to keep moving.

"They'll announce when your train is ready for boarding. You're on your own now, Mat. Be ready." She squeezed both of his arms and rubbed them, finding it difficult to let him go.

Zeemat stared at the tickets, then at Deltare before wrapping his arms around her in a long, hard hug. She closed her eyes and felt faint. Her heart raced even faster, and she hugged Zeemat back, bear-hug tight, wanting desperately to stay with him. She buried her face in his chest.

"Go now, Linda. They'll be coming soon," he said.

Deltare pulled herself away, and she reached into her purse for one final thing. She made sure no one was looking before retrieving a thick envelope.

"This has a lot of money," she said. "Don't let anyone see it. They'll want to take it from you. Use it to buy what you need until we meet again."

"Next year, like we planned," Zeemat said.

"Independence Rock on the Fourth of July. And you know how to contact me in an emergency," she said, more as a fact than a question.

"Through the Pastor at Mission Dolores in San Francisco," Zeemat said. "I memorized the address and phone number. Now I just have to learn how to use a phone!" He emitted a short burst of gurgling Torkiyan laughter.

Deltare sighed again. She looked into Zeemat's eyes and fumbled with her wristwatch, anxious about the time. She searched her mind for anything else she had to tell Zeemat before she left.

"Never stay too long in one place, especially at the beginning while you're figuring things out. Blend in. Don't stand out. Keep moving . . ."

"Stop," Zeemat said, placing a gentle finger on Deltare's lips. "I know."

She kissed his finger. *He has no idea*, she thought. But there was no time for the millions of things she wished she could say or do. There was so much for him to learn and so much she could show him. But he was right—it was time.

"I can't bear to let you go," she said.

Zeemat's breathing suddenly hastened, and his eyes glowed pink. He brought his hands to the side of her face, like he had seen human lovers do on TV shows, and he kissed her . . . and she kissed him back, melting into his arms. She held his face, too. She explored his mouth with her tongue. They pressed their bodies together, and they both felt the growing bulge in his pelvis. She held him even tighter.

When the kiss was over, Deltare pulled away, in tears—tears of love, of fear, of anxiety.

Zeemat replied. "I love you, Linda. May the stars lead us back to each other as we've planned."

"I love you, too," she managed to say, fighting another surge of tears welling up in her eyes. She started to walk away, then glanced back to see a blurry image of Zeemat standing at the boarding dock watching her leave, waving.

She waved back, wondering if they would ever see each other again, when she was suddenly startled by the piercing wail of a police siren heading in their direction.

FORTY-THREE

DELTARE'S DASH

DELTARE DASHED BACK to the car, shocked by the approaching siren, anticipating she would have to dodge police vehicles to make a run for it. At least she would lead them away from the train station and Zeemat.

She made it back to her car when the sound of the siren reached its loudest. She caught a brief glimpse of the police car as it zoomed by on the main street, and the siren's sound faded as it sped farther away. Her heart raced, and she tried to catch her breath.

Deltare took that as a sign. She didn't wait for the adrenaline rush to leave her body. She got into her car and hurried out of the parking lot, now focusing on her own escape.

She didn't need a map. She had planned and memorized her escape route carefully. She would take the 15 south to California and turn west on the 58 at Barstow, then north on the 5 for a short distance to west on the 46. That would lead to the 101 north to Salinas, and then the 68 to her destination—Monterey, a temporary hiding place until she got things settled. Her final goal was San Francisco.

Once she got out of Las Vegas and onto the road, she had to fight the impulse to go faster than the speed limit. Her eyes kept darting to the rearview mirror, still expecting to see someone chasing her at any minute. She reached for her purse and blindly rummaged through the contents, trying to keep her eyes on the road. When she felt the smooth plastic wrapper of the pack of Virginia Slims, her nerves began to calm. She felt even better when she lit one up and took a long, deep drag. As she drove for the next few hours, she chain-smoked the entire pack while contemplating her current crossroads in life. *You've come a long way, baby*, she thought to herself as she crumpled the empty cigarette pack in her hand, and a hint of a smile fought its way through her anxiety.

The Louis Vuitton briefcase lay next to her purse on the passenger seat. Deltare gently patted it, knowing the treasure it contained. She had Zeemat's ideas and drawings, and a list of tech executives who would lust for them, powerful people she knew personally. They would be glad to pay dearly for the information. These people and their companies had begun congregating in the San Francisco area, and she planned to be a part of it, even if only in a secretive way. She imagined doling out Zeemat's information little by little, gradually increasing the price. And she hoped to share the wealth with Zeemat someday, though she knew the chances of that were like her cigarettes—slim.

She continued to take inventory of what she had. Her bank account in the Caymans was funded by several executives who had pressured her for access to Zeemat's thoughts. She gloated a half smile, picturing herself as what she truly was—a broker of very strange commodities. She was already a multimillionaire. *And I'm just getting started*, she thought.

As she zigzagged her way toward the Pacific coast, she planned a personal makeover. She'd have to cut and dye her hair. She'd be able to wear more stylish clothes but would keep a professional appearance for her visits to the man's world of high technology. She'd have to change her name. *Maybe I don't need a name at all,* she thought, fidgeting to open a new pack of cigarettes. *I'm only a number on my Cayman account.*

A few hours later, fatigue settled in, and she made a few brief rest stops during her ten-hour drive. She stopped halfway at an all-night diner, enjoying an early breakfast of greasy eggs, bacon, and coffee, before pressing on.

The first light of dawn was peeking over the mountains when she arrived in Salinas. It was just a short way from there to Monterey, but she was exhausted. She checked her rear-view mirror one last time to be sure she wasn't being followed, and turned into a roadside strip motel. "Additional Parking in Back," the sign said, and a neon sign above it flashed "Vacancy."

She pulled into a parking spot in the back of the building, away from the sight of anyone driving by on the road, turned off the engine, and sat there for a minute. If they hadn't been found missing back at the base by now, they soon would be. Someone would bring Zeemat his breakfast and find an empty cell. Deltare imagined the panic and commotion that would ensue. She felt a different sort of panic, like what a rabbit might feel when chased by a wolf. Her tired heart managed to race again, and she thought of Zeemat, praying he would get on the train as they had planned. She might never know.

Deltare checked in, paying in cash and signing with a made-up name. When she found her room, she couldn't keep her eyes open a moment longer. She made sure the door was locked, dropped her bags and briefcase on the floor, and fell onto the bed fully clothed, exhausted. As she was falling asleep, she thought about the next part of the plan—having her Chevy Impala crushed at a junkyard, then buying a new car before making a trip to Santa Barbara, or even to LA, to buy some beautiful clothes and expensive suits. She fell asleep with those pleasant thoughts but soon tossed and turned with paranoid dreams of being chased and apprehended—not the refreshing sleep she thought she would get. By midafternoon she gave up trying, wrestled herself out of bed, splashed cold water on her face, and went outside to explore her surroundings.

To her surprise, a feeling of impossible freedom engulfed her as soon as she stepped out the door. A cool breeze off the low mountains to the east carried the delicious aroma of the local wine country. And she could go anywhere the breeze would take her—there was no one to tell her what to do. She decided to take a short walk, eat a quick meal, and linger in the valley for the day before finishing this part of her journey. She'd catch the setting sun that evening on the coast near Monterey.

She arrived in Carmel with the sun riding low in the western sky, with plenty of light yet remaining to witness the powerful beauty of the California coast. The rhythm of the ocean sounds—of the waves crashing hard against the rocks—was at once peaceful and anxiety provoking. The serenity of this wide-open space, the vast ocean, the salty breeze, and the sight of an occasional seagull in flight clashed with the sounds of the relentless waves pounding hard on the rocky shore. *War and peace*, she thought. She saw a mourning dove land softly on a gnarled cypress tree, and she thought of Zeemat.

"Mat," she said out loud, with a pang of pain gripping at her heart, and she wrung her hands in desperate worry. She didn't fight her tears. She hugged herself tight, her hair tousling in the cool, gusty breeze. She thought of him as the golden sun set, and the last of its brightness disappeared below the horizon. She ached for him, and she couldn't imagine how he could possibly survive.

FORTY-FOUR

IT HITS THE FAN

ON THE MORNING after their escape, a guard in Area 51 arrived at Zeemat's cell to deliver his breakfast, to be passed through the small door window per the usual routine. Promptly at 0730, the guard knocked on Zeemat's door. He waited a moment, but there was no answer, and he twisted his face into an impatient grimace. He knocked again, louder. Then a third time, even louder than before, and accompanied by a gruff, "Breakfast! Want it or not?"

Still without an answer from Zeemat, the guard cautiously unlocked and opened the cell door with a plan to leave Zeemat's breakfast on the desk. *Maybe he's sleeping more soundly than usual*, the guard thought. As he placed the tray on the desk, he looked over to see that Zeemat was not in his bed asleep. The bed was neatly made, and the sheets close to the window were dripping wet. His eyes flickered to the window, and suddenly he stopped short. His eyes widened, and his mouth dropped open, his entire body paralyzed in disbelief. Upon further inspection, he saw that the center bars were missing, chunks of broken cement and cinder block rested on the floor, and Zeemat was nowhere to be seen.

The guard drew his weapon and bolted out of the room. In his desperate confusion, he peered into Deltare's office to see if Zeemat was there, and when he didn't see him, he ran down the hall, looking into each room along the way, then out into the lobby, and eventually all the way outside, quickly inspecting the nearby grounds and terrain. There was no sign of the alien, but he did discover a body outside of Zeemat's window.

The guard rushed to the body and found him still alive but badly injured and barely breathing. He rushed back inside to call the medics, his trembling hands fumbling with the rotary dial and misdialing a few times.

Now in a rising panic, the cell guard called the main gate. The guard who had been on duty at the gate the night before was no longer there. His replacement was sipping on his morning coffee, and he took a few more sips before answering the phone. He picked it up on the sixth ring. "Hello, main gate," he said in a slow southern drawl.

"What's wrong with you, asshole? Why aren't you picking up the goddamn phone?" The cell guard could hardly choke out his words, as his mind whirled with thoughts about what he should do next.

"Excuse me?" the gate guard responded, more than a little irritated. "Who's calling?"

"I'm the guard at the cell block. I went to give our prisoner his breakfast, and he's gone!" In his panic, Zeemat's guard had forgotten the protocols for dealing with an escape. Suddenly, he was unsure who knew about the alien and who did not.

The gate guard knew that a prisoner was on the premises, and the scuttlebutt for years had been that the prisoner was an alien from space, but he was never formally briefed. That information was strictly on a "need to know" basis.

"What prisoner?" the gate guard asked, his own panic rising in his chest. "You mean . . . *the* prisoner?"

"Yes! *That* prisoner! Have you seen anyone leaving the compound this morning? Anyone at all?" Zeemat's guard was now yelling into the phone.

The gate guard dropped his coffee and rushed to inspect the gate log. There had been no comings or goings since he had assumed the post. "No, sir. The last person out was Dr. Deltare. It says here 'right after the storm.'"

Zeemat's guard and the gate guard agreed they should each call their supervising officers, and so began the waves of hectic, confused commotion at Area 51. With more people becoming aware of the secretive happenings at the cell block, the situation quickly escalated into a containment nightmare.

The immediate supervisors deployed Jeeps in all directions and launched search helicopters to comb the local area. At the same time, they contacted their own superiors. Word got to the Joint Chiefs of Staff and the president himself in short order.

When Special Agent Morgan returned to the base, he was detained and handcuffed on the spot. Despite his loud protests and claims of innocence, he was escorted into Zeemat's old cell until things could be sorted out. An armed guard was stationed outside the damaged window. The military was now in charge.

As the door was closed on Zeemat's old cell, Morgan yelled out, "Where the hell's Deltare?" The guards took note of the question but didn't respond, unwittingly giving her more of a head start.

When CIA Director John A. McCone learned of the problem, he exploded into a thunderous rage that sent shock waves through the agency. This was now priority number one.

"The subject must be recovered!" he yelled. "This will cost lives!" McCone called Marine Corps Commandant Wallace M.

Greene to alert him to the fact that many, many people would need to be kept quiet.

After his call, Nellis AFB became a central hub for intense military and intelligence activity. President Lyndon B. Johnson took immediate action, ordering the army to cover all roads and exits radiating from Area 51. Roadblocks and checkpoints were established over the ensuing hours. He ordered the Air Force to search the surrounding area. More helicopters and planes were in the air at once.

Late in the day, attention was finally directed toward an irate Special Agent Morgan, still held in Zeemat's cell. Director McCone flew in from Washington to conduct the interrogation of his agent himself. He marched right up close to Morgan and pointed a threatening finger in his face. "You're in a world of shit, Morgan! What the hell happened here?"

Morgan didn't even bother answering the question. He repeated his own question from hours earlier: "Where the hell is Deltare?"

McCone scanned his agent's angry face and concluded that his question was sincere, that he was not a part of the escape.

"She checked out of the compound yesterday evening," McCone replied. "Then she called in from the hotline phone in her room two hours later. That's the last anyone's heard from her. She didn't check in to the compound today. We checked her room at the Dunes. It's empty. Her car's gone. What do you know of all that?"

"Goddamn her!" Morgan yelled, marching around the room, punching at the air. "She always had a soft spot for that alien bastard."

"How'd they break the bars?" McCone asked, pointing at the window.

"No idea."

"The bars were wired up from the TV antenna. What do you make of that?"

"I don't know anything about it," Morgan said.

"Well, I need you on this—now! The military has already begun their own investigations. I want you out there to find them first. Capture him if you can but shoot him if you can't. I don't really care at this point. He's given us all he can or all he wants to."

"I'll talk to Dooley. He knows the alien as well as anyone. I want him with me on this."

"You haven't heard? He was almost killed during the escape. A guard found him outside this morning, unconscious, just on the other side of this wall."

Morgan leaned back, eyes wide. "How bad?" he asked. "Can we still use him?"

"He's already coming around—got some broken bones and a small crack in his skull, but he'll make it."

"He's got a hard head," Morgan said with a smirk. "He'll recover quickly if I know Dooley, and he'll be extra motivated."

"He's already awake, cussing, yelling, and pulling at his restraints. He wants at the alien."

"Good," Morgan said. "We'll set him loose as soon as possible. He'll kill Zeemat if he finds him, you know."

"I'm counting on it," McCone said.

FORTY-FIVE

LEAVING LAS VEGAS

AGAINST DELTARE'S INSTRUCTION, Zeemat left the train station to meander down the Las Vegas strip. It seemed activity bustled in the sparkling city all night long, and he wondered if these humans ever slept. He wore his wig and hooded sweatshirt, and he kept his sunglasses on to avoid eye contact, but he was oblivious of the curious looks he got from passersby.

When he returned to the station, he saw a few people sleeping on benches but decided he should stay awake to be sure he didn't miss his train. At 7:30 a.m., they called for boarding. He had to ask several people who were waiting for their own trains about how to find the right car and his seats, but the boarding seemed to go smoothly for him. *So far, so good*, he thought.

He laid his duffel bag on the floor in front of him, placing his feet on top. He hoped to sleep as soon as the train got going.

Two Mexican migrant workers took the seats across the aisle from him. They nodded a silent hello as they took their seats, and Zeemat did the same. They looked in his direction several times and whispered to themselves.

Zeemat had no time to register any concern about the men because at the same moment, the roar and vibration of a military helicopter flying low grabbed his attention. A short while later, the sounds of several vehicles with sirens speeding down the street pierced the air, one right after the other. He cleared a spot on his foggy window to peek outside and saw a military Jeep careen into the train station parking lot, just as a loudspeaker announced, "All aboard!"

Two soldiers jumped out of the Jeep and scanned the parking lot, then the people and the buildings, briefly laying eyes on his train. Just then, the loud blast of the train's whistle surprised Zeemat, and he jumped in his seat. His train groaned and jerked into motion, slowly leaving the soldiers behind.

The train picked up speed as it left Las Vegas, heading east to Flagstaff. As they chugged along, Zeemat counted several helicopters and planes in the air and numerous military and police vehicles on the streets and roads they passed. He left it all behind as the train crossed the outer limits of the city and wondered if all that military and police activity was normal, or if it maybe had something to do with his escape. He thought of Deltare and hoped she was safe.

As he continued to look out the window, he watched as the frenetic activity in Las Vegas gradually gave way to the peace and quiet of the desert country. At first, Zeemat couldn't help but examine every detail—the occasional Joshua tree and sparse sagebrush on an otherwise dry, barren land. There was something soothing about it all, but the sameness of the Mohave Desert and the rocking movement of the train gradually lulled him into much-needed sleep. His eyes dimmed, and he faded away.

Several hours later, in the midafternoon, the train whistle startled him awake. They were approaching Flagstaff. He looked around the train car to see if anything had changed. He registered little activity in front or behind him. The migrant workers across from him were sleeping in their seats across the aisle. Zeemat noticed one of them had dropped his wallet on the floor, so he picked it up.

He looked out the window, and his eyes opened wide at the drastic change in scenery. He saw snow on the ground. He craned his neck to follow the tree trunks up to the tops of tall ponderosa pines. He looked right and left to take in the expanse of the mountainous terrain. He saw an icy stream running parallel to the railroad track. The land was completely different from anything he had seen so far on Earth. He plastered his face to the window to see the occasional buildings becoming increasingly frequent, until they organized into lines forming the streets of the town. A sign zipped by, and he caught it just in time: "Welcome to Flagstaff."

A few minutes later, the train slowed as they approached, stopping at a station much larger than the one in Las Vegas. People on the train gathered their things and stood in the aisle of the railcar, preparing to deboard, and he did the same. He loomed over the Mexican men who were still sleeping and gently shook one of the men's shoulder until he awoke.

"*Que pasó?*" the man said, startled.

"We have arrived," Zeemat said.

The man looked out the window to orient himself.

Zeemat handed the man his wallet. "I saw this on the floor."

The man snatched the wallet from Zeemat's hand, noticing the oddly long fingers and the grayish coloration of his skin. He rifled through the wallet, confirming all the contents were still there. "*Muchas gracias,*" he said, twitching a cautious smile.

Zeemat nodded and smiled back. He picked up his bag and followed the other passengers off the train.

Briefly distracted by his steamy breath in the cold mountain air, he found himself in a bustle of people hurrying in all directions. Remembering Deltare's instructions, he headed to the board that listed arrivals and departures. Along the way, he noticed several advertising signs and stopped at one with an enormous picture of the Grand Canyon. He looked back toward the schedule board, then back to the picture of the Grand Canyon, and back and forth, until he'd made an impulsive decision to change his plans. After asking a few questions, he found his way to the tour bus company across the street and purchased a ticket. He was finally exploring his new world, and he didn't want to miss a thing.

He had some time before boarding the tour bus, and he was starving, so he drew a few bills from the envelope of money Deltare had given him, and he walked back to a small restaurant he had passed along the way.

Entering the restaurant, he was surprised to see the same Mexican men again, now with their families. The waitress showed him to a small table next to theirs. When the men noticed him, they waved him over to their table, and he accepted their invitation to join them. One of them, a young girl, spoke a broken English with a heavy accent and translated a few things for Zeemat, while the others jabbered away in an animated Spanish. They shared their tortillas and refried beans with him. The girl squinted and analyzed Zeemat, realizing he was somehow out of place. She showed him how to load a tortilla and what to order.

Toward the end of the meal, as the waitress was delivering the check, the young girl said to Zeemat, "My father theenks you're a *marciano*—a Martian."

Zeemat looked around the table at the group of curious faces regarding him, people who had welcomed him to their family meal, his first friends on planet Earth aside from Deltare. "Tell them I'm not a Martian," he laughed, unconsciously uttering a few Torkiyan *gurgles*. "Tell them I come from much farther away."

The busy waitress stood still for a moment. She shot Zeemat a sideways glance and raised an eyebrow.

FORTY-SIX

MILITARY MOVES

SHORTLY AFTER ZEEMAT was discovered missing, Army General Maxwell D. Taylor, Chairman of the Joint Chiefs of Staff, discussed the disaster at Area 51 over the phone with President Lyndon B. Johnson. Johnson decided not to deploy the National Guard this time, as Truman had done during the Roswell incident in 1947. They couldn't justify the public becoming aware of the alien. Instead, the military would deploy sufficient forces to recapture him. The CIA would assist in the effort, and the FBI would remain in the dark as always about these matters, to keep the intrusive Director J. Edgar Hoover from meddling in these affairs.

Taylor coordinated the rapid creation of an army field office in Area 51 to join the Air Force presence. Troops arrived and were dispatched to roads radiating in all directions, searching for a man and a woman driving a 1962 gold Chevy Impala. They had the license plate number, and a picture of the woman but not of the man.

They established checkpoints at all the entrance ramps to roads and highways leading out from Las Vegas, the last known whereabouts of the escapees. Over the ensuing hours, with the arrival of more troops, they widened the radius of the search to approximately three hundred miles. The military search stopped short of Phoenix, Arizona, and Los Angeles, California, crowded places where the military begrudgingly handed over the search to the CIA. The search radius extended east to Winslow, Arizona, a town just past Flagstaff.

They paid special attention to modes of public transportation in case the fugitives had ditched their vehicle. They halted all taxi, bus, train, and airplane traffic until the military knew who was traveling where.

They deployed helicopters, searching the highways for a gold sedan, possibly driving at a high speed in any direction away from Las Vegas.

President Johnson reminded General Taylor that this was a national security concern of the highest order.

"The goddamn alien and Deltare must be recovered—dead or alive," the president said in a booming Texas drawl.

Examining a map, General Taylor knew he had all exit points covered. He was confident his troops would succeed.

"Don't worry, Mr. President," he said. "We'll get 'em."

FORTY-SEVEN

MORGAN AND DOOLEY

DOOLEY'S HEAD THROBBED. It was wrapped in a bandage, covering the jagged cut on the top of his head that the medics had repaired with a mess of stitches. The crack in his skull would slowly heal. Fortunately, he hadn't suffered brain damage. What he had suffered was the humiliation of two black eyes that declared to the world he had lost a fight, that someone had beaten him up.

"I'm gonna kill him," Dooley said through clenched teeth.

Morgan sized up his agent in the clinic's hospital bed and determined that even injured, he was ready to go. In fact, his injuries seemed to energize him.

"Let's go find them," Morgan said.

"Hell yeah. Let's get that little shit and his lady friend." Dooley groaned, finding his balance as he stood up from the hospital bed.

"You gonna be all right?" Morgan asked, only slightly concerned for his agent.

"Nothin's gonna stop me," Dooley replied, to Morgan's satisfaction. He needed his agent on this.

"They got a big head start," Morgan said. "By this time they're probably outside the three-hundred-mile road-check zone the military set up. We have to track them down before the trail runs cold, so we'll start at the Dunes, their last known location."

"Someone saw her there?" Dooley asked.

"Maybe. Hopefully. She placed her usual check-in call yesterday evening."

"I assume we have orders?"

"Yeah. McCone wants us on it immediately, with full agency support. And anyway, we're being kicked out of here."

"So the Air Force wants their base all to themselves now," Dooley said, not surprised.

"Yep. Now that the alien's gone, we have no reason to be here. They want to run things their own way, without CIA interference."

"Can't say I blame them, and I'll be glad to get out of here—I hate patrol duty." Dooley groaned again, holding his head with one hand and his ribs with the other as he took his first few steps.

"Headache?" Morgan asked.

"I've had worse."

"Tough guy." Morgan grinned, imagining his agent in a boxing ring in his youth, then picturing him during Zeemat's interrogations. He was glad to know Dooley was still in play.

The medic offered Dooley a strong pain medication, but he refused, wanting to keep his head clear. He took three aspirin instead and checked himself out of the clinic. The pair hurried to their car, wasting no time leaving the desolate base, as if escaping a captivity of their own, and in hot pursuit of their prey.

"I packed up all we need." Morgan pointed to a few items in the back seat.

"And the agency will clean up the rest?"

"Like we were never here."

They raced to Las Vegas and questioned people at the Dunes. Indeed, Deltare had been seen at about the time of her check-in phone call, and she had emptied her enormous gaming account at the casino.

"How much?" Dooley asked the cage boss, wincing in a flash of pain as his jaw dropped.

"Let's go," Morgan interrupted. "That's a question for another day."

Morgan and Dooley split up to canvass the area at the transportation and exit points of the city. They asked for detailed logs and lists of every activity between Deltare's check-in call and the time the military had set up their checkpoints.

Dooley found nothing at the taxi station, bus station, and airport, but Morgan found a possible clue at the train station. They reviewed their findings when they met back up a few hours later.

"I think I found something," Morgan said.

"Good," Dooley replied. "Cause I've got nuthin'."

"The numbers didn't add up for the morning train to Flagstaff. Two hundred eighty tickets were purchased, but only two hundred seventy-nine people boarded the train."

"That could mean anything," Dooley observed.

"It could mean that Deltare and the alien split up."

"But that doesn't make sense. He'd have a hard time making it on his own."

"It makes a lot of sense if you think about it. They know we'd be looking for a couple traveling together. If they split up, and Deltare ditched her car, they wouldn't fit the description we're looking for."

"Hmm . . . maybe. It ain't much, but right now it's all we got."

"We haven't found Deltare's car, so I assume it was Zeemat who boarded the train. I also assume they took different directions, to throw us off even more. So I'll head west toward LA. You go east toward Flagstaff and see what you can find," Morgan said.

"I'm on it," Dooley said, feeling the weight of the loaded gun in the shoulder harness under his jacket.

FORTY-EIGHT

HAVASUPAI

AFTER A FINE meal with his new friends, Zeemat strolled along the streets before boarding the tourist bus to the Grand Canyon. He got in line behind a Native American man dressed in clothes Zeemat had seen "Indians" wear on TV Westerns.

Before boarding the bus, he saw military Jeeps race into the train station across the street. He hid behind the Native American man, peeking over his shoulder to see what was going on. He saw one Jeep pull into the nearest parking spot in the train station. A soldier jumped out and stood guard at the entrance to the parking lot with a rifle in hand, looking up and down the street, while another sprinted toward the ticketing office.

Zeemat didn't know whether this military activity was normal, or if they were specifically looking for him, but he didn't want to take any chances. He adjusted his wig and sunglasses and tried to make himself look small as the Native American man observed him. The man looked at the soldiers who were clearly searching for something, or someone, and his stoic face betrayed a faint squint of suspicion. He had no love for the US government and its military, so he adjusted his body position to keep Zeemat as hidden from view as possible, and they boarded the bus as soon as they were allowed. The Native American man took a window seat and motioned for Zeemat to join him on the aisle seat of his bench, and to stay low. They peered out of the tinted window, observing the small platoon of soldiers gather together, pull out maps, and point in several directions. Soon, after a few short minutes that felt like an eternity, the bus pulled away, leaving the soldiers scurrying around like a swarm of ants.

Ninety minutes later, they arrived at the Grand Canyon. When they got off the bus, Zeemat thanked the Native American man before he went his own way, and Zeemat followed the flow of foot traffic, trying hard to blend in and not make an impression. Luckily everyone's attention was focused on the marvels of the spectacular Grand Canyon and not on him. He walked right to the brim and looked over the rocky ledge, way down to the deep, jagged canyon floor below, then farther to the meandering line of the Colorado River. He focused his gaze on a tiny spot that seemed to be moving down the river, until he realized it was a raft holding a group of people. The sight gave him a better feel for the massive size and expanse of the canyon.

On the other side of the canyon, and to the right and left as far as he could see, he observed layered bands of reddish rock in what looked like a deep crack in the planet's crust. He tried to imagine how this magnificence had come to be, and whether this was the typical geography of planet Earth. He stood there in awe, feeling small and insignificant in this vast expanse, and at the same time, fortunate to be alive to witness this special moment. Zeemat was so drawn in that he didn't notice that the Native American man had been tracking him from a distance.

The group spent hours walking back and forth along the canyon's rim. He made his way to the visitor center and enjoyed the displays of local animals and birds, and he took note of the explanations of how the canyon's geography had formed over eons of time. He picked up pamphlets and brochures to read later, stuffing them into his bag. At the end of the tour, Zeemat stopped at a small stand on his way back to the waiting tour bus. An older Native American man and woman were selling colorful blankets and trinkets, and as he began to inspect them, the Native American man he'd met on the bus joined them, surprising Zeemat.

"These are my mother and my father," the Native American man said, uttering the first words Zeemat had heard him speak.

Zeemat sensed that the man was being protective of his parents, so he took a moment to bow deeply in their direction, trying to transmit a sign of respect and peace. It seemed to work.

He turned his attention back to the blankets and trinkets. "These are beautiful," Zeemat said, admiring the colorful patterns and feeling the rough texture of the woolen blanket.

The old man gave a subtle nod, not moving a muscle but watching him closely, alternating his questioning gaze between Zeemat, his wife, and his son. Eventually, the woman approached Zeemat with a trayful of silver rings and bracelets decorated with turquoise stones.

Zeemat took a bracelet to examine it more closely as the man from the bus whispered something into his parents' ears.

The woman's expressionless face did not betray what she might be thinking. Without saying a word, she approached Zeemat to show him the bracelets she herself was wearing, then she took the bendable bracelet from Zeemat's hand and wrapped it around his wrist. She noticed his long fingers and the unusual texture and color of his skin.

Zeemat's face brightened, flashing a broad smile as he admired the bracelet on his wrist.

"Five dollars," the older man said.

Zeemat paid for it and thanked the couple profusely, again bowing deeply. He continued to browse around their store.

The woman followed him, noticing every detail of Zeemat's face and mannerisms. She wondered what he was hiding behind the dark sunglasses.

"We see travelers from many places but never one like you," she said, shooting him a hard look. "Why are the soldiers looking for you?"

Zeemat felt a rush of alarm. He looked over to the Native American men, who continued to stand motionless, like patient lions waiting for their moment to lash out.

"The soldiers are no friends of ours," the woman reassured. "And it seems as if they're no friends of yours either. Our son says it's not safe for you to return to Flagstaff until they're gone. So for a while, we can offer you the safety of our reservation. If you accept, I ask that you honor us with your story."

Zeemat tensed up, his limbs itching to run. He felt like a rabbit surrounded by hungry wolves. He had just gotten free, but he'd already come dangerously close to screwing up the escape plan. He didn't know what to do. *Linda would not want me to be here*, he thought. *She would want me to run, blend in, go unnoticed.* But in the end, he agreed with the concern about the soldiers. He didn't know where else he could go, and these people seemed friendly enough; at least they were not on the soldiers' side, so he took a chance and accepted their invitation.

The Native American couple closed their shop, then led Zeemat to their old pickup and told him to jump into the bed of the truck. The man from the bus sat behind the wheel and his parents sat next to him on the bench seat. As the truck engine started, Zeemat was enveloped in black smoke pouring from the exhaust pipe. He coughed it out of his lungs as the truck lurched forward. He grabbed hold of the icy side of the cold truck bed for balance and spent the next few hours bouncing around while they drove the truck through several roads, some paved, some not. Zeemat was glad when they finally reached their destination. His body was freezing, sore, and tired from the bumpy ride, and his lips were parched from the cold, dry air. He was glad for his army coat but made a mental note to purchase gloves.

"This is the Hualapai Hilltop," the old woman told Zeemat. "We leave the truck here and hike the rest of the way. It's not far." She noticed Zeemat's parched lips. "Here," she said, handing Zeemat a large plastic container. "Have something to drink." Zeemat took long, delicious gulps of the plain water.

"Not far" turned into a four-hour hike because Zeemat had to stop frequently to sit and catch his breath. The man and woman stood waiting for him, with puzzled looks on their faces.

"You're young," the woman said, scratching her head. "And it's downhill."

But despite the difficulty, Zeemat found the hike down the rough, snowy trail to be spectacular. The formations of dry red rock, and the clean river coursing through the land took his breath away in a different manner. The setting sun threw hard shadows against the red stone that seemed to change the canyon by the minute. And the dramatic waterfalls were beyond anything he had ever imagined. It seemed as if the sun had set in a matter of minutes, the temperature dropping noticeably, and the sky darkened to a pitch-black. They stopped at the shimmering Havasu Falls under a blanket of stars and a bright half-moon, taking a moment to share several bites of beef jerky. Zeemat ripped off a piece of the tough dry meat with his teeth like he saw the others do. He was so hungry that even this tasted good.

They marched on and finally reached the village of Supai, deep in the Havasupai reservation, where they made a place for him to sleep. He stayed several nights with them in their small house, meeting their family and friends, who all treated him with courtesy and respect. They shared their stories and their history. He learned of their defeat one hundred years earlier at the hands of the "white soldiers," the loss of their freedom and their lands, and of their current plight on the reservation, stories very different from what he'd seen on TV. He listened with great interest, ate their food, drank his first beers, and smoked pipes of a fragrant smoke that made the world seem dreamy. He felt safe. He showed them his eyes and told them his story.

". . . and so now they're after me," he concluded.

The dreamy people sat on their lawn chairs around the campfire, drinking their beers and puffing on their pipes and nodding their heads in sympathetic understanding.

"So we must help you get away," one of them said. "But Flagstaff's full of army men—you can't go back there."

"So I'll walk," Zeemat said. "It'll take longer to get to Florida, but I can walk."

Laughter broke out at Zeemat's naive comment.

"It's too far, man," a young Native American man said. "But some of us are going to Albuquerque. You can ride with us in the truck. Maybe the army isn't looking for you way over there."

"What's in Florida, anyway?" another one asked.

"Rockets and spaceships," Zeemat replied. "I helped create them. I want to see."

"No, man! Are you leaving us already? Are you going back home?"

"I don't think so," Zeemat replied. "Earth is my home now. But maybe I can send a message to my people."

FORTY-NINE

THE CIA PURSUIT

MORGAN SPOKE WITH Dooley from his motel room's telephone. "A woman fitting the description, traveling in a gold sedan, filled up her gas around midnight in Barstow, California. The station attendant thought it was weird seeing a woman traveling alone at that time of night. He said she looked tired and stressed."

"Good," Dooley said, sitting behind a card table at the makeshift CIA field office in Flagstaff. "You've got the bitch in your sights."

"Not really. I lost her trail . . . for now. She could have gone in several directions from Barstow, but I think she's trying to lose us in LA, or to cross the border in Tijuana. We're covering those bases. It's only a matter of time before I find the next clue."

"That's a lot of territory."

"She had a big head start."

"Well, I found something here in Flagstaff," Dooley said. "A waitress says she saw an odd-looking fellow eating with some Mexicans. He said something strange about coming from a place very far away, farther than Mars."

"That was pretty stupid of him," Morgan said.

"And I'm gonna catch the stupid little shit."

"You keep working on him, and I'll keep working on her," Morgan said, then paused. "I'm getting a lot of heat from above," he added.

"Yeah, yeah, the boss man always talks a big game."

"Don't underestimate him. He can fire us at any minute."

"I ain't worried. If anyone's firing anyone, it's gonna be me!" Dooley said through clenched teeth, while spinning the barrel of his .45 Colt revolver.

FIFTY

ON THE BUS

AFTER HIKING BACK up the canyon, Zeemat rode in the back of a pickup truck with his Havasupai friends all the way to Albuquerque. They took Route 66 most of the way, purposely staying off Interstate 40. Despite the brisk, bumpy travel, he enjoyed riding in the back, holding on to his wig so it wouldn't blow off in the wind.

The picturesque countryside and the occasional small towns dotted with shops, motels, and gas stations were like nothing he had ever seen on Torkiya or on TV. They made short stops for burgers and hot dogs and long stops to admire the colors of the Painted Desert and ponder the mysteries of the Petrified Forest. Zeemat was mesmerized by the steady flow of people and road traffic, and by the mere fact that he was traveling with humans. He hadn't established himself yet, but he felt as though his mission was finally underway. He'd begun to see his new world and understand it better. And the world was affecting him—he noticed the sun gradually turning his grey skin into a brownish color.

They arrived in Albuquerque, relieved not to see a military presence when they dropped him off at the bus station. It was warmer there, though he could see peaks of white snow at the top of the Sandia Mountains to the east. Before saying their goodbyes with hugs and well-wishes, his new friends helped him purchase a ticket to El Paso, Texas. From there, he planned to follow the southern border of the United States all the way to Florida.

So he was on his own again, certain now that the military activity in Las Vegas and Flagstaff had indeed been in pursuit of him. His Native American friends had encouraged him to be cautious. They reminded him of the military atrocities against their own people over the years.

They were clever enough to follow me to Flagstaff, Zeemat considered. He looked all around as he boarded the bus, searching for any sign of trouble. The bus driver noticed Zeemat's suspicious behavior, and then his hands, as he took his ticket. He tried to get a better look at Zeemat's face but couldn't because of the hooded sweatshirt and the sunglasses, but he made a mental note of where he sat on the bus.

Once they were on the road, Zeemat relaxed and nodded off despite wanting to watch the scenery out the window. The bus ride was much smoother than the train and the pickup truck trips had been, and he was able to doze off in a comfortable sleep. When he got to El Paso, he bought a ticket for the next bus to Houston.

He had a few hours to kill before the bus departed, so he ate at a nearby Tex-Mex restaurant, the food burning his tongue like an open fire that he extinguished with an ice-cold Coke. Next he explored a few shops in the area. He felt people staring at him while he browsed a Western apparel store, and he became self-conscious about his clothing, of his not fitting in. He examined what other people were wearing and bought himself a pair of snakeskin boots and a ten-gallon cowboy hat, thinking these would help him blend in better.

Before boarding his bus to Houston, he also bought a tour book of Texas. It had a picture of the state flag and a map of the "Lone Star State." The name appealed to him. He studied every detail of the book during the ride to Houston.

But Houston was not what he'd expected. It was a big, crowded city. The air was hot, but it had a different feel than the air in Area 51. It felt heavy and wet. He didn't like it, and he was happy when boarding was called for his bus to New Orleans, Louisiana.

He was making steady progress toward Florida, but he was getting increasingly tired—sleeping on buses and on benches in bus stations had proved very uncomfortable. He surprised himself by missing the bed in his cell.

He arrived at the bus station in New Orleans on a bright, sunny day among people in high spirits. Even though the air was just as humid, somehow, he enjoyed it more. He bought a local map and a tour book, which was becoming a habit upon arrival at every city. He saw billboards of places in New Orleans he wished he had time to explore, promising himself he would return someday. The idea of exploring made him realize he would need a different mode of transportation to move around more easily once he arrived at his destination. So he began to scrutinize traffic to learn the rules of driving.

He bought a bus ticket to Mobile, Alabama. On his way there, while looking out the bus window, he compared different vehicles as they passed by, trying to determine which would best suit his needs. He decided he could use one in which he could sleep comfortably but that was more maneuverable than a big motor home.

Arriving in Mobile, he made a decision: no more buses. He followed other passengers out of the bus station and stood in line at the taxi stop. A porter asked him if he could help him with his luggage and Zeemat refused, holding his duffel bag tight against his body. The porter scowled at him and walked away while muttering something under his breath. Zeemat waited for his taxi and asked the driver to take him to the ocean when he slid into the back seat. He knew it was close, and he was aching to see it. He remembered the pictures of boats and storms he'd seen in the *National Geographic* magazine.

He also remembered the large bodies of water on the day he'd made his crash landing, but it was nothing like what he finally saw up close—the Gulf of Mexico. He stood at a beach, dropped his bag at his feet, and took in the view with his hands on his head in awe and wonder. The water's vast expanse stretched out to the horizon. As he compared the new experience to what he'd known on his home planet, he found that the blue of the water was different from the greenish oceans on Torkiya, but the sound of the waves was the same.

He took off his boots and dipped his toes in the water. It was warm. He heard seagulls, and inhaled lungfuls of the salty ocean air. He looked around again and saw no one, so he took off his coat and cowboy hat and enjoyed the feeling of the sun on the skin of his face and arms. He took off his sunglasses, his optic sensors automatically dimming in the bright light, and he basked in the sunshine for a moment. He hoped Florida would be just like this, and he decided he would travel the rest of the way along the coast, off the major highway.

I need a vehicle, he confirmed.

Zeemat found a phone booth and learned how to use the phone book like he had seen humans do at the train and bus stations. He discovered the *Yellow Pages* and figured out that types of businesses were listed in alphabetical order. He searched under *A* for automobiles and used his map to find a location close to him. He circled it on his map, tucked it in to his pocket, strapped the handles of his duffel bag over his shoulders like a backpack, and started walking.

When he arrived at the used-car dealership, he strolled up and down the aisles of the parking lot to examine the myriad of options. A man came out of a small building and asked if he could help. Zeemat told him he needed a vehicle that he could also sleep in.

"Ah," the man said. "I have exactly what you need."

The dealer led Zeemat to a 1962 Volkswagen camper van. He couldn't see Zeemat's eyes glow bright behind the dark sunglasses. The dealer made his sales pitch, but Zeemat interrupted him even before he mentioned a price.

"I'll take it!"

"It's a beauty," the salesman said, noting Zeemat's enthusiasm and mentally adjusting the price he would ask. "Everybody wants one. This won't sit here on the lot for very long."

"How do I obtain it?" Zeemat asked, hurrying the man along.

The salesman squinted, looked Zeemat over, then looked at the van, then asked for twice as much as the van was worth.

Without a word, Zeemat rifled through his wad of money and peeled off enough bills to pay the man.

"You must really want it," the man said, raising his eyebrows and counting the bills, examining them to be sure they weren't counterfeit.

Meanwhile, Zeemat climbed into the driver's seat, feeling as excited as Deltare had been when she brought him a new present. He thought of her as the man went over the details of the vehicle and its general operation, then handed over the keys.

"I don't know how to drive," Zeemat said.

"What?"

Zeemat was smiling and fumbling with the keys, and they both laughed.

The man took off his hat and scratched his head. "You're serious, aren't you?" he said. After a moment, he climbed into the passenger seat. "C'mon. Let's go for a ride."

Zeemat got behind the wheel, cautiously at first, but he quickly became more daring as he got the hang of the steering and pedals. The man took him up and down an empty side street until Zeemat had stopped jerking the car to a stop. He gave him a crash course in road signs and traffic lights. He could tell Zeemat was telling the truth—he had never driven before. He was concerned about the legality of selling him a vehicle and letting him drive away, but he wasn't about to lose this sale.

"So I take it you don't have a license."

"What's that?" Zeemat asked.

The man seemed stunned for a moment and stared at Zeemat again. After a moment, he broke out in laughter again.

Zeemat was puzzled, not knowing what was so funny and still waiting for an answer.

The man squinted and cocked his head, examining Zeemat even more closely, his curiosity piquing. He was now more concerned about himself, but he wanted to keep the money from the sale.

"You can't tell anyone I sold you this car," he said.

"I won't," Zeemat replied. "And you can't tell anyone I bought it."

"Deal!" the man said, offering his hand.

Zeemat shook it, drove the man back to his used-car dealership, and dropped him off.

"Thank you," Zeemat said.

"Safe travels," the salesman said, scratching and shaking his head.

Zeemat jerked the car out of the parking lot and weaved his way down the road, almost hitting a parked car.

FIFTY-ONE

NEAR MISSING

DOOLEY WAS HOT on Zeemat's trail. He didn't know how Zeemat could have slipped past him in Flagstaff, but he assumed he would continue heading east. He stopped at every likely place along Interstate 40, asking if anyone had seen a strange traveler.

"What's he look like?" someone asked him.

Dooley furrowed his brow and ground his teeth, irritated he couldn't give the man any specifics.

A few days later, he finally got a lead in Albuquerque. A bus driver had noticed a strange man boarding his bus. "He was looking around when he got on the bus . . . like someone was after him," he said.

"What can you tell me about his face and head?" Dooley inquired.

He had a big, messy Afro coming out of his sweatshirt hood, and he was wearing dark sunglasses. I kept looking at him in the rearview mirror to get a look at his face, but he never took off the hood or the sunglasses.

Dooley took notes. "What else was he wearing?" he asked.

"A long army coat, and he was carrying a large army duffel bag. Oh . . . and I noticed he had these weird, long, skinny fingers as he handed me his ticket."

"Where were you headed?"

"El Paso," the bus driver said.

Dooley thanked the man, then hurried to a phone booth to place a call to Morgan at the CIA field office in Los Angeles. He knew that was where Morgan would be headed. He left a message notifying him he was going to El Paso. "I have a decent lead," he said.

When he arrived at the bus station in El Paso, he questioned the ticket clerks and the bus drivers but got no new leads. He canvassed the local area, and before long, at the Western apparel store, someone told him that a strange-looking man had purchased snakeskin boots and a ten-gallon cowboy hat. Dooley snickered through a half smile. *Dumbass. He'll stick out like a sore thumb*, he thought.

Dooley kept heading east, stopping at the next large bus station—in New Orleans. It didn't take long for him to find several people who had seen a man in a long army coat carrying a large duffel bag, wearing dark sunglasses, with a curly Afro sticking out from under a cowboy hat.

"I think he was standing over there, in line for the bus to Mobile," a bus driver said. "He stood out in a city like this, and that's saying something. I gave him a lot of credit. The dude had style!"

Dooley frowned, taking notes, and raced to Mobile, Alabama. *I'm catching up, you little shit!*

In Mobile, a porter at the bus station replied to Dooley's questions. "Yeah, a guy just like that was in line right here for a taxi." Within a few hours, Dooley had located the taxi driver who had taken Zeemat to a beach on the Gulf. Dooley ordered the man to take him to the same spot.

Arriving at the very beach where Zeemat had stood just a few days earlier, Dooley looked in all directions and cursed at the irritatingly high-pitched calls of the seagulls. The sound of each ocean wave startled him and sped up his heart, reminding him of D-Day on Normandy Beach. The memory sent a pang of fear through his gut as he remembered that fateful day when so many in his platoon had died. He thought of himself as a brave man, and he hated himself for feeling fear, even if just from an old memory.

He shielded his eyes from the bothersome sun as he looked up and down the soft sandy beach. He spat out the taste of salty ocean air. Finally, frustrated, he sat down in the sand, shut his eyes, and concentrated. "Where are you going, you little shit?" he murmured to himself.

FIFTY-TWO

FLORIDA

ALL TORKIYAN SPACE Academy cadets were taught to seek the nearest spaceship launch center, if there was one, in case they were stranded anywhere. On Earth, all the launches Zeemat had seen on TV or read about in newspapers and magazines happened in Cape Canaveral, Florida—or Cape Kennedy, as they now called it.

Zeemat read a road sign as he crossed the state border.

"Welcome to Florida!" he yelled over the music he had blaring from the van's radio speakers, a big smile on his face. He pounded on the steering wheel and emitted loud *beeps* and musical *chimes* of Torkiyan joy.

He made a stop at the first exit, the Florida Welcome Center.

"Welcome!" a cheerful woman in an orange uniform said. She greeted him with a warm smile and a cheerful voice. "Welcome to Florida. We're glad you're here!"

Zeemat saw that she greeted everyone in the same manner, with the same words and the same tone of voice, but nevertheless, her cheerful attitude and hospitality felt personal to him.

"Please," the woman said, pointing to a table against the wall, "have a glass of delicious Florida orange juice. It's complimentary."

Zeemat accepted a small glass of orange juice, drank it, and bowed deeply as if this completed some sort of human orange juice ceremony. "It's nice to feel welcome," he said to the orange juice minister who was already busy passing out samples to other visitors.

He explored the visitor center, gathered a few maps and brochures of interesting places in the area, bought a newspaper, and made his way back to the van.

He decided to continue his slow drive along the coastline, as close to the water as possible. He read in the newspaper that the next launch from Cape Kennedy was to be the Gemini 1 mission on April 8, 1964. It was a new spacecraft and rocket, and Zeemat knew he had helped design it. He wanted to see how the humans had implemented his ideas. But he was a couple of weeks ahead of schedule, so he took the time to enjoy this beautiful part of his new world. He stopped at every beach to look around, making several overnight stops along the Gulf Coast.

He stayed the first few nights at campgrounds, sleeping in his van. He noticed no one was wearing cowboy hats, so he gave his away to a man in Pensacola who'd commented on it. The temperature was getting much warmer, and he saw no one wearing long army coats, so he gave his away to a homeless man in Destin.

He enjoyed the ocean, beaches, and sunshine so much that he stayed a few days in Panama City. He took his first boat ride, a half-day fishing trip. After that, he purchased a fishing pole, fishing line, sinkers, floaters, hooks, and bait, and fished from the long piers jutting far into the clear blue gulf water. He rented a room at a beachside motel, enjoying a real bed and a hot shower for the first time since his captivity. He walked down to the beach for every sunset. He kept the window open at night so he could hear the soothing sound of the waves. He witnessed his first ocean storm and felt the familiar tingling on his skin. He saw his first Earth rainbows. *I could live here with Linda*, he thought. *No one would find us here.* He would have stayed longer if not for the approaching launch date.

Zeemat left Panama City and drove east on Interstate 10 across the state to the city of Jacksonville on the Atlantic coast. He was shocked and impressed by the immense Navy installations, by the grandeur of the Navy ships, and the excitement of the noisy Navy jets zooming by overhead. It was different, of course, but it reminded him of the Space Academy on Torkiya. He felt a strange connection to the young men he saw walking around town in their crisp white uniforms.

He spent the last few days before the launch exploring the area around Jacksonville and the St. Johns River. He found a nice park along the river and enjoyed a leisurely stroll. He stopped at a bench under the shade of a poplar tree and enjoyed the peaceful view.

Florida is a peaceful place, he decided. *A place where I can settle.* He left the park feeling hopeful, as if his life had made a turn for the better, and he hurried back to his motel to make the final preparations for the last leg of his long trip.

On the morning of April 7, 1964, the day before the launch, Zeemat sprang out of bed, washed up, packed, and checked out of the motel—as usual, raising some eyebrows along the way.

He found a beachside restaurant and sat at a small table to enjoy breakfast and the sunrise, making a face as he tried again to drink a cup of coffee. He couldn't understand why humans relished in such a bitter fluid, but everyone seemed to drink it, and he was trying his best to blend in. After a few sips, he set the cup down, pushed it aside, and gulped from the tall glass of orange juice he had also ordered, to drown out the coffee's taste. A waitress chuckled at him.

After breakfast, Zeemat opened a map, and with a long finger, he traced the short line south on Interstate 95 to his destination—Cape Kennedy.

FIFTY-THREE

GEMINI 1

ZEEMAT STOPPED BRIEFLY to see the old Spanish fort in Saint Augustine, imagining Spanish ships moored nearby and soldiers defending their new colony in this beautiful part of the world. He did the arithmetic and realized that those events had happened while he was in space on his way to Earth. Inside the fort, the stone walls were cold despite the warmth of the day outside. Along the battlements, the rusty cannons pointed to the harbor, and somehow, despite their long silence, still issued an ancient threat.

At Daytona Beach, he dipped his feet in the ocean, making mental notes to return to this place someday so he could thoroughly enjoy it, as he seemed to feel everywhere he went. He sighed deeply and gazed to the west—toward wherever Linda was at that very moment. He felt as if this entire world was full of places where he and she could live and be happy.

But time was now drawing short—the launch was set for the following day, and he focused his attention on the matter at hand: reaching his destination. He was much closer now, so he slowed the van's speed, inching his way past Titusville to get a good feel for the lay of the land, until finally he saw the roadside sign he was looking for—an ad for the Kennedy Space Center.

He drove around the area for the rest of the day, getting his bearings. He explored the Merritt Island marshes just to the north of the space center complex. He came back to the mainland and took the NASA Causeway to cross over the Indian River. He drove by the space center, noting the location of the visitor center and the parking areas. Then he drove back across the Indian River to the mainland, around to the south of the gigantic space center complex, stopping at Cocoa Beach. He stepped onto the soft sand, feeling a cool breeze and ocean mist on his skin. He saw kids playing in the surf and overheard people on the beach talking about the next day's launch, excited like the flocks of gulls he saw squawking and squealing all around.

"Will we be able to see it from here?" he heard a young girl ask her mother.

Zeemat realized he was about twenty miles from the launch site and wondered how close he would get to the actual rocket.

As the evening waned, an exhausted Zeemat drove back to nearby Titusville to spend the night, but "No Vacancy" signs discouraged him at every turn. He learned that most of the hotels and motels in the area were packed with tourists visiting for the launch.

Zeemat finally found a run-down motel flashing an orange "Open" sign. He paid for his room and examined the rusty key wired to a wooden tag with a faded print of the hotel's name, which the clerk had handed him. He pushed open the door to his room—an old wooden door splintering at the edges, its red color long washed out. The orange "Open" sign shone on and off, on and off into his tiny room through the thin curtains, changing the color of the walls from a dirty gray to a dull orange, but he didn't mind. He was happy to have found a room at all. He got out of his clothes and into the squeaky bed. But he had trouble sleeping that night, excited about the next day's events.

At dawn on April 8, 1964, he couldn't stay still any longer. He bolted out of bed, took a long, hot shower, dried off with a threadbare hotel towel, and looked at himself in the foggy mirror. He hardly recognized who he saw staring back. His face and body were tanned from his days on the beaches. By comparison, the top of his head was a light gray where the wig blocked out the sun.

His body had changed, too. He was no longer as thin as he used to be. Zeemat ran his hands over the muscles of his arms and chest. They were more prominent than when he'd lived in Torkiya, even after the regular exercise at the Space Academy, certainly an effect of Earth's stronger gravity. Every little thing he did on Earth was harder to do than it had been on Torkiya, and his new muscles showed it. He felt stronger. He flexed his biceps a few times and inspected himself at different angles in the mirror.

He pulled out a few items from his duffel bag that he'd purchased the day before—a new Hawaiian shirt for the occasion and a windbreaker with pockets that would cover his arms and hands. He donned his wig and sunglasses, and stepped out, taking a deep breath of salty ocean air. He put his bag in the van and went to check out at the office.

He saw a different receptionist behind the desk, a pleasant young woman with smooth, glowing skin as dark as coffee, and she had a mane of black hair in tight little curls like his wig. She smiled warmly at him. "I hope you had a nice stay," she beamed. She seemed to exude happiness, and he liked her immediately.

Zeemat read the badge on her lapel—"Hello, My Name Is Irene.".

"I'm going to miss the launch today," Irene lamented. "I have to work." Her happy face changed for an instant to a dramatically sad expression, then converted right back to her happy smile.

"Yes, too bad," Zeemat said. "Have you seen many launches?"

"Sure! Are you kidding? This is my hometown. We're all about the space program around here."

Irene stopped what she was doing and focused her attention on Zeemat. Her lips kept a thick smile, but her eyes narrowed. "Have you been to a launch before?"

Zeemat was just about to answer yes, thinking about his own launch back in Torkiya, but he caught himself in time and simply said, "This is my first time here."

"Well, keep your radio tuned to WRKT 1300. They have continuous updates on launch days."

"I'll do that," Zeemat said, fumbling with his sunglasses that were slipping down his nose.

Irene eyed him closely but didn't miss a beat of conversation. "The best place to watch is from the observation area at the space center. You can get a ticket at the visitor center. They'll take you on a bus. But you better get there soon. It'll be a late-morning launch."

"Thank you," Zeemat said. "After everything I've done to get here, I wouldn't want to miss it now."

Irene kept her pleasant smile as she took her time carefully inspecting Zeemat from top to bottom. She made a decision. He was odd, but she liked him and his boyish enthusiasm.

"I just know you're gonna love it," she said. "And you come back to visit us again for another launch someday."

"Thank you," Zeemat said, bowing courteously. "You make me feel welcome."

"Anytime!" Irene said as Zeemat turned to walk out of the motel office. As he left, Irene's smiling face morphed into a serious look. She reached under the counter to remove a note she had taped onto the top of the desk a few days earlier, when CIA Junior Special Agent Kenneth Dooley had come to call. She read the note again: "Afro haircut, wears dark sunglasses even indoors and at night, drives a VW van." Irene watched as Zeemat boarded his VW van and drove off. She looked down at the note again, at the phone number to the local CIA office the agent had left, with instructions to call if she encountered anyone even vaguely meeting that description.

Zeemat drove to the NASA Causeway and crossed over the Indian River to the Kennedy Space Center. Compared to his drive-by the day before, there was a bustle of activity at the complex. He purchased a ticket and found his way to the buses taking people to the observation area of Launch Complex 19.

He stood in line with a group of animated people, abuzz with a nervous energy like a swarm of bees around a honey hive. People chattered nonstop as they waited in line, boarded the bus, sat in their seats, and were driven all the way to the outdoor bleacher area. On top of all the conversation, a voice from a loudspeaker added to the commotion. The voice was announcing the moment-to-moment progress of the launch preparations, which were nearly complete.

Zeemat found a perfect viewing spot on the highest bleacher bench. Itching with excitement, he scratched his arms, feeling an unusual tingling in his body. There was something thrilling in the air around him. His eyes were glued to the launchpad five miles away and his ears to the loudspeaker. He placed his open hand on his forehead over his sunglasses to further shield his eyes from the bright sun as he tried to pick out the details around the launch site.

As he scanned the crowd of people around him, he noticed a certain woman at the opposite end of the bleachers and a few rows down. She wore stylish sunglasses, and she had a head of full reddish hair protected from the breeze by a clear plastic polka-dotted bonnet. Her skin had a beautiful bronze tone, smooth, and glistening. He thought her cheekbones, jawline, lips, and mouth were very attractive. She had been repeatedly looking in his direction and not toward the launchpad like everyone else. He thought that was a little odd, so he looked from side to side and over his shoulder to see if she was maybe looking at someone around him, but that did not appear to be the case.

The voice on the loudspeaker continued to make important announcements. "All systems are 'go' for launch," the booming voice said, followed by an explosion of loud cheers from everyone on the bleachers. "T-minus ten minutes and counting."

A large, gregarious man sitting next to Zeemat took a swig from a small metal container and yelled, "All right!" He patted Zeemat hard on the back and shouted in his ear, "All right, man! This is it! It's happenin'!" He offered Zeemat a sip from the small metal container.

"No, thank you," Zeemat said, hoping he wasn't offending the man for refusing his generosity. But the man didn't seem to mind at all. He put the container away in the inside breast pocket of his jacket.

"Less than ten minutes to go! Aren't you excited?" the man asked.

"Yes, so very much," Zeemat responded. For once, he didn't want to observe this interesting human. He angled his body away from him to discourage further communication. He was here for the launch and he was already distracted by the presence of the beautiful woman.

The loudspeaker voice said, "T-minus nine minutes and counting." Then he glanced back at the woman just in time to catch her looking his way again. Her unexpected attention was starting to worry him. *Maybe I'm not blending in well enough*, he thought. He looked around to see if anyone else had him under observation. He became increasingly self-conscious as the time to launch continued to count down.

Regardless of what was to happen with the mysterious woman, the excitement of the moment at hand overwhelmed everything else. Smoke and steam were now visible on the launchpad. A few minutes later, the loudspeaker voice announced, "T-minus sixty seconds and counting." The excitement was palpable. People were jumping up and down, rocking back and forth, clapping their hands, yelling and whistling, then finally counting down along with the loudspeaker voice.

"Ten, nine, eight, seven, six, five . . ." Now the engines turned on and the launchpad was engulfed in flame and smoke. ". . . four, three, two, ONE!" The loudspeaker voice exclaimed, "WE HAVE LIFTOFF!"

Gemini 1 lifted off at 11:01 a.m. EST. In no time, the spacecraft and its rocket became a distant dot of light before disappearing altogether into flaky clouds high in the sky, and the roar of the engines faded to silence, leaving only a thick trailing flume of smoke as evidence that this incredible event had just happened.

The announcements continued, but the show was over. The cheering crowd gradually became quieter and settled into a conversational hum. Suddenly, Zeemat felt an urge to hurry and get away. He found he wasn't the only one, as everyone quickly left the bleachers and returned to the waiting buses.

Zeemat looked around for the mystery woman, but she was nowhere to be seen. If she had gotten into one of the buses, he didn't know which one. He didn't find her on the bus he boarded.

The buses took them back to the visitor complex, where he searched for her again in vain. There was something about her—both dangerous and attractive. He thought about staying there for a while, in case she suddenly appeared, but decided to return to his van and get going. He planned to return to the motel and talk to Irene about the launch, then figure out how he could maybe find the woman from the bleachers.

Zeemat left the visitor complex and worked his way back to the van. He started the engine and adjusted the volume on the radio which was still tuned to WRKT "Rocket 1300," as Irene had suggested. He was listening for any updates about the launch when his attention was suddenly drawn to the sound of screeching tires. He looked at the parking lot in front of him and what he saw threw him into a panic.

A man jumped out of the car that had just screeched to a stop one row over. Zeemat recognized him immediately. "Dooley!" he gasped, raising a hand to his mouth. Dooley was yelling something in his direction and pulled out the gun from his shoulder holster. To make matters worse, Zeemat noticed the mystery woman standing by her parked car directly in front of him, between him and Dooley. She turned her head back and forth to keep both Zeemat and Dooley in her sights. She yelled something at Dooley and pointed at Zeemat. He assumed they were working together and didn't hesitate. He slammed the transmission into drive, stomped on the gas pedal, and peeled out of the parking lot with the smoke of burning rubber coming from the van's screeching tires.

FIFTY-FOUR

DOOLEY'S FOLLY

ZEEMAT'S MIND RACED. *How did he find me?* he wondered. But there was no time to ponder—he drew his attention to the immediate task at hand—to escape. He dodged several cars and pedestrians as he exited the space center parking lot. Once he was back on the causeway, he floored the gas pedal and took the bridge over the Indian River back to the mainland.

Dooley jumped back into his vehicle in pursuit. He fumed as a group of slow-walking people and cars pulling out of their parking spaces blocked his quick exit. He rolled down his window and yelled at people to get out of the way. He laid on his horn to warn drivers he was coming through. He dodged and weaved around cars, picking up speed as he navigated the maze. He grazed a couple of cars, leaving shocked and angry people in his wake.

By the time Dooley got on the causeway, Zeemat had gotten a head start. He couldn't see Zeemat's van but he knew he had to be headed back to the mainland, the only way out. He kept honking his horn as he passed slower-moving vehicles in front of him. When he reached the apex of the bridge over the Indian River, he spotted Zeemat's van a short distance ahead, and he trained his eyes on it as Zeemat turned north on Highway 1.

Back at the space center, Zeemat's mystery woman also hopped in her car and hurried onto the causeway, joining the pursuit. She weaved through the traffic, racing to keep up with Dooley. She reached under the car seat to retrieve her weapon.

Zeemat sped as fast as he could, running red lights, narrowly missing crossing traffic. When he reached Titusville, he had to decide. He was running low on gas. He could either stay on the busy mainland or try to lose Dooley in the maze of roads on the Merritt Island marshes. He chose the marshes. He looked in his rearview mirror and hoped Dooley didn't see him making the turn onto the bridge to Merritt Island.

But Dooley had seen him in the distance ahead, turning onto the bridge. The agent was just a few minutes behind, frustrated by the heavy traffic leaving the space center after the launch.

Zeemat sped into the Merritt Island marshes. Anxious about his gasoline, he noticed that the needle on the gas gauge was below empty. Several miles into the marsh, he looked around for where he might turn off to hide the vehicle. But he was on a straight part of the road and there was no place to hide in the wide-open space. Suddenly, the van sputtered, and his speed slowed even though he'd had the gas pedal to the floor. The engine gave a few final knocks and finally fell silent. Zeemat looked in his rearview mirror as his van coasted to a stop, and in the distance behind him, he saw a vehicle catching up quickly.

Zeemat bolted out of his car and looked around. He saw miles of road east and west, and alligator-ridden marshes north and south. There was no place to run.

Dooley came to a skidding stop twenty-five yards behind Zeemat's van. Throwing the door open, he launched himself out of the vehicle and was engulfed by a trailing cloud of dust and exhaust. "I got you now, asshole," he yelled. He raised his gun and walked toward Zeemat.

Zeemat saw the menacing look in Dooley's eyes. At the same time, he spotted movement behind Dooley. Another vehicle was rapidly approaching. Dooley stopped as he heard the vehicle charging from behind. He wanted it to pass them by, but he heard it pull to a stop behind him. He didn't take his eyes off Zeemat, keeping his revolver aimed at his fugitive.

It didn't surprise Zeemat to see the mystery woman come out of the car. *They were working together*, he thought. He noticed she was holding a metal rod in her right hand. The rod had two sharp prongs at the tip.

"Do not shoot!" the woman commanded. "He's important."

"Get back in your car and drive away!" Dooley yelled back over his shoulder. "This is official business." Dooley knew he would have to "contain" her as well, once he "contained" Zeemat.

The woman didn't heed Dooley's order. Instead, she ran toward Dooley and reached him just as he was pulling the trigger. At the same moment, she stabbed him with the cattle prod she held in her hand. She squeezed the prod's trigger, sending a strong electric current into the back of Dooley's right shoulder.

Dooley's shooting arm went into a spasm, wrecking his aim as his gun discharged. Zeemat heard the bullet whizzing past his left ear as the gun dropped from Dooley's numbed hand.

Zeemat saw the woman stab Dooley again with the weapon in her hand, like the one they'd used on him in Area 51. This time he heard the familiar sizzle of another electric jolt. This one buckled Dooley down to his knees.

The woman calmly walked around Dooley, who was kneeling on the ground, stunned, rubbing his arm and hand. She picked up his gun. She looked at Zeemat and smiled, then turned back to Dooley and cocked her head, taking a few moments to observe his behavior before slowly raising the gun. She shot him twice in the head, the shots echoing across the lonely highway. Dooley's body jerked before slumping to the ground, lifeless.

Zeemat stood frozen, shocked and paralyzed. In that moment, he realized that as much as he disliked Dooley, he hadn't wanted to see him dead.

The woman dropped the gun by Dooley's body, looked at Zeemat with a spirited smile, and swept toward him in broad, buoyant strides. Zeemat was still in shock, appalled by what had just happened.

As the woman approached, she took off her polka-dotted rain bonnet, then a red-haired wig, revealing her large, smooth head. When Zeemat noticed her long fingers, his mouth dropped open. She stopped two steps in front of him and took off her sunglasses, revealing a set of large, familiar eyes.

"*Zzzt*. Welcome, Torkiyan," she said, in beautiful *buzzes*, *beeps*, and *tones*.

PART THREE

THE WAY HOME

FIFTY-FIVE

CLOSE ENCOUNTERS
OF A COMMON KIND

THE FEMALE STANDING before him was a vision of Torkiyan beauty, though she had a hard, suspicious look in her eyes. The planet Earth had endowed her with prominent muscles and a tan skin, just as it had Zeemat. But everything else—the shape of her head like an inverted teardrop; the almond-shaped eyes; the fine, tapering jaw; the fluid way she moved—remained fully Torkiyan. What impressed Zeemat the most was her intoxicating attraction aroma, a sign of a powerful Torkiyan female in her prime. His skin tingled wildly as she approached.

He almost doubted his own senses, standing face-to-face with another Torkiyan, both so very far from their home planet.

"What . . . Who . . ." Zeemat stammered, his voice trembling. He had so many questions but couldn't quite put one together.

"I've been here for years," she said calmly. "You're the new one here. Who are you?"

"My name is Zeemat. I was on the crew of Mission 51. I'm the only survivor."

"Well, that's a surprise," she buzzed suspiciously. "Considering I arrived only seventeen years ago—in Earth year 1947." She took a few moments to make mental calculations before she offered her name. "My name is Gerra, the Science Officer of Mission 50."

"Of course you are!" Zeemat bristled excitedly. "I learned all about you! I saw the images of your launch. I studied the details of your ship. I know all about your crewmates." Zeemat paused and looked toward her vehicle. "Where are they?"

By the sudden change in Gerra's posture and facial expression—and recalling Deltare's description of their ship and a dead fellow Torkiyan—Zeemat sensed the answer to his question. He knew it all too well. He waited for Gerra to compose herself.

"We miscalculated the landing. We were using ancient, incorrect data about the mass, density, and atmosphere of this planet. We crashed hard. Half the ship, along with two of my crewmates, disintegrated on impact due to the remaining antimatter in the tank. The other half of the ship was thrown clear, with Captain Agos and me." She paused for a moment, and Zeemat saw the faraway look in her eyes.

"I know he didn't survive," Zeemat said, recalling Deltare's description of his autopsy.

Gerra eyed Zeemat with a hard look. "No, he didn't. He died from a crushing blow to his head, and I was incapacitated by multiple injuries. I survived with the help of a few local native humans in Roswell, New Mexico. They found me, kept me hidden and safe, and helped me heal."

"So there are people out there who know you exist?"

"*Grrk*. Of course not. *Gllk*!" Gerra said, emitting guttural *clicks* of irritation.

Gerra cocked her head and squinted at Zeemat. The timing of his arrival still had her confused. "So did you depart Torkiya a mere seventeen Earth years after our mission? The tradition is more like every one hundred."

"We did wait one hundred. But ours was the first ship capable of entering 5D, doubling the speed of your ship, so we planned to arrive here before you. But something damaged our ship during the time we spent in 5D. I awoke from cryo to find the three other beds empty of fluid, and my crewmates were long dead. Only my bed remained intact. Janusia, our ship's Synthetic Soul, cut our speed back to a slow 4D for the rest of the voyage. She kept me in cryo for all but the last year. Then I also used wrong data for my landing calculations. I crashed and was injured, just like you."

Gerra nodded, but Zeemat saw no sympathy in her face.

"Humans helped me heal, too, and then held me captive until my recent escape," Zeemat added.

Gerra looked at Dooley's dead body. "But I can see humans know about *you*! *Gllk*," she scolded.

Zeemat hung his head and dropped his shoulders in a show of Torkiyan shame.

"Tell me more," Gerra said. "When did you arrive? What have you learned? What have you done?"

"I arrived ten years ago, in Earth year 1954, and—"

"*Zzzt*. Only seven years after me!" Gerra interrupted. Then she held out her hand in the universal sign for "stop" as she looked up and down the road. "I want to hear every detail, but we can't stay here in the open. Take what you need from your vehicle. Bring it to my car."

"And leave my van here?"

"This human knew to look for it," she said, flicking a dismissive finger in Dooley's direction. "Others may know of it as well."

Zeemat agreed. They went back to the van to gather his things and loaded them into the trunk of Gerra's car.

Gerra drove ahead to a wider point in the road and turned the car around. They had to return the same way they came and cross the bridge back to the mainland. Zeemat said a silent goodbye to his van and to Dooley as he passed them.

Once they were on Highway 1 again, they turned south. They passed the road leading to the space center. Shortly after, they came up to the small town of Cocoa. Gerra turned right onto a main street and then made several other turns, eventually reaching open lands on the far side of town to the west.

Gerra slowed when they reached their destination and pulled into a long gravel driveway. "Here we are," she said. "This is where I live and work."

They pulled up to a small farmhouse, flanked by a large barn on one side and a small toolshed with a tin roof on the other. She parked her car behind the barn, out of sight of passing traffic, and noticed Zeemat's inquisitive look. "This was a dairy farm when I took it," she said. "I was attracted by the cows. I needed them to continue the work I started in Roswell."

Zeemat looked around. There were no cows.

Gerra shrugged. "The cows are all gone, but I don't need them anymore. The work is far beyond that."

She kept talking as they stepped out of the car and retrieved his belongings from the trunk. "The barn has several stalls they used for milking the cows, and there is a large cold-storage room with thick walls they used to keep the milk cold. I'll show you later."

They walked past the barn and headed to the farmhouse. It was a small, two-story building like most other farmhouses he had seen in the country along the way. The most impressive part about it was the generous front porch, furnished only with two dusty rocking chairs. The porch looked over the empty, overgrown pasture fields, with the barn off to the side.

As he entered the house, Zeemat's first impression was of the messiness. Papers were scattered on the dining room table. A pile of dirty dishes filled the kitchen sink. Her bed lay unmade.

Gerra noticed Zeemat's look of vague disapproval.

"Washing the dishes is a low priority when there's more important work to do," she said. She led him back to the dining room table and snatched up the papers she'd been working on earlier in the day. Zeemat caught a glimpse of several sketches of heads and brains. They sat down at opposite ends of the small table, and Gerra leaned in.

"Tell me more about your journey and your time here on Earth," she said.

Zeemat sat back and gave her a long, detailed account of his previous ten years—the crash, his injuries and recovery, his interrogations, his unexpected friendship with Deltare, his awareness that the planet had copper, his involvement with humans who would enable technologies to connect their planets, his escape, and his trip across the country. At last, he took a deep breath and let out a long sigh. "*Zzzt*. And now I'm here . . . with you, against all odds."

But Zeemat couldn't tell whether Gerra was satisfied with his story.

"So we can communicate with Torkiya now?" she asked. "Have you already done it?"

"I don't have a transmitter, but it's only a matter of time. We now have satellites in orbit. We have the start of a space program. We're making progress."

"*Grrk*! 'We'? Or 'they'?" Gerra scolded again.

Zeemat turned defensive. "Advancing their technology is a mandate of our missions, to connect our worlds. That *had* to be the focus of my mission. It was all I could do as a prisoner. And we made progress. If I had a functioning Trangula to access our knowledge base, I could have advanced their technology faster, but mine was destroyed in the crash." He looked around the room, as if expecting to see one lying around somewhere.

"*Dominating* them and finding copper are the main mandates of our missions!" Gerra said with unmasked anger. "Advancing their technology is a secondary concern," she added, pounding her fist on the table. "And don't bother looking. My Trangula was destroyed, too. If I had access to my Trangula, my work would be much further along."

Zeemat cowered in his chair, intimidated by Gerra's force of conviction. He swallowed hard, his throat dry like it had been in the Nevada desert.

"Tell me about your work," Zeemat said, hoping to change the subject.

"Have you asked yourself why we would even want to connect our Torkiyan people to these miserable humans?" Gerra asked, inspecting Zeemat's reaction.

"Of course we want to connect," Zeemat replied. "That's the whole reason we're here!"

"Connecting our worlds, yes, but connecting our peoples? Now that you're here, after how they treated you, after seeing how they behave, do you still think we could use these humans?"

"What are you saying?" Zeemat asked, with a crackle of color in his eyes transmitting his confusion.

"We can't work with them!" Gerra proclaimed. "They're too volatile, unpredictable. They're prone to anger and hostility. They destroy themselves. They are not of one mind."

Zeemat sat motionless as Gerra continued to rave.

"I know Earth has copper," she said. "And I also know we can't use these humans the way they are." She pounded her fist on the table again. "But maybe we could use them if they were . . . different. And that's the nature of my work."

Gerra stood up and paced back and forth within the confines of the small room, speaking with an animated voice and broad gestures, like a roaring, agitated tiger about to strike out after its prey.

"If you study human history, you learn that humans created many successful civilizations and societies, but none of them lasted. None of them became the one true human civilization. They all rose and fell. The simple reason is that humans haven't evolved. They've done the opposite—they've devolved. They remain trapped in their primitive way of thinking, focused on self-survival or the survival of their particular tribe, not of the entire species."

"I've seen them work together as a group, accomplishing complicated tasks," Zeemat countered.

Gerra shot Zeemat an angry look. "You can't deny it. There are too many examples of violence in their history and at this exact moment. Too many examples of humans hurting one another. How can we control a species like that?"

Zeemat understood her logic but didn't share Gerra's view.

"I've met several good humans, and one in particular," he said.

"*Grrk!* You sound like one of *them!*" Gerra shouted, chiding Zeemat with guttural *clicks* and harsh *buzzes*.

Zeemat remembered the years of abuse he'd endured. Yet he still didn't feel as anti-human as Gerra did. He had strong feelings for Deltare, and he remembered how he'd felt when he saw Dooley die.

"They know how species survive—the universal concept of 'survival of the fittest,'" Zeemat argued. "And they've been successful. They colonized the entire planet. Their population grows. Maybe their behavior is exactly what it should be."

"We can't work with them!" Gerra interrupted. "We aren't compatible. If we're ever to connect our worlds, something has to change."

"And what might that be?" Zeemat asked. He suspected Gerra had an answer. She was the Science Officer of Mission 50 after all, one of the brightest scientific minds of her generation. She was an expert at identifying problems and finding solutions.

"*They* have to change," Gerra said. She picked up the pile of human-brain drawings and turned to Zeemat. "Follow me," she said. "I'll show you my work."

FIFTY-SIX

SAME BUT DIFFERENT

GERRA LED ZEEMAT to the barn. She inserted a key into the sturdy lock holding together the heavy chains on the outside door.

As soon as Gerra opened the door, Zeemat heard the muffled sound of a man screaming.

"What is that?" Zeemat asked.

Gerra escorted Zeemat down a wide hallway, passing a row of cow stalls along the way. The stalls were dirty and emanated a foul stench, like food gone bad. Two of the stalls had fresh hay on the floor and chains with shackles attached to the wall. They kept walking until they reached the center of the barn, stopping at a large metal door.

"This was once a refrigerated room. I like it because it has no windows and is nearly soundproof," Gerra said. She worked the lever to open the heavy door. Instantly, the screams grew louder. Once inside, Gerra turned on a bright dome-shaped light on a mechanical arm positioned over a wild-eyed man strapped to a gurney in the center of the room, struggling violently against his restraints. A metal halo wrapped around the man's head, preventing any movement. The halo was secured to his skull with screws.

"Welcome to my research laboratory," Gerra said, raising an eyebrow and beaming with pride. Zeemat was speechless.

"After my recovery in Roswell, I disposed of my human hosts and wandered the area for a while. My options were limited. I concluded that the best way to serve my mission was to learn more about these humans—how they think and behave, and I soon realized they are deeply flawed. They are not at all ready to accept Torkiyan Knowledge, Wisdom, and Truth. Unlike you, I couldn't advance their technology. So I decided that my job, difficult as it may be, was to help humans evolve to a point we can use them."

The man in the gurney continued to scream for help, struggling violently against the heavy straps that bound him. As Gerra continued talking, she walked over to the man and placed a cloth gag inside his mouth, holding it in place with a length of duct tape.

"The first thing I did in Roswell was to study their behavior and the workings of their brains. I practiced certain techniques on local cows. Then I gathered my first human specimens and got to work.

"As you might suspect, my first efforts failed, but step by step, I discovered the areas of the human brain that changed their behavior. I improved it and released several of those first specimens back into the wild. In retrospect, that was premature. They didn't function like I had hoped, and I exposed my presence. I became a target. They nearly caught me, and I had to change locations several times. Finally, I realized I had to leave the area and reestablish myself somewhere farther away. At about that time, I learned the humans had started a space program in Florida. So I left the Roswell area and settled here, so I could continue my work and keep an eye on the space program, like they'd instructed us at the Academy." Gerra seemed pleased at the retelling of her story. Zeemat was stunned, bewildered by how their common missions had taken such different tracks.

"Even though I hate this miserable planet, this area has proven to be an outstanding location for my work, and I've gotten better at identifying subjects. There's an endless supply of Mexican migrant workers and Cuban refugees around here. No one seems to care if they disappear. My work has proceeded without interruption."

Gerra was still standing over the struggling man. She pointed to a mark on his head. "I am using this primitive stereotactic equipment to place pinpoint lesions in specific parts of their brains. That's not exactly what I want to do. I would prefer to change things at the genetic level, so they can pass characteristics on to their offspring, but they don't have the genetic technology yet, and I don't have a Trangula. When I do, I plan not only to diminish certain functions but also to enhance certain others. And I will do exactly that someday, but for now, I have to start somewhere."

"So you're hurting these humans, placing targeted lesions in their brains, for what you believe is the greater good?" Zeemat was trying to wrap his mind around Gerra's concept.

Gerra scoffed at his use of the word "hurting."

"All progress requires hard work and suffering," Gerra replied, quoting ancient Torkiyan wisdom. "It's for their own good and the good of this planet."

"Yes, but the suffering is theirs alone, not yours." Zeemat bore a questioning look on his face, and it irritated Gerra.

"Of course it's *their* suffering. This is *their* problem, of their own making. Either these few will suffer now, or the entire human species will suffer until the day they destroy themselves and their planet along the way."

"You know we are more advanced than they are, and you believe you are wise enough to change their essential being," Zeemat said.

"Exactly. Their genetic makeup is changing anyway, by the random forces of mutation and by infestation of viral particles. It's created a wide diversity in their species that promotes tribal behavior, which no longer serves the purpose of 'survival of the fittest.' Quite the opposite—they're on a path of self-destruction. So what do you think is better—random mutations and viral infestations of their genetic code, or the purification and improvement of their genome by an agent of superior Knowledge, Wisdom, and Truth?"

Zeemat remained silent as he pondered Gerra's rationale.

"I'll demonstrate," Gerra said. While she spoke, she manipulated the stereotactic equipment to position a fine drill at a precise point on the human's head. The drill was attached to a complicated set of levers and mechanical arms. The man's eyes opened wide with terror.

"This apparatus allows me to reproduce identical lesions on different subjects," she explained.

Gerra turned on the drill. The man struggled even more violently, but his head remained motionless inside the metal halo and its attachments. Gerra brought the screeching drill up against the man's head and pressed in. The man's screams were muffled by the gag in his mouth. The duct tape held firm.

Once the drill pierced the entire thickness of the skull, Gerra felt the resistance give way. She stopped and removed the drill. Then she passed a thin wire through the tiny hole in the skull to a predefined depth within the man's brain. Tears rolled down his cheeks.

"Now that the wire is in the proper depth and position," Gerra explained to Zeemat, "all I do is give it a small jolt, and this part is done!" She closed her eyes and focused energy into her hand and fingers holding the end of the wire. She grunted and a small electric charge from her fingers sizzled through the wire and into the man's brain. He remained awake while his body suddenly relaxed and went limp.

"*Zzzt.* What just happened?" Zeemat asked.

"The subject is no longer resisting. I found a single site in the frontal lobe that accomplishes this. At first, it took me several jolts in different spots to achieve this result. Now I can consistently reproduce this effect with just one jolt to one spot." Zeemat noticed how proud Gerra was to demonstrate her accomplishments.

"So what now?"

"Now we jolt another spot in its brain, in an area they call the hippocampus. After that, it won't remember any of the things that happened here." She repositioned the drill and repeated the same maneuvers.

Zeemat nodded, trying his best to hide his horror, while memories of the miserable, conquered Senechians flooded his brain.

"And finally, we jolt several other brain locations, spots which have taken me years to identify. These will render the subject more compliant, more willing to follow orders."

"Will he be able to follow his own path?" Zeemat asked.

"To a degree," Gerra responded. "It's been difficult to find just the right combination of lesions to allow them a certain degree of free will and self-direction, while increasing their willingness to follow orders and assume a group mentality."

"Do you think you're on the right track with your approach?"

Gerra snapped her head around to look carefully at Zeemat's face, trying to determine the intention of his inquiry.

"Do you disagree with what I'm doing to these humans?" Gerra asked.

"I didn't say that," Zeemat responded. "I just wonder if this approach can ever give you the results you envision."

"Ah. Then that's an astute question. No, I don't think this is enough. I need to not only inhibit certain areas, as I am doing with targeted lesions, but to also stimulate certain others, which I will eventually do with implanted generators."

"Very creative," Zeemat said. He certainly disagreed with what Gerra was doing, but he didn't want to tell her so. He wanted to get a precise idea of the entirety of her plan.

"For now, I'm just identifying the areas that need to change. After that, the bigger job will be to alter the human genetic code, so this same effect can be passed on to subsequent generations of humans. We'll have to wait years for humans to develop that genetic technology, or for one of our ships to arrive with an intact Trangula. But I'm laying the groundwork now."

"I understand," Zeemat nodded, clenching his teeth as he tried to maintain control over his words. "Have you made any progress with the stimulators?"

"I needed a way to track the specimens once I released them back into the wild. I devised a simple radio-frequency transmitter that I implanted into their bodies to monitor them from a certain distance. I'm now developing a network of receivers so I can track their movements over a wider area. I plan to adapt that technology to use those devices as stimulators for certain spots within their brains. That's the next step."

"Unbelievable—the things you've done," Zeemat remarked.

Gerra flashed a half smile of Torkiyan pride. Zeemat could see that her creativity and resourcefulness knew no bounds, and he could almost taste the passion she had for her work. In a strange way, he was impressed by her Torkiyan determination. But then he thought of Deltare—and he couldn't imagine losing the essence of who she was, losing her humanity.

Gerra continued. "I've been implanting the tiny tracking devices in their perirectal tissues. It's unlikely other humans would ever think to look there. I can show you that procedure later," she said, pointing to a different set of tools on a table across the room.

Zeemat looked over to Gerra's "specimen," now resting peacefully on the table, awake and alert, with wires still protruding from his brain. He removed the gag from the man's mouth, and the man didn't squirm or scream, his eyes staring ahead vacantly.

"Do you plan to change all the humans, or to leave some of them as they are?" Zeemat inquired.

"Once we have altered the genetic code of enough humans, the original ones who remain won't be needed. They would only cause problems," Gerra replied. "When one of our ships arrives intact, I'll use its Trangula to speed up my work, and we can start reducing the human population."

Zeemat trembled inside.

"Now let me show you some results." Gerra walked away from the human, leaving him strapped, haloed, wired, ungagged, and cooperative.

They stepped out through the cold room's back door and entered another large stall area on the other side of the barn. These stalls were spotlessly clean. Zeemat stopped in his tracks, surprised to see two human beings plodding out of a stall at the far end of the barn. One had a broom in hand, the other a rag. They had bandages on their heads, one of them slightly bloody. Zeemat looked to Gerra, who didn't look surprised. She observed the behavior of her specimens, now with a full smile spread across her face.

"Who are they?" Zeemat asked. "What are they doing?"

"They're doing what I instructed them to do," Gerra replied. "I keep the subjects here until they have completely healed. I keep them fed, clean, warm, and dry. They stay here until they've learned a useful behavior. Some of them are even learning several behaviors! If I'm successful, they'll be ready to serve our fellow Torkiyans of future missions."

Zeemat stood openmouthed, shocked.

Gerra beamed, understanding Zeemat's look of surprise as a compliment, and she chimed a few *gurgles* of Torkiyan delight. She never imagined or hoped she would ever share her work with anyone.

She looked closer at Zeemat, gazing deep into his familiar eyes and studying the complex expressions written on his face. Suddenly she became concerned, uncertain whether she was seeing awareness and admiration or disgust and disdain. Gerra watched as Zeemat's eyes relaxed into a pinkish orange, his frown easing into a sort of smile. She came to the satisfied conclusion that Zeemat approved.

Zeemat felt like he just passed the most difficult test of his life, successfully hiding his disloyal feelings. "Excellent work, Gerra," he lied. But he couldn't stop thinking about Deltare, and he worried about his new world, which he had just begun to explore and to love. He hadn't even started painting again yet, and now he felt like all his plans were at risk.

Zeemat felt as if two versions of himself were fighting within. He and Gerra were fellow Torkiyans and fellow space travelers with a common mission, but he completely disagreed with what she was doing, and he hated himself for feeling a strong chemical attraction to her. He took a few steps back to separate himself from her dominant aroma. He didn't underestimate Gerra's skill, determination, and creative accomplishments—quite the opposite—he respected and even admired them, but he feared them. He knew she was wrong about the humans, and she was wrong to try to change them.

Gathering all the courage he could muster, Zeemat fought against her chemical attraction and against his communal instinct, which felt akin to trying to tear out his beating Torkiyan heart. He felt impossibly torn—he was Torkiyan, and he loved what he'd found on planet Earth. Right now, those things were not compatible, and he felt lost in a fog of confusion. He had to buy time to try to figure things out.

He glanced at the helpless man on the table and hid his feelings of pity. He shook his head to try to clear his mind, took a deep breath, and looked Gerra in the eyes.

"How can I help?" he said, rolling up his sleeves.

FIFTY-SEVEN

HELP IS ON THE WAY

ZEEMAT FELT TRAPPED—again. His mind felt lost in a dream much of the time, especially when Gerra was near. The loss of control felt like a living nightmare. She acquired new specimens, and he did everything he could to take good care of them while they were held in the stalls before Gerra used them in the lab. He wanted to help them escape, but Gerra kept a watchful eye, and only she had the keys to all the locks. He tried in subtle ways to change her mind, to alter the direction of her work, but Gerra was single-minded and determined, like a good Torkiyan. There was nothing Zeemat could say to change her mind.

Zeemat gravitated to the thing that always had brought him joy and peace—painting. Gerra helped him obtain some paints, canvas boards, and drawing pads, and he produced images of the farm and the surrounding lands, of the house and barn, of the humans in their stalls, and of Gerra's lab.

"Painting is a waste of time," Gerra told Zeemat, almost scolding. Though irritated, she tolerated his painting, as it somehow seemed to calm him. "Why haven't you painted my final results?" she asked.

But Zeemat couldn't get himself to draw the humans after Gerra had performed her procedures on them. They were somehow not human anymore, and they didn't belong in the landscape he wanted to draw.

He continued to witness every sunrise and sunset. The colors were there, but the joy he'd once felt had diminished. He gazed into the sky at night. When there were no clouds, he could make out the faint glow of Torkiya's star in the northern sky. He pictured his planet in orbit around it—fifty light-years away but somehow it still kept a hold on him. He recalled memories of home, culminating in the launch of Mission 51. That was now old history, and he had to assume Mission 52 was on its way, somewhere in space at that very moment, and that gave him an idea.

One day over breakfast, while Gerra worked on the laboratory notes from her previous session, Zeemat said, "I'm going to try to contact the Mission 52 ship."

"How do you plan to manage that?" Gerra replied without looking up from her work.

"I have ideas," he said. "First I'll build a communication tower. Then I'll need one of your transmitter devices."

Gerra looked up to gauge Zeemat's enthusiasm for the project. It was the first time he'd come up with something she thought might be useful. She nodded her approval.

Over the following weeks, Zeemat figured out how to prepare his communication setup. He installed the tallest TV antenna they could find in a clear open area in the field behind the barn. He installed the transmitter at the top. The transmitter was too weak to transmit through the Earth's atmosphere and send messages into deep space, so he and Gerra procured weather balloons capable of reaching the upper atmosphere, like he had learned from Lyman Spitzer during his consultations at Area 51. He secured the needed electronics to a cardboard box on the balloon's harness. He tuned the equipment to relay information through the balloon by using the electronics on the antenna, and to a receiver-transmitter he controlled on the ground.

When everything was set, he waited for a clear day with little to no wind, and when that day came in early June of 1964, he filled the balloon with helium gas and released it into the air.

The balloon gained altitude and had soon left his sight. Over the next hour, as the balloon reached the stratosphere, it transmitted the messages Zeemat was sending from the ground. The messages were sent in all directions since Zeemat hadn't yet figured out how to focus them in a specific direction toward Torkiya. But at least the messages were unimpeded by the static of Earth's atmosphere. The equipment on the balloon sent confirmation back to Zeemat's receiver on the ground. Less than an hour later, the communication went silent and Zeemat knew the balloon had burst—the equipment would fall to the ground, lost. He planned to repeat the entire process at regular intervals in hopes of someday receiving a reply from the ship of Mission 52.

Several weeks and several balloons later, that day came and Zeemat raced to the barn.

"Gerra! Gerra!" he screamed, short of breath after his all-out sprint, excited as a young horse finding his legs.

She furrowed her brow, studying Zeemat.

"I got it—a response from Mission 52!"

Gerra snapped to attention and stopped what she was doing as Zeemat read the transcript, the notepaper shaking in his hands.

"This is from their ship's Synthetic Soul—'*ZZZT*. Message received! I am thrilled to hear from you, Zeemat of Mission 51. Thank you for your comments and the information regarding your location and Cerulea's gravitational force. I have adjusted the landing formulas. We are at this moment decelerating as we approach Cerulea's star system. I will soon retrieve the crew from cryopreservation. You'll be pleased to know I carry a special crew memb—'"

The communication had been lost at that point, as the weather balloon burst and the electronics failed. But Zeemat was ecstatic. His message had been received—with not only the location and gravitation information but also his comments about Cerulea's people being friendly and capable of cooperating in peace with Torkiyans. There would be no need to genetically alter and dominate them. He hadn't told Gerra about that part. He was certain she would disapprove, but he felt hopeful he would get the support he needed from the crew of Mission 52.

Zeemat was thrilled to share the moment with Gerra, but in his heart, he wished he was sharing the joy with his best friend on Earth, Linda Deltare. Then he had a flash of a thought—he imagined himself and Linda lying side by side in their own cryo beds on the Mission 52 ship, fulfilling the ancient promises and bringing the first Cerulean treasures back home to Torkiya. He shook his head and drove that idea out of his mind.

FIFTY-EIGHT

ZEEMAT AND GERRA

A MONTH LATER, in mid-July, Zeemat looked out the window and squinted his eyes, a new habit he'd formed—anxiously looking for movement in the distant sky.

He figured the arrival of Mission 52 would be imminent, now that they were in Cerulea's star system. He grew increasingly anxious about it with each passing day, feeling as if time had slowed down.

Meanwhile, he continued to keep an eye on Gerra and the humans. He was leery of her intelligence, strength, and resourcefulness, and he hoped desperately for moral support from Mission 52—he needed it. He continued to fight the strong chemical attraction he felt whenever she was near. It hit him like a violent dizziness that tried to shake his will away. He wondered if she felt the same way, but she certainly hadn't acted like it.

Gerra was working on the laboratory's gurney and lights, setting things up for the next subject, and facing away from Zeemat when he entered the barn and the lab to check on the humans.

"I've been thinking of our mission to establish a colony here on Earth," he said. "Why haven't we mated?" His words were devoid of feelings, in typical Torkiyan fashion. He preferred the way human men and women interacted on TV, with passion and emotion. Though he sensed Gerra's aroma, he thought of the kiss he'd shared with Linda at the train station.

"Yes," she replied, not looking away from her work. "I've thought about it since you arrived. I was to mate with Captain Agos, but when he died, I put that part of the mission out of my mind. Then when I met you, I naturally assumed we would become a mating pair someday, since we're the only ones here."

"So why haven't we?"

Gerra stopped what she was doing and turned her head to meet Zeemat's gaze. She analyzed him for a moment. "Because I'm not sure about you."

Zeemat didn't respond, afraid to give anything away about how he really felt.

She turned her whole body to face him. "You have a sympathy for these humans, and I sense you're anxious about the arrival of our people, almost as if you dread it. You should be thrilled with anticipation."

Zeemat tried to keep a straight face, but the color of his eyes wavered erratically.

"And I see what you draw and paint," she continued. "Things about this planet—places you've seen and humans you've met, yet still no drawings to document the results of my work."

"We see different things," he admitted.

Gerra ignored his comment. "And I see how you treat our captives—with excessive care. They're just human animals."

Zeemat couldn't help but bristle at the comment. "*Zzzt.* I see something more in them. We may be smarter and stronger, but we're similar in more ways than you think. We could make them our allies, not our enemies."

Gerra growled and reddened her eyes into a focused glare. "*Grrk.* I bet you're talking about one human in particular."

An image of Linda flashed through his mind—the look on her face the last time he saw her, the worry for his safety, the tears in her eyes.

"But she's not Torkiyan, like you are," he said.

"Exactly, yet you talk about her as if she means something to you, so that's why I haven't mated with you. And when you told me Mission 52 was on the way, I put any idea of our mating on hold. I want to see my options."

"But I do feel attracted to you," Zeemat confessed, angry at himself for feeling that way, but somehow relieved for having admitted it.

"Then make up your mind!"

He eyed his beautiful and remarkable fellow Torkiyan, forcibly exhaling. Could she not see he had already decided?

FIFTY-NINE

MISSION 52

TWO MONTHS LATER, in August of 1964, a fast-moving object broke through the upper atmosphere. Mission 52 dropped out of orbit and managed a successful descent through Earth's powerful gravity. The hot, glowing ship was named Tamarz, after the Torkiyan god of war. It arrived in the dead of night and settled just over the water's surface in the middle of the Atlantic Ocean, due east from Cocoa, Florida. At the same time, Hurricane Cleo was in full force just to the south of their position. Tamarz teetered and swayed as Cleo's wild winds swirled around them.

All four crew members had survived the long journey in cryo and the rough deceleration through Earth's gravity. Now that they had arrived, their captain wasted no time in barking out his orders.

"*Zzzt.* Check all systems and prepare yourselves," he said. "Keep the cloaking shield at full power."

"Yes, Captain Yonek," the ship's Synthetic Soul responded in her calm and soothing voice.

Tamarz and the crew confirmed all systems were intact, and they prepared themselves for battle, uncertain of what was to come.

"Engines, computers, and shock-wave generator at full capacity," First Officer Maneg announced. He was a large, strong Torkiyan male, with a permanent scowl etched upon his brutish face.

"Life systems functional," Science Officer Lykle said, her efficient fingers and hands flying through the computer's interface, snapping sparks of electricity as they moved through the controls on the translucent image in the air in front of her.

"Captain Yonek, may I have your destination orders?" Tamarz politely inquired.

"Proceed to the coordinates you received from Zeemat," Yonek said. He squinted out the windows, trying in vain to get a glimpse of anything through the dark, windy storm in the middle of the ocean. "I want to see my son."

Tamarz ignited her small positional engines and pierced the stormy skies toward the Florida coast, silent and invisible.

Yonek kept his gaze fixed straight ahead until the Florida coast shadowed into view. He sat up straight and leaned forward to get a better look out the ship's small windows. He saw a flicker of lights in the distance. His scanners identified them as a small group of native habitations.

"Prepare the shock-wave generator," Yonek commanded.

"Shock wave ready and awaiting your orders," Navigator and Chief Engineer Nygni said. Her body posture was fierce, her focus intense, as she managed Tamarz's position with one hand, ready to deploy the ship's weapon with the other. Her uniform had the insignia of an experienced fighter pilot.

They continued in a straight line toward Zeemat's coordinates. When they flew over the lights of the small community that had evacuated in advance of the hurricane, Yonek ordered its destruction. "Fire!" he said.

Nygni fired a medium-beam shock wave over the community. A low *hum* developed into a loud, deepening *growl*. The buildings and streets trembled and shook until they collapsed into a fine rubble. Broken water mains erupted with tall geysers of water, and ruptured gas pipes exploded into flames, leaving the tiny community utterly demolished.

When they were satisfied that the destruction was complete, they continued. A short way inland, they observed a string of streetlights defining a road immediately below them. They crossed over the road as a single car was passing by, its headlights illuminating the road for a short distance ahead. Nygni again placed her hand on the shock-wave trigger and looked to Yonek for direction. Yonek nodded. The engineer tapped the trigger button, sending a narrow shock-wave beam focused directly onto the passing car. The car and the road beneath it vibrated wildly for an instant before disintegrating in an explosion.

The ship continued toward the coordinates Zeemat had provided, which led them to the pasture behind Gerra's barn. They arrived at sunrise, just as Zeemat was looking out the breakfast-room window, a glass of orange juice in hand.

Zeemat dropped the glass and stood motionless as the spinning ship dug its way into the topsoil, leaving only a small part of itself exposed. He remained semi-paralyzed, with an unchewed piece of toast hanging from his mouth, watching four Torkiyan soldiers exit from the top hatch, weapons in hand. Acting as the leader, one of them looked around, saw the barn, and waved for the others to follow him.

"*ZZZT.* GERRA! GERRA!" Zeemat finally managed to yell out. He'd known this moment would be inevitable, but now that it was here, he didn't know if he wanted it, or what to do. He quickly straightened the papers on the kitchen table and threw some dirty dishes into the sink, as if that mattered.

Gerra came running. "*Zzzt.* What's going on?" she asked, echoing the tone of alarm she'd heard in Zeemat's voice.

Zeemat pointed out the window. "They're here!"

Gerra saw the four soldiers coming and the small protrusion in the pasture, knowing with certainty what lay hidden beneath. A smile beamed across her face, and she let out a squeal.

"They're here! Nothing can stop us now!" she said, shaking Zeemat by the shoulders.

Zeemat gasped as the soldiers neared the farmhouse and he could make out their facial features. Suddenly, a shock wave of dizziness overwhelmed him. His legs buckled and he almost fell before steeling himself against the windowsill. A whisper wheezed from his mouth.

"Father?"

SIXTY

TWO WORLDS

GERRA HEARD ZEEMAT'S whisper and noticed the color drain from his face.

"What? One of them is your father?" At first, she seemed to be as shocked as Zeemat, but then she broke into a broad smile. "Excellent!"

Gerra dashed out of the house to meet the new arrivals as they emerged from the field into the backyard, still out of sight of any potential passersby. "*Zzzt*. Welcome, Torkiyans!" she shouted.

Yonek and the others instinctively raised their weapons, not having expected this sort of welcome, but they quickly lowered them as they confirmed that Gerra was indeed Torkiyan.

"This is unexpected," Yonek said. "Explain yourself," he commanded.

"I'm Gerra, Science Officer of Mission 50. I'm here with Zeemat from Mission 51. And you are his father?"

As if on cue, Zeemat stepped out of the house and approached the group with caution, twitching a confused and nervous smile.

"Father?" Zeemat said.

Yonek dropped his weapon on the ground and raced toward Zeemat. After a brief two-handed handshake, Yonek wrapped his son in a long, tight embrace.

"My son . . ." he said. He held Zeemat by the shoulders at arms' length and inspected him up and down, noticing his healthy, suntanned skin and the bulging muscles strengthened by Earth's gravity. "You survived! You look well."

"And you look... the same as when I last saw you," Zeemat said, his eyes emitting a puzzled wave of random colors.

"I'm the same age as when you left Torkiya," Yonek said. "Soon after you left, I had them place me in cryo until the day came for Mission 52. I couldn't live without knowing you had either found your strength or died trying."

Crazy as that was, Zeemat understood his father's reasoning and the drastic measures he had taken. The family legacy of military warriors had always been the most important thing to him, and Zeemat had always disappointed.

"What about mother?" Zeemat asked. "You left her behind?"

"She didn't feel the same way I did. She always trusted in your success. So we said our goodbyes."

Zeemat fought back a tear as he thought of his mother and felt the echo of her love beyond the vast expanse of space and time.

"All of you, come inside," Gerra said. "We've been expecting your arrival. There's so much to discuss."

The crew of Mission 52 marched behind Gerra's bouncing steps, with weapons still at the ready, looking in all directions, taking in their first sights of this alien planet.

Gerra and Zeemat made their guests comfortable while Yonek barraged them with nonstop questions. Zeemat gave his father details about how he had spent his years on planet Earth.

"So you know there is copper, and you helped improve their technology. That is good, Zeemat. You make Torkiya proud," Yonek said.

"The problem is," Gerra interrupted, "that these humans can never be our partners in space commerce, and they would be useless as slaves the way they are. They are impulsive and unpredictable. They fight among themselves and are self-destructive. That's why I focused my mission on changing them as a species, so they can at least be of some service."

"What's your plan?" Yonek asked, intrigued by Gerra's observations.

"My plan is to alter their genetics, to render them docile and compliant, to have them think as a group and follow orders. I've already made progress in that direction. All I needed was the ability to work with their genetic code, but they don't have that knowledge and technology . . . and I *didn't* have a Trangula." Gerra flashed a sinister smile, looking in the direction of the buried spaceship.

"And now you do," Yonek said.

"Now I have everything I need to complete my work. The new humans will benefit from our Knowledge, Wisdom, and Truth—and we will benefit from them."

"And what about the humans who are not changed?" Yonek inquired.

"We must destroy them," Gerra said, cold.

Yonek nodded.

"The ship is armed," Yonek said. "On our way here, a micro-shock was enough to destroy one of their vehicles. A medium shock wave eradicated a small community. They showed no defense. A larger pulse will destroy a much larger area."

Gerra looked thrilled.

Yonek glanced over to Zeemat. He was pleased with his son's efforts, but he was much more in tune with Gerra's ideas. "Tell me more about your work," Yonek said to her.

Gerra was excited to describe her work in the human research lab. She paced the floor, elaborating her story with sweeping gestures with her arms and hands. When she finished, Yonek emitted satisfied clicking sounds and vigorously nodded his approval. He liked her enthusiasm.

"Well done, soldier," he said.

Gerra stood up military straight, enjoying the compliment from a superior officer.

"I need access to your Trangula," she said.

"And you shall have it," Yonek replied.

Zeemat tried to hide it, but the flow of their conversation alarmed him. The support he'd hoped to get from Mission 52 had moved in the opposite direction. As his hope for the future evaporated, he realized in horror that the humans had no idea what danger they were in. Their lives were doomed. Gerra's plan would destroy their very nature. He had to do something!

"*Zzzt.* Father," Zeemat interrupted. "These humans can cooperate with us the way they are. There's no need to alter them."

Gerra shot him a look of disbelief, which morphed quickly into one of anger.

"*Zzzt.* I've had my doubts about you, and now you confirm them in front of your own father! You have a weakness for these humans," Gerra shouted at him.

She turned toward Yonek and added, "He's in love with a human female."

Yonek's eyes darted back and forth between Gerra and his son, analyzing her accusation, the weight of their stories, and their motivations. He came to the conclusion that Gerra was right, and that his son continued to be a deep disappointment.

Yonek pounded his fists on the table. "*Grrk!* Fifty-two missions! Many good Torkiyans paid a great price for us to be here at this moment, and we are here to stay! Change is inevitable for this planet and its people. These humans will either change, submit, or die—like the Senechians."

He glared at Zeemat with a face of disgust. "I sense Gerra has been faithful to her mission. I'm disappointed to see that you are still a lesser Torkiyan."

Zeemat's eyes darkened into a shameful purple. More than that, he felt defeated, and his anxiety was so strong he felt he might explode. How could he stop such a formidable force? People of his own kind—especially his own father, a renowned Torkiyan warrior. And he realized they were right. Zeemat no longer felt like a pure Torkiyan. He felt he was also a citizen of the planet Earth. And yes, he loved Linda Deltare.

Zeemat drooped his shoulders and bowed his head in submission. The worst of his fears had come. Now he would have to fight for his chance at a life of peace and freedom on planet Earth, and for Linda, and he would either live or die, win or lose in the fight.

While the others discussed their plans, Zeemat began to formulate a plan of his own, and it felt good. He felt as if he'd discovered a hidden room in his mind, filled with useful and valuable things.

SIXTY-ONE

ORLANDO

GERRA ARRANGED SLEEPING quarters for the new arrivals in the clean part of the barn. One of them always stayed with the ship to keep watch and guard the Trangula, the key to their technological superiority and dominance. Gerra made a bed for herself in the barn along with the others, a clear statement of her commitment to the group and her loyalty to Torkiya.

Zeemat told them he would stay in the farmhouse to guard it, though he had other plans.

That night, once he saw the lights turn off in the barn, Zeemat hurried to pack his things in the military duffel Linda had given him six months earlier. He extinguished the lights inside the house, grabbed his bag, and snuck out. Shuddering at every crunching step, he tiptoed across the gravel parking area to the Jeep and threw the bag into the back seat. After slowly opening the squeaky door, he put the transmission into neutral and pushed the car with the driver's door open, turning the steering wheel right and left to keep the Jeep aimed in the proper direction, all the way down the long driveway to the paved road. When he got to the road, he jumped inside, turned on the ignition, making his escape.

It didn't matter how far he went. What mattered was making a plan and recruiting the help he needed. He needed Linda.

Zeemat left Cocoa on State Road 520 and made his way northwest. He found a small motel with a flashing "Open" sign as he approached Orlando, so he pulled in. He parked the Jeep in the back, out of sight of passing traffic, and under a stand of trees, out of sight of a searching spaceship.

Once in his room, he sat at a small desk to compose the telegram he would send the following morning as soon as the Western Union office opened.

He tried to get some rest, dozing on and off for a few hours, but he was unable to fall into a deep sleep, so he gave up. Instead, he showered, dressed, and drove to the telegram office at the break of dawn. When it opened, he was first in line.

As he had discussed with Deltare before their escape from Area 51, he sent her a telegram in care of the Pastor of Mission Dolores in San Francisco. After that, he went to a nearby grocery store to stock up on a supply of food and drink. He returned to his motel room and sat by the phone to wait for Deltare's call, meanwhile drawing a series of pictures and maps of the farm, illustrating his battle plan.

SIXTY-TWO

SAN FRANCISCO

LINDA DELTARE STOOD on the balcony of her new house on Scott Street overlooking the San Francisco Bay in the distance. Her stylish bob waved in the gentle breeze. She looked beyond Alcatraz and Angel Island, trying to picture the vineyards she planned to purchase in Napa Valley farther north. A sad smile settled on her face as she swirled the luscious cabernet in her wine glass and took a whiff of its fine aroma before taking a sip.

She had settled into a two-story house in fashionable Pacific Heights, which she would decorate with beautiful, expensive things, none of which would replace the joy she'd felt when she was with Zeemat. She had accomplished much in the short time since leaving Area 51, but she felt desperately lonely, and she worried about Zeemat all the time. She assumed the government was still searching for them, so she remained anonymous and stayed away from people as much as possible.

Her only human contacts were her driver, her pilot, her personal trainers, and the businessmen who craved her dwindling supply of Zeemat's notes—the information that had made her filthy rich.

Thoughts swirled in her mind like the cabernet in her glass: *What good is all this if there's no one to share it with? Where's Mat right now? What's he doing? Is he safe?*

To distract herself, she considered making an extra appointment with her martial arts trainer, or maybe she would spend more time at the shooting range. If the CIA or the military found her, she wouldn't go down without a fight. But a loud, irritating telephone ring startled her out of her thoughts, pulling her from the view of the bay. She narrowed her eyes. She hadn't expected any calls, so she picked up the phone with some trepidation.

"Hello?"

"Hello. This is Father Perón, the Pastor at Mission Dolores. Is this Miss Judy Barton?" the priest asked.

Deltare nearly dropped her glass of wine. She recognized the voice on the other end and the alias she had used with him. The priest was to call for only one thing—if he ever received a telegram addressed to her.

"Yes, Father. This is Judy Barton."

"I have a telegram," he said.

"Don't move. I'll be right there," Deltare said, sounding more forceful than she would have liked.

She slammed the phone down and picked it right back up. She dialed her driver. "I need to go somewhere. Now!" she shouted.

She checked herself in the dresser mirror, grabbed her purse and sunglasses, and raced downstairs. By the time she walked outside, the driver was pulling up with her Mercedes. He came to a quick stop, got out of the car, and opened the back door for her.

"To Mission Dolores, as fast as possible," she said as she hurried into her seat.

The car sped down Fillmore and worked its way to the old Spanish mission. They screeched to a stop in front of the mission's ancient church, and Deltare dashed out of the car. After searching the premises, she found Father Perón in the adjacent cemetery, and he held out an envelope as she rushed to meet him.

"Thank you, Father," Deltare said, breathing hard. "This is important."

"You're welcome, Miss Barton. And we are grateful in return," he said, waving his arms around to focus attention on the cemetery itself. "The restoration is complete, thanks to your generous donations."

Deltare gave the cemetery a cursory look. It was beautiful as far as cemeteries went—a lasting monument to the lives and challenges of old. But she could only focus on the telegram.

The priest was about to say something else, but she ignored him, apologizing for her impoliteness. She inspected the envelope to confirm it had remained sealed.

"I didn't open it. I called you the moment I received it," the priest said. "As you instructed."

"Thanks again," she said over her shoulder. She was already walking away and ripping the envelope open, her anxious eyes darting over the message.

HELLO I NEED YOU NOW HURRY BRING HEAVY COPPER WIRE SALT AND EXPLOSIVES FOR SPECIAL PROJECT RUBBER GLOVES AND SUIT FOR YOURSELF HURRY NOW - - - JOHN FERGUSON ORLANDO FL 4072836706

Zeemat had used the alias they had agreed upon, and she was to call the phone number only when she arrived at her destination in case they were somehow being tracked. *Heavy wire and explosives? Rubber gloves?* Deltare wondered. She rushed through the possibilities of what it all meant. *And a suit? What kind of suit? Does he mean a rubber suit or a business suit?*

Deltare wasted no time. She made calls to several of her business connections, leaders of companies with military contracts. They would do anything she asked to ensure continued access to her knowledge of advanced technologies. She made several other phone calls before dialing the airport to arrange her flight.

"Prepare my plane," she said. "We're leaving as soon as possible."

"Destination?" Her pilot spoke in his usual calm and confident voice.

"I'll tell you when I arrive," Deltare said.

"Just trying to save time registering the flight plan, ma'am."

"No flight plan!" she exclaimed. "We can't register this one. And don't call me 'ma'am.'"

"Yes, sir, ma'am," he teased. "Transponder?"

"No . . . Completely incognito. This is the one we've been waiting for."

"Roger that. Stealth mode. The plane will be ready when you arrive," the pilot said, his voice lighting up in his signature boyish excitement, the quality that had endeared him to her when they'd met in Area 51.

She hung up the phone, hopped back into her Mercedes, and rushed to her plane at the Oakland International Airport.

She was met at the airport by several vehicles arriving simultaneously to deliver the items she'd requested from her business contacts. Some were private vehicles, and some were military. Deltare inspected the items and loaded her selections into two large military duffel bags. She instructed the pilot to load them onto the plane.

In the middle of the night, her Learjet broke through the thick San Francisco fog and made an unregistered beeline flight to Orlando, Florida.

SIXTY-THREE

CONVERGENCE

DELTARE'S PLANE MADE a rough landing at Herndon Airport in Orlando in the early morning of August 27, 1964. A riot of dark, tumultuous clouds rumbled their way through the threatening skies, an effect of the looming Hurricane Cleo that had already made landfall in Miami, leaving a wide swath of destruction in its wake—flooding, fires, millions of dollars of property damage, uprooted trees, overturned aircraft, and crop losses. It was now headed north toward Orlando, where a herald of uncertain winds buffeted Deltare's Learjet from several directions.

The plane made its way to a rental hangar that Deltare had reserved before departing from San Francisco. Once in position in the hangar, the engines spun down, the doors opened, and Deltare stepped out, standing tall at the top of the gangway steps. She was dressed in military-issue camouflage pants, a dark green T-shirt, and army boots. She had a prototype Beretta 9-mm semiautomatic pistol strapped to a holster on her right thigh. Her hair tousled in the gusty winds that snuck into the hangar from the gathering storm outside. She donned a pair of sunglasses she retrieved from one of her pant pockets. A cap served to control her wayward hair and as a disguise. She had no idea what Zeemat had in store, but if his request for supplies was any sign, they were in for a fight, and she intended to be prepared. She turned around to reach for the two large duffel bags she'd brought along, slinging one over each shoulder and marching down the jet's short gangway steps.

She looked for a phone and spotted one on the hangar's wall. There was a call she was itching to make. She spun the numbers on the rotary dial as fast as they would turn.

Zeemat answered on the first ring, listening intently without saying a word.

"Mat?" Deltare asked, surprised by the shake in her voice.

"Linda!" he replied. "I'm glad you're here! There is so much to tell you. How fast can you get here?"

"Give me an address," Deltare said. She jotted it down in a small notebook she pulled out from her shirt pocket. "I'll be there in a few minutes," she said, and hung up the phone.

Just outside the hangar, a driver stood by a parked limo. He was waiting for Deltare as she had arranged. Before jumping in, Deltare paid the driver three times what they had agreed upon. She looked the man in the eye and said, "No word about any of this to anyone—ever! Is that clear?"

The driver tried to speak, but the words choked in his throat. With one look at Deltare's gun and her threatening expression, he simply nodded, unable to hide the fear in his face. He opened the door, helped her with the bags, and closed the door behind her after she stepped in. When he was sitting behind the wheel, Deltare gave him an address, and he remained silent the rest of the way. Something was about to happen, and the less he knew about it, the better, he thought.

The limo rushed to Zeemat's location as fast as it could, with the driver weaving and dodging in and out of traffic. "Faster!" Deltare prodded.

When they arrived, Deltare threw her bags out onto the ground and pulled out another fifty dollars for the driver. She glared at him one last time, just to be sure he had gotten the message. The driver nodded again and made a zipping-up gesture with his fingers across his lips. He got back into the limo and drove away, looking into his rearview mirror, grateful to be done with that mysterious affair.

Deltare picked up the duffels and found Zeemat's motel room number. She reached up to knock on the door, but it opened wide before she could strike the first knock.

For a moment, they stared at each other, Zeemat's eyes an anxious orange, while Deltare panted heavily to catch her breath. She dropped the heavy duffels on the ground, and after a few hesitant moments, they fell into each other's arms in a desperate embrace.

Zeemat wanted to hold her forever, but he had to break off the hug. He looked quickly in all directions, pulled Deltare into the room, dragged the duffels inside, and slammed the door shut.

"What's going on?" Deltare asked, allowing her worry to finally show.

"I have a lot to say," Zeemat said. "But before I do, I want to hear about your escape, and what's happened since the last time I saw you."

Deltare also had a lot to say, but she knew this was not the time for details. "Let me just say that they haven't found me. I made it to California. I destroyed my car so it could never be found, and I settled in San Francisco. I made contact with several businessmen we met at Area 51 and sold them some of your ideas. I already had a lot of money from before, but now I'm *crazy* rich . . . I mean, *we're* crazy rich. I have a house, a fancy car with a driver, a jet plane, and I'm buying land in Napa Valley."

"Wow!" Zeemat said. He was certain all of that was impressive, though he couldn't quite picture any of it in his mind.

Deltare finished by mentioning that the technical information Zeemat had given her was almost gone, so her sales to the businessmen would soon come to an end.

"Maybe not," Zeemat said.

He wasted no time blurting out a summary of his travels to Florida, finding Gerra, the horror of her research lab, and the arrival of Mission 52. Deltare shook her head in wild-eyed, slack-jawed disbelief, listening until Zeemat had finished.

"What?" she said. "There are others like you? And a ship? Here? Now?"

"A ship with a Trangula," Zeemat said. "An *intact* Trangula—with a vast amount of Torkiyan knowledge they will use against us. They aren't here in peace. They want the planet and to destroy everyone."

"What do you mean 'everyone'?" Deltare asked.

"Everyone!" Zeemat replied. "*All* the humans. *Everyone!*"

Deltare's shoulders dropped. She could tell by Zeemat's agitation that he was serious, and the gravity of his accusations nearly bowled her over.

"So what can we do?" she asked, slowly lowering to sit on the edge of the bed.

"Here's my plan," he said, producing the pile of drawings he'd been working on—maps of the Torkiyans' location in Cocoa, details about the land around the farm, and the exact location of the farmhouse, the barn, the human captives, and the spaceship.

"First, we have to free the humans they're holding *here*," he said, pointing to a spot on the drawings. "We have to get the Trangula *here*, and then destroy the ship and the weapons."

"Weapons?" Deltare exclaimed.

"Yes, the ship carries a sound weapon that will destroy entire cities, and an antimatter device that can be used as a weapon of last resort. Antimatter is useful for our main engines, though it's unpredictable as a weapon. But my father will not hesitate to use it. He's ruthless. He's a warrior."

"Your father?" Deltare gasped. She brought her hand up to her mouth as the color drained from her face.

Zeemat smiled wistfully, pausing before he filled Deltare in on more details. He told her about his father and reminded her about how he had been such a disappointment to him back on Torkiya.

"I'm still a disappointment," he said.

"Not to me." Deltare reached for Zeemat's hands as she met his gaze and held it.

"We have to stop them," he said. "Were you able to find any of the items I requested?"

"I think so," Deltare said with a twitching, uncertain smile. She walked over to the bags on the floor and unzipped them. Zeemat's eyes widened as she revealed the contents of the bags.

"Maybe this will help," she said. First, she pulled out two backpacks that were covering the contents underneath. Then she produced large rolls of copper wire, as Zeemat had requested, and wire cutters. "You wanted explosives?" she asked. "Well, how about this?" She produced dozens of sticks of dynamite, several wired and remote detonators, and a dozen hand grenades. After that came walkie-talkies, duct tape, a bag of salt, knives, a handgun for Zeemat, and two M16 rifles with several loaded twenty-round magazines.

"I got everything I could gather quickly," she said.

Zeemat shook his head, his mouth agape. He wrapped his hand around the handle of the Beretta pistol, just like the one in Deltare's thigh holster. He aimed it in several directions, feeling the weight and balance of it in his hand. He placed his index finger on the trigger.

"Careful with that," Deltare said. "It's loaded."

Zeemat moved his finger off the trigger. "I really don't want to use this . . ." he said, handing the gun to Deltare, ". . . but teach me how it works."

Deltare showed him how to operate the handgun, then they spent the rest of the day poring over Zeemat's hand-drawn maps and plans. They filled their backpacks with everything they would need. The rest of the supplies stayed in the duffels.

The evening was short, and night came early under dark, gathering clouds. Outside, the gusty winds of the approaching storm rattled the windows, and the first meandering raindrops began to fall. They were as ready as they would ever be. Zeemat inspected the backpacks for the hundredth time, until he finally seemed satisfied. He took a deep breath and caught Linda gazing at him.

"We should try to get some rest before the big day tomorrow," he said. "But I don't think I can sleep."

Deltare looked over to the bed, then over to Zeemat. "I can't imagine sleeping right now either," she agreed.

They stared at each other for a few moments, before Deltare nodded her head toward the bed. "But maybe we can lie down and rest."

Zeemat nodded, and they took hesitant steps toward the bed.

She took off her boots and laid down first, on top of the fully made bed, with the rest of her clothes still on. Her face flushed and her heart began to race.

Zeemat did the same, and soon they were lying side by side, alternately gazing at the ceiling and at each other.

"I've actually thought about this moment many times," she confessed. "But I never imagined it quite like this."

"I missed you very much," Zeemat said, reaching over to hold her hand.

Deltare squeezed his hand hard and didn't let go. She brushed her leg against his.

"This is different from seeing you in my cell," he said.

"Yes, very different," she replied, her voice now coming in more of a whisper. She turned on her side to face him, inching closer.

He turned on his side as well, now facing her, and stroked her cheek with his other hand.

She closed her eyes and pressed her face against his palm, nuzzling it in. Almost without thinking, she brought up her free hand and rested it on his chest.

"This is nice," he said.

Deltare opened her eyes and gazed at the rainbow of soft colors waving across his eyes. "What are you feeling?" she asked.

"I'm just trying to forget everything else for a moment," he said. " Because right now I feel warm and safe. I haven't felt like this in a very long time."

With that, Deltare melted. She brought her body close to his and held his face in her hand, like he held hers with his. She swept her lips against his, closed her eyes again, and settled into a soft, lingering kiss.

Zeemat felt a wave of energy course through his body. He felt his body's charge rearrange itself somehow—to his face, his hands, his pelvis—and Deltare sensed it.

"Your body's humming," she said. "It's like a cat purring."

"I wasn't sure if I could feel this way with you," he said. "I'm so happy!"

She kissed him again, breathing harder, and then pulled away. "We have way too many clothes on," she said.

Zeemat watched as Deltare unbuttoned her shirt, tugging it off her smooth skin, and he kept watching as she slipped out of her pants. She left her underwear on as she slid under the covers.

Zeemat followed her lead and did the same.

"Oh my god," she said, her hand now exploring the bare skin of Zeemat's chest.

Zeemat did the same, feeling dizzy as his hands moved across her shoulders, her chest, the small of her back, and farther down.

She kissed him hard, and they held each other tight.

"I want to be with you," Zeemat said.

Deltare nodded.

"But this isn't the time," he added.

"I know," Deltare said, letting her breath slowly settle. "I hope we get the chance."

"It all depends on tomorrow. If we can . . ."

Deltare brought a finger up to his lips so he would stop talking. "But I'm here now," she said. "And I want to enjoy these moments if they're the last ones we might have." She kissed him gently again, letting herself melt into his strong embrace.

They kissed and held each other for hours.

Later that night, Zeemat said, "Maybe someday, our love can be more."

"Let's try to make that happen," she replied.

"I think our bodies will work together."

"We're going to try to find out." Zeemat caught her smirk in the moonlight filtering through the hotel window.

They kissed and caressed until their bodies relaxed, and they fell into a light sleep.

Meanwhile outside, the storm gathered strength and pelted the roof with thick sheets of heavy rain.

SIXTY-FOUR

ANOTHER STORM

ON THE MORNING of August 28, 1964, Zeemat and Deltare awoke to the sounds of distant rolling thunder. The wind picked up speed, and the rain pounded steadily against the thin motel roof.

They held each other tight in bed and kissed one last time, wishing they could stay that way forever—but there was no time.

"More of this to come," Mat promised, hoping that it was true.

"But first things first," Deltare said.

They bounded out of bed, dressed for battle, and loaded the backpacks and the duffel bags into the Jeep's back seat to set their plan in motion. They were already soaked in rain after rushing from the motel room to the Jeep, but they ignored the minor discomfort, knowing what lay ahead, as they headed in silence to Gerra's farm in Cocoa. Deltare checked her guns one last time, removing the safeties.

When they were about one hundred yards away from the farm, still out of direct sight, Zeemat pulled over and parked the car as far off the road as possible.

He jumped out of the car and back into the pouring rain. Strapping the backpack over his shoulders, he adjusted to the heavy weight on his back and helped Deltare don her own pack. She surprised him by how well she managed the heavy weight. She was strong.

"Ready?" he asked.

"Ready! Let's go!"

They hurried down the road toward the farm as fast as they could under their heavy loads, staying low and trying to make as little noise as possible. The rain drowned out most of the noise they made, and the poor visibility helped to conceal their approach. As they approached the mailbox at the border of the farm property, they stepped down into the drainage ditch that separated Gerra's farm from the neighbor's. Their boots squished at the bottom of the ditch, already muddied by the rain. Zeemat looked up to examine the worsening weather.

"Who cares about the weather?" Deltare said. "We have to get this done."

"I *am* worried, Linda. I know the storm is headed this way. I hear thunder, and my skin is tingling, but I see no lightning. I'm counting on it."

Hurricane Cleo was moving up the Florida coast after making landfall with destructive force in Miami the day before, but it was losing strength, devolving into a tropical storm.

As they approached the farmhouse, Zeemat saw what he expected—a thick cable of wires coming from the direction of the communications tower. The end of the cable was attached to a makeshift Torkiyan sidewalk built with sheets of tin from the roof of the toolshed. Four Torkiyans stood on the tin sheets, looking up to sky toward the advancing storm, waiting for lightning to strike. He could make out Gerra among the group of four. His father was the only one missing.

Zeemat took advantage of their distraction and snuck up to the propane tank on the side of the farmhouse. He swung the backpack off his shoulders and removed three sticks of dynamite he had taped together the night before. He used duct tape to attach them to the metal support under the propane tank and carefully attached the remote detonator. After turning on the receiver switch on the detonator, a blinking red light confirmed it was ready to go.

He snuck back to the ditch where Deltare was waiting, and they pressed on. The barn was just twenty yards ahead.

When they got to the level of the barn, Deltare army-crawled out of the ditch and attached a similar set of dynamite sticks to the side of the barn, careful not to get too close to the area where the humans were being held captive. She turned on the ignition receiver, confirmed it was blinking red, then slowly crawled her way back to Zeemat.

A bolt of lightning now shone in the distance to the south. Several seconds later, a crack of thunder ripped through the countryside. The four Torkiyans standing on the tin sheet howled in anticipation.

Zeemat and Deltare quickly headed toward the tower, closer to the spaceship that lay buried in the field a short distance beyond. They were farther from the four others now, and the pouring rain provided some cover. They crawled out of the ditch and ran in a crouch toward the tower. They froze for a moment when another flash of lightning lit up the sky.

Deltare looked to Zeemat. "I don't think they saw us," she said.

"I hope not," he replied.

Once they reached the tower, Zeemat retrieved the wire cutters from his pack and snipped the individual wires of the thick cord that led to the tin sidewalk where the others were standing.

Meanwhile, Deltare retrieved the heavy coils of copper wire she and Zeemat had brought along. She twisted them together as he finished cutting the cable.

"There! It's cut," Zeemat said. "Now at least they won't charge up."

"But maybe you can," Deltare said. She tried to help Zeemat attach their new copper wire to the cut end of the cable from the tower, but he pushed her away.

"Where are your rubber gloves?" he asked. "If lightning strikes . . ."

Deltare fished them out of the emptying backpack and snapped them on before they finished securing the copper wire to the tower cable.

"I wish I had a metal sheet to stand on," Zeemat said. He looked around but found nothing to which he could attach the end of the copper wire.

"Water conducts electricity," Deltare said.

"Yes, it will have to do," Zeemat said. They both looked back to the ditch, which continued to swell with the pouring rain.

They headed back toward the ditch, unrolling the remaining wire as they went.

A bright bolt of lightning hit somewhere close. For a moment, it lit the sky as if it were daylight, and the thunder roared.

Zeemat and Deltare looked over to the Torkiyans standing on the tin sheets, who were now looking in their direction and pointing at them.

"They've seen us!" Deltare exclaimed.

They hurried with unwinding the rolls of copper, now in a bit of a panic. Suddenly, the last of the wire fell from the empty wire containers when they were about ten feet away from the ditch, and it didn't reach. The water in the ditch was now flowing ankle-deep—it would have been perfect.

Zeemat held the end of the copper wire in his hand. He thought about putting it on the ground and just standing on the bare metal, but then he noticed a puddle forming just a few feet away.

"Get away, Linda," Zeemat said. "Go back to the barn and wait for it."

Deltare looked at Zeemat and nodded. She ran to him, gave him a quick hug and a peck on the cheek, then raced back toward the barn.

Zeemat made sure she was at a safe distance, then focused his attention on the wire in his hands. He pulled the heavy wire toward the puddle of water, looking up to the sky as two bolts of lightning struck nearby at the same time. The storm was upon them.

Zeemat pulled the wire with all his might and reached the middle of the puddle. He dropped the wire into the water, which was deep enough to cover a good length of it. Then he removed his backpack and rummaged through it until he found what he was looking for—the bag of salt. He tossed the backpack aside, ripped the salt bag open, and poured its contents into the puddle. He slopped his feet around to mix it in as best he could. It was done. All he could do now was wait . . . and hope.

Tropical Storm Cleo was now directly overhead. Lightning bolts struck all around the farm, lighting up the sky in a dazzling display of nature's power. With each bolt, Zeemat could clearly see his four fellow Torkiyans standing ready on the tin sheets, unaware they were disconnected. They had their eyes fixed on him, hands on their weapons, ready to pounce as soon as they were energized. He wondered again why his father was not with them, then looked back toward the spaceship, where he thought he saw movement at the doorway hatch.

At that moment, a thunderous bolt of lightning struck the TV tower. The four Torkiyans raised their arms and cheered for a few moments until they realized they'd received no part of the bolt—no charge at all.

The TV tower shook violently, and the shock of electricity roared down the tower, burning along the copper wire until it sizzled into the puddle where Zeemat was standing. His body vibrated as the electricity coursed through his every atom, both fists clenching in a violent spasm. His skin glowed, and his eyes shone bright.

After the rush of lightning passed, Zeemat had transformed. He let out a ferocious roar. His crimson eyes raged as he looked around to see upon whom he could unleash his fury.

The four Torkiyans still stood on the useless tin sheets, and Yonek, who was peering out from the ship's open hatch, had seen everything that happened.

"Attack!" Yonek yelled over the noise of the storm.

Without hesitation, the Torkiyans rushed toward Zeemat. It would be four against one, even though the one was fully charged.

At that moment, Deltare pressed the first detonator. A loud explosion rocked the farmhouse, knocking the four attacking Torkiyans to the ground. The exploding propane engulfed the house in a flash of fire. Then Deltare hit the other detonator, and the second explosion opened a gaping hole in the side of the barn.

With the distraction of the farmhouse engulfed in flames, Deltare ran to the burning barn and covered her face as she charged through the flaming hole created by the explosion. She coughed and blinked her way through the smoke until she found the cold room, just where Zeemat had drawn it on the map. She turned the large handle to open the door. Four people were inside. Three of them huddled together, cowering with a look of wild-eyed terror. The other had a wrap around her head and wandered around the room, oblivious to what was happening.

"Hurry!" Deltare said. "We have to leave! Now! Run!" The three people huddled together leapt to their feet. Deltare pointed to their exit, and they ran. She looked back into the cold room to see the other human standing there, looking at her with a blank expression.

"C'mon, friend," she said. "Let's get you out of here." Deltare helped her out of the barn and tried to hurry to follow the others, but the injured woman could only shuffle her feet, dragging them along the ground. Deltare wrapped her arms around the woman, trying to lift her as she led her out of the barn. She looked around, hoping the Torkiyans hadn't rushed in to find her.

After the explosions, the four aliens got to their feet and charged at Zeemat, who let out another angry growl as he rushed forward to meet them, zigzagging to avoid their gunfire.

Maneg and Nygni reached Zeemat first. One lunged at his body and the other at his head and neck in a coordinated attack. But Zeemat met them with a powerful fury. He thwarted their first blows and struck his own. He sent both flying to the side. Lykle came at him next. She was the same size and every bit as ruthless as the others, attacking Zeemat with both hands in a rapid series of blows. Zeemat absorbed her punches, fended off some others, and fought back with his own series of blows. She collapsed to the ground, dizzy and bleeding from her mouth.

Gerra had heard a commotion behind her, from back at the barn. As she whipped around to investigate, she spotted three of the humans running toward the road.

"*Zzzt.* They're getting away!" she cried. "Lykle, follow me!"

Gerra raced back to intercept the fleeing humans, but Lykle hobbled a few times and fell back to the ground, still dazed after her encounter with Zeemat.

Zeemat saw Gerra heading back to the barn. He looked for Deltare but couldn't see her through the rain. Distracted, he didn't see Maneg and Nygni coming back at him as they regrouped for their second assault. One pounded the side of Zeemat's head with the butt of his weapon. The other wrapped his arms around Zeemat's body with the full force of his run, tackling him to the ground. They pounded Zeemat's with relentless blows.

But even in the pain of the attack, Zeemat worried more about Deltare than for himself. He tolerated a few blows, then exploded into a rage. He kicked Maneg off him, sending him flying backward. He grabbed Nygni in a choke hold and squeezed hard until he felt something break within his grasp. Nygni collapsed, holding his neck and barely wheezing through his damaged windpipe.

Zeemat directed his attention to Maneg, who hesitated after sensing Zeemat's power. But Zeemat did not. He attacked Maneg with speed and fury, punching him hard in both his head and body. Maneg tried to defend himself but was no match for the strength of Zeemat's charge. Zeemat wrestled him to the ground face-first in the mud. Maneg struggled to turn his head to the side so he could breathe, but Zeemat held him down. He didn't let up until Maneg stopped struggling, then turned him over and allowed the unconscious Torkiyan to gasp a breath of air. The copper wire lay at their feet. Zeemat took hold of the wire and ripped a piece off with his bare hands, using it to tie Maneg's hands behind him, and then to bind his feet. "Here's your precious copper," he said to him. Then he looked up toward the barn and saw Gerra disappear into the heavy rain, charging toward the structure.

Zeemat tore off another length of wire and restrained Nygni as quickly as possible, then rushed back to the barn, hoping he could reach Deltare in time.

He caught up to Lykle, who was wobbling her way back to the barn to meet up with Gerra. Zeemat punched her in the back of the head as he raced by, knocking her to the ground again.

He rounded the corner of the barn and halted as he realized, in horror, that he hadn't gotten there in time. In front of the burning farmhouse, Gerra had caught up with Deltare, who was helping a struggling human. Deltare couldn't see Gerra rushing from behind, holding a metal rod in her hand. Zeemat recognized the cattle prod at once.

"Linda!" he yelled. "Look out!"

Before Deltare could look back, Gerra jammed the cattle prod into her back with a powerful jab. The two prongs hit their mark. Gerra pressed the prod's trigger and didn't let go, sending pulse after pulse of disabling electric shocks toward Deltare's spine.

"NO!" Zeemat screamed. He bolted in an all-out sprint to catch up to Deltare and Gerra.

Deltare felt the force of the cattle prod ramming her in the back, and she heard the *crackles* of the electric impulses, but she didn't feel them. She wheeled around and glared at Gerra, who looked back at her with shocked surprise.

Deltare didn't hesitate. With a swift motion she'd learned from her martial arts instructor in San Francisco, she disarmed Gerra and threw the cattle prod off to the side. Continuing with a smooth, deliberate movement, she swept her legs around and knocked Gerra's feet out from under her. Gerra fell to the ground, landing hard on her hip. On her in an instant, Deltare struck Gerra's side in a sharp kick with her heavy army boot.

Then she reached down to her holster, drew the Beretta, and pointed it at Gerra's head.

"NO!" Zeemat repeated. "Linda, stop!" He caught up with them, breathing heavily after his long sprint through the muddy field.

"*Grrk*! How did she not fall?" Gerra asked Zeemat, her Torkiyan speech heavy with angry, guttural *clicks*.

"She wonders why the cattle prod didn't work," Zeemat translated for Deltare with a knowing grin.

Deltare loomed over the fallen Gerra, with fire in her eyes and her finger on the trigger of the pistol she kept pointed at Gerra's head. She glared at Gerra as she pulled her T-shirt down at the collar to show Gerra the top of the rubber skin-diver's suit she was wearing underneath.

"*Zzzt*. A rubber suit," Zeemat told Gerra.

Gerra tried to move, but Deltare fired a warning shot into the ground right next to Gerra's head. Gerra froze, baring her teeth, growling at Deltare, then she glared at Zeemat.

"So this is the human you love so much?" she asked Zeemat in angry *buzzes* and *clicks*. Then her face softened. "You said you wanted to mate with me. You can still have me," she said, pointing to herself, then to Zeemat, then joining her hands and rocking them from side to side as if holding a baby, smiling at him. She made sure Deltare could see.

Deltare registered it loud and clear.

"I don't believe it! Were you two together?" she asked Zeemat.

"She's trying to trick us. We discussed becoming a mating pair, but she was against it," Zeemat said.

"Oh, and you weren't?"

Zeemat watched as Deltare's pained expression quickly turned to anger.

Gerra saw her opportunity and jumped to her feet. She dashed the few steps to Zeemat and held on to him to shield herself from Deltare's gun, her face darkening once more.

"*Grrk*. You *can't* choose her over me!" she shouted into Zeemat's ear. "We have to kill her!"

Zeemat pushed Gerra away from him, keeping her at arm's length.

With that, Deltare changed the aim of her gun . . . toward Zeemat.

"Linda! What—" Zeemat said.

"Duck!" Deltare screamed. But the word confused Zeemat. All he could think of was a duck waddling in water.

Deltare didn't hesitate. She fired off two rounds in rapid sequence. The shots whizzed by Zeemat's ear, just like Dooley's shots had done on the day he met Gerra.

Zeemat and Gerra heard a gasping sound behind them. Lykle had finally caught up to them in the pouring rain. Deltare had seen her at the last moment as she staggered toward them, raising her weapon. She had pointed it at Zeemat, preparing to shoot.

Deltare's double-tap hit Lykle like a professional shot, as she had practiced a thousand times at the gun range. One hit dead center in the chest, and the other in her large forehead. Lykle's head snapped back, and she dropped in a lifeless heap.

Gerra ran to her, and both Zeemat and Deltare gave quick chase. Deltare kicked Lykle's weapon out of reach. But Gerra didn't reach for the weapon—she went to help her fallen comrade. It didn't take long for her to realize she was dead.

"We have to tie her up," Zeemat said to Deltare. He ran over to the tin sheets on the ground, where the Torkiyans had hoped they would recharge in the storm. He ripped off a piece of the attached wiring and used it to restrain Gerra's hands and feet.

"I have to get back to the ship," Zeemat said, looking over his shoulder to the field where the hidden spaceship lay. "My father could escape!"

"I'll drag Gerra into the room where she was holding the humans," Deltare said.

"Don't hurt her!" Zeemat said, his voice more commanding than he would have liked. He worried about the fury in Deltare's eyes, knowing some of that was directed at him. But that would have to wait for later. He took off in a run toward the spaceship, toward his father.

"We have to talk about this!" Deltare yelled after him.

SIXTY-FIVE

HIS FATHER'S SON

ZEEMAT RAN THROUGH the heavy rain toward the buried ship. The hazy outline of the protruding upper hatch became clearer as he approached it through the pouring rain. He saw a figure standing just outside—his father, weapon in hand.

"*Zzzt.* I knew you would come back," Yonek said. "But I hoped it would be to rejoin us. I see now that it's not the case."

"Why weren't you with the others during the storm?" Zeemat asked.

"After you left, we talked about what we should do with you. We voted on your fate. It was four against one that you should die. I had to comply with the group's decision, but I refused to be a part of it. So I chose not to charge in the storm. I didn't want my anger to dominate my actions."

"Well, I'm still alive," Zeemat said.

"And the others?"

"Lykle is dead," Zeemat said.

Yonek took a deep breath. He knew what was coming. "What do you want, Zeemat?" he asked.

"The ship," Zeemat replied.

"As part of my crew?" Yonek asked, his eyes fizzling with a confusion of colors that gradually brightened to an even green. "We can use it to establish ourselves here, to defeat the Ceruleans, and then to return home! With copper and slaves . . . as conquering heroes . . . father and son. Is that what you want? Nothing would make me happier." He spoke the last words softly, as he knew the chances.

Zeemat took a moment to admire the ship and his father—his broad, intimidating presence, strong, with his famous boots on alien ground, rifle in hand. Yonek was the very image of a Torkiyan hero here in the flesh. Zeemat's mind raced with plans and possibilities, while Yonek waited anxiously for his son to answer.

"You misunderstand me, Father," Zeemat finally replied. "Like you always have. What I really want is the Trangula and to destroy the ship."

Yonek's eyes dimmed, and a wave of anguish erupted on his face, like the agonizing throes of a dying star. "I can't let you do that," he moaned, struggling to fight his emotions. Reluctantly, he raised his weapon and pointed it at his son, his hands shaking.

"You just said you don't want to kill me, Father. We don't agree on much of anything, but I'm your son . . . and I love you."

Now Yonek's entire body began to shake. "*Arrrg.* I know . . . and I love you, too."

Yonek released a roar as he struggled with his thoughts. The most important battle of his life now raged in his own mind—to fulfill the mission or to save his own son.

After a lifetime of indoctrination and training, the warrior in him won out. "I can't allow you to have the ship," he said. "The mission is more important than either of us."

Zeemat nodded. He understood his father and knew that he put his sense of loyalty to Torkiya above everything else, and in truth, Zeemat respected him for that. For an eternal moment, they looked at each other, believing this would be a final goodbye.

Zeemat charged his father. As he ran, he pulled his right arm back with a fisted hand, ready to deliver a powerful blow.

Yonek had no choice. He knew he could not match his son's charged strength. He fired his weapon.

Zeemat felt a sharp pain hit him on top of his left thigh. He crashed to the ground in a forward roll.

Yonek hesitated with a second shot, and Zeemat ignored the blood spurting out from a hole in his pant leg, but the violence of the shot had thrown him into a rage. He leapt back on his feet, ignoring the pain.

They clashed together in a fury of Torkiyan growls, punches, and kicks. Zeemat landed a series of heavy blows to his father's head and chest, driving him backward. He ripped the weapon from his father's hands and threw it to the side.

Yonek's soldier reflexes kicked in. He didn't have Zeemat's charge, but he had a lifetime of experience in fighting—and winning. He fended off Zeemat's next attack and threw several well-placed punches and kicks of his own. Zeemat fell to the ground and rolled back onto his feet. He took a moment to size up his opponent.

Zeemat rushed his father again and this time tackled him to the ground. They wrestled, each trying to find a hold that would neutralize the other. Yonek drove Zeemat's face into the mud, but Zeemat turned his head, heaved his body, and Yonek lost his hold. Zeemat grabbed Yonek's arm and twisted it to the breaking point, but Yonek escaped with a backflip and yanked himself free of Zeemat's bracing grip.

Yonek began to circle Zeemat, jabbing and distracting him with his left hand while hiding his right fist to catch Zeemat off guard with his powerful punch. When they came close enough together, Yonek unleashed his famous right uppercut, aimed squarely at the underside of Zeemat's jaw. If the blow landed, Zeemat's teeth would break, his brain would rattle inside his skull, and his neck would snap.

But Zeemat remembered watching his mother and father's fight moves during Torkiyan storms. He knew how they danced. He loved how they danced. In a microsecond, he recalled all their beautiful kicks, punches, and counterpunches. He could feel them in his bones.

Like his mother had done before, Zeemat made a graceful spinning move to the left, avoiding his father's deadly blow. He used the force of his spin to add impact to his own powerful blow aimed at his father's exposed right side. The blow landed, and Zeemat felt the crunch of ribs protecting important organs underneath. His father screamed in pain and collapsed to the ground, holding his side. Zeemat landed a roundhouse punch to the side of his father's head, rendering him unconscious.

Zeemat stood over his father with fire in his eyes. He was breathing heavily, and his fists shook. He waited for his father to resume fighting, but he didn't move.

Zeemat allowed himself a few moments to settle down. Now that he'd neutralized his father, Zeemat wasted no time in entering the ship. It was a little different from Janusia, but the components and the arrangement were basically the same. He located the antimatter fuel tank, dropped to one knee, and set his backpack down.

Zeemat removed the last of the explosives from the pack and secured them near the antimatter tank. He reached again into the backpack for the last of the detonators. This one was not a remote—it had a timer. He wired the detonator to the explosives and set the timer, giving himself two minutes to snatch the Trangula and get away.

Once he had everything assembled, he pressed the button on the detonator. The clock began to count down from two minutes. Zeemat hurried to the main control panel, where the glowing pyramidal Trangula was attached to its receptacle.

As Zeemat reached for the Trangula, he sensed movement behind him. He turned his head in time to see his father's shadow, wielding his weapon.

Zeemat lunged to the side, barely missing Yonek's shot. The errant energy shot sparked off a metal support beam close to where Zeemat had secured the explosives and ricocheted several times around the close quarters of the spaceship.

In mid-lunge, Zeemat twisted his body and threw his backpack with full force into Yonek's face, blinding Yonek for an instant. By the time he shook the backpack off his face, Zeemat was upon him. Several other errant shots fired from the weapon before Zeemat wrestled it out of Yonek's hands. Zeemat knew he was running out of time, so he hit Yonek hard on the top of his head with the butt of the weapon. For a second time, Yonek collapsed.

Zeemat looked over to the timer to see that a minute and a half remained. Zeemat ripped the Trangula off its base and threw it into the backpack. He slung the backpack over his shoulder and hurried to his fallen father. With a powerful heave, he lifted him off the ground and carried him over his shoulder up the ladder to the top of the hatch. He jumped off the ship and ran toward the barn as fast as he could under his father's heavy weight.

Zeemat heard a thunderous explosion behind him, followed a second later by a ripping, sizzling sound. The earth vibrated wildly for an instant, sending Zeemat and his father tumbling to the ground.

With the explosion, antimatter flashed out of its ruptured tank, and in an instant, the material spread through the ship and beyond, annihilating everything that stood in its way.

Zeemat looked back in time to see the ship vibrate for a moment and then disappear into thin air, as if it had never existed. A huge chunk of earth around the ship also disappeared, leaving a deep, gaping hole in the ground. The perfectly smooth sides of the hole quickly turned muddy as rain continued to fall.

Zeemat got back up to his feet and lumbered forward. Before his father woke up, he restrained him with a segment of wire that still stretched from the antenna.

Zeemat took a deep breath. His father was no longer a threat, and he was safe . . . and alive. Same with Gerra, unless Deltare had hurt her.

He carried his father to the barn, finding Deltare waiting for him outside of the cold room. She was standing guard, rifle in hand.

"Gerra?" Zeemat asked.

"She's in there, safe and secure," Deltare responded, her eyes smoldering.

Zeemat heaved a sigh of relief. "Let me place my father in there, too," he said. "Then I'll get the other two. They're still out in the field where I left them, struggling to get free."

Zeemat retrieved Maneg and Nygni and threw them in with the others. Now Gerra, Yonek, Maneg, and Nygni huddled together in the cold room. Zeemat and Deltare left them tied up, blood oozing from their wrists and ankles as they struggled against their wire restraints.

"*Grrk*! You'll die for this!" Maneg said.

"We'll hunt you down!" Nygni added.

"We already called for other ships. Next time, an entire fleet will come. You won't have a chance!" Gerra said.

"Silence!" Yonek commanded in a booming voice. The others looked in his direction, confused by Yonek's clear disapproval of what was being said.

Yonek turned to face his son.

And it surprised Zeemat to see a satisfied smile on his father's face.

SIXTY-SIX

THE WAY HOME

ZEEMAT COCKED HIS head sideways, as if that would somehow restore the angry grimace that normally decorated Yonek's face, but his father's unusual smile persisted. Zeemat was unsure what to make of it—a trick maybe—so he ventured a cautious comment.

"I'm sorry, Father. I'll never be the Torkiyan you wanted me to be."

"You *are* the Torkiyan I always hoped for," Yonek said. "I'm proud of you, Zeemat. If I die now, it's with our family's honor intact."

Zeemat looked at him, puzzled. He wanted his father to say more, but he was worried that the local authorities could arrive at any minute. Someone must have heard the powerful explosions or felt the aftermath of the antimatter reaction. He had to keep moving.

"I hate what you've done, but you fought like a Torkiyan for what you believe," his father said. "And you won. That is something to admire and respect."

Zeemat could almost feel the embrace and the two-handed handshake his father would have extended if his hands weren't restrained behind his back. And he couldn't help but notice the outraged expressions on the faces of the others, who did not share Yonek's sentiment.

"Thank you, Father." Zeemat cracked a tiny smile. "And I mean you no harm," he said to the others.

Zeemat left them growling and tugging at their restraints as he hurried out, with Deltare slamming the door shut behind him, dampening a tirade of Torkiyan obscenities. She pulled on the handle to be sure the latch held. She knew there was no lever or handle on the other side. Now the Torkiyans, like the humans before them, were captives in the barn's cold room.

Zeemat and Deltare raced out of the barn, down the long, muddy driveway, and made their way back to the Jeep. Deltare drove, and Zeemat took the passenger seat, keeping the backpack on his lap, protecting it and its valuable content with both hands.

On their way out of Cocoa, they stopped at a corner phone booth so Deltare could place an important call. She had the number ready.

A young woman on the other end of the line answered the phone. "CIA Orlando," she said in a cheery voice. "Please state your name and the reason for your call."

Deltare smiled at Zeemat. "This is Dr. Linda Deltare, and I'm calling to report the presence of aliens on a farm in Cocoa, Florida."

Deltare heard a long pause on the other end. Then the young woman replied, this time with a serious tone and a trembling voice.

"Where are you, Dr. Deltare, and where are these aliens?"

Deltare gave the young agent the farm's address and hung up the phone, long before they had a chance to trace the call.

Zeemat and Deltare sped back to her waiting plane at Herndon Airport. On the road to Orlando, they saw police vehicles and unmarked black sedans racing past them, heading in the opposite direction back toward Cocoa.

Arriving at Herndon, Deltare brought the Jeep to a sliding halt outside the hangar. She grabbed the remainder of their supplies and raced to board her waiting Learjet. Zeemat clutched his backpack. They took their seats and strapped in while the plane pulled out onto the tarmac in the pouring rain. The pilot revved up the turbines and strained to see well enough to keep the plane on the taxiway heading to the runway.

"Hold on to your hats," he said when the plane was in position. "This is going to be interesting."

The pilot slammed the throttle all the way down, instantly pressing them into the backs of their seats as the powerful jet accelerated. The plane swayed from right to left as the pilot fought to keep it from sliding or blowing off the runway. When the jet had enough speed, he pulled at the control wheel to lift it off the ground, then kept his eyes on the instruments and continued making instant adjustments as the jet zoomed through hectic winds and the lower layers of stormy clouds in zero visibility.

Zeemat tossed from side to side in his seat, glancing repeatedly at the ominous sky outside his window, seeing nothing but a collusion of dense dark clouds. Thunder and lightning shook the very skies and rattled the plane. He felt a pressure in his chest, as if he couldn't breathe. Then he spotted a brief hint of blue far above him. A few moments later, another larger spot of blue expanded into the sky. As the plane gained altitude, they gradually left all the clouds beneath and behind them. Now, above them, the sky was a peaceful, clear cerulean blue.

Zeemat and Deltare sat in a stunned silence, catching their breath, deep in thought. Finally, Deltare broke the silence with the question she had been dying to ask.

"What about Gerra?" she said.

Zeemat looked at his dearest friend and reached out to hold her hand, but Deltare pulled it away.

"We never mated," he said. "I made a choice. I chose you."

Deltare studied his face for a clue, with a look of worry in hers. "Will you go back to them, or will you stay with me?"

"There was no place for me on Torkiya, and now there is no place with my Torkiyan people here on Earth," he replied.

Deltare noticed the undisguised pain and sadness in his eyes.

"You're my people now," he added, holding her gaze. Then, with a soft voice he asked, "Do you have room for me at your new place?"

Deltare allowed a tenuous smile. "Only if you'll stay forever. Can you promise?"

So many promises, Zeemat thought.

"Yes, Linda. I promise."

Deltare reached out to hold his hand, and Zeemat squeezed hers tight. Yet he could tell that it still didn't feel quite right between them.

"You could have a baby with Gerra," she lamented. "We can't."

Zeemat and Deltare looked at each other and laughed at the audacious improbability of it all. "Who's even thinking of that?" he said, making gurgling noises.

After a few moments, the laughter settled, and Deltare's face turned serious. "I am," she said. "I'm thinking about *us* . . . and the future."

He thought about it for a moment, then reached inside the backpack. He rummaged inside until his fingers wrapped around the prize. He drew out the glowing Torkiyan Trangula, handing it to Deltare with great care.

Deltare gazed at the object with eyes wide-open, holding it gingerly in her hands. "So this is it? The famous Trangula!"

"This is our baby," Zeemat explained. "It holds our future. Our gift to humanity."

"Yeah, but can it make a baby?" she asked teasingly.

Zeemat gurgled some more and flashed a mischievous smile, a universe of emotions sparkling through his unfathomable eyes. Then his smile faded.

"You'll have to wait and see. But first, there are other promises I have to keep."

SIXTY-SEVEN

EPILOGUE

FIVE YEARS LATER, on July 20, 1969, Linda Deltare sat in the living room of their country estate in Napa Valley, watching a historic event unfold on live TV.

"Mat, come now! It's about to happen," Deltare called out.

Zeemat was on the outside deck, painting a picture from memory: a moment forever etched in his mind when he'd first arrived and established orbit around the planet Earth. The painting had an image of a part of the planet to the left and a full moon on the right. After Deltare called out, he used a cloth to wipe the colors of paint from his fingertips as he hurried to the TV. He found Deltare pouring two glasses of sparkling wine.

"That's one small step for man, one giant leap for mankind," Neil Armstrong said on the TV. They watched as his grainy image jumped off the lunar module's ladder and stood on the moon's surface for the first time.

They clinked their glasses of wine together and sipped in triumph as they witnessed Armstrong bounding along in the moon's low gravity.

"You did it," Deltare said.

"You mean *we* did it," Zeemat replied. "And anyway, I can't take much of the credit. This was a human achievement."

"Ha! 'Can't take much of the credit.' Only the propulsion system on the Saturn V, the computers, the idea for the lunar module, the space suits . . . Should I go on?"

"It would have happened anyway," Zeemat said. "We only helped it happen faster."

Zeemat's humility warmed her heart. "How do you feel?" she asked.

He pondered the question for a minute as he examined his emotions. A lot had happened in the fifteen Earth years since his arrival.

"Thankful . . . happy . . . sad . . ." He paused.

"Me too," she said, giving him a warm hug. "But mostly happy . . . and hopeful."

They walked back out onto the deck and finished their wine under the waking stars of the evening sky. Zeemat looked north to find the faint light reaching out from his distant Torkiyan star, then to the brightness of the moon.

"I've earned my freedom, and my right to be here," he said.

"You always had a right." She wrapped an arm around Zeemat's waist as he draped his own across her shoulders.

"So, what now?" she asked, nudging an elbow into his side. "A baby?"

He raised an eyebrow and a mischievous smile lit up his face. A world of possibilities sparkled in his gleaming eyes.

"Yes. Now we focus on the genetics labs," Zeemat said. "Everything is possible."

The End

AUTHOR'S NOTE

MY MOTHER AND FATHER first came from Mexico to the United States as resident aliens in 1954. After I was born, we moved back and forth between the United States and Mexico for several years, long enough for me to establish lasting relationships with my extended family and to feel the pain of separation when we finally left Mexico for good.

My parents came to this strange new land in search of a better life for themselves and their children. Their biggest cost was losing day-to-day contact with family, friends, and everything about one's native land. Arriving with nothing, they worked hard and accomplished much. Now they are the root of a multigenerational Mexican American family, and we are still significantly bicultural, thanks to them.

Several ideas came together when I first imagined the story of *Mission 51*. First and foremost, I wanted to honor my immigrant parents. I also wanted to contribute to the immigration narrative in general, even if it was in some small, obtuse way. In telling the story, I wanted to be honest about human nature, about our virtues and defects. I thought about how invaders have decimated native cultures all over the world and across recorded history. I thought about the throngs of immigrants who have come into the United States, and how they have changed the very face of America. And then it all crystalized when I thought about the old Spanish missions in California, and when I realized the notorious events in Area 51 occurred at the same time as my parents' immigration to the United States in 1954. The story simply had to be about missions and aliens! But it would have never happened without my "legal alien" parents' immigration experience.

So first of all, my deepest gratitude is for my mother and father. Pa, you can read this in heaven, and I'm sure you know how much I emulated, loved, and respected you my entire life. I won the lottery when I was born, when you and Ma became my parents. Ma, your total dedication, love, encouragement, and support are legendary, beyond compare. You instilled in us a positive self-esteem and confidence that we could accomplish anything. I credit you for all the successes I have enjoyed, and there isn't a moment when I don't feel the warmth of your love.

To my wife, Gail: Thank you for giving me the time and space I needed to get this done, because it was a much longer project than either of us expected. Who knew there was so much to learn about creating and publishing a first novel, and that the process would take more than five years? Your patience, acceptance, and heartfelt encouragement were essential every step of the way. Thank you, and I love you very much!

To my children, Megan, Ginny, Kelly, and Kevin: Little do you know how much you affect and influence every part of my life. Surely it comes from the years when we all lived together as a young family. Yet now that you are all grown and have children of your own, leading your own lives, you remain a constant in my mind and heart, an indelible part of me. You influence what I think and do in subtle and wonderful ways, and there were many moments where memories of you sparked a writing idea. Thank you for being the warm, caring, intelligent, hard-working, fun-loving, fun-to-be-around, and generally amazing people that you are.

Beyond my children, there are countless family and friends who have supported this effort, and I am truly grateful. In the early stages, several of you showed such enthusiasm, even for the bad first drafts, that I dared to think I could maybe do this. I think of Irene Asare in particular, who personifies that early enthusiasm (and in whose honor I named a character). Encouraging words from many people kept me going, but what really committed me to the project was the Inkshares/Nerdist Science Fiction Contest in 2017. Many of you supported this project with money from your pockets, purchasing the preorders that determined the winners of the contest, of which I was one. Without this very real support, *Mission 51* would not be where it is today. It was a truly humbling experience feeling the love of so many people, and as a result, I felt obliged to deliver. It gave me the drive to persevere. I will be forever grateful for that experience.

Thank you to Inkshares, the innovative, modern publishing company with a great idea—choosing projects to publish based on readers' choice as evidenced by preorder support. It is a unique crowdfunding platform. A huge thank-you goes to Matt Harry, my first editor ever. Matt, your initial insights were priceless and right on the money. You dissected a very rough first draft, written by an author wannabe who really didn't know the first thing about writing a novel. You began my writing education, helped me hammer out a workable outline, and set me on a better path. You opened my eyes to a body of writing knowledge I never even knew existed, and gave me the structure with which I could start to develop as a writer. You taught me the way to reshape *Mission 51* into a proper story. Thank you!

More huge thanks go to Sarah Nivala, my second editor at Inkshares, who took over when Matt left to pursue his own projects. Sarah, you saw me through several drafts, refining the structure of the story and guiding the development of character, plot, setting, scene, dialogue, and my basic prose. I felt myself grow as a writer under your direction. Thank you!

Avalon Radys, as director of editorial and publishing operations at Inkshares, you oversaw the final steps. It was a pleasure working through your masterful and insightful copy edit. I felt the love you have for your work, and I thank you for the book's final look and polish.

Delia Maria Davis, thank you for your outstanding proofread. I appreciate your thorough inspection of every grammatical detail, your insightful editorial comments, and your suggestions for optimizing the readability of *Mission 51*.

Noah Broyles, I appreciate your meticulous attention to the final parts of production.

Thank you to Christian Akins, who designed *Mission 51*'s remarkable book cover. It was a special joy creating it with you, Chris, and I hope we can collaborate again in the future.

Special thanks to Chris Pyke and Idan Carré, unique artists who created original artwork during the early promotional part of this project. It was great fun working with you both!

Today, as a result of my experiences at Inkshares and beyond, I am fortunate to be surrounded by a group of highly imaginative, creative people who I'm happy to call friends. Honestly, you are too numerous to mention, and I would hate to inadvertently exclude someone important to me, so I give a general thanks to my writing friends at Inkshares and Writing Bloc. Our interactions and mutual encouragement are an important part of my life today. Thank you!

Despite the hard work, writing this story has been a joy on multiple levels. I never lost the feeling that I was doing this for fun, and in an effort to honor my immigrant parents. Throughout the ups and downs of this five-year project, I received countless unexpected gifts and treasures through interactions with many wonderful people, and for that I'll be forever grateful.

GRAND PATRONS

ABOUT THE AUTHOR

Fernando Crôtte came to the United States at the age of six, with his immigrant parents in search of the American Dream. With one foot in his native Mexico and another in his new adopted land, he assimilated into American culture while still honoring his Mexican heritage. Along with wife Gail, he resides in Winston Salem, North Carolina, where he practices medicine. In his spare time, he enjoys traveling, birding, and general aviation. *Mission 51* is his debut novel.

INKSHARES

INKSHARES is a reader-driven publisher and producer based in Oakland, California. Our books are selected not by a group of editors, but by readers worldwide.

While we've published books by established writers like *Big Fish* author Daniel Wallace and *Star Wars: Rogue One* scribe Gary Whitta, our aim remains surfacing and developing the new-author voices of tomorrow.

Previously unknown Inkshares authors have received starred reviews and been featured in the *New York Times*. Their books are on the front tables of Barnes & Noble and hundreds of independents nationwide, and many have been licensed by publishers in other major markets. They are also being adapted by Oscar-winning screenwriters at the biggest studios and networks.

Interested in making your own story a reality? Visit Inkshares.com to start your own project or find other great books.

CPSIA information can be obtained
at www.ICGtesting.com
Printed in the USA
JSHW031922140122
22027JS00002B/2